I0777505

the Twilight THEFT

JANET OPPEDISANO

The Twilight Theft
ISBN Digital: 978-1-998251-00-1
ISBN Paperback: 978-1-998251-01-8

Copyright © 2024
Cover Art Copyright © 2024

Cover Designer: The Book Brander

This is a work of fiction. Names, characters, places, and events are from the author's imagination or are used fictitiously. Any resemblance to actual persons, living or dead, business, companies, events, or places, is purely coincidental.

All rights reserved. No part of this publication may be used or reproduced in any form, whether by printing, photocopying, scanning, or otherwise without the written permission of the author, except for the use of brief quotations in a book review.

For everyone who's climbed out of the darkness
to find the light in someone's heart

FREE NOVELLA

To instantly receive the free romantic suspense novella *The Phoenix Heist*, the prequel to the Reynolds Recoveries series, claim your copy at
https://bf.janetoppedisano.com/smbari40im.

Chapter 1
Jayce

If you've seen one billionaire's office, you've seen them all. Lots of leather, marble, and dark wood. Plus a wall of windows overlooking the Potomac. Clean as a whistle.

I hopped off Gideon Tremaine's gargantuan desk and stretched my back. My watch buzzed with a notification.

Step one complete.

"Can I take out the card now?"

"The Trojan is in. Now we wait for it to find a way into his data." The distracted female voice over my earpiece was punctuated by a keyboard clacking in her background. "Give me five minutes to be sure I don't need to intervene."

"Five minutes, check." I smoothed out the cleaner's uniform I wore. It was a simple baby blue button-front shirt with black pants. A bit stuffy for my taste, but it ticked the most important box—designed for movement.

Five minutes.

Two large paintings hung on the wall opposite the windows, with a four-foot-tall sculpture on a short pedestal between them. Books and knickknacks that probably cost more than my condo. But it was the huge red and black graffiti-like painting on the other side of the room that had been calling to me since I'd arrived. I had time for a peek.

I strolled across the expanse toward the black leather couches, dragging a hand over the smooth surface of the one in my way, as I detoured around it. "He's got a giant piece of art, I'm sure's a Basquiat. Would it be a total cliché if he hid a safe behind it?"

"Don't touch," drawled a male voice over my earpiece. "We're here for intel."

"Except…" I let the word hang in the air. Good thing it was only Brie and Emmett on the line. Anyone else and they'd be putting a stop to the job.

"Jayce?" he said. "We're not here looking for trouble."

"I never go *looking* for trouble."

"Just tends to find you somehow?"

Sometimes. I knelt on the couch beneath the painting and pressed my face against the wall. It was perfectly flush. Hard-mounted. Maybe there was a catch somewhere? A button to press? More likely a false trigger with an alarm. "What if I have it open in less than five?"

"You only have four left," said Brie.

"I can see the catch." Halfway up on the right side, I'd only have to flick it and the painting would swing away from the wall, revealing whatever marvel Gideon Tremaine had hidden behind it.

Emmett cleared his throat. "You know he made his money in tech securi— Shit! Abort. Abort."

I flew away from the wall, leaped over the coffee table in front of me, and vaulted over the back of the other couch. We were supposed to have another hour. *Grab the drive. Grab your phone. Grab the cleaning cart. Go.* "Which abort?"

"Plan F."

"What?" Brie's quick response heightened the rush of adrenaline through my bloodstream.

Nectar of the gods.

"I'm not done," she said.

Plan F was an emergency backup, not a plan. Only to be used when—"Who's with him?"—someone was coming who'd recognize me and not let me slip away.

"Drew Donovan." Emmett was so quiet. They must have been passing by his sentry position.

That changed everything.

I had a minute, tops.

With the tiny drive tucked into a small compartment in my bra, I snatched a bottle of cleaning fluid and a rag from the cart and darted to the bathroom at the far end of the room. I closed the door and pressed an ear to it. Two male voices filtered in from the other side of the door. They were already in the office.

"I'm in the bathroom. Hit the alarm." I pulled on a simple pair of headphones from around my neck and turned to the sink. A quick spray from my bottle and I started wiping the vanity. If the alarm didn't come fast enough, I'd look like a distracted cleaner.

Plan F was a solid one, but it hadn't accounted for Drew. He was a bigger variable than expected.

"Brace yourself," said Brie over the earpiece, and the piercing cry of the fire alarm began.

"Tell me when I'm clear."

A firm hand landed on my arm.

Showtime.

The man behind me said, "Don't even pretend you're—"

"What are you doing?" I squealed, spinning to face him while tearing the headphones off. I might have been loud enough for Gideon to hear over the alarm. The corner of my mouth refused to stay down as I lowered my volume. "Well, if it isn't Drew Down-ovan."

A muscle ticked in his jaw. His annoyingly sexy jaw with the short light-brown beard. The kind of beard that made you want to rake your fingers through it—if it weren't attached to such a sour, miserable face. Let alone the way it was paired up with his equally annoying, gravelly, low voice. "Donovan."

Yeah, a voice that settled deep in my stomach. "Right, I keep forgetting."

"Emmett needs to find a better lookout spot next time." His rich brown eyes bored into me and he leaned close. So close I got a hit off his cologne. Just as irritating as the rest of him, the heady scent of sandalwood and leather. His hot breath brushed over my ear that sported the earpiece. "And Brie, if you're listening in—turn off the fire alarm."

"Jayce?" Brie asked. "You good?"

I slid my hands up his chest—brushing over his lapels that hid rock-solid pecs—and eased him away from me. *Phone in your inside breast pocket, Drew? You're going to make this too easy.* "But Downie—"

"Donovan," he growled.

There was a knock at the door, and a man's voice said above the din, "We should get outside."

"One minute," called Drew, not taking his eyes off mine. "Tell her to turn it off."

"If we do that, I'll lose my fire alarm cover and have to sneak out the window before Gideon catches me."

"We're on the fifth floor." He straightened, folding his arms over his ridiculously broad chest. Intimidation pose? *Seriously, Drew?* "You are not about to scale the building."

The answer was always to scale things. Climb them or go over them. Walking in a straight line was too predictable. I leaned toward the window and pointed upward. "Five floors down, but only two up. Child's play."

The loud wail stopped, and Drew nearly cracked a smile.

Brie said, "I'll turn it back on if you need it."

"Now what are you doing here?" he asked.

"Does it matter? Anyone Washington's best fixer—"

"Crisis manager."

"—meets with must have secrets someone wants." I moved into his space, tilting my head back to look up at him. I was only six inches shorter, and he wasn't about to scare me off. "Is Gideon Tremaine a proud papa of a kleptomaniac?"

Another jaw clench. Had I hit a nerve by bringing up our last job? The one he completely botched? "Is that why you're here? Are you after his son?"

"As much as I'd love to hang out and chat..." I clapped his upper arms, making a show of sucking in a tiny breath at how solid his biceps were. "I really need to get going."

He grabbed one of my wrists, removing it from his arm. "Did you take anything?"

"Me?" I batted my eyelashes at him, clasping his wrist with my free hand. *Nice watch.* "I didn't take anything."

"Intel only?"

I pulled closer to him, increasing contact points and breathing in his cologne. "You going to rat me out?"

"Don't antagonize him," said Emmett over the earpiece.

Drew just stood there, looking all serious, not moving. Not separating from me. The former spy was waiting me out.

He knew waiting wasn't my forte.

How long would he stand there?

"Jayce." Emmett said my name so purposefully, it was obvious I wouldn't like what he was about to say. "I want you to tell him we're not there for Gideon."

Give that smug jerk info? No way.

Drew took a step, moving us backward like a dance. Another and another until my back touched the wall and he'd sandwiched me in place. That six-inch height difference seemed like a lot more all of a sudden.

I would have pushed against him, but he wouldn't budge if I tried. No way was I giving him that satisfaction. "You missed the side and together part of the waltz, Downie."

"I gave you an order." Emmett's voice grew sharper. "Follow it."

Drew exhaled slowly. "Gideon isn't my client yet, so I don't owe him anything. Just tell me whatever contract you're on isn't something that's going to put me on your tail."

How many smart quips could I make about him being on my tail? As tempting as they all were, I did my job. "Emmett wants you to know we're not here for Gideon."

His gaze roamed over my face, and an unexpected wave of heat flushed through me. I had to get control of that. Sure, he was sex on a stick, but he was also a stubborn jackass who didn't play nicely.

"It's the truth." And I wasn't saying more than that.

With the barest nod, Drew loosened his grip on my wrist and stepped back. "All right."

This time, I kept step with him, grazing my fingers over his watch. *Think you can outplay me, do you?* One hand to pocket, other hand to pat his chest. Distractions. "You need to work on your people skills."

"I have plenty of them. Try acting more civil and maybe I'll show you." The corners of his lips remained tight, slightly down-turned.

I gave him a wink and returned to the sink, retrieving a mint from a crystal holder. Popping it in my mouth, I rolled it around with my tongue while I stared at Drew in the mirror. "You know, billionaire mints aren't any different from discount store candies."

"For someone who eats so much, you don't have a particularly discerning palate."

Drew Freaking Donovan. It had to be him, didn't it? I picked up the bottle with the cleaning fluid. "CIA teach you the finer points of mints?"

"Jayce," said Emmett. "Stop taunting him and get out here."

"Emmett says I'm supposed to go now." I turned and leaned against the sink, swirling the blue liquid in the bottle. "You going to let me leave?"

"By all means." Drew stepped aside and gave a slight bow, offering me access to the door. "Better than having to explain why we're scraping you off the sidewalk."

Like I would have fallen.

"I'm so"—I pushed off the sink—"grateful you"—took one step and slipped.

The cleaning bottle flew toward Drew's head.

I stumbled forward, flailing for balance.

His gaze stayed on the bottle, and he caught it, just as I slammed into him.

We careened into the wall together.

Hands to chest.

He latched an arm around me, keeping me upright.

Look flustered. Slide a hand up his lapel.

His arm tightened.

I gave a weak laugh and averted my eyes, dragging the spotlight of attention to the bottle he held next to him.

He looked with me.

Reach for the bottle with left hand. Hook under his breast pocket with right-hand thumb.

Slide.

Slide.

I tilted my head closer to his neck as I eased my grip on the bottle, brushing his fingers and breathing hard. "Well, that's embarrassing."

"Are you all right?" He didn't let go of me or the cleaning fluid. Just held me, staring at our hands.

Final slide with the hand. Hand to my pocket. Back away. Look at the floor. Be embarrassed. I tucked my hair behind my ear, a futile effort as it fell back down to cover part of my face. "Can I have the bottle back? I need to at least pretend I'm still the cleaner, right?"

He released the bottle. As he scanned the length of me, I straightened my shirt and pants, surprisingly uncomfortable under the scrutiny.

"Are you sure you're all right?"

"Fine." I headed for the door. "No funny business? I get to walk out?"

"You swear you weren't here for Gideon?"

"Cross my heart." I traced an ex over my left breast, drawing his gaze.

Did he think I fell into him as a come-on?

You've been out of the CIA too long, Drew.

That muscle ticked in his jaw again.

A taunt bubbled up inside me, but I tamped it down and hurried out of the bathroom.

Gideon Tremaine stood at the bank of windows, surveying the city. He was a tall man of average build with dark brown skin and tightly cropped gray hair.

"Monsieur Tremaine, I am so sorry!" I kept my eyes off him, hurrying toward the cleaner's cart by the door. Face down so my hair obscured my features.

I'd used this cover before and the ultra-rich usually looked right through me. But as someone who'd built his empire from the ground up, our team's research determined he wouldn't be so oblivious. He'd pay attention and possibly engage me in conversation. If I was stressed, he was as likely to sit me down and ensure everything was all right as he was to kick me out.

But throw in the fifteen minutes I'd been in his private en-suite with his fixer? Hopefully, he'd be more interested in talking with Drew than slowing me down.

"I did not think you would be back so soon." My hands landed on the cart. "I'll return later."

"One moment—" Gideon began, his deep voice soft.

Footfalls sounded behind me, and Drew said, "It's all right, Gideon."

I pushed the cart toward the door at double-time.

Drew continued, "We need to discuss business."

"Of course."

I pulled open the door, slipped out with my cart, and bustled down the hallway. After the first corner, I started down a thirty-foot escape route to the service elevator.

Emmett appeared at my side. "That was too close."

I waved it away and blew a raspberry.

"You were baiting him, which was an unnecessary risk."

"Nah." A strange mixture of warmth and something uncomfortable skittered around my stomach. Not the normal high after a job well done, but something tinged with... something else. "He totally thinks I was flirting with him."

"And what were you really doing?" Emmett sounded as unimpressed with me as Drew had.

"Getting even." I plucked the beautiful watch from my pocket. Smooth black calf leather with a gold face. "He pissed me off."

Emmett chuckled to himself. "You can't keep that."

"Yeah, I know." I sighed theatrically and jogged back to Gideon's assistant's desk. Passing the watch to him, I maintained the thick French accent. "I found this in the office of Monsieur Tremaine. I was too nervous when I saw him after the fire alarm and the noise and... Could you return pour moi?"

He smiled his polite little smile and I hurried back to the cleaner's cart, dutifully heading for the service elevator. Emmett had vanished down a separate hallway. We'd meet up outside and head back to the jet, then fly home.

If everything went the way Brie said it would, her Trojan program was enough to access the information we needed. Gideon hadn't gotten a good look at me, but his assistant and security would have. I wouldn't be able to try that game a second time.

And no doubt Drew was already working out a plan to ensure I couldn't.

Chapter 2
Drew

Gideon crossed the room, heading for the sideboard opposite the windows. "Do I need to worry about a sexual harassment suit?"

"I'll handle it."

"Of course you will. You're good at your job." He lifted two cut crystal glasses from a shelf at the back. "That's not what I'm worried about. You were in there with her for a long time."

"Nothing happened." I joined him at the sideboard. "The fire alarm rattled her. I was calming her down."

Rather than selecting one of the bottles on display, he slid open the lower section and withdrew an oak presentation box with a purple and gold imprint across the front.

"Would you rather wait for Craig?" I'd run into Gideon in the lobby downstairs, so we'd come up early for the meeting. My boss wouldn't be more than another few minutes.

I flipped over my wrist.

And sighed.

No watch.

That explained Jayce being so handsy. When had she taken it? When I grabbed her wrist and then she grabbed mine? Or after I'd stepped back from pinning her against the wall?

I'd played right into her devious little hands.

"Let me pour. I've been looking forward to tasting this one." He unlatched the case and withdrew the smooth, simple bottle. Gideon poured while I reviewed my adventure in the bathroom.

I could read just about anyone. But somehow, that ball of sarcastic energy—despite two separate targeting packages I'd prepared—always surprised me.

If it had been her team lead, Scarlett Reynolds, we could have had a reasonable discussion and she likely would have told me what her team was doing in Gideon's office. At least Emmett had forced Jayce to tell me the bare minimum.

There was a knock at the door, and Gideon's assistant opened it. "Mr. Tremaine, you asked me to let you know when Craig Bishop was here?"

Gideon waved a hand. "Show him in."

"Oh, and Mr. Donovan?" The assistant held up a watch. "Does this belong to you?"

"Yes, thank you." I put down my glass and retrieved the watch, turning it over. Jayce hadn't planted something inside it, had she? "I must've dropped it on my way in."

"The cleaner returned it. She said she found it on the floor in here, and I knew it wasn't Mr. Tremaine's."

"Thankfully, she found it before I left." It had to have been when she grabbed my wrist.

Or when she tripped? No, given her skills, she hadn't tripped at all. I revisited her movements. She hadn't fumbled the cleaning fluid bottle. She'd thrown it.

As the assistant retreated, I did a quick pocket check. Keys still in my left. Wallet in my right.

Phone in my—

Shit.

She'd taken the watch when she grabbed my wrist and then taken my phone when she stumbled into me. How hadn't I noticed?

Because you were too busy wrapping your arm around her slender waist. Holding her tight against yourself like the white knight you think you are, ensuring she was all right.

And she'd stolen my fucking phone in return.

"Drew." Craig breezed into the room, patting my upper arm on his way by. CIA legend, my mentor, and my boss for the past two years. He was lean and roughly my height, with light brown hair highlighted with gray you could only see close-up. With sharp eyes that missed little, his easy smile hid many secrets.

I closed the door behind him, maintaining the most neutral expression I could manage. Would my phone be at the front desk? In my office? Dropped off at my apartment by courier?

"Gideon!" Craig crossed the room to our prospective client, and the two embraced, clapping each other on the back. "You two didn't start without me, did you?"

"Of course not." Gideon poured a glass for Craig and the three of us made our way to the sleek black leather couches at the far end of the office. He sat and leaned back, crossing his legs. "Drew, I've already given Craig a high-level summary of the project, but it's fairly simple."

Craig chuckled. "Maybe on your end it is."

"I'm going into production with a new chip, designed as a permanent data storage and retrieval mechanism. Think of it as an archive for eternity. I won't bore you with the technical details, but I'd consider this my legacy."

"Tremaine Industries is a pretty good legacy all on its own." I took a sip of my whiskey. The rich heat burned its way down my throat.

"That it is." Gideon smiled, swirling his own drink. "Are you familiar with the seed vault in Norway?"

"Svalbard? The doomsday vault for seed genetics?"

"This chip will fill that role for the collective data of humankind." Gideon sat forward, placing his glass on the table and leaning his elbows on his knees. "There are those who wish to see me fail. Not because the endeavor isn't a noble one, but for the same reasons a segment of the population wants me to fail at anything. Because I've done government contracts. Because some believe my employees around the world aren't all paid equitably. Maybe because I grew up poor and built a fortune on my own. The reason doesn't matter. What *does* matter is I've received several threats aimed at this data chip."

"Which I'm sure you receive all the time?" I offered.

"True." Gideon looked at Craig. The two of them had been friends for years, and Bishop and Associates had completed two jobs for Tremaine since I'd joined the firm. "I've increased security at my plants, but someone specifically threatened the unveiling event."

Craig sat forward, mirroring Gideon's pose, but looking at me. "Tremaine Industries is throwing a charity gala next weekend and the messages Gideon showed me indicate that will be the place and time."

Why steal it during a charity event, where security will be high and it will be surrounded by people? "You suspect it's about you, not about the chip itself?"

Craig tapped the side of his nose and pointed at me. "Precisely."

If my boss knew so much, why bother with the meeting? Why not tell us this was our next job? For that matter, why call our team in at all? "I assume you already have security in place for the event. I further assume you won't cancel for exactly the reason they're targeting the event: You don't want to risk your reputation."

"Yes, on both counts." Gideon stood, heading for his desk.

Was there something I knew? Something from my past that tied me to this event? Some reason Craig would bring me here? "Do you think your son's mistress has something to do with it?"

Gideon chuckled as he returned to the couch with a thumb drive.

His son's mistress had attempted to blackmail him with a pregnancy story. It hadn't taken me much mental effort to identify the true father and put that to rest. Plus, I'd instilled enough fear in her about crossing the Tremaines that Gideon's daughter-in-law would never find out about the affair.

"Craig tells me you have experience with thieves."

My hand gravitated to my watch. *A little too much experience.* "I do."

"This drive contains a listing of all event personnel, blueprints of the location, and a schedule of activities." He passed the thumb drive to me. "I'd like you to head up a special security detail designed to keep this chip safe."

"And your reputation?" I slid the drive into my inside breast pocket, where my phone should have been. Maybe I needed zippers added. "That's what we're really protecting here?"

"The charity gala is my wife's brainchild. The merging of art and technology." Gideon swept a hand through the air, shaking his head slightly at the scope of his wife's vision. "Complete with auction and display."

"Will any of her pieces be included?"

"She's been working on something for six months. I've hardly seen her the last few weeks." Gideon's wife was a well-known artist, renowned for industrial-sized work. "I won't let her efforts be spoiled because of my tiny chip."

"It's not our normal type of contract, but Gideon came to me personally." Craig hadn't touched his whiskey. He normally nursed his drinks, fitting in with anyone who held a glass but keeping his senses sharp. "I've already agreed to the contract. My focus is on crafting a campaign to deal with the fallout in case the thief or thieves are successful. While I'm working on that, I'd like you to coordinate our team. Bring in any specialists you deem necessary."

In other words, he wanted more than our team of five involved. There were several local contractors we'd worked with on other jobs, but when Gideon Tremaine hired you, you used the best.

And it was going to hurt.

I rolled the crystal tumbler between my palms, watching the liquid swirl, appreciating the scent of raisins wafting from it.

"If you want to prevent a heist, your best defense is another heist crew—if you can find one you trust." I took a sip, barely tasting the fine whiskey over the flavor of irritation coating my tongue. "I think we should call in Reynolds Recoveries."

Craig nodded at Gideon and his curious look. "They're smart, fast, and, most importantly, discreet. We've worked with them twice. Your chip would be in excellent hands."

With the decision made, our conversation veered toward the weather, a minor scandal brewing for a junior senator, and the shopping habits of the other men's wives. I smiled at the right places, laughed with them, and contributed an anecdote about my ex and her handbag fetish.

The memory of my encounter with Jayce intensified as the conversation turned increasingly mundane. Scarlett, her team lead, was a gorgeous woman. Tall and slender, with long brown hair, she dressed in designer clothes and had a smile that could melt the polar ice caps.

I knew her type. Trained from an early age to best men like me, she knew what to say and when to say it, whether it was with words, her body, or a simple glance.

Still, it was the little spitfire who did what she wanted when she wanted, consequences be damned, who'd captured my attention. Average height with light olive skin, brown eyes, and broad shoulders, her background couldn't have been more different from Scarlett's. Instead of working in the shadows where she lurked now, Jayce had grown up in the spotlight. Three World Gymnastics gold medals, five silvers, and a vault routine named the Monroe which had more flips and twists than I could wrap my head around.

It all came to an abrupt halt at twenty, only months before her Olympic debut. That's when the information about her grew sparse. One car accident, and she went from international champion to... an irritating thief who'd stolen my phone.

"I'll call my pilot," said Gideon, snapping me back to the room.

How much had I missed?

Craig tossed back his drink and stood. "We'll be in touch in a couple of days."

I followed suit and shook Gideon's hand, thanking him for the drink and conversation. Craig and I walked out together.

"Reynolds is a good idea," said Craig. "Are you sure you can work with them after the last time?"

The last time, we hadn't set the boundaries as tightly as we should have. I'd deferred to their expertise and Jayce had taken advantage of that.

This time? I'd be running the show and she'd either do as I told her or she'd be off the team. "It'll go smoothly."

"Exactly what I wanted to hear."

And if it didn't?

At least I'd get my phone back.

CHAPTER 3
JAYCE

The ping of the door chime announced my arrival with Emmett. The Reynolds Recoveries headquarters was a large office in a nondescript building in a nondescript business park in Halifax. From the outside, it looked the same as the dozens of companies surrounding it. Even from a glance in the windows, it was nothing more than cubicles and a few dozen workers.

Those workers weren't a cover—they were the day-to-day bread and butter. They kept the lights on between high-profile cases that our small crack team handled.

A trio near the entrance might have been tracking down someone's birth parents. A quiet woman in the corner could have been dealing with a call to open a safe the owner had forgotten the combination to. The group laughing by a water cooler could have been celebrating the return of a lost dog.

We did a lot of good in our community and far beyond.

But hidden behind the walls of private offices and a couple of laboratories was a different type of recovery agent. A white hat heist crew that did dangerous work, skirted the law, and always brought home stolen items for their rightful owners.

Emmett nodded to me as he broke off toward his office, and I paused, letting out a long sigh.

Stolen items.

Why did I take Drew's phone? *Because he was trying to prove he was better than you.* Trying to throw his weight and control around. Showing off that sexy jaw and those smoldering eyes. I should have returned his phone when I returned his watch.

We'd come directly from the airport for our debrief with the team. I wheeled my small suitcase toward Yvonne's large desk with its chest-high cubicle walls.

Our logistics manager looked up with a smile, her straight, light-brown hair swishing over her shoulders. "Hey, Jayce. How was Washington?"

"Fast." We'd arrived last night and left just after noon. The flight was only two and a half hours, bringing us home before the office emptied of regular staff. "I need something shipped back, though. Small package. Any chance you can get it there tomorrow?"

"Probably." She turned to her computer, fingers dancing over the keyboard in that strange three-finger way she did. "Address?"

"Don't know the details, but—"

"Jayce!" called Scarlett from somewhere in the office. "Boardroom."

"It needs to go to Bishop and Associates." I didn't have his home address, although someone surely did. Best I let everyone think it was professional—a delivery for a company we'd worked with before. Of course, if Emmett caught wind of the shipment, he'd figure me out.

"Oh?" Her fingers paused and she glanced up at me. "That's convenient."

Convenient? What did that mean?

"Jayce?" Scarlett appeared next to me. She wore a black pantsuit, her sleek brown hair hung in easy waves. She always looked like she'd stepped out of a fashion magazine.

I appreciated my body. It was strong and flexible, and it let me do a job no one else in this company could. But my stretchy jeans and blue T-shirt were practically rags compared to her stilettos and skinny pants. She hadn't dressed down at work a single day since Malcolm joined us.

"Sorry, Yvonne," said my glamazon team lead, "but Jayce is late for a meeting. She'll be out in an hour."

With a flick of my wrist for a wave, I left with Scarlett. "Just let me drop my things off first."

"If I told you Evelyn had the profiteroles from Russo's sitting on the table for you, would that change your priorities?"

I snorted a laugh. "I'll park my bag in the corner."

We made the short trek to the main boardroom, where the two glass walls were frosted over. On a normal day, they were clear, but when the secrets came out, privacy was paramount.

The boardroom table seated twelve, with paintings decorating one wall and a big-screen television dominating the other. Emmett was already there, as was his and Scarlett's mother, Evelyn.

Scarlett may have been my boss, but Evelyn was the Big Boss. She wore her platinum blonde hair in a short bob and dressed like her daughter. The two of them had a tense relationship, likely because they were so similar—although Scarlett would have throttled me for saying that out loud—but something had changed between them over the last couple of months.

After Emmett's kidnapping, a lot changed for the Reynolds team.

Emmett had an extra edge about him. Aftereffects of his ordeal, maybe? Maybe not. But he was different.

Scarlett expressed emotions every now and again—mostly around Malcolm, her overly devoted boyfriend, who'd just received his work permit after moving up from the States. She also got along with her mother far better, and even sat next to her in the boardroom most days. The decrease in tension was a welcome change.

As for Evelyn? She may have acted like she was more boss than mother at the office, but after someone had messed with two of her kids, the woman was out for blood—in her own silent and ultra-scary way.

I rolled my suitcase past Emmett and into the corner. The white box of treats was in front of him, so I took the chair beside him, dragging the box to its rightful position in front of me. Chocolate and sugar invaded my nostrils. It was good to be home. "Brie joining us?"

Our tech wizard's office was upstairs, directly above the boardroom. Hurried footsteps on the stairs nearby announced her approach. Evelyn's youngest bore little resemblance to her mother or siblings. She was plain compared to Scarlett's glamor, gentle compared to Evelyn's intensity, and hesitant compared to Emmett's smooth-talking ways.

"Can't stay long." Brie was already speaking before the door closed behind her. "The Trojan's making its way through his layers of security, but we're being careful. His programming's amazing. We're mapping the parts of the network we can safely, with about thirty percent of our steganographic messages getting through. First step is upping that to fifty. Nothing useful yet—nothing on the scarab, nothing on the location of the data center. Can I go now?"

I popped a profiterole in my mouth, biting down slowly on the crispy exterior, sinking into the airy dough, then the creamy middle. The chocolate drizzle over the top was divine.

"Is Will monitoring it?" asked Evelyn.

Will Reaney was our gadget guru, Brie's backup, and her lifelong bestie. I didn't know a quarter of what they did about computers, but despite all his talents, the one thing I did know was that she was better than him in this arena.

"He is." Brie held up a tablet, tapped it a few times, then looked back at us. "Ash is on her way in, and she can cover me when I have to sleep."

I selected another treat, letting it hover in front of my mouth. "It's that touchy you can't sleep while it's working?"

"It is. One wrong step and his AI finds us, then the Trojan gets destroyed. We need to go slow." Brie shrugged. "And if Tremaine Industries has gone through all this trouble to hide that data warehouse, it's going to be behind a lot of security. Who hides something like that if it's completely above board?"

We had two targets at Tremaine Industries. First, we'd received a tip that an ancient Egyptian scarab, stolen from a museum in Cairo, was on its way to Tremaine. A museum patron of some sort requested we retrieve it, so we were searching for details before signing a contract.

Second, and the higher priority for the people in this room, was tracking down a data storage center in the Arctic Circle that didn't exist according to the Internet. Word was that many criminals housed information there, including the Fenix Group. After Emmett's kidnapping, Scarlett's near-fall from grace, and our recent adventure in the Roman Catacombs, Evelyn had the shadowy organization in her sights.

Brie had started with hacking into low-level employee computers, but she'd been working all her angles for a month with no results.

Which had given me my chance to shine.

"Tech billionaires do whatever they want." I tossed the profiterole in my mouth and covered it with a hand as I kept talking. "He seemed like a nice guy, though. Surprised he'd be collaborating with such lowlifes."

"I doubt he's collaborating. More likely, they don't do extensive background checks." Brie stretched her neck and rubbed at it before glancing at Scarlett. "We'll find those photos."

Her older sister shook her head. "Even if you do, I'm sure they've been downloaded all over the world."

"Which means I can remove them and trigger a cascading delete to every synced computer and phone." *That* was Brie's primary goal. Protect Scarlett by destroying the photos Fenix had of her stealing something in London. Brie was the shy Reynolds, a dramatic contrast from her siblings and mother. But somewhere deep inside, she had the same cutthroat instincts.

What was it like to have people who loved you so much?

"Moving on." Evelyn tapped a tablet in front of herself and the television came alive. "We have some positive news."

"Can I go back to my office?" asked Brie.

Evelyn nodded and her youngest slipped out of the boardroom. "In case Brie's efforts don't yield the results we want, Scarlett and I have negotiated a contract that brings us closer to Gideon Tremaine."

Leaning forward, I grabbed another pastry and slid the box toward Emmett, who shook his head. "I doubt I can get into his office again."

"True." Evelyn's lips thinned and she hit play on an audio of my bathroom waltz with Drew. We listened to the whole thing, from him whispering in my ear about the fire alarm to our chat about the window, confessing we weren't after Gideon, and the dance over the mints and cleaning spray.

It was hard not to smile. I'd come up with some awfully clever lines.

"Jayce," she said, all her frost on full display. "Get some self-control."

Not my strong point, boss. "It was all Donovan. You can't hear it on the audio, but he was harassing me."

Just by standing there, glowering at me, wearing his tailored suit and yummy cologne. What else did they expect me to do?

"Perhaps you should spend some additional time with Scarlett on the next job, so she can show you—" A knock at the door cut off Evelyn's mini-lecture. "Come in."

One of the front office staffers whispered to her from the doorway, and Evelyn stood, walking out with him.

Uninterested, I eyed the white box. There were six profiteroles left. Did I want more? Or did I want something else? What was in the staff kitchen? Did I have time for a bagel? "Any idea how much longer we'll be, Scarlett?"

She cocked her eyebrow.

God, I hated that eyebrow.

It was *Be patient* mixed with *Do you seriously need more food?* and a hint of *Sit still for a minute.* Maybe a little *I have no idea, but my mother will kill us both if we leave.*

I swiped some cream stuck to the side of the box and licked it off my finger.

Just as Evelyn walked through the door.

Followed by *him.*

Drew.

And I totally had pastry cream on my face.

CHAPTER 4
DREW

A near-empty bakery box sat in front of Jayce, who was hastily licking something from her finger and the corner of her mouth.

Chaos.

Personified.

"Drew, good to see you again." Evelyn's voice was a purr, always smooth and controlled. I wouldn't have said I liked the Reynolds matriarch—more that I respected what she'd built. A team devoted to rectifying the wrongs of others. Despite that goodness, she exuded a special kind of power. Hidden—like a snake bearing its belly so you thought it was dead—but it was watching and waiting for the opportunity to strike.

"And you." Instead of sitting in the seat she gestured to, I walked past two chairs and stopped beside Jayce, who swiveled to look up at me. I held out my hand, palm up.

From the way she met my gaze, her light brown eyes flickering with mischief, it was clear I didn't have to tell her what I wanted. She placed another finger in her mouth, sucking the residue off it. Without a word, she bounced out of her chair and headed past me to a corner of the office, opened a zipper on a suitcase, and returned to place my phone in my hand. "Thanks for saving me the shipping cost."

There were many things I wanted to say to her. Cuss her out for taking it, congratulate her on how seamlessly she'd done it, or tell her she wasn't welcome on this job. I pushed it all into my mental locker—along with the way my gut had tightened when she licked her finger—and took the seat next to her.

Jayce rocked back and forth on the chair. "How'd you get here so fast?"

That was the part of my conversation with Craig and Gideon I'd missed while I was busy fuming about my phone. One of the Tremaine Industries private jets was ready for me the moment we finished. I'd only had enough time to pack an overnight bag. "I flew."

"You get your watch?"

I pulled up my suit jacket's sleeve for her to see. *Don't get drawn into another snarking match.* I looked at Evelyn. "Do you have the files I sent?"

She nodded and tapped on a tablet in front of herself. All eyes turned to the television at the far end of the room, which displayed a 3D mock-up of the housing around Gideon's data chip. A specification list appeared next to it, including its size and weight. Two inches square, weighing four-hundredths of a pound.

"This is—"

A knock on the door cut me off.

"Come," said Evelyn.

A tall, broad, haunted-looking man came in first. His dark, shaggy hair brushed his black golf shirt's collar, long enough to pronounce he was done with the military life, but short enough to say it wasn't fully behind him. Rav LaPierre, the head of

Reynolds Recoveries security. He nodded at me and took a seat on the far side of the table.

A blond man followed him, wearing a white Oxford shirt, casually unbuttoned at the neck.

"Malcolm Sharpe?" I stood, approaching him with an extended hand. "What are you doing here?"

He was a private investigator based in New York, the last I knew. Bishop and Associates had hired him for a few jobs over the years. He took my hand and pulled me in to clap my shoulder. "You already know the rest of the team?"

"I've worked with them before." Twice. Once successfully, and once screwed up so badly by Jayce that we'd had to toss our plans out the window and run.

"Lucky you." He grinned and rounded the table, his fingers brushing over Scarlett's neck as he passed her. A faint smile crossed her lips. The way she looked at him when he sank into the chair next to her telegraphed a close relationship. *His* smile told me it was sexual.

Did Evelyn approve of something like that? Did he sleep his way into the company? That made little sense when he had a business in the States. Unless it was more than sex. In love? Malcolm Sharpe? Surely not.

In their line of work, on their more covert ops, a relationship between team members would be a weakness. They'd be too concerned about the other's safety to do their job properly. Although she'd been working with her brother for many years, so maybe caring what happened to each other was part of their strength.

"Anyone else joining us?" I asked as I took my seat.

"This is the full team we're sending," said Evelyn. "I'll read tech support in later. Scarlett?"

Scarlett took over. "I'll be brief. This is a short timeline. You all know I don't like those, but Drew and the team from Bishop have provided us with enough information that we're going ahead. Next weekend, Gideon Tremaine, the head of Tremaine Industries, will be hosting a charity gala in Washington, DC."

Emmett's glance at Jayce was hard to miss. He must not have known about the location, and he was tying the news to... to what? Their visit to Gideon's office earlier today? Or something else?

"We'll be working for Bishop and Associates on this one." Scarlett looked at Jayce this time, as did Evelyn. "*For* them. We're contractors with a specialized skill set, and Drew's point on this."

Jayce's shoulders visibly dropped. She recovered quickly, pulling the box of chocolate-covered pastries closer and shoving one into her mouth whole.

They looked delicious. But were big enough they should have required two bites.

"Drew? Want to take it from there?" asked Scarlett.

I nodded to her and stood, approaching the television. "This is a prototype of a data storage chip—inside a protective housing—which Gideon says will revolutionize information management. He'll make the first public demonstration of it at his gala on Saturday, and he's received several threats that someone will steal it during the event. Since there haven't been credible threats against any of his research labs or production facilities, we suspect the goal is to embarrass him publicly."

At my nod, Evelyn tapped her tablet, and the image on the screen shifted to a floor plan, split into three parts.

"Gideon's wife, Liana, is organizing the event. They're hosting an art auction and there will be a VIP room where non-auction items will be on display."

Jayce lifted a hand to cover her mouth, talking around another mouthful of food. "Why's he unveiling tech at an art gala?"

"Liana's a sculptor and will be..." I was unsure of the details. This was the part Gideon hadn't even known. I hadn't met his wife, but from my research, art was more important to her than anything else, and if she wanted to make a show of things, it would be grand. "One of her pieces will be in the VIP room and the chip will either be on it, in it, or attached to it."

Jayce lifted in her seat, curling a leg underneath herself. "You don't know?"

I glanced at Scarlett, checking for a hint of her '*I don't like rush jobs*' rejection. Nothing. Good. "The venue is a high-end restaurant on the Potomac River, which they've rented out for a few days to install everything. You can see here"—I began pointing out high points—"there's a main dining room, where most of the artwork will be on display. This adjoins a banquet room which will function as the VIP display. There is also a second-floor mezzanine which overlooks the main dining area and a three-tiered outdoor balcony."

Jayce tipped the white box toward herself and frowned. How much sugar had been in there when she arrived? "Sounds swanky."

Emmett nudged her.

She turned to face him, so all I saw was the back of her head as it rolled, but no doubt from an exaggerated eye roll. The woman had no control.

"It will be. Black tie, three hundred in attendance at five thousand a ticket, live music, and a technology-assisted silent auction. All proceeds are being split between his charity, which gives children an opportunity to explore STEM, and hers, which sponsors artistic residencies."

Scarlett added, "Drew's provided personnel details, including all private security, and a partial list of attendees."

"We should have the full picture in a couple of days." One missing piece of the puzzle was a target list. Who was most likely to want to see Gideon—or Liana, since she was the host—fail?

"Good." Scarlett surveyed her team. "I know this is short notice, but happy Monday folks. We'll be flying to Washington tomorrow afternoon, and the gala is on Saturday."

"Only five days to prep?" said Rav, in his low, French-accented voice.

"Five days." Scarlett leaned toward Evelyn's tablet and tapped a few buttons. The television switched to display the guest list, and she highlighted the first attendee. An expanded view of the man's career profile, marital status, and family information appeared. "The Bishop team has provided an excellent starting point, and they'll work with us. Our team will do independent vetting of all attendees and staff."

"What's our job?" asked Malcolm. "Figure out who's behind the threats? Consult on the security?"

Scarlett's lips curved into a grin. "We're going undercover."

"Posing as partygoers?" Malcolm gave her a similar sly look.

"Why am I here?" asked Jayce. "I don't do undercover. I do the shadows."

I sat again. "It'll be a little of everything. The Reynolds team will go in with full access ahead of time, make a plan for how you'd recover the chip, then we shut down every opening you can find. *That's* where you come in."

"Plus," said Scarlett. "You'll be at the event posing as a guest, Jayce. You'll keep an eye out for anyone with slippery fingers."

Jayce frowned, then rubbed a spot above her left knee. "Okay."

So long as she also kept her own slippery fingers to herself.

Evelyn said, "The analysts have started their initial pass and you can expect reports in your inboxes by start of day tomorrow. Review the files. First step is identifying if there are faces, names, or aliases we recognize. Be at the airport for three o'clock when the jet leaves."

"Do you need a flight back tomorrow?" Scarlett asked me.

"I'd appreciate it."

Jayce stood suddenly. "We're done?"

Evelyn nodded.

Jayce grabbed her bag from the corner and was out of the meeting room before anyone else stood. What was with her? She'd been full of her normal cocky attitude when I'd arrived. She'd fidgeted and moved around the entire time, her mood gradually deflating. Something about this job didn't sit right with her.

Did it matter?

No.

There were files to review, discussions to have with my team, and plans to make with the Reynolds crew. I'd get a start on things from my hotel room, take a morning run, then continue the team prep on the flight.

That's what mattered.

Not Jayce Monroe's opinion.

CHAPTER 5
JAYCE

My suitcase hit the doorframe on the way into my office. Stupid roller bag. I shoved it into the corner and flopped into my chair, staring at the desk.

Mondays sucked.

I leaned back and stared at the ceiling. Spun the chair to look at the walls with their simple paintings and photos, none of them mine, except one selfie of me and my friend Leigh. Pulled open the drawer where I'd hidden my logic puzzle books, which normally did wonders to calm my nerves, but they weren't what I needed, either.

What was it about Drew? The entire time he'd been in the boardroom with us, I'd felt like ants were crawling over my body. I couldn't get comfortable. The profiteroles weren't sweet enough. The mint I found in my pocket wasn't minty enough.

Now, I was supposed to go undercover with the team to some fancy gala in Washington, DC? One trip to Washington a year was too much already.

But this time, we'd be there more than one night. There'd be downtime. I'd get the itch to explore.

To visit.

I pushed out of the chair and faced the back wall, where a small plaque hung. I put a hand on it, the one piece of my past which had moved everywhere with me.

Simple white background with black letters: *Never fear the leap. Fear standing still.*

Coach McInnis used to say that every time I was too scared for a new aerial movement. 'Just jump. I'll catch you if you need me to.'

This wasn't a floor routine or the beam. This was work, and the only reason I was with Reynolds was because I was good at my work. I didn't do undercover. I didn't get dressed up in fancy clothes and wear death-trap shoes like Scarlett. Keeping my mouth shut and using pretty words was a skill I'd never needed at Reynolds.

"Okay…"

I spun, startled by Emmett's voice. Should have closed the door.

"What's the deal with you and Drew?"

I exaggerated an eye roll and dropped back into my chair. "Is he gone?"

Emmett leaned against the doorframe, looking over his shoulder in such a blatant way it was obviously a dig at me. "He left right after you stormed off."

"I didn't storm."

"It was less elegant than how you normally leave a meeting."

"Elegant." I snorted a laugh. "Now there's a word that's never been applied to me."

"You rarely leave with a great deal of stealth either, but I think half the office was wondering what happened."

"I don't trust him." No, that wasn't it. What was?

He came into the room, closing the door behind himself. "Are you pouting about the undercover thing?"

"I'm probably just hungry."

"Or crashing from a sugar high?" He sat in the chair on the other side of my desk, crossing his legs like the smooth operator he'd been groomed to be. "I know the last job we did with him didn't turn out the way you envisioned it, but it was still successful."

Successful, my butt. Our anti-heist had wound up as a staged break-in. All to cover Drew's bad decisions. "You don't think this is a conflict of interest? We were just hacking into Gideon Tremaine's computer five hours ago. Now we're working for him?"

Emmett shrugged. "I had a brief chat with the team once Drew was gone. It's a perfect opportunity to get close to Tremaine if Brie's Trojan doesn't work."

"Scarlett and Malcolm will focus on Tremaine himself?"

"I expect so."

Still sounded like a conflict of interest to me. That's what we did, though. Ran the fine line between legal and not quite, to do good in the world. So why did this feel wrong? "And we're not telling Drew any of that?"

"Of course not."

"So we end up being the ones no one can trust?"

He uncrossed his legs and sat forward, setting his hands on my desk. "If it's not Drew, what is it? Tanner?"

I needed a snack. Something less sugary. "I'm going for food." I stood, but he did the same, barring my way to the door. "What are you doing?"

"How did I miss it?" He folded his arms, looking down at me.

Pity? No thank you.

We were not discussing me. "Trusting people outside our team hasn't turned out well for us lately." Too many double-crosses and surprises.

"Worked out well with Malcolm." He pointed to a photo on my wall. "And Leigh."

"They're not Drew." I held up a finger. "They were team players. He's not."

"He is. Just because he questions your quick decis—"

Another finger. "He's too grumpy and serious for undercover work."

"So is Scarlett, but she's exceptional at undercover."

"He second-guesses everything I do."

Emmett swatted my hand. "Stop using Drew as an excuse and admit it. You always get this way when we go to Washington."

Fear standing still. "I'm going to the kitchen. Don't make me knee you."

"You have a whole drawer devoted to food." He didn't budge, just pointed at my desk. "If you want us to check in on Tanner, we can. Or if you prefer, you can visit him while we're there."

"I don't know what you're talking about." Rather than continue the battle to leave, I knelt by my desk and rummaged through the food drawer. Beef jerky? Hazelnut energy bar? Dried mango slices? I yanked out a small jar of peanut butter and a spoon. *Focus on the food*. Anything was better than thinking of Tanner.

Of the screams.

The blood.

The tears.

"I can visit him, if that helps." Emmett stayed put. "Then I can report back."

Even thinking about Drew was better. "I don't have clothes for black tie."

Emmett sighed and leaned against the door. Afraid I was going to bolt the second he gave me a chance? He was probably right. "And you're eating more than usual. You only do that when you're stressed."

"And you're psychoanalyzing me." I took a spoonful of peanut butter, rolling the creaminess over my tongue. "That usually means you're bored."

"Worried." He scratched at his short brown beard. He'd shave it off soon—he always complained it got too itchy after a month. "Drew's watch, I understood, because you returned it right away. That was a taunt. But his phone?"

I waved the spoon around as I swallowed. "Also a taunt."

"What was your plan?"

"Ask Yvonne to ship it back?" Not that I'd come up with that plan until I'd stepped through the office door.

"Why?"

Why did I do anything? Because it was interesting. Because it was a challenge. Because... Maybe because he pressed me up against the wall, and something in his sandalwood cologne fried my brain? Why did Drew Donovan have to be such a hottie and such a jerk at the same time?

"You should talk to Scarlett."

I took another mouthful of peanut butter, which wasn't satisfying whatever craving I had. I covered my mouth with a hand. "About what?"

"Your outfit for the gala." He pushed off the door and opened it, signaling he was done grilling me. "I'm sure she'd love to dress you."

"I prefer black spandex." Anything I could climb in and go unseen. Nothing with a skirt or that included words like *drape* or *slit*.

"Careful what you wish for," he called over his shoulder as he left for wherever he was going.

Good riddance. I took one more taste of the peanut butter and closed the container. I *was* eating more than usual, and that was saying something.

Another trip to Washington meant fifty more times I'd consider visiting Tanner. It'd been twelve years and there'd hardly been a day I hadn't thought about him.

Let alone seeing him in my nightmares.

Nightmares that included my mother forbidding me from seeing him. Or me lying about staying with friends for a weekend and sneaking down to check on him. Then his parents blaming everything on me.

I reopened the jar and took a spoonful I barely tasted.

Thinking about Drew was safer.

Thinking about neither of them was even better.

I closed the jar again and picked up my phone, dialing Leigh's number.

"How's Washington?" Leigh's cheery voice was what I needed. "Any leads yet?"

She'd gotten caught up in a job we did in Rome last month and fell in love with our team's safe cracker in the process. She didn't get to hear the details of our jobs, but knew what we did and was hopeful we could track down Fenix. They'd screwed her over, too.

"It was good, but short, and not fruitful yet. I'm already home, but we're flying out again tomorrow."

"That was fast. You only went last night."

"You wanna catch a movie? Or dinner? I'm hella hungry."

"I would, but..." She paused, her speech growing muffled, then cleared up again. "Declan's making lasagna. Do you want to come over? He always cooks too much."

Right. Visit the two new lovebirds? "No thanks. Maybe I'll go to bed early. I've got a lot of prep work to do."

"Okay. Let me know if you change your mind."

I hung up and considered the peanut butter again. Maybe I'd head to Pizza Corner and eat my weight in greasy pepperoni and donairs. I took off my shoes and curled my toes against the short-pile carpet. The floor was too cold, like always. It didn't make anything better.

Maybe you should hit the climbing gym?

I needed to get rid of this energy and get some sleep.

Tomorrow was going to be a long day.

CHAPTER 6
DREW

Breathe in two three. Out two three.

My feet pounded the gravel, breath coming steady and even.

In two three. Out two three.

Trees and bushes lined the right side of the path, grass and lawn stretching out to the Halifax Harbor on my left. Other runners passed in the opposite direction, giving small waves as they went. I sped by a couple of strollers and random early-morning walkers. Men and women taking a yoga class stretched by the shore, saluting the sun an hour after it had risen.

In two three. Out two three.

A monument, wide at its base and topped with a huge granite cross, stood sentinel ahead of me. Next to it, a Canadian flag hung on a nautical flagpole, barely stirring in the breeze. This was my objective. I slowed, veering off the path onto the grass and a green park bench. One foot at a time, I stretched out my calves and hamstrings while checking my watch.

My sports watch—the one no one had stolen recently.

Heart rate was on target, but my pace was twenty seconds too slow.

I hadn't been able to shake the memories of my altercation with Jayce in Gideon's office. All evening and most of my morning, my brain had been playing a near-constant loop of Jayce's smirk, her stumble, and how gullible I'd been. The way her gaze dipped toward my lips or how my stomach had clenched each time she ran her hands over me.

Recommending her team for this job hadn't been one of my smarter ideas.

Be honest.

For the job, they were perfect. For everything else, it was a mess.

Focus on your work, man.

Despite the hour, the harbor was alive. Two cruise ships were in port and the downtown had been thick with tourists last night. This morning, it was fishing vessels, some small sailboats, and a military RHIB. A container ship was heading out and word on the street was an American aircraft carrier would arrive sometime this afternoon.

My running belt had two water bottle holders, and I pulled out the only bottle I'd brought with me, taking a quick sip.

I pushed my sunglasses to the top of my head and absorbed the view. Inhaling the sea air, I sank onto the bench and breathed in the serenity. It was a beautiful city, so much quieter than the constant buzz around Washington. Sure, Washington was quieter than somewhere like New York, but it was full of power brokers, all the same.

When I left the CIA, my plan had been for a simpler life. Put my parents' death behind me, marry my gorgeous girlfriend, and start a family.

Instead, I traded a career in lies for a career in spin. Discovered the truth my parents had hidden. Found out what my girlfriend had been doing while I wasn't watching. And I wound up alone.

At least my old career was about standing up for something and preserving the Nation. That was a positive. My new career was about preserving reputations and bank accounts.

My watch vibrated and I shut off the alarm, stowing the water in my belt. I took the phone from my armband and held it to my ear.

"Hello?" I said to the silence on the other end as I pulled my sunglasses down again. "You caught me in the middle of a run. How's New York?"

I nodded a few times, made noises of assent. To the outside world, I was having a wonderful chat with my sister, who was on a trip with some friends. In reality, I was counting down the final seconds until my contact arrived.

Gideon had offered to fly me back yesterday after I'd met with the Reynolds team, but I had a meeting I'd already rescheduled for this morning. One I'd been waiting for six months to have, as other intelligence officers did their thing without me.

Another runner approached, sweat collecting at her hairline. She breathed deeply and pointed at the bench. When I nodded, she put a foot on it and leaned over. In an RP accent so smooth she must have cultivated it for years, she said, "Nice shoes. I have the same model in pink at home."

"Can't talk." I gestured at my phone. "I'm talking to my sister."

With the recognition phrases out of the way, she untied her shoe, keeping her head down. Her long blonde ponytail fell forward as she fiddled with the laces, adjusting, as though her shoe were horribly uncomfortable.

"Sorry for the last-minute location change." My trip to Halifax had been a surprise, although not a wholly unwelcome one. Being near the water always calmed me. Something I'd need after this conversation.

"I don't mind. I've not been here in ages. Plus, it's a lot easier for me to fly into the airport here than DC."

And easier for me to go unnoticed. "What's the news?"

"He *is* dead." Her voice was quiet, as though I hadn't known that part.

"I know." I watched the water, continuing to nod to my non-existent sister on the non-existent phone call.

The woman was in private investigations in London, a former MI6 agent, who'd served with the best friend I'd ever had. "And it wasn't the Iranian government."

I clenched my teeth. "I suspected as much." More like Craig had suspected and encouraged me to find out the truth.

When Alex vanished and then I got the news he'd been killed, it cemented my decision to leave the Agency. The story I'd been told was that Iranian forces had caught him sneaking across the border from Afghanistan. He hadn't told me what his mission was before he left, but he *had* told me he was flying into Tehran. Either he'd lied to me or the stories about his death weren't true.

Just like everything else in my life. All lies.

She finished re-tying her laces and switched to the other shoe. "All the data you requested on the drive."

"Including who and how?"

"Of course. You paid for everything." She twisted her torso, playing into the role of a tired runner, although her long, toned legs indicated she ran regularly. "I don't have to tell you how sensitive the information is."

"Did you know? What happened?"

"I didn't."

I bowed my head forward, staring at the grass which fought against the dirt around the base of the bench. How many people sat in this space each day, gazing out at the water, not a care in the world? "Does it bother you?"

"My psychiatrist would say yes." She took a seat next to me and pulled out one of her water bottles, maintaining the ruse. "There's a comfort in knowing your government's behind you, in case something happens. But..."

But sometimes that government then claimed the Iranians killed your best friend, rather than truly being there for him. Although I hadn't seen the information, so there might have been nothing anyone could have done. Maybe Alex got into a situation he couldn't get out of. Maybe he trusted the wrong source.

She chuckled. "But if someone like Craig Bishop tried wooing me away, I'd have left a lot sooner and likely been happier for it."

We'd traveled in the same circles and worked with many of the same people—some even by the same names. She and I had never met before, but she knew who I was and who I worked for. Most people thought I'd left the Agency for Craig, but he'd only approached me after I'd decided to leave. It was a mistaken impression I didn't care to correct.

A lie of omission, isn't it, Drew?

She leaned back to take a swig from her bottle, paused, and stared at it. Shook it. Empty? She placed it on the bench between us and grabbed her other, taking a long pull. Once she was done, she stood and tucked that water bottle into her running belt. She bounced on her toes a few times, testing the fit of her shoes. "That's better!"

Back to her performance, in case anyone was watching.

With a wave, she jogged off, leaving me to the morning noises. Waves. Gulls. Wind in the trees. Joggers, walkers, and children.

I hung up the fake phone call, slipped the phone back into its carrier on my bicep, and stared out at the harbor fading into the ocean. Land jutted into the water at the right and an island sat at the harbor's mouth to the left, ensuring the waves remained gentle.

Another deep breath.

The park was as much a part of this city as the waterside trails I ran in DC, but there was something different here. More buffer from the cars and buildings, more trees, more something. More water.

I turned to look at the monument, but my gaze landed on the bench. The runner had left her water bottle. As casual as I could make it, I picked up the bottle and shot up from the bench, searching for where she'd gone. Mouth open, as though to call out, 'You forgot your bottle!'

But she was out of sight, vanishing faster than my leisurely appreciation of the scenery.

I slipped the bottle into the empty slot on my running belt and resumed my run.

Exactly as we'd planned.

Hopefully, the data hidden inside would keep me distracted until I met the Reynolds team at the airport.

Chapter 7
Jayce

The aft cabin of the Reynolds jet had four plush leather seats on one side, two across the aisle, and a table which extended the full width of the plane. A sea of tablets littered the surface, vying for space with the folders and printed sheets. Lists, photos, and bios—all required reading.

We'd each reviewed everything independently before boarding. Flight time was collaboration time.

"This one"—Malcolm zoomed in on a photo on the tablet between him and Rav—"has had at least four mistresses I'm aware of." Malcolm's work as a PI for the elite along the East Coast came in handy. He recognized half the people who were attending the Tremaine's gala.

"Can we talk perimeter security?" I stood from my seat, carrying my tablet and stretching my legs. We'd been at cruising altitude for an hour. All the talking and sitting was driving me batty. "The obvious ingress points are the doors to the patio, the balcony off the mezzanine, the elevator, and the emergency stairwell."

Drew, on the opposite side of the table, watched me as I moved, while everyone else—accustomed to my pacing—focused on the work in front of them. "We'll have security on those doors."

"What's the weather forecast?"

His miserable little face remained pinched, as though answering my questions was an inconvenience. "Rain Friday, but clear on Saturday for the party."

"That means a steady stream of partygoers heading in and out to the patio all night." Part of me wanted to sit back down behind the table, so I was invisible.

His gaze didn't flicker off me for a second.

I tapped a button on the side console of the divan in the mid cabin, which opened a drawer containing—nothing. I'd eaten everything I'd stashed inside. "Plus, I'd bet there's roof access that's not listed on the floor plan."

"Or that access is from connecting buildings," said Drew. The restaurant venue was part of a larger complex, with shops, a deli, a few professional offices, and a coffee shop. He could have been right. Maintenance would require access to the roof, and more than one part of the building might have provided it.

"We don't have aerial photos. We should get Brie or Will on that."

"If you mean by drone," said Drew, "they're not allowed in DC. If you mean satellite, that might work."

I'd meant drone. No need to say that out loud. "Of course I meant satellite."

"I'll text Brie." Emmett pulled out his phone and began typing.

Brie was likely too busy monitoring her precious Trojan—not that we could discuss that with Drew on the flight.

She'd probably pass it off to someone else on her team or over to Will if it would be challenging.

"When are we visiting the venue?" I asked.

"Tomorrow morning. We'll meet with my team…" Drew paused, his gaze finally dropping to the table again. What was that about? "Then we'll go."

"Drew?" said Scarlett. "Can you walk me through—"

I wandered the length of the private jet to the small galley. Our flight team kept it stocked with snacks—and they knew my favorites. A brief rummage pulled up a blueberry and pecan protein bar, plus a bag of chips. And a bottle of water. Perfect. I balanced it all on top of the tablet and sat in one of the forward cabin reclining seats, tucking my legs underneath myself.

There were too many doors to this location. If security guarded all of them, it would put the guests off. Since Gideon and his wife would want them to open their wallets as much as possible, they'd want the guests comfortable.

Instead of guarding the doors and preventing a thief from getting in or out, the best bet would be to increase the security for the chip itself. I funneled food into my mouth, savoring the crispness of the chips first. Sweetness would come later from the protein bar.

The venue was long and had two stories. The chip and some other showcase items would be in a banquet room, forty-eight feet by fifty-three. Two doors on the south wall to the sprawling patio, one on the west to the main dining room, another to the west for stairs to the bathrooms, and finally one on the north wall heading to the kitchen. They were all double doors, save the one for the kitchen. The east wall was the only one not open to the world.

Could they have picked a location with more options for a thief to get in and out of?

It was a data chip. A tiny thing as easy to steal as a—well, as a phone. I took a sip of my water, glancing at Drew as covertly as I could. He was deep in conversation with Scarlett, the two of them pointing at things and shuffling papers and tech. Rav joined their discussion as Malcolm stood and walked past me to the heads.

I put the water bottle into the holder next to me and woke my tablet, staring at the doors on the floor plan.

Drew fit in with my team better than I did. He could handle hours of focus and analysis.

My eyes were already glazing over.

You don't have a focus problem, Jayce. I'd barely slept last night. If it was only *my* team on the jet, I would have snuck into the private cabin in the back and napped until we got to DC.

Although if it was only *my* team on this job, I wouldn't have been tossing and turning all night, thinking about Drew. Drew and his trim little beard and the lips that never curved up into a smile. The jaw that kept on flexing. The clever eyes that saw everything.

I chuckled to myself. They saw everything except me stealing his watch and phone.

Yeah, he fit in with my team. None of them would have caught me, either.

Malcolm appeared, taking the seat across from me. "What do you think?"

"They're like two peas in a pod." I kept my gaze fixed on Malcolm, but my attention was on Drew and Scarlett.

"They are." He didn't turn his head. "Same intensity."

I lowered my voice. "Doesn't that make you worry?"

"Worry?" Malcolm's eyes narrowed, dimming their ridiculous blueness. "He's worked with Reynolds before, right? Brie's done the background checks and ensured he's trustworthy?"

"Twice and yes, but that's not what I mean." I unwound my legs from underneath me so I could lean closer. "You know. The two of them?"

Malcolm's face relaxed and he chuckled. "Any sign of an attraction between them before?"

"No, but they were quick jobs."

"So was the one I did with Reynolds." He'd shown up on Scarlett's doorstep after Emmett was kidnapped. She'd pulled a gun on him, and somehow, within two weeks, Malcolm melted her normally frosty exterior. Now he lived with her and worked with us. "Why would I worry?"

"What if he can give her something you can't?"

"There will always be people who can do that, but it doesn't mean they can replace me or what she and I have."

How could he be so sure after so little time? He'd brought a special skill set to our team, but one that wasn't completely unique. Emmett and Rav had investigative talents, too. Emmett could talk anyone out of anything. Scarlett could plan any op within an inch of its life.

He and Scarlett didn't have the past she had with Rav. Malcolm was gorgeous, but so were the other men. Almost as hot as irritatingly sexy Drew.

"You can always be replaced." By someone more talented, more acceptable, more capable. I pulled my left leg underneath myself, kneading a thumb into the spot above my knee that would hurt if I sat much longer. I'd been replaced easily enough after the accident.

By everyone in my life.

"That's not how connections between people work. Chemistry isn't about similarities, it's about magic." He shook his head and slid to the edge of his seat, coming closer to me. "It's something you can't fake. It's either there or it isn't."

My throat tightened. I grabbed my water bottle, rolling my eyes as dramatically as I could. Maybe that was my entire problem. I couldn't fake anything. Words tended to fall out of my mouth before I realized I'd thought them.

That's why I worked in the shadows. The only people who ever heard me on a job were my teammates, and they could cover for me.

A sly smile slid up his face. No doubt at my silence.

I swung my protein bar at his smug grin, but he easily dodged. "You're such a cheeseball."

"No." Rav's harsh word pulled our attention to the group at the back of the jet. "Scarlett teams with me."

"You mean me," said Malcolm, already on his way to join them. For someone not worried about being replaced, he worked awfully hard to ensure it wouldn't happen. Or maybe that was the key. He'd fight for the woman he loved.

"I'm not trusting her security to anyone else," continued Rav.

Scarlett knocked twice on the table. "Enough."

Drew put up his hands, dipping his head slightly toward Rav. "You've already said you won't allow our two teams to share comms, Rav. We need to pair up my team and yours."

"Then you can work with Malcolm, and I'll take Scarlett."

"Rav?" Scarlett slipped into her command tone, no doubt highlighted by that eyebrow she learned from her mother. It sounded like a question, but it was an order. *Stand down, guard dog.*

They'd been friends since they were kids, and from what snatches of conversation I'd heard, something serious held them close. He was always protective of her, which had only become more intense over the last couple of months.

But watching Malcolm stand up to Rav over it? Maybe there was some truth about what he said about chemistry and not faking it. He hadn't hesitated for a moment to declare he'd take care of her, even though Rav could have snapped him in half without a thought.

"How many of your team members will be joining us?" asked Scarlett.

"Two who'll be working the party. My boss will coordinate."

Scarlett nodded, pointing as she spoke. "Malcolm's with me. Emmett and Rav will team up with your people."

And just like that, she'd decided, leaving Emmett and Rav nodding.

But wait, that meant—

"Drew, I want Jayce with you."

I shot up out of my chair. *No.*

"People in DC know you." Scarlett was talking like I had no say in the matter. Did no one else see what a terrible idea this was? "You'll have more reasons to be working the crowd in the banquet room, giving her a perfect excuse to monitor the chip."

"No." The word sounded weak coming out of my mouth. Why was I even objecting? I joined everyone around the table. "He can't be my partner."

Scarlett turned the eyebrow on me. "He can."

"You remember what happened the last time?"

"We're both professionals, Jayce." Drew's face held no expression. No smile, no irritation, not even a head tilt.

"Professionals work *together*, Drew. They don't order me around and screw up our entire job. You tanked that job on me."

At least his jaw flexed. At least he had some sort of emotion inside him. His mouth opened, but Scarlett stood abruptly.

She pointed one immaculately manicured fingertip toward the seat I'd been enjoying my snacks from, forcing me back there. Time for the reaming. At least she lowered her voice. "You remember what my mother said?"

I swiped my bag of chips from the tray table. "Get some self-control?"

She blew out a small breath and put a hand on my arm. "We're trying to stop a thief. We'll look at every angle and figure out how we'd take the chip, but in the end, your instincts are going to be the most important asset we have."

I tossed a handful of food into my mouth.

Scarlett was playing me, throwing out compliments so I'd agree to pair up with Drew.

Paired up meant posing as dates. How the hell was I going to pose as that man's date without making a fool out of myself?

Chapter 8
Drew

I stepped out of the elevator into our office Wednesday morning, the SD card in my pocket weighing me down. What was I going to do with the information? Did it matter the British government had lied about what happened to Alex? Could I have expected the same fate if someone found me where I didn't belong?

Just as well I had no family or close friends to mourn me.

The Bishop and Associates office was in a historic building, with soaring ceilings and semi-flush lighting fixtures. The polished concrete floor contrasted with the warmth of dark wood paneling and doors. We didn't have a receptionist or a front desk, but controlled access on the stairwell kept unwanted visitors out and the elevator announced every arrival.

"Drew?" Wyatt's unmistakable Texan accent carried from down the hall. "Is that you?"

The wide hallway led to our boardroom and Craig's office beyond. Two offices on either side housed the rest of us. Wyatt was also former CIA, Zaria had been a lawyer in New York for under a decade, and Byron was our tech guy who'd left Apple for Google and then for Bishop and Associates.

Rather than head for my office, I detoured into Wyatt's.

He stood behind his desk, reaching into a drawer, his blue eyes trained on me. "I can trust you, right?"

"That's a loaded question, don't you think?"

He eased the drawer shut and locked it, one hand balled up as though he were hiding something. He was a handsome man in his early forties with thick, sandy blond hair and a ready smile, all the readier if a woman walked into the office. Her looks didn't matter, just her sexual orientation and availability—or willingness to pretend on either account. "And that's why I know the answer's yes."

I stopped behind one of the guest chairs at his desk, placing a hand on the smooth leather.

Wyatt leaned into his Southern background to keep others off guard. He'd told me once the accent made people think he wasn't as clever as he actually was, which was one more advantage he could use. That extended to the way he decorated his office—artfully worn edges on his furniture and the painting of a cowboy herding cattle behind the desk. He used to wear big belt buckles and bolo ties but had switched last year to a subtle leather cuff bracelet with a longhorn. "Did you get the information you were looking for about your buddy?"

Other than Craig, my co-workers only knew small parts about my investigation into Alex's death. And the truth was too raw to discuss with them. "Did you need me? The Reynolds Recoveries team will be here soon."

"I know, I got the meeting invite." Wyatt rounded the desk and held out his balled-up hand, nodding at mine. When I held mine open, he handed me a small brass key. "Your story about him got me thinking. If something ever happened to me,

I wouldn't want some stranger poking around in my business. I'd want it to be a friend."

I held up the key, which had no markings on it.

He lowered his voice, the twang all but disappearing. "That's the backup key to my safe. The only backup."

A strange offer. "Shouldn't your executor have this? Or Craig?"

"Maybe." He patted me on the upper arm. "But for now—"

"Are we bonding, boys?" came Zaria's smooth voice from behind me.

Wyatt curled my fingers around the key before I turned to see Zaria. "I was trying to get some information about this new job."

"The event security for Gideon Tremaine?" Despite growing up in the States, her light accent hinted at her Nigerian heritage. She was a hair shorter than Jayce, but her high heels, draped blouse, and pencil skirt made her seem taller. Zaria was our contact with media of all kinds, her musician father providing her with an influence list almost as long as Craig's.

I nodded, sliding my hands into my suit pant pockets. "Is Craig here?"

"In his office." Wyatt ushered us toward the hall. "I have a quick call to make before the meeting, so if y'all don't mind?"

"Did I hear correctly?" Zaria followed me across the hall to my office. "You're the one who suggested the Reynolds team? Despite..."

"Despite their thief nearly getting me caught on Chase Harrington's job?" The room was minimalist, with sleek lines and simple surfaces, which I preferred. It was a stark contrast to Wyatt's, with his homey leather versus my ergonomic mesh-backed chairs.

She chuckled behind me. "Craig says she's going to—"

"Zaria," said Craig, who'd arrived without making any noise. "Can you give me a minute with Drew?"

"Of course." She inclined her head and retreated, clacking heels fading into the background.

I didn't turn around. Instead, I swung out the painting over a set of low filing drawers to reveal my office safe. "She confirmed Alex is dead."

"We were sure of that already."

If only that part of the story had been the lie. I pressed a thumb to the scanner on my safe, and a nearly inaudible click sounded. "But it wasn't the Iranian government."

"Who was it?" His volume was the only thing that told me he'd moved closer.

Inside the safe were documents, cash, and a few files from clients. I stored everything personally critical in my apartment. I placed the SD card, in its carrying case, onto a shelf at the back, then added Wyatt's key next to it. "A group called the Flame of Khvarenah."

"That sounds familiar." Craig swiveled one of the visitor's chairs and sat.

"I did some research while I was out of town." I closed the safe, swung the painting into place, and sank into the other visitor's chair, facing him. "A group of historians and archaeologists started it in the early 2000s to protect cultural heritage items from being destroyed or pillaged. Over the last five years, they've grown more aggressive and apparently violent."

"And Alex got mixed up with them?"

"From the sounds of it." I dragged my hands through my hair. "She couldn't find out what the link was."

"She gave you everything else?"

"It's all on the drive." I hooked a thumb over my shoulder, toward my safe.

"Do you know where they were?"

"The data package included details on their base of operations." Did I really want to know? Did it matter? What was I even going to do about it? "They've moved around a lot in the last five years, but they're currently based near Shiraz."

"That's a long way from the border with Afghanistan."

"No kidding." It was closer to the Persian Gulf. Claiming he'd been sneaking across the Iraqi border or in from the water made more sense.

"What's the key for? Something of Alex's?"

"It's for Wyatt's safe." Leaning forward, I let my head fall into my hands. I should have been prepared for everything I learned about Alex. I knew he was dead, so what did the details matter?

Because it was one more deception. There was no escaping the lies.

Craig placed a hand on my shoulder. "Are you all right?"

There was a knock at the door, and we both looked. Zaria, on the other side of the glass, inclined her head down the hallway.

"Guess I'll have to be." I stood, as did Craig. "I assume the Reynolds team is here."

We reached the door as Wyatt led Scarlett and her crew past my office. Each of them nodded to me, and then Craig and I fell into step behind them.

Our meeting room had floor-to-ceiling windows on two sides. The third wall included a table for coffee and small snacks tucked next to Craig's door and a large screen television on the fourth wall.

No surprise, Jayce made a beeline for the sideboard with the food, finding a bowl with fruit and granola bars. We didn't stock our office like the Reynolds team did, as we had significantly fewer employees and usually ate takeout.

Everyone took their seats around the table while she stood against the wall by the coffeepot, unwrapping a bar.

"I'm sure introductions aren't necessary, but a quick recap," I said. Our last job was four months ago, and no one in this room forgot people quickly. As a courtesy, I gestured to my team members in turn. "Craig Bishop at the end of the table, Zaria Okoye in public relations, and Wyatt James in investigations. They'll be joining us at the event."

Scarlett nodded and did the same. "I'm Scarlett Reynolds, my number two is Emmett Reynolds, I understand you all know Malcolm Sharpe, Rav LaPierre for security, and Jayce Monroe, who's our subject matter expert."

Subject matter expert. That was a new one.

With the pleasantries over, I dove in. "Did everyone review the information packet I prepared? Including this morning's update with the high-risk individual list?" Gideon's assistant had sent me the names of every business contact, former employee, and acquaintance the Tremaines suspected might want to see them fall. It was a long list.

Heads nodded around the table.

"Then we won't spend too much time here since we're work-ing under a tight deadline. At Scarlett's suggestion, we're going to partner up across team lines to improve communications and cover more ground. Zaria, you'll be with Emmett. Your first task will be to speak with the caterers who'll be working with the event staff. There are a couple of employees on their list who need further vetting. Start with management and go from there."

Zaria nodded and looked at Emmett across the table from her. Her smile told me there would be no complaints about that pairing.

"Scarlett and Malcolm, you'll be visiting the security team today."

"That should be my job," said Rav in his thick French accent. He'd served as a clearance diver for the Canadian Navy. Given the spotty information between when he finished dive school and when he left the Forces, he must have worked for CSIS or JTF2. "I served with one of the men in the past. I want to be certain that won't cause a problem."

That made sense. I'd have to adjust the plan. "Wyatt, you'll pair up with Rav—"

Wyatt, who'd been leaning back in his chair, rocked forward. "You are *not* telling me he's my date for the party."

"I am." And I'd expected this reaction. There simply weren't enough women on the Reynolds team to go around.

He sat back again, laughing. "No one is going to believe I'm attending with someone like him. Set me up with Jayce."

From her spot against the wall, she snorted. "Tried that al-ready."

Wyatt stood and walked over to her—no, that wasn't a walk, that was a swagger. His Texan was on full display. He sidled up next to her, giving her a blatant once over. "I think we make a perfect couple. We could go anywhere, including into a coat closet in the back."

Jayce smirked at him and his ridiculous innuendo. "Then Drew and Rav can scowl at everybody at the event. No one would question the two of them hanging out together."

A hard ball settled in my gut.

Zaria grinned, accustomed to Wyatt's overt flirting, and Emmett shook his head.

Before I could lay down the law, Scarlett spoke. "You raise a valid point, Wyatt."

Scarlett Reynolds had always impressed me. In particular, I appreciated how well she convinced people to do what she wanted. If I didn't know better—if I hadn't researched her background—I would have sworn she'd been in the intelligence community.

Obviously, she wasn't finished. Wyatt should have recognized that, too, but he waggled his irritating eyebrows at Jayce.

"However," Scarlett continued, "we've already discussed this. Jayce will only work with Drew or with Craig."

Wyatt, still smiling at Jayce, said, "Like a man in power, do ya?"

She crumpled her granola bar wrapper and held a hand over her mouth while she chewed. "I like the man who feeds me."

"Nothing personal, Wyatt." It definitely wasn't personal. I found her annoying, and she was the biggest variable on this job. Wyatt would have let her get away with anything. I was the one who'd keep her under control. "But we've already established the teams."

He pushed off the wall and retook his chair at the table. "Then I can partner with Craig. Or let me go solo. If I can't have a pretty young thing on my arm, I work best alone."

When his gaze landed on Scarlett, Malcolm sat forward, darkness flaring in his eyes.

Scarlett put an end to the conversation, clasping her hands on the table and appearing perfectly calm. "It's the most efficient way for our teams to stay in touch with each other. And I believe Craig is going to be coordinating the Bishop communications?"

Craig nodded. "Drew suggested I use the manager's office. That will allow me to watch their security feeds."

Scarlett said, "And our off-site team will plug into them as well, providing us with remote support."

Jayce finally joined us at the table, sliding in between Wyatt and Zaria. "What's the point of the event? Why are they unveiling a data chip at a charity art gala?"

"Did you not read the brief?" Zaria's lips tightened, no doubt in response to Jayce's lack of preparation—she had little patience. "Gideon's wife is a celebrated artist. They have respective charities in technology and art, so the event will highlight the fusion of both. It's a perfect opportunity to showcase Tremaine Industries' newest revolutionary product."

"Yeah, I read all that." Jayce's eyes rose heavenward. "But why? They've never held an event like this before, raising funds for both of their charities at the same time. They've never held an artistic event for one of his technology announcements before. Why now? What's different this time?"

Zaria's tense face loosened. "Constant evolution? New ideas?"

"Maybe?" Jayce shrugged and bounced out of her seat, heading for another bite of food. Not only had they been valid questions, but she made it clear she'd done additional homework. Maybe she was cleverer than she let on. Although she certainly didn't deliver any of her speech with the smoothness Scarlett would have. "I mean, what are they going to do? A bunch of paintings and sculptures and stuff and then some random data chip sitting on a table? And why put the real one there? Why not just put a decoy and leave it at that? Is Gideon going to give some giant slideshow presentation on everything it does? You don't need a functional data chip for any of that."

Zaria began, "I don't —"

"You're right." As much as I hated to say it, it was a conversation we had to have with Gideon. Why take the risk? "All we know is that the banquet room will have four special items on display, including the chip. Jayce, you and I need to get over to the venue to meet with Gideon and Liana to get more details on exactly this."

Chapter 9
Jayce

"I feel like I shouldn't touch anything."

"Don't worry, everything's firmly attached. You won't accidentally steal something." Drew clenched his silly little jaw, gaze flicking from the traffic ahead of us to the rearview mirror and back again. The sleek, black Lexus screamed his name. From the wood trim accents to the elegant lines of the leather interior with saddle stitching, it was—there was no other word for it—clean. Not a speck of dust in the cup holders, nothing on the dash, and not even a fingerprint on the huge display screen.

"How long have you had the car?"

"A year and a half." He looked at me, or maybe in the side mirror. It was hard to tell from behind his reflective aviators. "What's going on with Scarlett?"

What kind of question was that? "You have anything to eat in here?"

"Do you not carry your own stash of food?"

"I ate everything already." Normally, I'd be driving somewhere with Rav or Emmett and they'd stop for me. It wasn't my fault I'd been extraordinarily hungry the last few days. "Can we get a burger on the way to the venue?"

"Gideon and Liana are expecting us."

"What about a drive-through? It won't take long."

He touched the center console, which flipped open. "I have gum. Are you going to die without something else?"

I did my best to stop them, but my eyeballs rolled all on their own. It wasn't about surviving; it was about thriving. Didn't he know anything? I checked the center console. No surprise, there was a shallow sliding tray over an organized cavern underneath. A box of tissues, a perfectly spooled phone charger, hand sanitizer, and the package of gum. "Sugar-free spearmint? Even your gum is the most boring ever."

He rolled to a stop and tightened his grip on the steering wheel. "Do you have any filter between your brain and your mouth?"

"Nope," I said, emphasizing the 'P' as I popped a piece of gum out of its blister pack. Scarlett had tried to teach me when I first started working for Reynolds, but that was why she did the talking. Words weren't my strong suit. Actions were. I pushed off my shoes and crisscrossed my legs. I put the package back in the shallow tray, twisted it one way, then twisted it another. "Is it in exactly the right direction? Or should it be five more degrees clockwise?"

His jaw clenched one more time, but there was almost a hint of a smile. In his line of work, he'd have to win people over. Surely the man knew how to smile. Or maybe it was just me that brought out the Negative Nelly in him?

"I was asking about Scarlett? I couldn't help but notice Rav's more protective of her than when we worked together before. At first, I thought he disapproved of her relationship with Malcolm, but he seems content to let her work with him for the gala."

"I think I'm supposed to apply that filter now." As much as words regularly tumbled out when they shouldn't, this information was private. I wasn't just being courteous or trying to piss him off.

The light ahead of us turned green and he began driving again. "I want to make sure it won't jeopardize our job for Gideon. I recommended your team because you're the best, but if something's going on that would prevent that, I need to know."

"Some stuff happened a couple of months ago." Emmett's kidnapping, Fenix courting Scarlett, and then the double- and triple-crosses in Rome.

We sped down a divided roadway and fell into silence, other than the quiet news channel that droned out of his speakers. Also, so Drew.

I stared out my side, which overlooked the Potomac River, thick with trees on either bank. A trail for walkers and runners followed the river. Tanner and I had walked down there once, the last time we were in Washington together. It'd been late at night, the path illuminated by classical-looking lampposts. Reflections of building lights from the opposite bank had glittered across the water. We'd talked about our dreams, worked through a mental block I was having with one of my routines, and chatted about what we were going to do once we'd each won at the Olympics.

My mother had been so upset because we were out past curfew. Back when she cared.

I closed my eyes, fighting the memories lodged in my throat. I hated Washington.

"Did she get hurt?" he asked, pulling me out of my moment.

I popped open the center console and grabbed another piece of gum. "Not even a bottle of water?"

"We're almost there. The parking garage is close to the restaurant where the event's being held, but we can make a quick detour into the coffee shop in the building complex."

"That's more like it!" I swatted his chest—his rock-hard, broad chest—I had to stop doing that—and stowed the gum away again.

He glanced down at where I'd hit him and frowned. How often did he work out? His suit jacket hid the details, but it wasn't disguising arms as thick as Rav's. Was he lean underneath all that? Or was he chiseled?

And why was I thinking about this?

Why did such a ridiculously sexy man have to be such a downer?

The better question was: Why did I care? Not like anything would ever happen between us.

Or that I ever *wanted* something to.

My phone buzzed in my lap, and I pulled it out of my small crossbody bag. It was a text from Scarlett.

"Interesting," said Drew.

I immediately tilted the phone away from him so he couldn't see it. Not that he could have, because our gadget guy had designed the surface of our custom Reynolds phones so you could only see them head-on. "What's interesting?"

"Did Will design that?"

"Design what?" Of course he had. Will built everything for us. And with Brie's programming to back him up, we had the best tech available.

He slowed with the traffic as we passed into a more commercial area. "We have screen protectors on our work phones, but they're nowhere near that effective."

I knew that. I'd turned his phone on a few times after I'd taken it. Not sure why, since my goal wasn't to hack it. The lock screen image was—like Drew—boring. Standard, out-of-the-box view of the planet. No widgets, no personal photos, no schedule. Just a globe, a clock, and the date.

"Will's designs are the best." With the phone tilted, I checked the message.

Scarlett had sent: *Trojan failed. See if you can get close to G's phone. Don't take it, just stand near it.*

Great. "Do you think Gideon will recognize me?"

Drew shook his head. "I took his attention off you while you made your escape."

My first instinct was to snark at him about our altercation in the bathroom, but he'd made me a promise and kept it. Part of me had trusted he'd follow through. "His assistant might, though."

"The man who works in the office wouldn't be with him. He stays at the desk." Drew made a turn onto a narrow street with two single lanes, so tight oncoming traffic would have to crawl past to be certain they didn't collide. "He may have one of his other assistants there or possibly a team to discuss the event, but no one who'd normally be at his office."

I texted Scarlett back: *I'll do my best.*

"And I don't need to worry about you stealing anything from him?"

Note to self: Don't let him see you getting close to Gideon's phone. "Only if they're displaying something on our list of stolen items."

CHAPTER 10
JAYCE

I bit into the croissant, its buttery, flaky layers practically melting on my tongue. "So. Good."

"You can make it through the meeting?"

"Probably. But that's why I grabbed the oat bars. Emergency stock."

Drew held the door open for me as he took a sip from his clear cup. I'd expected him to order a simple black coffee. Plain, like his car and his gum. Instead, he'd ordered a cold brew with a dash of cinnamon. Caffeine with no sugar. What was the point?

"Do they seriously add nitrogen to that?" We stepped out onto the pedestrian street paved with red and white bricks. The buildings on either side were five stories high, all glass and stonework, but far enough apart the sun lit the walkway. Shops dotted the lower floors—like the coffee shop Drew had let me detour into—while professional suites lined the upper floors.

"They do. The microbubbles add a faint sweetness."

"I thought the cinnamon was for sweetness?"

"They complement each other." He took a sip of his coffee, one hand tucked casually into his suit pants. "It's not just sweetness, but depth, complexity, and a smooth mouthfeel. The best flavors are about subtle layers and contrast."

Contrast? Like him in his tailored suit versus me in my T-shirt and jeans? Or how perfectly he carried his cup versus me shoving a croissant in my mouth, with a water bottle stuffed under my arm and my beat-up leather crossbody bag?

Scarlett had told me to wear something nicer to meet with the billionaire, but I'd countered with the very logical 'What if I need to do some recon?' and she'd agreed.

Bullet cameras watched the space, providing full coverage from the third floor. Near as I could tell, no doorways were in blind spots.

Raised circular gardens dotted the middle of the walkway, crammed with flowers in whites and reds, surrounding potted trees. We passed a fountain with more stone planters for huge ferns at its edge. I took another big bite of the croissant—not as good as Russo's at home—and studied the shapes of the buildings. The Mosaic restaurant was still out of sight. It was set back from the large square at the end of the complex, which was dominated by an even larger fountain than the first one.

As far as Drew had planned, our goal was to get a walk-through of Mosaic from Gideon and his wife, Liana. I needed to brief the team on the conversation, but my primary focus was to look for every ingress and egress point. How could a thief sneak in? Where would the chip be? And how could someone make off with it? I needed to look at the roof. Which shop would gain me the quickest access?

Brie had sent me the highest-resolution satellite images she had of this area. The buildings on either side of the walkway connected to each other, simple and straight, but they hooked like crescents at the end—Mosaic was the tip of the crescent on my left. No rooftop gardens and no patios, but plenty of signs of industrial usage. There were vents, air conditioning units, and pipes, which meant someone needed to get up there at some point—to remove snow when it got too thick, if nothing else.

A square shape at the eastern end of the building might have been a bulkhead with a door, but the satellite image wasn't clear enough.

And what was the camera situation up top? There'd be cameras outside and inside the elevators, for sure. Bypassing them would be simple for Brie, but she'd be tapped into the Mosaic feed. Monitoring a single building in the complex would be easier than watching the whole thing.

"This is the quietest I've ever seen you," said Drew.

I held a hand up to cover my mouth while I chewed. "I'm eating."

"Has that stopped you before?"

Fine, I was working. Inspecting buildings. Trying to take my brain off Mr. Cinnamon Coffee. The croissant was good, but it hadn't done that job. Nothing I'd eaten in the last two days had cleared my head.

Try fasting? I snorted. *That's not going to happen.*

"Everything rolls right off you, doesn't it?" He was looking straight at me, eyes shielded behind his sunglasses. At least when he was acting all aloof and moving his head around, I could see his eyes from the side.

"What do you mean?" Obviously, it was about the criticism rolling off me. Growing up as a star athlete, people critiqued me every day. At some point, it became part of how people communicated with me.

'You need to tuck that arm tighter,' and 'You're too tall to add the half-twist, so stop trying,' and 'If you can't run faster, your roundoff won't have enough power for the vault.'

The tears stopped by the time I hit eleven.

'Your leg isn't healing properly. You can't compete at this level anymore.'

Then the tears had started again. I took another big bite of my croissant. I should have gotten the chocolate one.

He shook his head and pointed to where the buildings opened to the square. "The restaurant's down by the river."

Wide stone steps led to the second fountain, at least sixty feet across its base. It was adorned with modern sculptures with harsh angles, two large plumes of water, and flags. So many freaking flags. A hundred feet beyond the fountain was the Potomac, with trees and more glass buildings on its opposite bank.

The square was full of people enjoying the warm mid-June day, with promises of summer in the air. "They keep the fountain filled in winter for ice skating."

"Nice spot."

"The views are spectacular in the evening." Drew slowed on the steps, an oddly whimsical tone in his voice. "In the warmer months, there's a water display in the fountain on the hour, and the outdoor patios are lit with tiny lights."

Again, I wanted to snark at him or tease him about the way he was talking like it was some magical fairyland. *What romantic sap's stolen your body, Drew?*

Instead, I took an even larger bite of my pastry and scanned the restaurant's exterior. As we descended the stairs, a drop of at least twenty feet, the building's profile became more imposing. Four stories grew to five, but the walls weren't smooth. Around the square, protrusions and balconies dotted the second and third floors. Plenty of handholds to go up, not far to fall if you made a poor choice, and each balcony meant additional access.

I mentally reviewed the floor plan.

The ground floor was under construction, being converted into a whiskey bar. Mosaic took up the second and third floors, with a multi-tiered patio climbing gradually from ground level outside up to the restaurant's main floor. Above that, two floors of offices. The restaurant walls facing the square and the river were floor-to-ceiling windows with too many doors. "They'll have a lot of security working the doors and the ground-level patios, won't they?"

"They will."

"Numbers?"

"Wyatt and Scarlett will have the head count once they're finished. There'll be at least one person near each door and others floating through the crowd."

As I stepped off the bottom stair, I ran into his outstretched hand. A kid darted in front of us on a scooter—I'd been too preoccupied with the upper floors. Drew didn't budge, just watched the kid go by, with the back of his hand against my abdomen. I didn't move either. I was frozen mid-chew, with the ant army skittering over my skin again.

I took a step back. *Chew your food, girl.*

Drew continued talking like nothing had happened. "But each of the special pieces in the banquet room will have their own security. Liana's been tight-lipped on those details."

I nodded, bracing my water bottle against my body, fumbling to open it with my free hand. The croissant wasn't going down my throat properly.

He took the food from me, carefully wrapped it in its napkin like he was doing me a favor, and I gulped down a third of the bottle.

That's better. Now move. Do something. Clear your head. "I need to check out the roof."

"The roof?" His brows pulled down behind his sunglasses so I couldn't see them, but his tone was obvious. *There goes crazy Jayce again*, he must have been thinking.

"Yeah." I held out my water bottle, which he took under his arm. "But I need to see it close up."

Enough people milled around that anything truly bizarre would be too much of a spectacle to be suspicious.

I strode across the square, craning my neck up as I visualized my path. The first floor would be easy. Hop onto a tall concrete planter, one foot onto the pillar next to it, spring back, grab the edge of the awning—it looked sturdy enough—and a simple kip would have me on top with access to the second-floor balcony.

From there? I'd figure it out once I was on the second floor. But there were lots of architectural details I'd be able to use as foot and handholds.

Or I'd look like I didn't know what I was doing.

And *that* was not about to happen.

I took a few steps toward the restaurant with Drew, then removed one shoe, a few more steps, and the other shoe. I curled my toes against the paving bricks, dragging along the gap between a red and white stone with my right foot. "Nice and warm, just the way I like it."

"What are you doing?"

We made an even more entertaining sight now. Him with his fancy nitrogen coffee, my water bottle under his arm, and my croissant in his hand; me enjoying being out of shoes.

I took the croissant back and scarfed down the last few bites—just what I needed—and handed him my black sneakers. "Hold on to these for me."

"There's broken glass over there." Drew jutted his chin toward a garbage can nearby.

"Kevlar." I extended my leg so he could see the gold threads woven into the bottom of my socks.

"Will design those for you?"

I nodded, pulling my knee to my chest for a stretch. "He thinks of everything."

"Still, you should be wearing shoes when you meet Gideon."

"Meh." I stretched the other knee and bounced on the balls of my feet a few times. "They'll appreciate my thoroughness more than they'll care about my footwear."

"Wait." Somehow, despite all the things Drew was carrying, he pulled his sunglasses down to glower at me over the rims. "What are you planning?"

"Planning?" I winked at him. "You obviously have me confused with someone else."

"Jayce, I—"

Showtime.

I darted off, gaining enough momentum to launch myself at the planter. My right foot landed firmly on the edge, and I pushed off. My left hit the pillar, bent, extended, and I flew up to the awning.

"Jayce Monroe!" Drew sounded so pissed.

Good.

The gasps and hollers from the crowd barely registered.

Swing legs up, shift balance, pull up, bring my hips to the front bar of the awning. It had more give than I was expecting, but it held. *Right foot up, push, leap, and grab the railing of the second-floor patio.*

This was going to be child's play.

CHAPTER 11
DREW

She was climbing the building.

Jayce was literally scaling the outside of a five-story building in the middle of Washington, DC, in broad daylight. Mosaic—the high-end, ultra-posh restaurant where the charity event would be held—was nothing more than her afternoon entertainment.

And what was I doing? Holding her fucking shoes?

She hadn't said a word. Not a goddamn word to me about what she was doing.

No plan?

More like no fucking brain cells.

"If you fall, I'm not calling 9-1-1!" I yelled.

She was halfway to the third floor, giving no reaction to my words.

"What's she doing?" A frantic woman grabbed my arm, almost sending Jayce's water bottle careening to the ground. "Is this a movie set?"

"No, it's..." *A woman with a death wish.*

The one next to me held up her phone and began recording. Not so frantic, after all. At least, not frantic enough to be worried. And she wasn't the only one. Several people spoke quietly at their phones, likely all live-streaming Jayce's antics.

Rather than become part of the spectacle, I walked casually to the restaurant's front door, ensuring nobody thought to film *me*. I dropped my coffee and her water into a garbage bin by the entrance, so my arms weren't embarrassingly laden.

Should drop her shoes in there.

That would make a wonderful impression on Gideon and Liana. Maybe she should have left me her purse, too.

Jayce was on her way up to the fourth floor, moving slower than when she'd started.

I couldn't watch. I wanted to watch, wanted to be sure she was all right, but I tucked that inside my mental locker and moved on. The fifth floor protruded from the side of the building. She'd get that far and realize this was a stupid idea without any safety gear or prep work—let alone actual climbing shoes—and she'd make her way back down.

Jayce was competitive to her core. There was no way she'd admit that defeat. Instead, she'd sneak in through the patio doors on the second floor and skirt around the walls. Maybe she'd confess. Maybe she'd lie about it.

No, she wouldn't try that. She'd evade rather than admit the truth. Jayce Monroe couldn't keep her mouth shut long enough to be a convincing liar.

One last check. She was at the fourth floor, head rolling back and forth, scanning the floor above her. *If you'd had a plan, you might have been able to do it.*

I pulled open the glass door. Inside, I had three options—the heavy wooden doors leading into what would be a whiskey bar

I'd check out once it was open, an elevator with access to all floors, or the wide staircase heading up to Mosaic's main floor.

Option three, it is.

At the top of the stairs, I made my way through a small welcome area into the spacious, elegant dining room. Red leather chairs surrounded long tables which normally sported white tablecloths. Men and women, in black staff shirts with the Mosaic logo, buzzed around the area, which was being cleared for the party.

More floor-to-ceiling windows lined two walls, providing natural light and a view straight down to the river. Hardwood floors provided warmth to the room, while a white, branch-like glass sculpture dominated the space above.

The one time I'd been for dinner, the sculpture had been lit with thousands of tiny lights, the same way they decorated the three-tiered patio. The food had been exquisite, deserving of the rave reviews their head chef had received. A world-class sommelier, brisk and efficient staff, and light classical music. The evening had been near perfect.

But the company?

Eight months ago, I would have said Vanessa was the perfect date. The perfect girlfriend. The most beautiful woman in the room.

Open locker. Shove memories in.

I continued to the middle of the main floor, dodging between tables, to check the mezzanine above. Several more tables hugged the railing, which led to the upper floor's patio. That's where Jayce would come in.

"Drew!" Gideon's deep voice brought me back to my reason for being there. He stood in the open doorway to the banquet room at the far end of the restaurant. He wore a casual white golf shirt with a black logo.

One last look at the mezzanine. No sign of her.

I waved to him, rather than yelling over the noise of the people working, and tucked the shoes behind my back.

The main room was over a hundred feet long and sat at least two hundred and fifty. A bar closer to the stairs had seating for more than twenty. I dodged staff members, watching an efficient woman with upswept blonde hair and bold cat's-eye glasses direct several men hanging paintings on the walls.

"Quite the undertaking, Gideon." As I shook his hand, he clapped the other one against my upper arm, as though we were old friends.

"As long as we bring in a profit for the charities, I don't mind." He flipped over his watch. "Is it just you? I was expecting someone else."

I stopped myself before looking over my shoulder again. This was a time to exude confidence, not concern or irritation. "She'll be in soon."

"One of the contractors you hired?"

"Their team's spread out today, doing some additional vetting of attendees and staff."

"Sounds like we're in excellent hands." He pulled me farther into the room and gestured at a slender woman in a flowing white pantsuit. "Drew, have you met my wife, Liana?"

I hadn't, although I'd read a lot about her. Before the job we did for their older son, I'd done my research and knew where she'd gone to high school, college for pre-law, and every job she'd had. Knew she'd married Gideon at thirty—his second wife and her first husband. Knew they had two children—one with a philandering problem—and all the details about those kids. Knew her voting history, where she lived, and about her charity work.

"It's a pleasure to meet you, Mrs. Tremaine." I took her hand to shake, but her grip was palm down. I shifted to a slight bow as she gave my fingers a gentle squeeze.

"Craig speaks highly of you." She smiled, glancing at my arm hidden away.

I *should* have thrown the shoes out. Or at least put them down in the main dining room. I unwound my hand from behind my back and gave her a rueful smile. "The woman I'm working with today is doing some reconnaissance. She insisted the shoes slow her down."

Liana looked around the room. "What kind of reconnaissance? Didn't Giddy provide you with the information you needed?"

A wall of windows faced the river, with two sets of double doors leading onto the top tier of the patio. The easternmost wall was also windows, facing a small street that separated the restaurant from a minor embassy. From the floor plan, I knew the door in the back corner led to the kitchen, while another door provided access to a set of stairs to the mezzanine and the washrooms.

"He did. However, it's crucial we identify all possible ways a thief could get in."

"Or out," came a voice from behind me.

I jolted in surprise—I was facing the only two people in the room. I spun, knowing who it would be before I laid my eyes on her.

Chapter 12
Drew

Jayce held out her hands. "Where's my water?"

"How'd you get in?" My words were more abrupt than they should have been.

She pointed vaguely upward. "Through the door in the roof."

"You did not." There was no way she'd gotten up over the fifth floor. Maybe she had more lies in her than I thought.

"Needed the lockpicks I keep in my underwire, but the lock was pretty simple. The view was amazing from up there." She fished her phone out of the small bag she'd secured around her waist. Without bothering to introduce herself or acknowledge the other parties in the room, she played her video for me. Sure enough, it was a survey of the roof, including the view of the river, and the service door. "We should tell the security team about it. That door leads to the emergency stairwell, which provides easy access to every floor of the building. There was only one camera on the whole route. It also lets out onto the street. Huge risk."

"I'll send the details to Wyatt." I texted him the information, and he acknowledged the message immediately. "He's with the security team now and will fill them in."

Liana came closer to Jayce. "Are you from the heist crew Giddy told me about?"

"Recovery crew." Jayce took one of her shoes from me and balanced on one leg to put the shoe on. "We recover things for people after they were stolen—not after the people were stolen. After the things were stolen. Although we do get people back after they were stolen sometimes. Or kidnapped, I suppose."

She was rambling. Nervous? Or too much sugar?

"So you're, what?" continued Liana. "The security expert?"

Jayce snorted as she took her other shoe. "Our security expert is about eight feet tall and five hundred pounds. I'm the grease man."

Liana's eyes widened. "A thief?"

Gideon stepped closer, holding out a hand to shake. Before their hands touched, he said, "Do I know you?"

Maybe Jayce was right. Maybe I hadn't gotten Gideon's attention off her fast enough on Monday.

"Doubt it," she said, vigorously shaking his hand. "Pretty sure I'd remember meeting a billionaire."

She had no tact either.

"I'm certain. Your face is so familiar."

I should have prepared for this. "It's part of what makes her good at her job; she has a common appearance—average height, ordinary features."

Jayce's broad smile faded, and she pulled her hand back from Gideon. Everything about her seemed to collapse all at once.

"I know!" Gideon snapped his fingers and pointed at her. "I used to sponsor a gymnastics event here in DC. You're a gymnast, aren't you?"

Somehow, the light inside Jayce dimmed even further. "That would probably be it. I stopped competing about twelve years ago."

"I remember now." Gideon nodded slowly, his face softening. "I'm sorry."

He remembered? He must've meant her accident. It had happened in Washington the evening before the gold medal day.

Jayce straightened and smiled a fake, plastic smile. She needed to learn how to mask things better. "Why don't you tell me how you're setting everything up?"

Liana threaded her arm through Jayce's and steered her toward the center of the room. Green tape had been stuck to the floor, making four Xs in a diamond pattern, fifteen feet apart from each other. "The display items will be here. Everything must be just right when we unveil the chip."

"And what's the deal with the unveiling? How does the chip fit in with the sculpture?"

"It's going to be a masterpiece." Liana swept her hand through the air. "Steel and fire meet ingenuity and eternity."

Jayce shriveled her nose. "That didn't answer my question."

"I hear your team's the best, so I'm sure you can work with me on this." Liana patted Jayce's arm. "Now, my sculpture will be over here, on the green X closest to the patio doors."

Jayce frowned, then scanned the windows facing the river. "What will the security be like on the doors?"

Gideon said, "Someone will be stationed at each one."

"All the doors? Including the one to the kitchen?"

"Yes, and the security personnel assigned to this room will all be on the inside."

Jayce nodded. "So they can monitor partygoers, staff, your sculpture, and each other?"

On our previous jobs, I'd witnessed Jayce switch into professional mode several times. It was the side of her that irritated me the least. I even had a grudging respect for it—when it was genuinely professional and not just an attempt to mask her hotheaded reactions.

Not moments when she went against the plans because she thought she knew better, as she had on the Harrington job.

It had been an anti-heist. Our goal? Return a high-value baseball card my young client had stolen during an alcohol-infused party. She and I had snuck into the owner's house with her team's support, but found one person awake who shouldn't have been. We'd ended up staging a break-in and leaving the card on the floor.

I clenched my jaw at the memory. Alarm blaring. Running through the woods while house lights flicked on around us.

Up until when she'd smashed the glass doors, her skill had impressed me. But if I hadn't been with her, she would have made a stupid choice and gotten caught.

"How big's your sculpture?" asked Jayce. "Is it going to be easy to slip into a pocket?"

Liana's gaze rose toward the ceiling and she let go of Jayce, her hands expanding above her head. Before she said anything, she pulled the arms back down and folded them. "It needs to be a surprise. A performance. Something worthy of Giddy's amazing invention."

Jayce walked the distance between the Xs and the closest door. "It's hard to formulate a plan without specifics."

"The last thing I need is for someone to ruin the event." Liana was known for several things. First, as Gideon Tremaine's wife. Second, for her charity work. And only third as an artist, primarily for work in resin and metal. The latter were almost exclusively larger-than-life junkyard pieces, which regularly took her a year to construct out of scrap. Despite her immense wealth, she was often quoted as saying she enjoyed working with materials anyone could access. She could have built everything out of gold but usually turned junk into beauty. "One slip of the tongue, one cowboy spouting off a rumor that's too close to the truth, one reporter who digs too deep and asks the wrong questions... I have a vision of the event and that vision is how we raise so much money."

"My tongue doesn't slip," I said. "And neither will Jayce's."

Liana turned to me. "People fly to my events from all over the world to find out what the big surprise is. I'm not risking millions of dollars to satisfy your curiosity."

"It's not curiosity. Your husband hired me to ensure no one steals his data chip. Not to ensure the amount you raise."

Gideon put a hand on my shoulder. "Consider them both your job."

Jayce had stopped listening. She walked the perimeter of the room with long, intentional steps. We had the floor plan, but she was measuring anyway. She studied the door frames, the windows, the floor, and the ceiling.

"All right," I said. There were three other Xs on the floor in the banquet room. "You provided an inventory of the paintings and sculptures that will be up for sale, but what about the other items that won't be? I assume the tape marks mean you'll have four display items in total?"

Liana slipped her arm into mine this time and steered me toward one of the Xs. "Since our theme is the merging of art and technology, Giddy spoke to some of his friends and we have three items on loan. We'll have the Obsidian Mirror, an ancient relic owned by a Welsh lord, which reflects light in a way that current science can't explain."

"More a baffling of science and technology than a merging of them?"

"Precisely!"

Jayce opened the door that led to the stairs for the bathrooms and vanished through it. Where was she going now? Upper floor again? Mezzanine? Out a window? This was always the problem with her. Lack of communication. Lack of coordination. When it didn't matter, she'd talk endlessly, but when I needed to know what she was doing?

Maybe it was my fault for not setting the ground rules in the car. Or I should have grabbed her before she scaled the building.

We'd have to work on some hand signals before the event.

Or a tether. At least that way, if she climbed something, I could catch her if she fell.

"—from London." Liana laughed.

I joined in the laughter, despite having missed everything she'd said after telling me about the mirror. *What is wrong with you, Drew? Trust Jayce to do her job and you do yours.* "Can you send the specs on those pieces?" *Good cover.*

"I'll have my assistant email you."

"What about the bathrooms?" Jayce must have snuck in while I was covering my lapse. She continued taking deliberate steps along the back wall.

"We've arranged for lavatory attendants," said Liana. "For hand towels and lotion, not as security."

"It's an obvious staging point." Jayce didn't write anything down and didn't have her phone out to take notes. Was she recording everything in her head, or was it all a show? "Changing outfits, prepping decoys, or hiding stuff. If they can keep an eye out for suspicious behavior, that should suffice."

Gideon pulled out his phone and made a call, asking someone about attendants for the party. The conversation carried on and he excused himself, stepping outside onto the patio.

"There's some loose spots on the carpet here." Jayce was on her knees in the back corner. "Looks like some damage from a leak. Might be somewhere to hide something, too."

Liana's brows drew together. "There will be too many people here for someone to crawl around and hide things under there."

"You'd be amazed what people overlook when the room's crowded and the alcohol's flowing freely."

I said, "Or when there's only two people in a bathroom?"

"And that's why you always need an attendant." Jayce rocked back on her haunches, flipping her short hair from her face. The grin she shot me sat low in my stomach. "So, I get the artsy thing where you don't want to reveal too much, but can you confirm if someone can easily remove the chip from your sculpture?"

"They cannot."

"And will the sculpture be more or less than twenty-five pounds?"

Liana's gaze rose to the ceiling again. "More than."

"I can work with that." Jayce dug a thumb into her left quad, just above her knee, and stood. "I'm done for now. Scarlett will want to do a walk-through with me once everything's in place. What's the schedule, Liana?"

"Everything will be set up by Friday for a preview that evening."

"I'll be back that afternoon with my team." She gave me a faux-salute and wandered toward the exit. "I'm going to the coffee shop. Meet you there."

Don't get into trouble.

Once she was out the door, Liana tilted her head. "She's a clever one, isn't she?"

"She is." And dangerous. I had to do something about how she constantly distracted me. Was there any way I could get past Rav and Malcolm so I could pair up with Scarlett for the gala? No, probably not.

Don't let her get to you, Drew. You've been trained to shut down your feelings.

Unfortunately, the training wasn't working.

"About the preview," I said, dragging my attention away from where Jayce had vanished through the main dining room. "I'd like to discuss some changes."

CHAPTER 13

JAYCE

I stepped into the sunshine outside Mosaic, let out the longest breath I could, and sucked all the oxygen back in. My head was a jumbled mess. Climbing hadn't fixed it. Inspecting the restaurant hadn't fixed it. Chatting with a billionaire and his wife hadn't fixed it.

All I needed to do was survive one car ride with Drew.

He'd drop me off at the hotel where the team was staying and I wouldn't see him again until tomorrow. I'd work with *my* team—the one that didn't make me feel like I needed to run—and we'd review everyone's separate meetings from this afternoon. We'd make plans.

My phone buzzed and my stomach dropped. *Shit.*

Scarlett's message was predictable: *Brie's still waiting to sync up with G's phone. Are you having connectivity problems?*

She'd told me to get close enough to Gideon's phone that Brie could try tapping into it. All that Drew energy in the room made me forget.

What was I supposed to do now?

I'd already left. I'd told them I was finished. How was I supposed to go in without making anyone suspicious? I wandered around the edge of the fountain, toward the river. From there, I watched Gideon in my peripheral vision.

He was pacing on the patio's mid-tier, voice growing louder with each word—not enough I could make anything out, but it was obvious something had displeased him.

I could approach him and explain I needed more information about the sculpture if we were going to protect it. Maybe he'd laugh about his artsy wife and agree to tell me. Maybe he didn't know what she was planning.

Gideon fell silent and shoved his phone into a pocket, shaking his head as he did. He called through the open door into the banquet room, "Liana!"

Her response was too quiet for me to hear.

"I need to go. There's a problem for Saturday." He marched into the restaurant, removing most of my options. Other than accosting him on his way to his car—wherever that would be.

Not a smart plan. What were my options?

I texted Scarlett back, *He's leaving. Will Liana's do?*

She responded, *If that's the only play, give it a shot.*

That meant going in and facing Drew. No matter what reason I gave, he'd silently judge me, wondering why I honestly came back. Looking at me with that frowny face. Throwing my brain off kilter.

You're a professional, Jayce. You can do this. I'd worked with Drew before. Hell, I'd even stolen his phone and watch. I was getting too in my head.

I climbed over the patio's railing and jogged its length, past wooden tables and chairs, huge potted plants, and under the twenty-foot metal sculpture of... a cross between a bird and a giant letter T? Up the wide, shallow stairs, to the door into the banquet room.

Drew stood alone in the middle of the room, between the four taped Xs on the floor, with his back to me. He dragged both hands through his hair, the subtle wave fanning into place perfectly when he was done. He clasped his hands at the nape of his neck, taking slow breaths. Stress wafted off him.

If I tiptoed backward, he'd never know I was there. Ignoring my better judgment, I said, "Where's Liana?"

He turned to face me, and my heart skipped a few beats. He'd loosened his tie and undone the top buttons of his dress shirt. "I thought you were meeting me at the coffee shop."

"I forgot I wanted…" What did I want? What was my plan? *You don't have plans, remember?* Nothing came to mind, other than his open collar—open low enough to show off a hint of chest hair. I should have tiptoed away.

"Gideon and Liana left." He stripped off his suit jacket and held it over his arm while he unbuttoned his shirt cuffs. "There was a customs issue with one of the items coming in for the gala, and they need to deal with it."

"They didn't pass me on their way out."

He rolled the cuffs up as he spoke, sending the ants skittering over my skin again. "Staff entrance at the back of the kitchen."

"Right."

"How did you get up to the roof?" He walked closer, the veins and light hair on his forearms on full display. He always wore suits or fully buttoned dress shirts, so I'd never seen them before. How did Mr. Grumpy have such muscular arms?

Because they go well with that muscular chest, Jayce. And those broad shoulders.

"Skills." I shrugged and gestured to his clothes. "You overheating?"

"I needed to breathe."

I needed something to eat. "If she's not here anymore, I'm going to—"

"How do you do it?"

What were we talking about now? The fifth floor still?

"Go through life without caring what anyone thinks." He hooked a thumb over his shoulder. "Crawling around inspecting the edge of the carpet like one of the world's richest men wasn't standing right there?"

"That's what they're paying us for."

He stopped less than a foot away from me. In this huge room, just the two of us, we didn't need to be so close. His jaw flexed as he looked down at me, his intense brown eyes roaming over my face, searching for something. For what?

"Drew, you're in my personal space."

"I know," he whispered. "And I don't have the faintest idea why."

Heat pooled low in my belly, threatening to drop lower. He was so... so... I stepped back, out of his reach, so he couldn't do what he looked like he wanted to—either smack me, shove me, or kiss me.

Maybe that last one was what I wanted him to do.

Except I didn't. Definitely didn't.

"I need to talk to Scarlett about what I found here."

He nodded, not moving closer. "I don't agree with your approach, but it sounds like you accomplished your goal."

All but the special one Scarlett had given me. "I can take a cab. Don't worry about me."

"We need to learn how to work together better." He slid on his sunglasses and headed for the door as a woman with a clipboard entered, followed by a setup crew in yellow T-shirts. "I don't like my partners wandering off without giving me a heads up. We can talk about it in the car."

CHAPTER 14
DREW

Thursday morning, I rode the elevator to my apartment, sweat rolling down my back after an aggressive workout in the building's gym. I'd run too fast, too far, and lifted weights heavier than I should have.

Nothing was working.

Jayce and I hadn't figured anything out on the car ride to her hotel yesterday. On the ten-minute drive, she ate two oat bars and a pain au chocolat, finished a bottle of water, and commented on fifteen different buildings we drove by. Every time I'd tried to start a real conversation, something else caught her eye.

She'd been avoiding me.

Now I was working out too hard, trying to forget about it. About the worry consuming me while she'd been climbing the building. What if she'd fallen?

A broken leg twelve years ago had ruined her life and still she took foolish risks like that? What would she do if she fell? A sprained ankle would put her out for this weekend's job, but another broken leg? Paralysis? Fuck, death?

The elevator stopped at the tenth floor and I got out, walking past five doors before arriving at mine. I guzzled my recovery drink while unlocking the door.

Before it swung all the way open, movement inside the apartment caught my eye.

A blur of black.

I never brought my gun to the gym, but I—

The blur halted, transforming into my favorite black Imagine Dragons T-shirt, draped over full breasts. Sky-high black stilettos and bare legs that went on forever. Vanessa.

"Ooh," she purred. "You're still sweaty, just the way I like you."

I closed the door behind me.

Her long blonde hair fell loose around her shoulders. She turned and leaned over the coffee table in the living room—far deeper than she needed to bend, but it revealed the thong she wore under the shirt—and picked up two glasses of red wine. After giving me a blatant once-over, she walked toward me, crossing her legs with each step. The woman knew how to use her—if I was being objective—jaw-dropping figure. "You're normally only in the gym for an hour. I was starting to think you'd never come back."

"What are you doing?" I took the glass she offered me, no doubt one of my special stock she chose at random. "It's only ten a.m."

"I need to get laid, stud muffin." She took in an overdramatic breath, swelling her breasts intentionally.

Instead of drinking the wine, I sipped my tart lemon-lime recovery drink. "How'd you get in? You gave me your key when you left."

She brought the glass to her nose and inhaled, batting her eyelashes over the rim. "I gave you *a* key. It's possible I had another one."

"I knew I should have changed the locks."

"Oh, honeybear." She returned to the table and put her glass down, using the same bend-and-extend technique she'd done before.

I averted my eyes from the overt display. Focused on the blue and white plaid throw pillow at the end of the couch. At the dark gray curtains. The small writing desk by the door to the tiny balcony. This was *my* space, not hers anymore. I'd need to cook up a storm—or fumigate—to get rid of the cloying scent of flowers she wore.

She straightened, and I felt her frown as much as I saw it. "How about it? For old time's sake?"

I took another swig of my lemon-lime drink as she closed the distance between us.

She traced a finger down my chest, along my abdomen, and slid her hand down the front of my shorts.

Fortunately, my cock agreed with my brain. *Never again, Vanessa.*

"That was always the problem..." She sighed and took the glass from me. "Your libido needs serious work."

"My libido wasn't the problem. It was the other men you were sleeping with."

"What can I say? You were away a lot." We'd started dating while I was still in the CIA and it was understood that sometimes I had to leave and not tell her what was going on. "You changed after your last mission."

"I'm not having this argument again." I pulled up the hem of my shirt to wipe the sweat from my forehead. Part of me had left because of Alex's death, part because of Vanessa, and a whole host of other shit. "Commitment means commitment."

"Looks like you're committed to working out harder." Her fingers found my abs, raking her nails lightly across the skin. "I like this."

I released the hem and gripped her arm, removing it from my body. How had I stayed with this woman for almost three years? How had I been so blind? *Because she's right and you were away a lot, and then because you refused to acknowledge all the hints she gave you.* "Go find someone else. I'm not interested, and that won't change."

"Want to tie me up? Play good spy bad spy?"

I rolled my eyes heavenward as though there'd be an answer somewhere. "What I want is a shower. I'm going to have one now—and no, you're not invited—and I expect you to be gone when I get out."

She put my wineglass down, huffed, and balled her hands on her hips. "My clothes are in the bedroom."

"Fine." I walked into the bedroom with her hot on my heels. Rather than give her the opportunity to undress there, I grabbed everything from where she'd placed it on a wing chair in the corner and tossed it out to her.

"Drew! That's a Prada bag!"

"Don't care." I closed the door and locked it for good measure. "Now go home or wherever the fuck you want to go."

Vanessa muttered and complained from the other side of the door, rattling off a list of everything I'd ever done wrong, not well enough, or even slightly less than perfect. And for bonus points, a shot about how smart my birth parents were to give me up.

Why had I told her about that? *Because she was supposed to be your partner in life.*

"And take the shirt with you." It would smell like her, and I'd think of her every time I saw it.

I went into the ensuite, turned on the hot water in the shower, and snuck back into the bedroom. She'd leave eventually, but there was an off-chance she'd wait me out, so I listened to be sure.

"Your decorating sense sucks, Drew!" she yelled.

I'd sent most of the furniture with her—equal parts good-guy gesture and not wanting to see anything we'd shared anymore. I'd replaced the white duvet cover with steel gray. The white shag rugs with thin woven ones in dark blues. The entire apartment was now strong and masculine, rather than fluffy and feminine.

I'd kept the wine hutch, the wineglasses, and everything in the kitchen—those were mine and heaven help the woman who got between me and my things.

"It would have been the best orgasm of your life!" She smacked a hand against the door. "Asshole!" Her high heels clicked on the hardwood floors and she finally left, slamming the front door.

Push that into the emotional locker, too. Her cheating had stung, but I'd spent a lot of years learning to compartmentalize. With her, it had never been a problem.

Maybe that was the reason we'd stayed together so long—I'd pushed everything between us into that locker.

I removed my running shoes, stripping off layers of clothes to drape over the wing chair Vanessa had sullied with her things.

The bathroom, decorated with white subway tiles and antiqued black fixtures, included a see-through shower curtain that opened up the space. Steam hung heavy in the room already. Exactly what I needed.

I stepped under the scorching water, letting it pelt onto my back and neck. I was so used to working late hours that when she had to stay late at her co-working office, I suspected she was doing the same thing I was—working.

How many times had that actually been true? How early had the lies started?

It was ten in the morning and I had a meeting at two with the Reynolds team. Craig had some other clients booked into the office, so the Reynolds crew was coming to my place. Liana's assistant had finally emailed the details of the VIP items, so we'd meet, discuss, and split off for more analysis.

I could have forwarded the email to Scarlett.

Should have forwarded it.

Really, really should have, Drew.

But I wanted to see Jayce. Why? I could do my job better if we kept our distance from each other. Why couldn't I compartmentalize her like I could Vanessa?

Why did she get under my skin so much?

Because she was different. No filter between her brain and her mouth. Or between her brain and her body, for that matter.

My cock twitched.

That mouth. That body.

Jayce Monroe was confident and brash. Talented. Used to people paying attention to her. But I'd seen a vulnerability in her yesterday. Something about the way she looked at the river on our drive to Mosaic. A sadness.

When I'd done the first background check on her, that was what I'd expected. A former champion turned thief turned recovery agent. She'd fallen so far, I'd assumed it still haunted her. Instead, I'd found a woman who fit in with her remarkable team, easily taking every criticism and rolling with every challenge that presented itself. She was flexible—

My cock twitched again. How flexible could the gymnast be?

Emotionally, Drew. You meant flexible emotionally.

An hour ago, I'd been debating whether I was losing my touch or if Jayce was frying my brain. Considering my body hadn't reacted when Vanessa groped me, it wasn't my touch that was the problem.

I turned toward the water, dipping my head so it could pour through my hair. I stroked my dick, gently at first, while images of Jayce flooded my thoughts. The way she'd looked at me yesterday after Liana had left. Jayce was supposed to be gone—wasn't supposed to see me breaking down like that. I'd stood so close to her, wanting to touch her. Needing to get her out of my system.

In my head, she was waiting for me when I'd opened the apartment door, not Vanessa. But Jayce wouldn't be a thong and high heels kind of woman. What would she wear to seduce a man? Or would it be all about the taunts?

I groaned, gripping myself harder, thrusting into my fist.

Would she be the one pushing me onto the bed, demanding I tell her what I wanted while she teased me? *Good luck with that, Jayce.*

I fucked my hand, thinking about the feel of her body, her toned muscles, her tongue tangling with mine. She'd taste like sugar, for certain, considering how she ate.

My breath started coming faster.

I couldn't fight it. Couldn't fight her. I had to come. I imagined her underneath me, felt her hands on my ass, guiding me as if we'd done this a thousand times.

"Yes, Jayce," I whispered. "Yes, take me deeper."

Squeezing my eyes shut, I felt her wrap a leg around my waist, meeting me thrust for thrust. My whole body tensed and I growled her name through my climax, coming with a hard shudder.

When I finished, I slumped against the shower wall, trying to slow my heart. She irritated the shit out of me, but I couldn't stop wanting her. The last thing I needed was to lose focus because of a woman—but here I was, completely distracted by her.

Even after the orgasm.

What the hell was I going to do?

CHAPTER 15

JAYCE

I'd walked up and down the street five times already. I had it all paced off and could do it blindfolded, tapping each fire hydrant and power pole as I went.

The meeting at Drew's was in an hour and a half. I could call for a rideshare and be there in thirty minutes. I could walk up and down this street at least seven more times and still be able to ring the doorbell, say hello, and leave. Maybe even ten times.

I was in a residential neighborhood in Alexandria, Virginia, with modest townhouses on one side and single-family homes on the other. Small green lawns, young trees along the sidewalks, and nice simple cars. There was a school nearby. People I passed smiled or nodded at me. It was kind of like being at home.

Except, if I were at home, Tanner's house wouldn't be the one at the midpoint of my pace.

How had I let twelve years go by? We'd practically grown up together. Tumbling at the same gym in Toronto when we were five, at the same gymnastics birthday parties when we were eight, and sharing coaches until we were eleven. We were in school together, traveled together, and competed at some of the same meets.

I stopped and looked across the street at his white two-story house with the arch over the front door.

And kept walking.

I should have had Brie give me all the information instead of just his address. There'd be no need to be nervous because I would have been prepared. But that would take a plan and...

More courage than you've got, you coward.

The truth was, all the planning in the world wouldn't have been enough. It couldn't have told me how he'd react if I showed up on his doorstep. If it could have, I wouldn't have been pacing.

I'd probably be pacing somewhere else, anyway.

Because today's meeting meant I had to see Drew again—and try to focus.

Plus, I had to face Scarlett after failing her yesterday afternoon. She'd acted like everything was fine and it was a minor inconvenience, but I didn't do failure. It wasn't a Jayce Monroe characteristic.

I stopped at the end of my circuit and looked back at Tanner's house.

You don't fear the leap. You don't cower on the sidewalk across the street.

"Let's do this," I said to myself.

Butterflies filled my stomach. What if he didn't remember me? What if he was angry with me?

I needed some food.

No, you don't. You need to do this.

One foot in front of the other, over and over, until I was knocking on his door.

Maybe he's not home. It's 12:35 on a Thursday. Maybe he's at work.

The door opened and my breath caught.

He was nineteen when I last saw him, but he still wore his straight black hair short. Light wrinkles and plain black glasses framed his brown eyes. His face had more angles.

"Hi." That wasn't what I'd rehearsed, but it was all I could think of.

"Jayce?" Tanner held the door partially open, not moving other than his eyes. He blinked repeatedly, looking me up and down.

No surprise. I may as well have been a ghost. "I probably should have called, but..." Not probably—definitely.

He lurched forward and threw his arms around me. "You're alive!"

"Um..." I patted his back, then slowly eased my arms tighter the longer the hug went on. I tucked my head against his neck—he was only a couple of inches taller than me at five-foot-eight—and the stress of the past week evaporated. I was eighteen years old again, hugging my best friend.

He pulled away, holding me by my upper arms, his eyes wide. "What are you—Where—How?"

"That was a lot of questions."

He let me go, bobbing his upper body as though nodding. The rods, pins, and whatever else they ended up doing to his neck must have limited his mobility. His sister had told me about the first few operations until she went radio silent. "Did you want to come in?"

"If that's okay? I know it's short notice."

"Of course!" He pulled the door open further and ushered me into a small living room off the entryway. "Have a seat. Can I get you something to drink?"

"Just water, thanks." I sat on a simple white couch, facing another, with a coffee table between them. A low propane fireplace decorated the wall to my left, with a narrow mantle crowded with photographs. I stood, scanning through them. Lots of two little girls, from babies up to six or seven years old.

Was he a dad? Were they nieces? *I should have prepared for this.*

"You heard about Coach McInnis?" He walked with a nearly imperceptible limp.

If I hadn't known he'd lost the leg, I might not have noticed it. "No."

"I thought that might have been why you came." He handed me a glass and sat on one of the couches, crossing an ankle over the opposite thigh. "He passed away last year."

My heart sank, and my throat tightened up. I should have asked what happened, but the words wouldn't form.

As though reading my mind, Tanner said, "Pancreatic cancer."

I nodded. Why did I come here? Why put myself through all this?

"He got in touch with me near the end." Tanner exhaled slowly. "He called off the chemo after a few rounds didn't help. Said he wasn't scared—it was just the next step in his life."

Part of me wanted to laugh. That was so Coach M. "Never fear the leap, right?"

"I think standing still would have been the better option that time." He stared down at his glass, rubbing it with a thumb. Even after we graduated from his program to higher levels, Coach M had attended every event he could, cheering us from the sidelines. "It got me thinking about old times. I made some calls and talked to some old friends, but I couldn't find you anywhere."

I wasn't exactly off the grid, but Evelyn Reynolds liked her teams to stay out of the headlines, despite the high-profile work we did. "I moved to Halifax about five years ago to work for a recovery company."

"Like collections?"

"Sort of, but not quite. We recover stolen property. Lots of travel, lots of happy customers."

"Like detectives, then?"

The more questions he asked, the more I'd answer, and the closer he'd get to truths I wasn't supposed to spill. "Yeah, that's the best way to put it. What about you?"

"Computer programmer by day—I work from home for a company based in Vegas—and devoted dad by night." He pointed to a wall by the window, where there were more photographs in frames of various shapes and sizes.

The girls *were* his. I moved from the mantle photographs to the ones on the wall, taking in Tanner's entire life. His parents were in some photos, his sister in a couple, but most of them were of his little girls.

"The top left is Marie and I on our wedding day—I met her at the clinic where I did most of my rehab. Top right is the girls from a gymnastics party in the spring."

They looked a lot like he had as a kid, just with longer hair. "Twins?"

"They're six now."

I pointed at another photograph, a candid shot of him standing next to a balance beam with one little girl on it. "You coach them?"

"Absolutely."

My stomach churned some more. I could run down the length of a handrailing but hadn't been able to look at a real beam in a decade. "Even though..."

"Yes, even though." He put his own glass down and stood slowly. "Or especially because. The first couple of years were pretty dark, but Marie was amazing and eventually convinced me there was more to life than what I'd lost."

How would my life have turned out if I'd had someone who'd stood by me? The only ones who had stood by wanted me for how nimble I was. How fast I learned to swipe wallets and pick locks. They wanted me for my skills, not for me.

Tanner joined me by the wall and tapped on a photograph of him in a suit, shaking hands with—

"You met President Obama!"

"I got involved with the First Lady's Let's Move campaign." He pointed to a framed newspaper clipping, where he stood at a lectern, while Michelle Obama sat off to the side. "I had the opportunity to provide input and do some talks to kids around the area."

"That's amazing." The accident had destroyed my life. The leg healed well enough for me to walk and run, but my tumbling took a nosedive. Four operations after that, and I eventually gave up.

"You never competed again. Why not?"

"I still feel this pain." I brushed my fingertips over the spot above my left knee. "Mom said it was all in my head."

Tanner leaned against the wall beside the photographs. "That's about where my phantom pain is."

I'd lost so little compared to him. But he was the one who'd moved on with life. "I'm sorry."

"You don't have to—"

"Not for that." For everything. "For not visiting. For never calling or checking in."

"You did. My sister told me you were there."

I'd tried before I was discharged, but his parents wouldn't let me near him. He wasn't supposed to have been out that night. Our coaches insisted on an early bedtime, so we'd be well-rested for the last day of the competition, but we had a tradition. We'd both broken curfew and taken my mom's rental car out for a stress-reducing quickie. Sex was good luck.

Then he'd told me he was done with our friends-with-benefits arrangement. He wanted more.

That wasn't part of the tradition.

That wasn't good luck.

"I'm sorry for what I said that night." I didn't want the complication. Breaking curfew was one thing—a relationship was a different matter.

"You told me you loved me." He put a hand on my arm and squeezed. "Don't apologize for that."

I swallowed hard. '*I love you, but I need to focus on London and so do you.*' Those words had haunted me for twelve years. If I'd said yes, he wouldn't have been upset and he would have been more focused on the drive back to the hotel. He would have noticed the other car. He would have…

"It wasn't your fault."

But it was. "Marie's a lucky woman."

He grinned, the little dimple in his left cheek showing up for the first time. "She is."

I'd spent the first two years after the accident trying to heal and get back into Olympic-hopeful shape. My mom helped, but with each operation, I saw less and less of her. My sister was busy with figure skating competitions and the spotlight moved from me to her.

Mom loved me, but she needed to focus on my sister.

One champion replaced by another.

"Did you ever settle down?"

The ache started in my thigh. I was standing still for too long. "Too busy to focus on that."

"Recovering things?"

"Exactly." I dug a thumb into the sore spot. "I should go—"

The front door opened and closed and a woman poked her head in. She was pretty, with short brown hair, bright green eyes, and a warm complexion. She gasped and smiled at me. "Jayce Monroe?"

Tanner chuckled, keeping his gaze on his wife. "Marie's seen lots of photos of our competition days."

"I didn't know you'd be stopping by."

"I'm in town on business. It was spur of the moment. I have a lot of meetings."

"How much time do you have before you have to go?" Marie placed some shopping bags on the floor and joined us in the living room. "My next appointment's not for a couple of hours, and I'd love to hear some of Tanner's stories from someone else's perspective. You were there when he kissed the Blarney Stone, right?"

I snorted at the memory. Before a competition in Dublin, when we were fifteen, our team had taken a bus to Cork. Normal people lay down and leaned backward, holding onto the railings while someone else held their bodies. Tanner? He'd decided a handstand was more appropriate and gave everyone a heart attack when one of his hands slipped. "I can stay for a bit, I guess?"

I just had to text Scarlett—no, I'd text Emmett and tell him I'd be a few minutes late. He'd understand. He'd encouraged me to come here.

And it would only be a few minutes.

Chapter 16
Drew

I sliced the Manchego cheese into wedges and placed it on the charcuterie board, between the prosciutto and the grapes. I popped a piece into my mouth, savoring its tangy nuttiness with its undercurrent of earthiness. It was the perfect cheese for the spread. I moved on to cutting bread into thin pieces and added them to the board as I went.

It was two o'clock, and the Reynolds team was heading up in the elevator.

I'd prepped the review materials on the dining room table. A blown-up floor plan of the banquet room, showing the four Xs on the floor, plus additional printouts of the information Liana's assistant had finally sent me. It had taken two requests yesterday and another this morning, but I had the details on the other three items that would be in the VIP showcase. Still no more intel on Liana's sculpture other than that it was over twenty-five pounds.

I pulled down the sleeves on my black Henley once I'd finished working with the food. No, Vanessa always said it looked better with the sleeves up. And rolling up my sleeves yesterday had exploded Jayce's pupils. She'd liked it.

Not that she was my focus for this afternoon. I washed all that stress down the shower drain. This was all courtesy. Hospitality.

And it wasn't as though I'd debated between four different aprons to wear. Vanessa had gifted me one each of our Christmases together—one with *Kiss the Chef* written on it from our first Christmas, *Mr. Good Lookin' is Cookin'* from our second, and another with the image of a bare-chested barbecuing man on our third. The last one should have gone in the garbage. It was a passive-aggressive suggestion that she wanted a house with a back deck and a barbeque instead of an apartment. She'd made it sound like it was a joke about having her man barefoot and shirtless in the kitchen, another red flag I—yet again—completely missed.

I'd chosen the simple black one. The one I'd bought for myself because it was professional. The boring one, as Vanessa called it.

There was a knock at the door. I put down the knife and made my way out of the kitchen, through the dining room, and passed into the entryway. A quick check through the peephole and I opened the door.

"Scarlett. Emmett." I looked past them, down the hall. "Just the two of you?"

Scarlett wore a long white wrap dress, carrying a bag like the one I'd thrown out with Vanessa. On the outside, there was a great deal of similarity between the two women. On the inside as well, except Scarlett used her powers for good, while Vanessa was a snake. "Malcolm found something disturbing in the background of one of the security men, so he and Rav are collecting more information before removing him from the team."

"And Jayce?"

Scarlett made no reaction, but a minor twitch of Emmett's right eye gave them away. Something wasn't right.

"She's running behind. She'll join us when she can," said Emmett. As they entered, he added, "Nice place."

"I was preparing some food. I assumed Jayce wouldn't be able to focus without a full sideboard." I led them to the dining room and the documents I'd printed out. "If you'll excuse me?"

The Reynolds siblings moved the chairs out of the way. Scarlett placed her bag on one of them, and they both leaned over the table.

I finished with the bread, added it to the end of the board, and stood back. Three cheeses, three meats, three starches, three fruits. Everything was balanced aesthetically. Beautiful.

"Where is she?" Scarlett's voice was the faintest whisper, not for my ears. If she didn't know, Emmett's easy reply at the door had been a cover.

He whispered back, "She texted me earlier she was going to visit Tanner."

"Tanner? That's good, but she's supposed to be here."

I froze, the voices far more interesting than what I was doing. Was it the same Tanner she got into the car accident with? Was I making a fool of myself preparing food and wearing this stupid Henley and apron when she already had a side piece? Or a boyfriend?

If Jayce were normal, she wouldn't have been flirting with me at Gideon's if she were in a relationship. Although no one in our line of business was particularly normal. Besides, my last girlfriend had made no bones about the fact she was sleeping around on me.

I moved the knife, making enough noise to seem as though I were oblivious to their discussion.

"Between you and me," continued Emmett, "I think she's avoiding Drew. I'm not so sure they can work together."

Avoiding me? More than just yesterday in the car? Why would she—

Unless that meant—

That meant she was just as distracted by me as I was by her. But what was the Tanner angle? Some of the news articles covering the accident claimed the two of them were in a secret relationship. There hadn't been any corroborating evidence, but it explained why they were out at midnight during a competition. Had the relationship continued? If not, was she starting it up again?

Mental note: Double-check Tanner's current marital status.

"She's a professional," hissed Scarlett. "She can work with anyone."

"Have you seen how much she's eating? Something's going on."

Rather than continuing the charade, since I'd already found out everything I needed to know, I raised my voice to them. "Can I get you two anything to drink?"

"Sparkling water, if you have it," said Scarlett. "Still water if you don't."

"What are you having?" Emmett sounded suspiciously close.

I turned from the refrigerator where I'd grabbed Scarlett's drink, and he was standing in the entryway.

"Nice kitchen, too. Did it come like this, or do you have a decorator?"

"I had a decorator in after my girlfriend and I separated. The place had looked too much like her."

He leaned against the door frame, folding his arms. He was even more casual than I was, in dark-washed jeans and a loose T-shirt. "I find relationships usually aren't worth the hassle."

Scarlett chimed in, "Because you haven't found the right woman yet."

Emmett grinned, shaking his head and rolling his eyes. "She would have agreed with me a few months ago. This whole Malcolm thing's ruined her judgment."

"Em, remember how we're supposed to be working?"

Emmett joined me in the kitchen, surveying the charcuterie board. "This looks fantastic. I'd ask if you made it yourself, but the apron gives you away."

"Cooking is my hobby."

"Can I take it out?" He lifted the wooden tray and I nodded. "I'm going to text a picture of this to Jayce. When she shows up, we should hide it from her."

I held back the chuckle. "She'd kill you."

"You know her well."

I hung up my apron and pulled two more bottles of sparkling water from the refrigerator, then joined Scarlett and Emmett at the table. "I apologize for having to meet here, but the boardroom at our office was in use."

"Understandable," said Scarlett.

True to his word, Emmett took a photo of the food. "What are the items for the gala?"

I opened my bottle, the black currant mixing perfectly with the scents from the sideboard behind me. I flipped open a folder at the end of the table, displaying the stack of stapled printouts. "The Obsidian Mirror is coming from Wales. It's four feet tall and two wide, a polished piece of—no surprise—obsidian. The details are in the information package, but there's something strange about the way light reflects off it."

Scarlett pulled the printout about the mirror closer. "And it's traveling with two security guards?"

"I sent some questions back to Liana about how that's going to be coordinated with the main security team. She hasn't replied yet." I took a sip from my bottle, the bubbles dancing over my tongue. "I suspect they'll add to the number of scary-looking men in the banquet room instead of swapping out any of the others."

Emmett pulled the next set of sheets closer. "A bird statue on loan from a friend of his in Germany. How does it tie into the theme of the event?"

"Some believe the statue's three thousand years old, but the granulation technique used to affix much of the ornamentation is too complex for that age." I flipped to the third sheet about the bird, which showed some of the scientific research into its manufacture. "There's some debate about where the statue is from. Some scholars claim it's a griffin and is genuinely from Western Europe, while most say it's a huma bird, of Persian origin."

Scarlett reached for the third stack of papers. "And an Egypt-ian scarab?"

Emmett's attention shifted, the golden bird statue forgotten. "Coming from Egypt, I assume?"

"No, actually. It's—"

"From a collector in Monaco?" Scarlett skimmed the doc-umentation. "Gold base... top carved from carnelian... hiero-glyphs on its underside. Dated to the reign of Khufu?"

"I love Egyptian relics." Emmett separated the papers, pulling them off the staple. "Not to mention how much I love Monaco. Where's the technology tie-in with this one?"

I plucked a grape from the sideboard. "That link is more tenuous. Legend has it the piece was a gift from the pharaoh to his chief surveyor, who used it in his measuring rod."

And I'd heard from a contact that Gideon pulled some strings when customs held it up in Dulles. Insufficient paperwork, apparently, but nothing a billionaire couldn't fix.

Scarlett continued skimming details. "It's only two inches long. And no additional security traveling with it?"

"That's one of the questions I sent to Liana. She told me each piece would have a specially constructed display, but I assume it'll be under glass. The mirror will be too big for that, but given its size, it may simply have a stanchion around it. By contrast, the huma bird is ten inches tall, but it weighs over fifty pounds since it's made of pure gold."

Scarlett straightened, focused on the scarab's information. "Can you forward me the files?"

"You're seeing something I'm not. What is it?" I'd hired them because they were good at what they did. They thought like thieves, covering the obvious angles and the ones most people missed.

She didn't look up. "It's the same size as the chip, isn't it?"

Emmett hummed in assent. "Interesting coincidence."

What did that mean? What kind of coincidence was it? "But the chip is going to be part of something much larger. Liana said over twenty-five pounds, but I suspect it's going to be taller than the mirror. Possibly taller than any of us."

"We're doing a walk-through tomorrow as a full team," she said. "Will Liana be there?"

"Do you want her there?"

Scarlett put the sheet down and picked up her water bottle, cracking the top and letting the fizz out. "What I want is Jayce's opinion on this."

"She's not coming this afternoon, is she?" So much for my food display.

Scarlett blinked slowly and gave me the faintest smile. "If she doesn't arrive before we're done, she can swing by this evening. If you can work another meeting into your schedule?"

"I can. This case is my highest priority right now." And if she'd be there in the evening, I had enough time to prepare something better than a charcuterie board.

CHAPTER 17
JAYCE

As I made my way down the hallway to Drew's apartment Thursday evening, Scarlett's words tumbled around my brain. *'Learn to work with him.'*

I could totally work with Drew Donovan. Not a problem.

All I had to do was review the plans I'd discussed with the team and get his feedback. Simple goal.

So long as I could forget the way Emmett had looked at me when she'd proposed it. He didn't think I could do it. He'd taken me aside and offered to come with me. And when I'd said I had it under control, he asked about my visit with Tanner.

I'd shared the highlights with Emmett, including Tanner's success, how amazing his wife was, and we laughed about how foolish I'd been for putting the visit off for so many years.

What I hadn't confessed was how I felt just as guilty as before.

But that was a thought for another day. As was Scarlett's additional threat of taking me off the team if I wound up on the news again, as I had after climbing Mosaic.

The only thing going right for me was the surprise appearance of the Egyptian scarab in the files from Liana's assistant. Since the scarab would be at the gala, my failure to clone Gideon's phone was less of a screw-up. We were still missing a lot of detail—such as specifics on its owner and where they normally kept it—but we had a few days to track that down.

I stopped in front of Drew's door, rolled my shoulders, and knocked.

You can do this, Jayce.

Mr. Scowly Face opened the door, as irritatingly sexy as always. His corded forearms were on full display below the shoved-up sleeves of a black Henley. "You showed this time. Excellent."

"I was busy earlier, but I—" With my first step inside his apartment, I cut off. A wall of intoxicating fragrance hit me. "What is that?"

It was roast beef or steak or some other red meat, notes of garlic, fried mushrooms, and fresh bread all melding together. I was officially in heaven.

"It's seven o'clock. I was starting to think you wouldn't show, so I started my dinner."

I walked past him in his cute little black apron, following my nose. Through a small entryway, past a piano in the corner, through an arched opening to the dining room—papers all over the table, that was what I was supposed to be doing, but I was powerless—through a single doorframe into a black-tiled and gleaming stainless kitchen. The aromas overwhelmed me and I stopped in the middle of the galley, closed my eyes, and inhaled.

Drew chuckled behind me. "Beef Wellington, potato puree, and I was about to put some vegetables in the oven to roast."

"Don't tell me you're an amateur chef." I couldn't handle that.

"There's nothing amateur about me."

Something about the way he said those words settled deep in my belly. Maybe a little deeper. Maybe I couldn't totally work with Drew. "Scarlett wanted me to review a few scenarios with you. Then I can leave you to your dinner. How long do we have?"

"It should be ready in a half hour or so."

"Then we need to work fast!" I turned to head back to the dining room and the paperwork, but he remained in the doorway.

"I made enough for you. I assumed if your stomach was full, you'd be more productive."

Working very hard to maintain a carefree attitude, I snapped my fingers and pointed at him. "That I will be. Is there dessert, too?"

His nostrils flared and he narrowed his eyes, a look that settled even lower than the amateur comment had. "I made sticky toffee pudding. But if you don't like that—"

"Hold up there." I raised a hand to stop him. "'Don't like' and 'sticky toffee' do not belong in the same sentence."

"Your palate may not be discerning"—the corner of his lip twitched—"but at least it will be appreciative."

"I feel like that was an insult." I leaned back against the opposite counter since he didn't appear to be moving. "But since you're going to feed me, I won't complain."

"That's all it takes to win you over?"

I shrugged. "I'm a simple girl."

He cocked an eyebrow. "I don't believe Evelyn Reynolds hires anyone who's simple."

"Emmett has his moments."

"I suspect Emmett pretends to have his moments but rarely does."

"Possible."

Drew approached me, slowly, stopping inches away from me, like he had yesterday. Like he had at Gideon's.

He leaned forward, his delicious cologne mingling with the scents of food. One hand landed on the counter next to me.

Don't inhale the cologne, Jayce. Don't do it. "Didn't the CIA teach you about personal space?"

"They did." He moistened his lips, and every cell in my body contracted. "However, you're standing in front of the bottle of wine I opened."

"Oh!" I shoved off the counter, darting through the narrow opening he'd left.

What was he doing? Pretending to flirt with me? Was this payback for messing with him at Gideon's office? For stealing his stuff?

Probably at least one of those.

I could mess with him back. "Let me guess. An uber-expensive, complex red from some private vineyard in France?"

He grabbed a glass from a top shelf, turned, and poured it without taking his eyes off me.

Goddammit, he was hot.

Or maybe it was the oven.

He placed the bottle on the counter and swirled the glass under his nose. Eyes fluttering closed, he said, "Yes, yes, yes, yes, and no."

I hadn't paid close enough attention to what I'd said to figure out what I'd gotten right or wrong.

"It's from Italy, not France." He held the glass out to me. The bowl on the glass was astonishingly large, so the serving was likely more than it appeared. "I'll spare you the details if you're more interested in the flavor than the history of the Cavallotto winery."

The stem was extraordinarily long, yet somehow, when I took it from him, our fingers brushed. He didn't seem phased by it—just poured a glass for himself. But me? My insides were melting.

The plan to mess with him wasn't going well. I made a hasty retreat into the dining room. A little distance would help. I sighed at the sheets on the table, already tired of the Mosaic floor plan. The measurements were in my head and I didn't need pictures anymore. That's what the rest of the team needed.

The dining room opened into his living room, where a large screen television hung on the wall by a small balcony door. On television? More news. No wonder he was always so grumpy. How could a person be happy with so much negative information bombarding them every moment they were awake?

I scanned the living room, an overly masculine space that resembled a show home. Structured furniture, everything in tones of gray and blue, including the barely there rug under the coffee table. After being in his car, it shouldn't have surprised me.

Shit. My shoes were still on. Did I track in any dirt?

Mr. Clean wouldn't be a wearing-shoes-inside kinda guy. I'd been too distracted by the kitchen when I arrived to think about common niceties. Not that it was only a nicety—I preferred feeling the floor. Another thing that centered me.

I kicked my shoes onto a small mat next to his door. He had one shiny pair of brown Oxfords next to a worn pair of running shoes, lined up perfectly.

That was a way to mess with him. I adjusted one of my shoes so it crossed over the other. Asymmetry. That was step one.

Unfortunately, the hardwood floors weren't as pleasant as I'd hoped. "Your floors are cold. Has anyone ever told you that?"

No response came. Either he hadn't heard or he was ignoring me.

I wandered to one of the tall windows, the curtains hanging open. The sun was still up—would be until we were done—and I could see for miles. "Nice view."

"It's better from the top of the building," he called from the kitchen. "You can see the Potomac from the lounge area by the outdoor pool."

"Swanky."

"We can go up there after we discuss Scarlett's ideas." The sound of metal slicing against metal came from around the corner. Not an amateur, for sure. He was sharpening his knife. "The city's beautiful at night, with all the lights twinkling in the darkness."

At night? Darkness? In the middle of June, that wouldn't be until after nine. How much did he think we had to discuss?

I took a sip from the glass, a hint of chocolate and cherries dancing over my tastebuds. It *was* fantastic. Not that I had to let that slip. It would go against my whole plan of messing with him. *Or you should talk about work, the reason you're here in the first place.*

"Scarlett thinks—"

"How's Tanner doing?"

My heart lurched.

The sound of sharpening switched to cutting, and he raised his voice further. "Emmett said that's where you were this afternoon."

Emmett, you jerk! You were supposed to cover for me!

Next question: What did he mean? He'd asked how Tanner was doing, not who he was or why I was there. Did they know each other? Did he know which Tanner I'd visited?

"He's good."

"Have you met his wife?"

I took another sip of the wine and moved from the window to a hutch tucked in the corner of the dining room, decorated with small framed photos. How was I supposed to play this game with him when I didn't know the rules? "Yeah, we had lunch together."

The chopping stopped, and something solid rattled into a bowl.

I skimmed the photos, all of them landscapes or monuments. No family, no faces, not even Drew. Except for one. I shifted two photographs out of the way to pull a silver frame from the back. Drew and a beautiful woman with long blonde hair, in a tiny black bikini on a beach. He was in swim trunks and they stood next to each other in the water, with their arms around each other.

"Lunch? That's why you missed the meeting?" he asked.

She was almost as tall as him, with full breasts and legs that went on forever. The kind of woman who reminded me I was five-foot-six and built like a hobbit. I should have been ogling

Drew in the photo, but I couldn't take my eyes off her. That's what sex-on-a-stick Drew Donovan dated.

"What are you doing?"

I startled, nearly spilling my wine. When I spun, he was right there. Too close again. "Is this your girlfriend? She's really pretty."

He didn't even glance at the photo I was holding. "I don't have a girlfriend."

"She's obviously not your sister."

His jaw clenched.

"Fiancée, then? You two look awfully close."

His nostrils flared again and a dangerous glint shimmered in his eyes. "I said I don't have a girlfriend. You assume that was a sidestep? A way to avoid your actual question?"

What *was* my actual question? "She's gorgeous."

"And she uses it to her full advantage."

I looked down at the photograph in the tiny space between us. "So you're the tall, blonde woman type? You like the living dolls?"

"She's not here, is she?"

"She dumped your grouchy butt?"

"I don't want to talk about her with you."

"Oh, but you wanted me to talk about Tanner?"

"You skipped out on a meeting for him." He reached for the picture frame, but I tucked it behind myself. "I need to trust you've got my back on this job."

"Like you had mine on the Harrington job?" *Weak attempt at changing the subject, Jayce.*

He inched closer. "Your plan sucked."

"Your slow thinking would have gotten us caught without my plan." I took a half-step away and ran into the hutch. *Throw the wine at him. That'll show him.*

As though reading my thoughts, he took the wineglass from me and placed it on the table behind himself. "She was sleeping with two other men."

Well, shit. I had to stop teasing him about her, didn't I? Maybe I should have gone back to harassing him about Chase Harrington.

Drew stepped up to me again, reaching behind my back for the photograph. When I didn't let go, he wrapped the other arm around me, grabbing the frame with both hands.

I was caged between his strong arms and his hard body. This wasn't how tonight was supposed to go. I released the frame. "We should discuss the gala."

With his chest nearly pressed against mine, his deep tenor reverberated inside of me. "Yes, we should."

I'd have to move for us to do that. But I didn't want to, not really. I wanted to stay there, warm from his body, the taste of the wine in my mouth, and his sandalwood and leather cologne fighting with the scent of the food. I wanted to believe he wanted me. That someone wanted me. "Bet you wish—"

"Screw this stupid dance."

"We're not dancing."

"We're dancing around each other." He shifted one of his hands from the photograph to my back, encouraging me closer. That hand was so big on my waist. "I need to kiss you."

I swallowed hard. What was I supposed to do? I was so far out of my league. I was a thief, not a con artist. My skills were in taunting and sneaking, but I damn well couldn't lie or tell him I didn't want the same thing. And I couldn't sleep around. That was a leap I couldn't take. It would ruin everything. "Need is an awfully strong word."

"It is." His breaths were deep and ragged. "I haven't been able to think straight since I saw you at Gideon's."

"That must be difficult for you."

"I'm always in control." His hard cock pressed against my lower abdomen. This wasn't an act. And it didn't feel like it was about a kiss. Let alone a game. "Except around you."

Chapter 18
Drew

Jayce's eyes flitted back and forth, confusion washing over her. "What are you talking about?"

"You feel the same way, I can tell."

"What if I say you're reading too much into things?" She licked her lips, and it took every ounce of self-control not to follow her tongue with my thumb.

"Then you'd be lying." I flexed my hand at the small of her back. This was a horrible idea. I should have stuck with the shower approach. We only needed to get through two more days. "And you're not a convincing liar."

"Why do you still have her photo here?"

"I thought I'd gotten rid of everything." Cracking open a drawer behind her, I dropped the photo inside. Before the decorators did their magic, I'd cleansed Vanessa from the apartment. She must have brought it this morning, thinking she could weasel her way back in subliminally. I shut the drawer and ran my fingers over Jayce's cheek, into her hair.

Her eyes fluttered closed, but her mouth tightened instead of opening for me. She didn't even move her limbs from where she'd held the glass or the picture. "This is wrong, Drew."

"Does it matter? We're adults and we can do what we want."

She laid one hand against my chest, the other explored my fingers on her back. "Then why haven't you kissed me yet?"

"Because I'd never force myself on a woman who doesn't want me."

Her eyes opened, and she let out a half-laugh. "I doubt that happens often."

Not the reaction I was looking for, but an invitation nonetheless. I dipped down, ghosting my lips along her cheekbone, wanting little more in the world than to please her. "What do you crave in a lover?"

Her breathing had picked up, and other than her lungs, she still barely moved. "Nothing."

I breathed next to her ear. "You don't like sex?"

She tilted her head so her cheek touched mine.

"Or is it me you don't like?"

There was no way. Desire vibrated off her, as strong as the impossible energy she lived every second with. Something else held her back. Maybe it was Tanner, maybe it was someone else. But if she belonged to another man, she'd have said so.

"Just say yes, Jayce." I caught my thumb around one of her fingers. "Let me touch you."

"You already are." Snarky responses were good. It meant she was settling into the idea of being with me.

"I want to touch more." I rubbed my hard-on against her, doubling down on my words. "I want to touch everything."

"No more standing still." She pulled in a long breath, like when she'd initially entered my kitchen. Her fingers threaded into my hair. "Kiss me."

I pressed my lips to hers, finding her tongue eager for mine. Not sugar. She tasted like red wine. Like complex and full-bodied Barolo-tinged perfection. I slipped my hand lower over the roundest, tightest ass I'd ever felt in my life.

As we continued to explore each other's mouths, a wave of heat spread through my body. Her tentative touch turned firm, fingers digging into my scalp, while her other hand balled into a fistful of my apron.

Why was I still wearing the apron? Why hadn't I turned the news off? The food, my clothes, the wine—and I'd forgotten the music.

Although it didn't seem to matter.

I tangled one hand in her hair while the other continued learning her curves.

She moaned and stepped forward, pushing me toward the table. Our tongues tangled in a frantic dance, and I picked her up, her legs effortlessly swinging around my hips. She wanted me, exactly how I wanted her.

Hard.

Fast.

And now.

The bedroom was too far away. I had to get to the couch. Had to get her clothes off. Had to taste her.

Her hands were in my hair, teeth raking my lips.

On our way, I pulled the curtains closed—maybe closed—I didn't pay enough attention. I rounded the couch and eased down, settling her on my lap.

She ground down hard, her arms wrapped around my neck. "It's been too long."

That answered my earlier question—there definitely wasn't another man sharing her bed. I leaned my head away, taking in her swollen lips and hooded eyes. "You're so fucking sexy."

"You're so full of shit." She lifted on her knees and hauled the apron out from between us. "Take this off."

"Yes, ma'am." I untied the apron and removed it, keeping my eyes locked with hers as I threw it away.

"And the shirt." She curled her fingers under the hem and pulled it up, her lips touching my chest while the shirt covered my face. "I was betting on more chest hair."

I finished stripping off my shirt with her eager help. When I could see her again, the heat pouring out of her was palpable—she liked what she saw. I grabbed the hem of her shirt. "May I?"

She dragged her fingers through my hair and kissed me, her hips continuing to stroke my hardness. "Yes," she said against my lips.

"No more standing still. I like that line." I pushed her shirt up off her body, barely able to contain my groan at the sight of her curves. Her bra was black, but not a hint of lace. It was utilitarian, exactly like I'd known it would be. My fantasy in the shower had gone from fully clothed to fully naked, but going through the steps, one by one? A thousand times better. I traced my fingers over her small breasts, and I had to move closer, kissing along her collarbone, taking one breast in my hand to squeeze.

"Drew," she groaned, writhing under my touch.

I wrapped an arm around her and pivoted us, landing her on her back on the couch. I crawled down her body, licking along the edge of her bra and kneading her thigh. My tongue danced over the top of her waistband, and her hips rocked up, demanding more. "Fuck, you taste so good."

Jayce cupped the back of my neck. "Get up here and kiss me again."

"I need to be inside you." Still, I inched my way up, easing down one bra cup to roll her nipple in my mouth. I sucked hard, pulling it taut, until she whimpered. "We need to get this out of our systems."

She tensed underneath me. "What?"

"If you're even half as distracted as I am every time we're in the same room together..." I undid the button of her jeans, revealing the sexiest pair of unassuming black cotton underwear I'd ever seen. I wasn't the only one who hadn't expected this tonight.

A high-pitched beep broke my focus. "Shit."

Jayce edged up on her elbows. "Is that the oven timer?"

"It is." I dropped my head to her abdomen and kissed it. "Don't move. I just need to take something out and I'll be right back."

"Yes, sir." She gave me a faux-salute and a tiny smile.

I straightened, eyes roving over her not-naked-enough body. "I have so much more I plan to do to you."

Her breaths continued coming quickly. "Don't let the food burn."

With a nod, I rushed to the kitchen. The Wellington timer had gone off, so I threw on my oven mitts and pulled it out, dropping it unceremoniously onto a cooling rack. The vegetables had a few more minutes, but I wasn't about to accept another interruption, so I pulled them early. Everything would be cold, but cold food and hot bodies went together well. The sticky toffee pudding would make up for it.

And maybe an extra orgasm.

Maybe a shower together. *Even better.*

I tossed off the gloves and did what I could to not run and leap over the back of the couch. This was going to be an amazing—

The couch was empty. My heart gave a tremendous leap and my dick led me down the hallway. She was already in the bedroom.

But when I got there?

Nothing.

Not in the ensuite or the main bath. Not in my office.

She'd left?

She'd left!

What the fuck? She'd left?

I stormed back to the living room, where I'd docked my phone hours ago, and called her.

No answer.

What had happened? She wanted me, didn't she?

Didn't she?

Chapter 19
Jayce

I sat on the roof of a building close to Drew's, staring down at the street from five floors up. Cars puttered by, people went about their lives—their perfectly normal, unscrewed-up lives.

"There you are," came a soft voice from behind me.

"Hey, Emmett." I didn't turn around.

"Not planning on jumping, are you?"

"Just watching." I sniffled. "You know. Living in the shadows."

He stopped, well clear of the edge. "You said you needed to talk."

I held up my great defeat, my red-wrapped chocolate shame. "I stole this chocolate bar."

"Oh, sweetie." Emmett sank down beside me and began rubbing gentle circles on my back. "It's been five years. What brought this on?"

A wad of cotton lodged in my throat, and the stupid tears started again. "Drew kissed me."

Emmett nodded slowly. "What happened?"

"I went into the jewelry store, but their security would be too tight without more prep time." I sniffled, pointing at the shops five stories below us. "But the antique store wouldn't be. They have some small items they'd never notice were missing."

"I meant, what happened with Drew?"

"I went to see Tanner."

"Yeah, you told me."

"Why did you tell Drew? How did that come up in conversation?"

"It didn't. I told—" He sighed. "I told Scarlett and he must have overheard."

"He's so happy, Emmett." I dragged the back of my hand over my eyes, the skin already raw. "His wife was amazing and he met the President and he's got twin girls he coaches in gymnastics. His life is perfect. The accident didn't stop him. Not for good."

He lost a leg and his Olympic dream, but he had the biggest things I lacked. Love. Family.

"Tanner, you mean?"

"Of course, Tanner."

"I thought I was here to listen to you complain about Drew kissing you."

"Oh my god, Emmett, I liked it." I could still feel Drew's lips. Could still taste the wine on his tongue, mixed with the savory sauce he'd prepared. The salt on his skin. "I liked it a lot."

"So you stole a chocolate bar?"

"I didn't know what else to do." I dropped my face into my hands, unable to clear my brain of the smattering of hair across his pecs. Or the faint trail leading from his chiseled abs to his waistband. And his hands, so strong, pulling me to him like I was the greatest need he'd ever had.

Emmett chuckled softly. "Normally, the answer is to kiss them back."

"My hands have been clean for five years."

"And so's your bed?"

"Sex just went with the stealing. I was afraid one would lead to the other and…" After my life fell apart, shoplifting small things gave me the rush I was missing. For a few minutes, at least. Then I moved on to bigger items and bigger thrills. To men who couldn't fill the place in my heart that Tanner once had. "He asked what I craved from a lover."

Emmett made a noncommittal noise.

"I mean, who says that?"

"A considerate lover?"

"Do *you* say that? As more than a pickup line?" Not as if Drew had to pick me up. I was already there and more than willing. "Crave? Lover? Not one-night stand or—"

"How about we talk about that chocolate bar again?"

"But then…" My stomach twisted tighter, and I choked out, "He said all he wanted was to get me out of his system. Said he can't focus when I'm around. Like I'm some annoying little bug flitting around his head that he can't swat away."

Like I was temporary.

Replaceable.

"I would have thought you both needed that. You've been off since you ran into him at Tremaine Industries."

"What?" I smacked him hard. "I'm not a bug."

"You verbally spar with him in Gideon's office, then you steal his watch and phone. He kisses you, you like it, and then you steal something else." He tapped the chocolate bar. "You're distracted. It's even worse than the last time you worked with him."

"I'm sorry." The tears threatened to start again. "I'm screwing everything up, Emmett. The Trojan failed—"

"Not your fault."

"—I didn't get the clone of Gideon's phone or even Liana's. I didn't tell Drew anything we talked about for tomorrow—"

"We rarely have a job go perfectly."

Everything in my life had been perfect twelve years ago. A lifetime of planning and hard work was about to pay off.

It wasn't only my life that fell to pieces.

I'd ruined Tanner's, too.

"His parents wouldn't let me see him. They blamed me for him being out that night. The accident wouldn't have happened if we were in our hotel rooms for curfew." I looked down at the street again, at the two shops I'd considered stealing from and the convenience store I did. "And when I couldn't bring in gold medals anymore, my mom started blaming me, too. Said I wasn't taking my recovery seriously enough. Said I needed more hours in physio."

"Your mom is a self-centered opportunist."

But she was still my mother. She was supposed to be the one supporting me through everything, not giving up when I couldn't reach the podium anymore.

She wasn't supposed to replace me with someone else, even if it was my sister.

"I just want someone to want me, despite my screw-ups."

"I want you." Emmett moved closer and put an arm around my shoulders. "Not in the same way Drew does..."

A tiny chuckle burst out of me. "That would be so eww."

"Watch it. I can still throw you over the edge."

I wiped more tears away. "Except you want me around, so you won't."

"Exactly."

"I can't work with him, Em. I couldn't even go over the scenarios Scarlett tasked me with or get any information about the scarab." I took a long, shuddering breath, trying to find some composure. "She was already pissed at me for missing the meeting. I can't imagine what she'll say about this."

"Don't worry about it. I'd hoped you and Drew could figure things out, but I warned her you might not."

"What about Saturday?"

He pulled me closer, subtly moving me farther from the edge. "Leave it to me. You're going to team up with Wyatt if you think you can handle his obvious come-ons."

Him, I could handle. He was all bluster and overt flirting. I could laugh at Wyatt. With Drew, it was all serious and tingles and now tears.

Emmett sat with me in silence for a few minutes, just being the friend I needed.

"He made Beef Wellington." The apartment had smelled so good.

"He called me ten minutes before you did."

Probably to complain.

"He was out looking for you. Said he was worried."

"Worried about his irritating little bug?" I scoffed. "Sure he was."

Emmett shrugged—what did that mean?—and stood. "Not everyone's your mother, Jayce."

"Well, duh."

"You say that, but you spent five years trying to get her attention, then five years with us, trying to pretend you don't care about anyone."

"You're psychoanalyzing again." And definitely wrong. Stealing bigger and bigger things, plus a few minor arrests, was about expressing my independence, not seeking my mother's attention.

"What else am I going to do at midnight two days out from the mission? Sleep?" He pretended to yawn, stretching his arms. "We should head to the hotel. I'll handle Drew—and my sister—tomorrow."

I stood with him, waving the chocolate bar. "Let me pay for this first."

CHAPTER 20
DREW

I'd thought I was distracted before last night.

But then Jayce ran off, ignoring every call I made to convince her to come back.

At least Emmett had taken my call, but his *She's fine* text at one in the morning was significantly less than I'd wanted. I'd had a fitful night, going over every moment she'd been at my place, searching for an explanation for her erratic behavior.

She's chaos personified, Drew. Don't bother looking.

I paced the length of the restaurant, rain pelting the tall windows. Most of the tables had been cleared to make way for a dance floor. At the western end, overlooking the fountain and the square, the staff had added a two-foot-high platform for the band and announcements. The Mosaic staff who'd dominated the space on Wednesday had all but vanished, replaced by the blonde event planner overseeing the last few paintings and sculptures being placed for maximum financial gain.

At the eastern end of the main restaurant, I peeked into the banquet room. The Reynolds team hadn't arrived yet, but Craig and Wyatt had. The patio doors along the southern wall were all closed against the rain, and I hadn't seen either of them come in the main entrance, so they must have used the staff entrance to the north, closer to the parking garage.

"Drew!" Craig waved me in and the three of us walked over to a man installing a four-foot-high pedestal where the northernmost X had been on the floor. "This is George. He tells me this podium is being built with a small acrylic stand at the top of it."

"For the scarab?" I asked.

Craig nodded. "I just got off the phone with Liana. She still wants to install the VIP items tonight."

The Tremaines were holding a vernissage this evening—a private, low-key viewing for the people with the deepest wallets—ahead of tomorrow night's gala. No alcohol, no food, no music, simply a tour of whatever pieces they were interested in and discussions with the artists. Then at the gala, the Tremaines would already know who wanted what and how badly, allowing them to stroke egos and incite bidding wars. Everyone knew that was the tactic, but the ones who'd be attending tonight were more than happy to be part of it.

"Did you shut her down?" I'd already discussed this with her. She told me the plan on Wednesday after Jayce's initial departure, and I'd said no. She'd argued it was too much for her team to do on Saturday before the event. I'd told her to get more staff.

"She said the scarab and the bird were small enough they could be brought in, then returned to their secure locations overnight."

"But not the chip?" asked Wyatt. "Isn't it only two inches wide?"

Craig inclined his head and we walked toward the glass wall overlooking the river. A half-dozen people bustled around the room, heading in and out through various doors, and the sounds of drills and saws hummed in the background. Still, Craig lowered his voice. "I got a look at her sculpture this morning. She told me not to tell anyone, but it's huge."

"Photos?" I asked.

Craig frowned. "The sculpture itself is a metal dragonfly about four feet across, mounted on the side of…" He swung his hands up and down, as though trying to describe it visually. "A giant tree trunk. It's ten feet tall and must weigh several hundred pounds."

Wyatt frowned. "Where's the chip gonna be?"

Craig's eyebrows rose and he shook his head in disbelief. "Embedded inside the dragonfly's head."

Wyatt mirrored Craig's expression. "Why are we worried about someone taking it, then?"

"With enough force, someone might be able to dislodge it, but I—"

"Sorry we're late." Scarlett entered with Jayce and Emmett. "Rav and Malcolm are double-checking the lower floor and emergency stairwell."

"Ladies." Wyatt's extra twang appeared. "And Emmett."

The Reynolds group joined us by the windows, with more nods than hellos. Scarlett and Emmett were in dark suits, matching my team's formality. Jayce stood between the two siblings, directly opposite me. Per usual, she was in skintight jeans with a dark T-shirt and black running shoes—always ready to bolt. Her pants were damp below the knee, so she must have hung up a rain jacket when she arrived.

"We should have a security patrol down there," Jayce said to Craig. "Explosives would be messy, but if the thieves don't care about a mess, blowing a hole in the floor to get the chip is an option."

"How many options does your team think there are?" I asked.

"The most obvious is the smash and grab." She shifted her gaze to Wyatt, then back to Craig. She didn't look at me and didn't acknowledge me, other than answering my question. "Take the chip and run."

Craig said, "It'll be inside a ten-foot-tall sculpture."

"So?" Her lips tightened. "If we only ever looked at the easy options, you wouldn't have hired us. Assume they dislodge it somehow and take off—you'll have enough security here that shouldn't be an issue."

"From there," said Scarlett, "we look at all the angles. What if a security guard was paid off? Maybe they let the thief go by? Maybe they make a convincing play for the thief, but accidentally tackle someone pursuing them?"

Jayce nodded at Scarlett. "With all the possibilities and those angles to account for, there's over a hundred options."

"And if *you* were going to take it?" I looked pointedly at Jayce, willing her to either meet my gaze or throw a taunt at me or something.

"I haven't even seen it yet." She stared out the window, toward the water or maybe the patio or the huge metal sculpture outside. "I'd go in with my list of one hundred scenarios and start crossing them off the more I learned."

Wyatt rocked back on his heels. "A hundred plans ain't no plan at all, darlin'."

"It's a flexible plan, is what it is." Jayce smiled at him. At him! "Minus the explosives. I don't like things getting messy."

"Speaking of which…" Emmett scratched at his short beard. "Rav feels Wyatt would be more convincing with Jayce as a partner tomorrow night—"

"No." The word was out of my mouth before I thought wiser of it. *Push it into the locker, Drew. At least until you can talk to her.* "We already went over this. You're with me, Jayce."

Scarlett cocked her eyebrow. "You hired us for our expertise and that's what we're giving you. Wyatt's more believable with a younger woman on his arm than with Rav. Drew, you're more likely the type of man who'd invite a friend."

Jayce wandered away from the group, heading for George the carpenter. "Is this to display—"

Craig tucked his hands into his suit pant pockets, speaking loud enough I couldn't make out anything else Jayce said. "You're right. That makes more sense from a cover standpoint."

Wyatt peeled off next, following Jayce. *Go after her, Drew.* If I did that, I'd have to concede the discussion on pairings for the gala.

Craig continued, "But your rotation of all groups had Drew and Jayce in the VIP room more than Wyatt and Rav."

"Exactly." I kept my peripheral vision trained on Wyatt, his hand winging out to touch Jayce's back. *Hands off.* "We determined it was more likely I'd be interested in the art than him, giving us a reason to linger in the VIP room. Wyatt would be more likely to have her out on the dance floor than paying attention to anything important."

"The decision's made," said Emmett.

Before I could protest further, Liana swept into the room, followed by a half-dozen men wearing tool belts, two of them carrying a five-foot wide slab of metal between them.

"This way," she said in a singsong voice. "Craig! You're here!"

People gradually filled the room. The coordinator with her clipboard escorted two men carrying wrapped paintings and two disinterested-looking men who may have been the artists. Another three women followed behind, in pencil skirts and tailored jackets, plus a man and woman in the black Mosaic shirts.

Craig introduced Scarlett and Emmett to Liana, while I made a beeline for Jayce and Wyatt.

"What are you wearing to the party?" Wyatt asked her. "I'll wear cuff links that complement your dress."

"Scarlett picked it out. It might be pink. Or blue. I'm not sure."

Liana's workers placed the platform over the southernmost X, the floor shuddering as it landed. One of them muttered, "Fucking heavy thing."

The carpenter said something to them, gesturing with a hammer, while two of Liana's followers debated whether it was in the right spot.

"Wyatt," I said, "can I have a minute with Ms. Monroe?"

"One minute only." He winked at Jayce and sauntered over to the women in the pencil skirts.

Jayce looked up at me, a defiant purse to her lips. "What?"

I kept my voice down. "What happened last night?"

"A mistake." She folded her arms, lifting her chin.

"It didn't feel like a mistake." I wanted to shake her. Pull her close. Kiss her again.

"And now I'm fixing it."

"Fixing it? By refusing to look at me?"

"By showing the professional work ethic I'm known for." She opened her hands in front of herself, emphasizing her feigned innocence. "That's why you hired us, isn't it?"

"Back to standing still, are you?" I didn't know what it meant, but it had meant something important to her last night.

Her lips quivered and she balled her hands into fists. "Fuck you."

Shit. It had meant *too much* to her. An unfamiliar shiver ran down my spine. Guilt? Regret? I reached for her arm and she pulled away.

"Walk-through time!" Scarlett clapped twice behind us. "If you don't work for me or for Craig, I need you to clear the room for fifteen minutes. Liana, please stay." She nodded at Jayce. "The floor's yours."

Chapter 21

Jayce

Drew freaking Donovan.

I was *not* standing still.

He was *not* distracting me. I was *not* 'off' like Emmett said. I didn't need to get him out of my system. And I definitely wouldn't be a little plaything he could throw away the second he was done with me.

I shouldered my way past him. I'd show him how professional I could be.

If only it hadn't been pouring rain and I could have ducked into the coffee shop first. I needed food.

Rav and Malcolm entered the room while Liana waved her people out.

We were just missing one. "Where's Zaria? She was supposed to be here for this."

"She won't be able to join us," said Craig. "Go ahead and I'll fill her in."

See, Drew? I'm more professional than someone. At least I'm here.

"You've all seen this on paper, so nothing should be a surprise. Everything boils down to three concepts." I held up my fingers, walking toward the patio. "Ingress, egress, and obtaining the chip."

"That's a lot fewer plans than a hundred," chuckled Wyatt, who settled next to Drew. Not only was he a massive flirt, but he was the class clown, too.

I could work with that. "Gotta keep it simple for you, Wyatt."

"Much appreciated."

"For the banquet room itself, we've got five doors—ingress and egress. We'll refer to these doors"—I pointed at the two doors in the glass wall, leading to the patio—"as river doors east and west. The door on the western wall, leading to the main dining room will be the main door, the other one on the western wall will be the bathroom door—"

"That leads to more than the facilities," said Wyatt.

Drew's scowl deepened—not that I was looking at him.

I would *not* look at him. "That's the primary reason guests will use it, so that's our term. The door on the northern wall, farthest from the action, will be referred to as the staff door, as they're the only ones who should use it."

Rav said, "We found five members of the security team with questionable backgrounds, and we've removed them from the detail. I've replaced two with friends of mine who'll be responsible for the main door and general security."

"Our second-tier concern," I continued, moving counter-clockwise around the room as I spoke, "is the eastern and southern walls. They're made of glass, which makes them relatively easy to get through, but that would alert everyone in the room. It would also be messy, but we can't eliminate the idea of a truck being driven up the tiered patio and straight through that wall."

Liana's hand flew to her chest. "My word!"

I nodded at her. "The metal platform your workers brought in—is that for your sculpture?"

"It is."

"That puts it closest to the patio. The odds of someone coming in that way are slim, but we'll have less opportunity to stop them if they do. I want it moved to the northernmost spot."

"But the sculpture is designed—"

"Nope." I popped the 'P' sound at the end, emphasizing there was no debate. I needed some gum. "Our third-tier concern would be the ceiling or the floor. Neither is likely, but the floor's more possible than the ceiling, so we'll have Rav's men do the initial sweep before the event, and then a rover will keep it on his circuit."

Liana pressed her palms together, as if in prayer. "I'm worried the extra security will detract from the event."

Scarlett said, "You wanted to make it a big event—talk of the town? Play up the security during your vernissage and drop some hints about the threats. It'll increase the intrigue and open their wallets further."

I added, "While keeping everyone on high alert for anything suspicious. Make it sound like one of those murder mystery nights, where everyone wants to solve the puzzle."

"That's a good start," said Drew.

"Also in this room, we have the risk to the chip." I turned to Liana. "Does it have a GPS tracker embedded in it?"

"No."

"I'll add one once we arrive tomorrow evening."

"Also no." Liana put her hands up. "Your job is to prevent it from being stolen. If you need to track it, you've already failed. And I will not have my masterpiece marred by extra material."

Artists. I held back the eye roll. That just meant I couldn't tell *her* that was the plan, but I'd easily sneak one onto it.

"All right." I made my way to the center of the Xs on the floor. They were fifteen feet apart, giving ample room for traffic flow between. "You'll move your sculpture, put the mirror to the west, closest to the main door—"

"That cannot be done." Did she have to be so difficult? "It has to be on the opposite side, so it can reflect people as they come in. I don't want anyone approaching it from the back."

"That's fair," said Scarlett.

I walked to the main door, the group gravitating with me. My goal had been to position the scarab furthest from the doors, so we'd be able to study it. We still had a client looking for it, and whatever detail we gathered at the gala would help plan its eventual recovery. I nodded—having it closest to the main door would give us several passes from behind and in front. "In that case, scarab to the west, and bird to the south."

Liana stood back, arms folded, tilting her head back and forth. "I think I can make this work."

"And I don't want those VIP items coming in tonight." I nodded to where George had been installing the stand for the scarab. He'd told me Liana's plan for the evening, but I wanted the center of the room as empty as possible for the early guests, to ensure potential thieves couldn't get a read on the space they'd be working in. The more variables they had to contend with, the more chances we'd have to stop them.

Liana glanced at Craig, who nodded, and she did the same.

"Next up…" I walked back toward the middle of the room, all eyes on me. They didn't follow this time. I was pacing. I had to stop that. "We'll have four teams on rotation, three that combine our teams and one that is Reynolds exclusive. Each team will have separate communications. Brie will coordinate ours from Halifax."

Craig said, "The manager's approved my use of his office to coordinate my team, and I'll be able to provide your tech support with access to the cameras."

Before my feet could whisk me toward the main door again and prove I really was pacing, I forced my body toward the windows at the eastern end. The rain continued coming down in sheets. Too bad it was raining today, not tomorrow. All the rain for the gala would have given us more control of the foot traffic in and out from the patio, plus the bonus of making it easier to track wet footprints.

"Each couple will do rotations in the banquet room, ten-to-fifteen-minute minimums, with Wyatt and I floating in more frequently and for longer." I was better in the shadows. This was going to be a long night. I paced back toward the group, looking at Wyatt. "I warn you, I'm a talker, but not a conversationalist. You'll have to handle any shmoozing required so we can stay close to the chip."

Wyatt tipped a non-existent hat at me. "My specialty."

"Since we have the extra Reynolds-exclusive team and we're not sharing comms, Scarlett will coordinate the banquet room times and Emmett will convey them."

Everyone nodded, even Mr. Sourpuss. Maybe that's why he left the spy world—people kept picking him out in a crowd because he was always too miserable to blend in.

"I want to review the main dining room, mezzanine, and kitchen next. Follow me."

Chapter 22
Drew

There were restaurants you frequented for the food and others for the price. In DC, many were where you went to see and be seen. But di Sano's, a dimly lit Italian restaurant near Dupont Circle, was about privacy.

The host greeted me at the door. "Welcome back, Mr. Donovan. We made your regular table available."

"Thank you, Luca." I followed him past intimate tables with pendant lights on long chains. I always sat in a circular booth at the far end. From there, I had a view of everyone else but was close enough to the kitchen that the chef could duck out for a chat.

He ushered me into the booth, and I slid to the rear of the worn leather bench. "Would you like a menu?"

I waved it off. "Ask Martina to surprise me."

"Of course." He left with a slight bow and a subtle nod toward a young female server who delivered fresh cutlery and a small candle in a stained glass holder.

Alex had introduced me to the restaurant five years ago, when he'd been in town. The head chef, Martina, was an ex-girlfriend of his he'd maintained close ties with. She'd originally opened the restaurant in New York, but it proved successful enough she opened this one a few years later.

The candle flickered and I ran a finger along the side. The Flame of Khvarenah. How had Alex gotten mixed up with them?

And what was I going to do about it? Anything?

"Would you look at that?" A male voice grew too close to my table and I looked up. Emmett Reynolds stood there, hands on his hips, with Rav LaPierre looming behind him. "He walked right past us without saying hello, didn't he, Rav?"

I blinked at the men. So much for privacy.

"Why thank you for the invite!" Emmett slid into the booth from the other side, stopping at the midpoint. "We'd love to join you."

Rav sat next to him, pushing the dark hair from his forehead as he did. "Better view from here."

Emmett nodded, taking the drink menu from the middle of the table.

"Better view of what?" I asked.

Emmett opened the menu and held it high enough to disguise the way he was staring at someone. "Yeah, perfect view."

I followed his gaze and my stomach tied in the most ridiculously large knot, which then rose progressively up my throat.

Jayce sat at a small two-person table along the opposite wall. She had one foot tucked underneath herself and she leaned forward on the table. From the side, she appeared more slender than usual, her athletic shoulders hidden by a pale blue silk blouse. She was smiling and laughing, without the malice or sarcasm I normally brought out in her.

Across the table from her—Wyatt James. He was also laughing, in that obnoxiously loud way he did. The way he did when he was playing up his Southern charm.

"We're chaperoning," said Emmett. "He called and invited her to dinner, she told us, and we snuck in. Our other table required craning necks, so when we saw you sit down, figured you wouldn't mind."

"You're spying on her?" I asked.

Emmett cocked an eyebrow. "You're not?"

"I came for dinner." Although I was no longer craving Martina's cooking. I waved to a server I didn't know—time for a drink. "Have you eaten?"

"Not yet." Rav folded his thick arms and leaned on the table, casually glancing in Jayce's direction. "I wasn't on the last job you did, so I'm not familiar with Wyatt. Is he trustworthy, you think?"

I shifted in my seat. "He's twice her age."

Emmett shrugged. "Only about ten years older, by my estimation."

The server arrived. "Have you had a chance to look over the drink menu?"

"A glass of the Barolo Cannubi, and whatever these gentlemen would like."

"I'm sorry, sir, but"—he gestured to the menu Emmett was hiding behind—"we don't have that variety. Is there something else I can interest you in? A Chianti, perhaps?"

A dozen tables beyond the server, Wyatt leaned forward, and Jayce canted her head. A subtle move that exposed her neck. She was flirting, whether intentional or not.

"Tell Luca the wine's for Drew," I said.

The server nodded, took Emmett and Rav's orders for scotch and water, respectively, and left.

Emmett put the menu down in front of himself. "Any chance you want to tell me what happened between you and Jayce?"

Of all the directions I expected my quiet evening to go, this was probably the last one. "If I knew, I wouldn't tell you, anyway."

"Well, that's a plus. At least you realize *something* happened."

"She's difficult to work with." That was true before yesterday, so it was a safe point of contention to share.

Rav grunted. "All the women on our team are. Women as strong and capable as our teammates often make men feel inadequate."

"That sounds like an insult." Although possibly true. "Trust me, I've worked with more than enough women who know how to wrap people around their little fingers."

Emmett considered for a moment. "Then you should be perfectly comfortable working with Jayce. And yet the two of you are like oil and water."

"She's irresponsible, reckless, and doesn't listen."

Rav leaned in closer, a snarl nearly forming on his lips. "She knows when to take the right risks. She reacts faster than any of us do and always moves at the right time."

He may not have been on our last job, but was that a dig? Jayce had complained when I stopped her from running headlong into someone who would have had us arrested. She thought her speed and agility made her a ghost—it didn't.

"She doesn't know how to keep her opinions to herself."

"This is true." Emmett put a hand on Rav's arm and the big man eased back. "I don't know about you, but there are days I think I've heard more than enough lies. I appreciate the fact she doesn't know how to insert a filter between her brain and her mouth."

"She doesn't know how to insert a filter between her mouth and anything." Whether that was between her brain and her mouth or food and her mouth.

Her mouth.

I was so irritated with her. So why was the soft touch of her lips against mine flashing through my memory? Jayce had made it abundantly clear she wanted nothing to do with me.

"And yet," said Emmett, "when Scarlett and I showed up at your place, you were preparing a feast so she could concentrate."

"I know how to handle a source."

Rav stood from the table suddenly. "I'm stepping outside before I break something."

As the Reynolds security specialist marched out of the restaurant, many gazes followed him.

"He means you, in case that wasn't clear." Emmett sighed. "Looks like you've alienated half our team a whole twenty-four hours before the gala."

"Making friends isn't the priority."

"Being convincing partners tomorrow night will be."

The server arrived with a special large-bowled glass and presented the bottle. We went through the ritual of presentation and opening the bottle, and he poured me a taste. I inhaled the rich scent and took a sip.

One of the muscles in my body unclenched.

I nodded to the server, who poured my glass and left once the other drinks were on the table. Once he was gone, I said, "I understand the reason for teaming up, but why bother with the undercover act? Half the city's elite know the Bishop team."

Emmett rested an elbow on the table and leaned his hand against his fist. "But they don't know us. That's why Craig will be in the manager's room and we're splitting the three of you up. Some people might figure out something's going on. If they do, they'll spend all night trying to figure out who hired you and what for."

It made sense. "If Reynolds wanted to steal the chip, you'd want as many distractions as possible. Keep people's attention off you and off the chip."

Emmett smiled and pointed at me. "And here I thought you couldn't teach an old spy new tricks."

"Crisis manager." Speaking of crisis, I couldn't hold back the tide of curiosity anymore and shifted in my seat to survey the restaurant.

Maybe not the entire restaurant.

Jayce sat with her palm face up, held out toward Wyatt. He took her hand, spread the fingers wide, and ran a fingertip down the middle.

Son of a bitch. "This is the point at which he's telling her about his grandmother from Louisiana who told fortunes, and how she taught him to do the same. Such a load of shit."

"Does that line normally work?"

A fire built deep in my belly. "Every time I've seen him use it."

"You didn't answer earlier—can I trust her with him?"

I didn't give a fuck if Emmett could trust Wyatt with Jayce. *I* didn't trust Wyatt with Jayce. "We're going back to the original plan."

"And which plan would that be?" Emmett straightened, picking up his glass. "The one where you and Jayce still can't work together?"

"She bloody well can't work with him, either."

Across the restaurant, a server delivered the bill to Wyatt, who paid. They didn't split the bill—he paid. And he'd expect something after this.

"In Jayce's immortal words, 'Nope.'" Emmett popped the last letter, the same way she had, and took a sip of his drink.

"Our contract clearly states I'm point on this. Not you. Not your sister. Me."

"And if Scarlett refuses?" Emmett grinned, like a man too confident in his bargaining position. "Jayce has already refused to partner with you twice now. Although I think there was also a third time before we left Halifax."

The fire inside me burned too hot.

Screw the consequences.

It was Friday night and the gala was tomorrow. If everything went at least close to plan, the Reynolds team would be gone again by Sunday. If *I* couldn't have Jayce before they left, there was no way in hell Wyatt would. "You can tell Scarlett she's fired if she won't agree to it."

"Say no more." Emmett threw back the rest of his drink and slid out of the booth. "I'll take the hit with Scarlett over this because Wyatt doesn't strike me as a positive influence on Jayce. But I promise you, if you screw this up—if she comes to me, telling me you hurt even one of her feelings, you'll be dealing with Rav. And I'm sure you know that is *not* a fate you'll survive. You hear me?"

I took another sip of my wine, the flavor sour on my tongue.

Wyatt and Jayce stood together and headed for the door.

Emmett positioned himself between me and them, stooping to get in my face. "No bullshit, Drew. Don't be a jackass. Be good to her."

"I'll be professional."

"That's not what I said." He raised his eyebrows expectantly, and I nodded. Without another word, he turned and made for the door.

From so far away, I couldn't hear what he said as he approached Jayce, but he flung his arms wide and threw them around her. He stumbled slightly, jostling his head.

She looked concerned, but held his arm around her shoulders, easing him to the edge of the nearest seat.

Was he pretending to be drunk?

She shook her head, then shooed Wyatt out the door.

I pulled an Emmett and held the wine menu up so she couldn't see me watching her.

A server brought Emmett a glass of water, which he chugged down. Overall, it was a convincing performance.

Emmett had stopped her from leaving with him. They could have been leaving in different vehicles, but Emmett had interrupted any private words between Jayce and Wyatt. As Emmett stood, he put his arm around her shoulders again and glanced back at me with a glare that repeated his order. *Don't be a jackass.*

CHAPTER 23
JAYCE

Mission prep was normally tactile. Was my outfit tight enough? Did it move the right way? With my eyes closed, could I feel the location of each tool strapped to my body or in my pack? I would run my hands over my hair to ensure it was flat against my head, with no risk of strands falling out.

But for the Tremaine gala? Mission prep was in front of a mirror. Was my makeup on straight? Did my hair look nice in the complicated knot Scarlett had tamed the short tresses into? Did my one-shoulder pale pink dress show off any panty lines?

Once upon a time, that had been my life. Living in the spotlight, wearing a skintight leotard, with my face and hair done up to match my team. Why did it feel so foreign now?

Because it's been twelve years, Jayce.

Tonight would be an adventure if nothing else. From the way last night had gone at the restaurant, it was possible the job wouldn't be the only adventure. Wyatt had worked hard, flirting up a storm—including the ridiculous palm reading he'd done about a handsome man whisking me away from all my troubles.

He likely thought he'd be rewarded tonight if we pulled everything off without a hitch. When I'd reviewed the levels of physicality allowed during undercover—level one was holding hands, and level two included touching the waist, back, or shoulder—he'd suggested we try level three. We were only going lightly undercover, so kissing was off the table.

His response? 'Gotta leave room for improvisation.'

But from the look in his eyes when he saw Emmett arrive, pulling his drunken act, Wyatt must have known the truth.

No one got close to a Reynolds woman unless the Reynolds men approved. They were the closest thing I had to a family. Better than family, considering my past.

But would they do the same thing if I was no good at my job?

There was a knock at my door. My 'date' had arrived.

"Coming!" I picked up my clutch and headed for the door. There was no way I'd give Wyatt James an excuse to come into my hotel room. When I peeked through the peephole, my legs almost gave out underneath me.

That's not Wyatt.

I flung open the door and snapped, "What are you doing here?"

Drew Freaking Donovan. Good thing I had so few words to say to him because my throat had completely closed over. I'd thought he was jaw-dropping before but in a tuxedo? With his hair styled just perfectly so it swept off to the side, begging me to run my fingers through it? And his delicious cologne invading my senses?

"You look..." His gaze slithered down my body, sending a trail of heat in its wake. In my imagination, his hands made that journey, his mouth sucked on my breast again, and the throbbing between my thighs grew with every second I ground down on his hard cock. It had been less than forty-eight hours, and I could still feel his hot breath on my belly. "Beautiful."

"Save it, Downie." I pointed to the door across the hall. "Your date's over there. I'm sure he'll appreciate the obligatory compliment."

I slammed the door—at least, I tried to.

He got a foot in the gap and pushed it open. "Emmett didn't tell you?"

"Tell me what?" I stepped backward into the room, maintaining my distance as he came in.

He closed the door behind himself but didn't pursue me. Didn't even reach for me. "He and I had a reasonable discussion about Wyatt's role on this job, and we reverted to the original plan."

I folded my arms rather than throwing something at him, like I wanted to. "Are you forgetting how much of a *distraction* I am? Can't have you screwing up another job because of me."

"I'm sorry." Drew raised his hands as if in surrender. "I let my emotions get the better of me and put you in a position you didn't want."

Yeah, right. I'd wanted it too much. But I wanted something different from what he did. *That* was the real problem. His need was purely physical and I was done with those kinds of relationships. Someday, I'd find a man who fit that small spot in my chest, but if not, I wouldn't compromise. Empty sex—hell, empty making out, apparently—brought out my darker side, and I needed more from life.

"I promised Emmett I'd be professional."

"That should be interesting." I walked away from him, to my suitcase on the other side of the king-size bed. There was one thing I'd forgotten. The chocolate bar I'd stolen, then snuck back in and bought legally. I'd been saving it as an end-of-job reward. But I was going to need it.

"There *will* be food."

"Cute little canapés aren't my jam." I peeled open the wrapper and snapped off a piece, tossing it into my mouth.

"So we're good?"

I'd said nothing of the sort. I held the rest of the bar between my teeth to free up my hands. Closing my eyes, I opened the far-too-small clutch and felt for each item. I spoke around the bar as my fingers navigated the contents. "Got my phone, my earpiece, the tracker, ID, room card, lock picks, gloves, zip ties, and some cash."

"Don't I feel inadequate? All I've got is a phone, keys, and my wallet." Drew walked deeper into the room. "Craig's distributing earpieces when we arrive."

I opened my eyes to ensure I didn't get cornered again. With my clutch under my arm, I took another bite of the bar.

He glanced at everything as he moved—the bathroom, the closet, the desk, the television. He was observant, no doubt an important skill in both his prior and current jobs. "Can you move in the dress?"

"It has lacing built in, so I can adjust it." I stuck out a leg, so the thigh-high split fell to either side. With a few twists and strategic ties, I hiked the dress up and reconfigured it into a short jumpsuit.

"That's brilliant."

I hastily undid the skirt so the dress was again floor length. "You didn't mention the invite. You have it?"

He patted his breast pocket, sending another flurry of images through my head. How his pecs and shoulders had flexed as I stripped off his shirt. His firm abs. How I'd run my fingers over the soft hair now hidden under the tuxedo shirt.

Brushing off Wyatt's advances would have been a lot easier than forgetting what Drew and I had almost done.

I needed more chocolate. I'd already devoured the existential crisis bar. "Did Liana give you a menu?"

"Do we need to stop for a cheeseburger on the way?"

"Nah." With my luck, I'd drop it on the dress and screw up the entire plan for the night. "May as well get my money's worth with the Tremaines' food."

"You're not paying to go to the gala."

"We're undercover. We're pretending to pay." I pointed to the door and he took the hint, leading the way, so I could take in the cut of his tux from behind. "It's only right I pretend to enjoy the expensive food."

"For the record." Drew gripped the door handle, turning it, but not opening the door. He glanced at me over his shoulder. "I also discussed with Emmett that I'm point on this mission. My word goes. Can you manage that?"

"And here I thought we were getting along so well." I put my hand on his—so warm and strong and big. *Don't think about all the places it was Thursday night.* Why did I do that? Why were the ants skittering up my legs at physicality level one? Why did I want to skip past two and three and stay in the room with him?

I pulled the door open. "For the record, I'm the subject matter expert, so you need to trust my judgment."

"Speaking of interesting ideas." Drew brushed his fingers across the small of my back as we left. It was nothing more than a gesture to keep me going, but my body paused—regardless of what my brain wanted—to enjoy it for a moment.

Our escapade Thursday night was the first time a man had touched me like that in years. I'd been fine without it—proud of my restraint, even. One-night stands and sleeping with men who didn't care about the real me were part of my dark phase. The one that saw me stealing anything and everything, getting as many dopamine hits from the theft as from the words of praise afterward.

The sex had barely mattered.

Even with Tanner, it was about little more than...

I stepped into the hallway with Drew right behind me and sighed deep inside.

Even with Tanner, it had been about getting it out of our systems so we could focus on our training and our routines.

I didn't need more of that in my life. Didn't want it.

The door across the hall opened and Emmett paused before joining us in the hallway. His gaze flitted between Drew and me, and he pushed the door open wider to reveal Rav right behind him. "You know, Rav, Drew *does* look better with Jayce than he would have with you."

Rav grunted in assent as he straightened his bow tie, not appearing to be the least bit surprised by this turn of events. He and Emmett also wore tuxes, looking just a hair less gorgeous than Drew.

I pointed an accusing finger at each of them. "I'm going to have words with you after this."

The door next to mine opened, and Scarlett joined us. She was stunning in a floor-length silver dress with a neckline that plunged far too low. She wore two-sided tape underneath to keep it in place, but most men wouldn't realize she had a face with all that cleavage on display.

Malcolm exited the room after her, sliding a hand across her back. The man was always touching her.

That was what I wanted. Someone whose world started and ended with me.

Scarlett's eyebrow quirked at Drew in a way that said, '*That's not Wyatt.*'

This would be interesting. Emmett rarely hid things from her on the job, but it was obvious he had.

"They make a cute couple." Malcolm took Scarlett's hand, and the two of them walked toward our group.

Scarlett's eyebrow rose higher the closer they got. "Is someone going to explain this to me?"

Drew turned to Emmett. "You didn't tell her, either?"

"Wyatt took Jayce out last night, and I didn't think they looked convincing together. It was too forced." Emmett scratched at the short beard he'd been too stubborn to shave off. "This chemistry's not forced."

"Chemistry?" I blurted out.

Emmett had been with me on that rooftop. He knew how I felt about Drew.

"C'mon, honey bunches." Malcolm had dozens of ridiculous food-based nicknames for Scarlett, every one of which made me hungry. He moved through the middle of our group, leading her down the hallway. "Little late to change things now."

It was never too late to change things.

I glanced at Drew.

Some things, at least.

CHAPTER 24
DREW

"I'm here. Drew and I are nearing the fountain." Jayce chatted quietly with her team while they went through their roll call.

The last job I'd done with them, I'd been the only one from my team involved, and they'd let me in on their comms. They were as polished as any team I'd worked with in the CIA, and certainly more than the group from Bishop and Associates. We were all trained to work independently, and the idea of using earpieces for continual conversation was foreign. Being subjected to hours of Wyatt's one-liners or Zaria's fashion commentary didn't appeal to me.

"Shit," said Jayce. "I hope she's okay."

I put my hand under her elbow when we reached the stairs. There were still pools of water dotting the walkway after yesterday's downpour. "What's that?"

The conversation distracted her enough that she didn't wrench her arm away from me. Either that or the moment the earpiece went in, she was in professional mode. Or she needed help to balance in the low heels Scarlett had forced on her. "Will isn't on comms with Brie tonight. His mom's in the hospital."

"Is it serious?" I'd only worked remotely with Will, who was living in London temporarily. He'd impressed me as a genius engineer, just as talented as their hacker guru, Brie.

She nodded and mouthed *Alzheimer's* to me, then added for her team's benefit, "She had a little fall. She'll be fine. Ash is filling in as Brie's backup."

"Ash?"

"Ashley. Former FBI. She knows her—" Jayce cut off, resuming the conversation with her team.

It gave me an opportunity to observe her from the corner of my eye. The pale pink dress flowed around her, hugging curves I'd had my lips on just days ago. Despite how much she leaned away from her femininity, she couldn't hide it from a man who'd seen her practically naked. There was a woman under her tough exterior—one with needs and wants I still couldn't quite figure out.

"Time for level two." As we reached the bottom of the stairs, I slid my arm around Jayce's waist. It was overkill—the goal was to look like a date, not a couple. Was it for my own selfish need? Anyone at tonight's party who didn't know me as Craig's employee would most likely know me as Vanessa's boyfriend or her ex. She was the socialite, although most of her overt charm had been about obtaining gossip to post online.

One more red flag I'd ignored.

Jayce didn't reciprocate. She held her clutch and swung her opposite arm freely as she walked. "I hate high heels."

"You've mentioned that once or twice." Or five times since we left the hotel. They were only an inch high, but as she pointed out, she always wore things she could run in. "Are your Kevlar socks hidden in them?"

"Yeah, Will needs to get on that," she said to her team, rather than to me. She snorted a laugh in response to something one of them said.

The regular crowd milled around the fountain, enjoying the warm evening. It was only eight, the sun was still barely up, and the light display hadn't started yet.

"Rav's just called in to confirm his buddy Marc has finished his sweep." Jayce's voice dropped to a whisper. This would have been easier if we'd all been on the same comms. "No one hiding out in the lower or upper floor offices. He's also confirmed the staff exit off the kitchen and the stairwell exits on the ground floor and to the roof had their locks upgraded. The guards on the stairwells will ensure no one gets to those doors from the inside."

Ten-foot-high swaths of canvas surrounded the perimeter of the restaurant's patio, providing increased privacy for the evening. Not to mention the distinct feeling of exclusivity. Men in tuxedos and women in long dresses made their way to the paved trail near the river, where an arch of rose bushes laden with red and metallic flowers provided entry into the event.

As Jayce and I followed the flow of traffic, I eavesdropped on the surrounding conversations.

"They've outdone themselves this year," said one woman in a floral gown to the man with her.

"Ostentatious," said another.

Both sentiments and everywhere in between rippled through the attendees. Few people on their way up the patio spoke of anything personal, instead marveling at the decorations. Tiny lights wound around the twenty-foot-tall metal sculpture and the potted trees decorating the patio tiers. A red carpet had been rolled down the shallow stairs up to the restaurant's main floor, with additional greenery dotting the path.

I let go of Jayce when we joined a short line at the rose arch, where four security personnel scanned invitations. One of them, Rav's other friend who'd joined the security team, discreetly waved us forward. He had us through the entrance quickly.

The inside of the canvas walls was black, decorated with a pattern reminiscent of stars. Here and there, light reflected off the stars, while others twinkled on their own.

Once we were on the long, multi-tiered patio inside the canvas walls, Jayce took my hand, twining her fingers with mine. My heart kicked up, but I refrained from staring at her. I'd thought *I* would be the one leading the physical portion of the job.

"I reviewed this with Wyatt last night," she said, her gaze everywhere and nowhere. "Three taps with any finger means danger—"

"Same as when I was on comms with your team?"

She glanced at me for a beat. "Same. Two taps with the thumb means going forward when we can't say as much."

That was also the same code as we'd used on the Harrington job.

"There are a few differences when we're in-person and you aren't on our channel. Two taps with the pinky finger means we need cover."

"From something we don't consider dangerous?"

Two women in wide cage skirts glided around the patio, each skirt decorated with metal hoops that held stemmed glasses filled with liquids of various shades. They brought to mind cyborgs in their own interpretation of Elizabethan gowns. Another woman in a silver breastplate and face mask had only two levels to her gown, carrying single-bite foods.

The second we got close enough to the latter, Jayce grabbed something that looked like a pastry dipped in chocolate. It vanished into her mouth before I got a good look at it. She held her clutch over her mouth as she chewed. "Two taps with the pinky means cover of a physical sort."

"How does that differ from the thumb tap?"

"Thumb tap means hide. Pinky-tap cover means…" She lowered her hand long enough to pucker up, giving me an obvious hint that type of cover would require us to get a lot closer again. Rather than discussing levels of tongue, she continued, "Deliberately squeezing each finger in order means make conversation."

"With someone other than you, I assume?"

She frowned, but it was quickly lost to a smile. After the way she'd greeted me at her hotel room, I wasn't sure I'd earn one of those all night. "If I'm holding your hand and need you to talk to me, I'm pretty sure I can just tell you that."

"What does this mean?" I stroked my thumb up and down the side of her hand, along her finger. It meant I was more invested in the cover story than the job itself. Wrong, but sadly true.

"It doesn't have a meaning, other than your fingers are twitchy." Her smile vanished. The red carpet would take us into the main dining room, where the two sets of double-doors were open. Jayce gestured to the twin doors to the banquet room. "We're the first ones from my team here, so we should set up in the banquet room for our shift."

Each door had one large man in a black suit and obvious wired earpiece. They could have worn something more discrete, but Gideon and Liana wanted a conspicuous security presence. Maybe it would be enough to deter whoever was behind the threats—or maybe they were only threats and nothing would come of it. Maybe I was in a tuxedo with a beautiful woman on my arm for nothing.

Nothing other than the opportunity to hold her hand.

And finish the night with a cold shower.

"Holy crapballs," Jayce breathed as we neared the open banquet room doors. "It's huge."

The interior of the banquet room was dim, with spotlights shining on the four VIP items at the center, as well as the paintings and sculptures around the perimeter for the auction. Even from outside, the sheet of black fabric towering over ten feet drew my attention.

"Liana's sculpture is under there, isn't it?" Jayce snatched a date stuffed with some sort of cheese and topped with—she ate it too fast for me to identify everything.

I tapped twice on Jayce's hand with one of my fingers and finally stopped stroking with my thumb. It was time for both of us to focus on the job—I had to pay more attention to my surroundings than her, and she needed to stop stuffing her face.

"There's fabric covering it," she muttered, likely to her team. "The fabric's twelve feet high."

I leaned close to her, toward the ear she was communicating from. "Craig saw it yesterday morning. He says it's ten feet tall."

"Why's this the first we're hearing of it?" asked Jayce.

Because I'd been too busy being angry about her disappearing on me, and then with Emmett's declaration that Jayce would be with Wyatt. *If she distracted you this much yesterday, you should have stuck with Rav for the evening.* "I assumed Craig would fill you in."

"I thought you were point on this job?"

"Which means counting on my team to do their job, including Craig."

"Did you *tell him* to tell us? If not, that's not exactly his job, is it?"

She had no filter. *Keep the emotional locker door open—lots will be going in there tonight.*

There were only thirty guests in the banquet room, while fifty or so perused white-draped tables with multimedia artwork in the main dining room. It was difficult to make out details from our location, but on the other side of the glass walls, light glinted off pieces of metal and glass combined with more matte materials. More of the women with skirt platforms and a few men with metallic masks carried flutes of champagne through the room.

None of our high-risk individuals stood out yet, but I'd need a closer look to be sure. A man as wealthy as Gideon had too many enemies. Liana's list was far shorter, but was still too long.

"At least Liana listened," Jayce muttered. "The items are in the correct position. You've got eyes on everything, Brie? Liana's sculpture to the north, farthest away from the patio, then the mirror, bird, and scarab clockwise."

The scarab and golden bird glittered under their spotlights, while the space around the mirror was surprisingly dull. As though it absorbed light instead of reflecting it.

Jayce slowed as we neared the golden huma bird.

I gave her two taps with a finger. *Move forward.* "We need to see Craig."

"We're the only ones here so far." She slipped her hand out of mine—which I certainly did *not* miss. "I'd rather stay and get a feel for the space with everything in it before the masses arrive."

"Good idea." Our teams were staggering their arrivals, so it wouldn't be as obvious we were working the event. "I'll be right back."

The farther I got from her, the clearer my brain became.

Maybe I'd made the wrong choice.

Yes. I'd been short-sighted insisting she spend the gala with me.

But no. It *was* the best decision to have her in the banquet room for more of the evening.

Be honest with yourself, Drew. You were jealous.

Maybe my brain wasn't getting clearer.

I dodged a server with a giant skirt and ducked out through what Jayce had deemed the bathroom door. Up the stairs from there and I hung a right down the hall to the manager's office.

Craig sat behind the manager's desk with two monitors off to the side. "Feed's good. I've got the kitchen, main dining room, banquet room, and the path to the washrooms visible."

"Good." I circled the desk. There were a few blind spots, but no way for someone to get through the restaurant without being seen. "The Reynolds team is piggybacking off your feed?"

"Brie Reynolds said it was the easiest job she'd ever had." Craig slid a small black case closer to me. "Your comms."

I pulled out a beige earpiece, roughly twice the size of those the Reynolds team used, and inserted it into my ear, twisting until it sat comfortably.

"It's not an open line." He pressed a finger to his ear and said through the earpiece and live in the room, "Press the small button by the volume control to transmit."

I did as instructed. "Testing."

"Loud and clear."

No one else responded, as expected, at the early hour. I checked my watch. "Zaria should be here in fifteen minutes and Wyatt in a half hour."

"If he shows." Craig dipped his head, raising an eyebrow as he did. "I hear he's plenty pissed with you taking the spotlight off him."

I waved the comment off.

"Emmett was right. Wyatt would be more convincing with Jayce than with Rav." He glanced at the video display, tapping the spot where Jayce admired the golden bird. "But you two? Holding hands on your way in? Even more convincing than Wyatt would have been with her."

"We're professionals." It was a pathetic excuse. Wyatt, for all his bluster and volume, had a decade more experience than I did. I'd seen him smooth-talk politicians, starlets, and dozens of lawyers over my two years with Bishop. He'd watch Jayce, absorb everything I'd written in the documentation I'd prepared on her, and learn how to treat her and get the response he wanted.

That targeting package had provided him with all the ammunition he needed to swoop in and steal her—

Not steal, Drew. She's not yours. She'd been very clear about that.

"Are your contingency plans in place?"

"Gideon and I already refined the speech." Craig chuckled to himself, turning to the screen again. "He'll ramp up production and release the chips a month early if someone sneaks off with the prototype. Plus, he'll match all donations to the charities tonight."

"With that spin, he may be hoping the thieves get away with it. That would be one hell of a PR campaign."

"Which wouldn't dent his pocket."

I joined him in watching the video feed.

Jayce snuck another bite of food from a server and wandered over to the scarab. She chuckled to herself—likely talking to her team—and took the snack in two bites.

Craig hummed. "Unapologetic."

"What's that?"

"The thief. Every time I've seen her, no matter who she's interacting with, she's always herself. Quite unlike..." He moved closer, pointing at another figure, this one a woman in a draped gown stalking toward the bar in the main restaurant. "I see Vanessa's here."

Shit.

"Don't tell me you got her invited, Craig?"

He leaned back in his chair. "If things go south, we need our contingency plan. Her"—he made air quotes—"editorial site will help spread the word about poor Gideon and how unfortunate the theft was for him."

Great. Now I had to focus with Jayce on my arm, keep Wyatt away from her, and keep Vanessa away from me.

CHAPTER 25

JAYCE

The longer Drew was gone, the sharper my senses grew. Kitten heels weren't so bad once you got used to them. The dress wasn't too uncomfortable, and it moved well enough.

But my hand already missed his. His arm around me had been one thing—ants skittering over my skin and all—but holding his hand? That had been strangely comfortable.

I'd *never* held hands with a man before. Not like that, with our fingers around each other's. Rav and Emmett a few times, but that was work.

Somehow, it didn't feel like work with Drew.

Wrong.

It was so very wrong.

Focus, Jayce. Remember your job.

The gold-and-carnelian scarab sat nestled in its custom-made display case. Under the spotlight, the orangey-red carved beetle on the front glowed almost unnaturally. The carpenter I'd spoken to yesterday had provided details on the security attachment that fed up through the base of the stand.

A small plaque glossed over its provenance, stating only that it was on loan from a private collection and that it had once belonged to Pharaoh Khufu's chief surveyor.

Our lowest priority for the evening was getting someone close enough to Gideon's phone, so Brie could try to lift some data about the scarab's owner, their transport plans, or where it was being kept in Washington.

"To think, this thing saw the Giza plateau before the Great Pyramid was built."

"And to think," said Scarlett over my earpiece, "the owner would loan it for an event when it's a stolen item."

Malcolm added, "Maybe they don't know it's stolen."

The display case was entirely glass, so I made a slow circuit around it. "The intermediaries are usually the ones who know. Brokers, gallerists, slick salesmen. But a lot of buyers take things at face value rather than digging as deep as they should into a piece's history."

"Can you take some photos?" asked Brie. "Will wanted close-ups from all angles in case we need to make a duplicate."

"We could call the police or FBI and have them pick it up?" said Malcolm.

"We've tried that before," said Scarlett. "Lots of posturing between local and federal authorities. This would probably bring in Interpol or reps from the Egyptian government. By the time they figure out what they're doing, the owner's lawyers will have stepped in and whisked it away."

Then no one would ever see it again.

We wouldn't recover the scarab tonight—the security was too tight. Instead, we'd use the opportunity for recon and construct a solid plan later.

"I may only get one." I pulled my phone out, acting as though I were reading a text. "Which side is more important?"

"Backside," said Brie. "There are lots of photos of the front, but he wanted a clear shot of the hieroglyphs in the gold. The museum will rely on that to verify the product."

I paced toward Liana's sculpture, hidden under its black fabric. No one seemed to pay undue attention to it. So long as it was under its cover, the chip should be safe.

The crowd in the banquet room had doubled since we'd arrived, which would help conceal any attempts to photograph the items. There was a strict no-selfie policy in place, and the second I pointed my camera at anything—person or item—someone would grab my phone.

We'd elected to keep Drew and me out of all meetings with the security team, so they wouldn't turn a blind eye to what I was doing. I recognized every one of them, but they wouldn't know me. The only exceptions were Rav's two friends—they received a full briefing. "Brie, load up a text chat."

"On it." She had complete control of everything from our office in Halifax. "Done."

I strolled back to the scarab display, opened my text app, and got into position. Facing the scarab, I began typing a reply to a convincing string of messages.

Brie also had full control of the camera in my phone, whether or not I was using it.

A large man in a black suit—not a tux, so not a guest, but not someone I recognized from the security detail—shot off the wall. His voice was quiet, in the same way a lion's growl was quiet. Ominous. "No photos."

"I was texting someone!" I fumbled with the phone, as though attempting to stuff it into my clutch. I wouldn't put it inside, in case he thought he could dig around in the bag and learn more about my true intent than I wanted. "Not taking a—"

"Show me."

"I've got the photo," said Brie. "You're good."

"I—I'm—I wasn't taking a photo," I stuttered, acting as flustered as I could. Fortunately, I'd been accosted by enough security guys in my past, so I had plenty of experience to draw on. "Leave me alo—"

He snatched the phone from me, flashed it at my face to unlock it, and jabbed meaty fingers on it to open the photos. He swiped through a few food pictures before I could take it back—Brie wouldn't have left any evidence. "Keep the phone in your bag, ma'am."

I nodded vigorously and made a hasty retreat to the bird statue, blowing out a few deep breaths.

"Good performance," said Brie. "You'll be taking over for Scar before you know it."

"No thank you." I snorted, admiring the golden bird. "Tell me the photo came out well."

"Crystal clear," said Brie. "Although we need Will to add more control over camera angles, so you don't have to be so obvious next time."

The bird looked more like a griffin, with a beak and tucked wings like an eagle, but a thick body like a lion. It was intricate, with distinct feathers and adorned with row upon row of hundreds, or possibly thousands, of tiny golden beads.

It stood barely more than a foot tall, atop another custom-made platform by my buddy, what's-his-name the carpenter. Unlike the scarab, which was tiny and could easily be palmed if someone disabled the security catch underneath it, the bird didn't have a glass case over it. That allowed the spotlights to hit it just right, so its beauty radiated.

"Fascinating, isn't it?" A woman sidled up to me in a draped, emerald green dress that barely hid her ridiculous curves.

A pit opened in my stomach. It was Drew's ex. An urge to cover myself festered in that open pit. I was too short, too thick, too strong. I was a thief, not a woman who should be in heels and an evening gown. "It is. The rows of granulation—"

"Not the huma bird." She moved closer, one impossibly long, toned leg revealed from the slit in her skirt. "I noticed you arrive with Drew. Hand in hand?"

"Yes?"

"He's working, isn't he?" She gave me a conspiratorial grin and looked around the room. "Who's the client?"

Feign ignorance, Jayce. "I don't understand."

"Well…" She tossed her long blond hair and eyed me up and down. "He's here with *you*, not me. You're obviously working with him."

Scarlett chimed in over my earpiece, "Is she as much of a bitch as she sounds?"

"Hold on…" I snapped my fingers and pointed at her. "I thought you looked familiar. You're Drew's ex who couldn't keep her legs closed, aren't you?"

Scarlett assumed the calming tone I probably needed. "Keep your cool. Malcolm and I are two minutes away if you need a distraction."

"Or I can call Drew," said Brie.

I loved my team. They had my back.

The Blond Betrayer's lip twitched. "Didn't have them closed last night at his place, either."

Wow, hadn't taken him long to move on to the next piece of ass. Or an old piece of ass. I craned my neck around, checking behind her. "And who are you here with tonight?"

"That doesn't matter, because I've got something better." She leaned close and her flowery perfume nearly choked me. "I know I'm right about you two, which means I'll be leaving here with a story."

"And I'll be leaving here with Drew." How was that a come-back if he was with her last night?

She ran her teeth over her bottom lip as she straightened. "Has he made you the Beef Wellington yet?"

The pit in my stomach gaped wider.

"Taken you to the roof to see the river and the city lights?"

Was that meal and the line about the Potomac his standard MO? How many other women did he need to get out of his system? Good thing I'd run from his apartment. I was *entirely* replaceable to Drew Donovan.

Not even replaceable.

Interchangeable.

Brie whispered, "Drew's on his way back. He'll be there in less than a minute."

"He offered to take me to the roof. Instead..." I glanced around, drawing her gaze toward the patio windows so she wouldn't see him coming. "You won't believe it, but we—"

"Vanessa," Drew practically growled. "What are you doing?"

"Just getting to know your little friend." She fluttered her overly long eyelashes and jutted out a hip. The neckline of her dress shifted, showing the profile of one irritatingly perfect breast.

Who had a body like that? Scarlett. Scarlett had a body like that. But the big difference? I'd never wanted to shove Scarlett into a server carrying three tiers of food.

"If you go anywhere near Jayce again"—he grabbed my hand, a dangerous glint in his eye—"I'll spill every bit of dirty laundry I can find on you."

"Oh, Drew." She chuckled, a throaty sound that was sexier than anything I could pull off, and swatted his chest. "You and I both know we belong together."

"How many times have I told you to go find someone else?"

"Good luck with whatever job you're on." She winked at me and left, finding another couple to speak with on the other side of the room.

Drew didn't take his eyes off her.

"We don't need secret communication right now." I yanked my hand out of his and reached for the server sweeping past us.

But Drew caught my hand before it landed on the food. He pivoted, so we weren't both facing Blondie anymore and he was partially obscuring her. "She's a lying, manipulative narcissist."

"There's a lot of people like that around here." I tried to pull away from him, but he didn't let go.

"Too many." He lifted my hand, turned it palm up, and pressed his lips to it.

A wave of heat shot through my treacherous body.

"Don't let her think she got to you, or she'll come back for round two."

Scarlett said over my earpiece, "He's right."

When I started with Reynolds, it had taken a month before I could sort out voices over our open comms. Every team member's ongoing discussions, picking up voices from their surroundings, and trying to make out what someone was saying to me in person. After the first year, I'd gotten to a point where all the extra chatter faded to the background and my brain zeroed in whenever someone was talking directly to me. Scarlett could have said that to Malcolm, Brie, or someone else around her—but I knew it was for me.

"I need you to smile." Drew looped his other arm around me, not letting go of my hand. "And tell me what she said."

There was no smiling. This was why I stayed in the shadows. I wasn't cut out for all the lies and pretending. "She's determined to find out who you're working for tonight. She doesn't think you're a guest."

From his expression, all soft lines and concern, I might've thought he was happy to be with me. But the grumble deep in his throat revealed the truth. Vanessa was right. This was just a job and I had to remember Drew hopped beds the same way I hopped between pastries.

"I need a snack."

"Vanessa won't get in the way, but she'll keep an eye on us." Drew's thumb stroked against the small of my back, like he'd been doing with my hand earlier. He was convincing at this game. "Have you noticed anyone or anything suspicious yet?"

Just you. I tilted my head so he'd lean in and I could whisper. "There's a man in a—surprise—black tuxedo who was paying more attention to the mirror than seemed necessary."

"That's not our target."

"The guilty party won't be obvious until they attempt to take the chip. And even then, maybe they manage to stay inconspicuous." How much time had I spent pretending to admire the bird to cover my interest in the scarab? "If they want to make a statement, they'll at least wait for—"

Around us, heads turned. A lot of them. I took a half-step back and Drew released me, likely seeing the same thing happen.

Drew finished my thought. "They'll wait for *them* to arrive?"

"Heads up, everyone," I said. "The Tremaines are here."

CHAPTER 26
DREW

Fucking Vanessa.

Jayce had been plenty comfortable taking my hand earlier, but there was no masking the tension in her muscles. Vanessa had said something other than asking about a job. I'd given Jayce the opportunity to tell me, but the woman with no filter suddenly wasn't talking.

Of all the moments for Gideon and Liana to arrive, this had to be the worst.

I touched the tiny button on my earpiece. "They're here. You see them?"

Craig replied, "I have them."

"Wyatt's late. Where is he?"

"I just handed him his—"

"Donovan, you son of a bitch!" Not only had Wyatt arrived, but he'd apparently received his earpiece from Craig. "I'm coming down there and—"

"Their cover's already established," Craig said in Wyatt's background, but the line went silent.

"Wyatt's here," I whispered to Jayce.

"So's Rav," she said. "He's currently complaining about Wyatt's reaction to working with him tonight."

A dozen people descended on the Tremaines as they made their way to the center of the room. They focused on those talking around them—Gideon on a man discussing golf and Liana on a woman who was asking about a spa visit—and walked past us without a second glance.

The hair prickling at the nape of my neck told me Vanessa was watching. Good thing we'd decided the Tremaines wouldn't acknowledge any of the Bishop or Reynolds team members.

"Wyatt," came Craig's voice over our team's comms. "Get back here."

"I've got a job to do, Craig." Wyatt was far more upset than I'd expected. Did he honestly believe something would happen between him and Jayce?

Had she given him some indication?

"Don't screw with Drew and Jayce. They've already interacted with people and shown they're together. Calm down and do your job." Craig's voice remained controlled, just as we'd all been trained to handle our emotions.

Why Wyatt couldn't keep his grievances to himself was another question. Maybe the ball of chaos next to me fried more brains than just mine.

More guests poured into the banquet room, which steadily grew stifling. Everyone wanted to see what was under the black tarp.

"I'd wager," said a muted voice behind me, "it's a tiny thing in an enormous glass case."

"I'll take that bet," said someone else. "Liana doesn't know how to make things small."

"But it's Gideon's chip in there. If it were that big—"

The two continued their debate as they moved past us. The gossip flowed around us, everyone wondering what the big surprise was. We were too close to the action, standing in the center of the room, in front of the golden bird.

I threaded my fingers around Jayce's and tapped twice with my thumb. Thumb was hide, right? Pinky was getting physical?

"I'm curious about that painting." Jayce inclined her head toward the back of the room, near the staff door. Three large paintings and two smaller ones stood on easels for prospective bidders.

The Tremaines' gravitational pull had practically cleared out that area as we moved toward it.

Jayce stopped in front of a painting, a shimmering gold swath of metal embedded in blue paint. "Watch over my shoulder."

I let go of her hand and pivoted, so I faced her, stroking the back of my knuckles down the length of her arm.

She tensed. "It's completely reasonable for you to look at the crowd. Everyone else is."

"That's what I'm doing." It was cover, that was all. If I wasn't admiring my date, it would have made more sense to look at the painting. "I'm a professional, too, remember?"

"Brie, what have you got?" Jayce asked, not taking her eyes off the artwork.

The room buzzed with conversation, and no one paid us any heed.

I said, "She's playing with the fabric. I recognize one tech giant, two senators, and three members of Congress. Opera singer. A couple of pop stars."

"Quite the crowd," said Jayce. "Brie says the House leader's in the main dining room. And some social media influencers who are worth a small fortune."

"They all belong." I stepped closer to Jayce, sliding my hand across her abdomen and around her side, sinking deeper into the cover. It placed my mouth next to her earpiece, so I could talk directly to her team. "Is Brie running facial recognition?"

"She is."

"Finding anyone who doesn't belong?"

She pulled in a slow breath. "She's been checking everyone as they come in from the patio. Everyone's on the guest list."

"No one from our caution list?"

She put her hand on my arm, pinning it against her. "Not yet."

The faintest scent of vanilla clung to her hair. In her line of work, she must have avoided anything that could give her away by lingering in the air. But I was close enough to catch a whiff.

I could have stood like that all night. *Get a fucking grip, Drew.* I pressed the button on my earpiece. "Craig, how are we doing with the schedule?"

Unlike the rest of us, he would communicate with Gideon through the evening. "Liana said she'd flutter the cover a few times before they reveal it. Looks like that's her signal."

"The cover's coming off soon." I continued talking into her ear for her team's sake, although they'd be able to hear me if I didn't—so maybe it was for my sake. "So long as the chip's still under there, the job starts when it's out in the open."

"Let's grab a snack." As though sensing food, she turned and began walking toward one of the masked male servers.

"Wait now." I gripped her upper arm before she reached her quarry. "Facial recognition isn't working on them, is it?"

She stopped, looking between two servers. "Get Craig to have security check them."

I tapped the piece in my ear and repeated the request.

Craig responded that he'd have the servers verified, but then Wyatt piped up over the comms. "I want to see what's under that cover. Rav and I are taking over in the banquet room."

I tapped my earpiece. "You are not. Scarlett is coordinating when we switch."

Had he and Jayce shared something at the restaurant last night? Or before that? He was acting like a child whose favorite toy had been taken away, not a man who'd lost his opportunity to flirt with her.

Jayce nodded slowly, shifting so she was facing me, her mouth and words blocked from the outside world by my shoulder. "Brie, check the guy who accosted me earlier, too."

"Someone accosted you?" I gripped her arm tighter, like an angry, vengeful boyfriend.

She shook her head this time. "I was taking some pictures of the food. He made me delete them."

"Security?" I shifted my hold on her arm, rubbing up and down where I'd held her too tightly.

"I didn't recognize him."

Hopefully, he was simply an overzealous rule follower.

The more time that passed, the more everyone in the crowd shifted. They were no longer the wealthy and influential of Washington—they were suspects. It felt like the old me, traveling through Eastern Europe, searching for people who had secrets I could take. In this case, I was searching for people who had secrets and wanted to take something from someone else.

Why had Craig accepted this job? This was so far outside our area of expertise.

Not that it was Craig's decision. He put me in charge and I was the one who opted for all of us to attend.

"Good evening, gentlemen," came Zaria's lightly accented voice over the comms. "Emmett and I have arrived and will be mingling on the patio."

My first instinct was to tell her where we were and what was going on, but if she had just arrived and was now in communication with the Bishop team, that meant she'd visited Craig. She would have reviewed the cameras, gotten an update on Wyatt's behavior, and was doing whatever was required. If I knew her, she'd hang off Emmett's arm while flirting with every man in sight.

My second instinct was to tell Jayce they'd arrived, but her team's communication was far faster than mine. She would have heard from Emmett when he was at least ten or fifteen minutes out.

The spotlights around the perimeter of the room dimmed slightly, while the ones over the VIP items brightened.

Jayce took my hand and gave two taps with one of her fingers—not her pinky and not her thumb. "Showtime."

Liana's voice rose above all the others, and a hush fell over the room. "I'm sure you're all wondering what I've been hiding. No one, not even my husband, has seen this masterpiece."

"Pretty full of herself?" said someone we passed.

I wouldn't argue, but from what I'd seen of Liana, she was a humble, wonderful woman. Despite her background studying law, she had the free spirit of an artist. She devoted a great deal of time to her charity work. But tonight, her goal was raising money, and she'd put on a performance that increased how much.

"As you all know, the theme for this evening is the merging of art and technology. I labored in secret for six long months, preparing. And now, I give you…" With the multiple rings of people surrounding her, it was hard to tell what she was doing, but she held her arms wide. The black tarp covering her sculpture flew to the ceiling, as though pulled by invisible strings. "Digital Twilight."

Gasps and applause filled the room.

As expected, it was ten feet tall. A black cylinder with grooves and indentations to make it look like a burned tree, with glowing amber sections of what must have been resin or plastic, covering it. It resembled sap running out of the tree.

The metal dragonfly stuck out from the side, its legs encased in sap, and its wings and head free.

"I'm too short," grumbled Jayce. "I can only see the top of it. What am I missing?"

"We'll have to get you closer." There were too many people surrounding the sculpture. And what about the chip? Craig had said it was embedded in the dragonfly's head. How secure was it? "It's basically a dragonfly getting caught in tree sap. The chip is in its head."

Jayce squirreled up her face. "Are we sure about this threat?"

"What do you mean?"

"How is someone going to make off with that? Or does the chip come out somehow?" She opened her clutch, fished around inside, and closed it again. "Maybe the threats simply meant they were going to vandalize it? Glue their hands to it? Throw soup on it?"

I put my arm around her back. They were all valid concerns, but without a better look, we'd still have more questions than answers. "Get your tracker out. Even if it's unlikely, you said we treat it like everything's possible, right?"

She turned her hand over, showing me the tiny metallic dot wedged between her fingers. "Two steps ahead of you."

We wove through partygoers, a blur of colors, fabrics, and jewels. Voices in various languages. People excited to attend, next to those bored by the same old same old.

And Vanessa, who was watching us again.

"Be careful on the approach. Vanessa is taking an interest in you."

"I'm pretty sure it's not me," muttered Jayce. She picked up her pace, almost losing me between a pair of women in black dresses with far too many diamonds. They stared at her as she walked through their line of conversation, her focus laser set on the sculpture.

I apologized to them on her behalf. I'd have to find out what happened between her and Vanessa. Her mood was growing progressively worse the longer we were here. Unless something was happening on her comms I didn't know about?

Brushing my fingers through my hair, I covertly tapped my earpiece. Unlike while we were at the back of the room, there were too many eyes near the hub of activity. "How is everyone doing? Jayce is acting rattled. Is something going on with the Reynolds team I should know about?"

Wyatt was the first to answer. "Other than her missing out on my company for the evening?"

Zaria opened her comms channel to laugh at us. "Let me know when the two of you are going to whip them out to compare. I'll see if I can find a tape measure."

Yeah, this job had been a terrible mistake. But as Malcolm had said earlier, it was too late to do anything about it now.

I shouldered my way between a senator and his aide and finally caught up with Jayce, who was only a few feet away from Digital Twilight. I grabbed her hips from behind and slowed her down, leaning to her ear without the earpiece. "You need to stay with me. I know you're not used to working the floor, but we're a team. "

"Then maybe you should try to keep up."

"What's going on? Why are you acting like this?"

"Professionals, remember? I'm doing our job." She twisted out of my grip and inched closer to her target.

No matter how fast her hands were, she would have to touch the sculpture to plant the tracker. And not just any part of the sculpture—she'd have to touch the dragonfly's head. People would see it and someone would try to stop her.

What could I do? Create a diversion?

Or did she have a plan?

Was she hiding a bottle of cleaning fluid in that tiny clutch?

I smiled to myself at the memory. She *was* unapologetic, like Craig said. Even when she handed my phone over at their office, she didn't apologize, just thanked me for saving her the shipping cost.

"Drew!" A man with light brown skin and gray hair blocked my path. A businessman who'd hired Craig—who tasked the job to me—to negotiate a messy divorce and spin it as an amicable separation.

"Vijay!" I shook his hand but didn't slow down. "Good to see you, but I'm—"

He held fast. "I was just speaking with your lovely girlfriend. She suggested you might be interested in a business proposition."

A business what? I glanced around, not seeing Vanessa anywhere.

"She said you're thinking about leaving Craig to go out on your own. I was surprised to hear it, but after the wonderful work you did for me, I wanted to make an offer. I'll bankroll you, for a percentage."

What kind of game was Vanessa playing? "I'm not—"

"I won't tell Craig." Vijay tapped the side of his nose and pointed at me. "I know a lot of people in a lot of countries who could use your expertise."

Did he want a crisis manager or a spy?

Voices rose behind me.

A woman. "What are you—"

A man speaking over her. "Get out of—"

I spun from Vijay to see the commotion. Bodies moved toward the sculpture—was the thief already making their play?

Digital Twilight rocked in its place. *Oh no!*

A squeal, a scream, a shout. "Watch out!"

I lunged forward, as the giant sculpture settled back in place.

Jayce was in the middle of a small crowd. One of the security men gripped her by the upper arms, her shoulders heaving up and down as though she was crying. When her gaze met mine, her eyes flew wide. "Drew!"

The man didn't release her, and I barged forward. "Let go of her!"

She wrenched herself out of his grip and flung herself at me, wrapping her arms around my neck. "Oh my god, Drew!"

I pulled back from her, running a hand over her face and my gaze over her body. Everything seemed to be where it belonged. No cuts, no scratches, no bruises. "What happened?"

"It was the shoes." She furrowed her brow as deep as it would go and sniffled, looking up at me. "Someone spilled their drink and I slipped on it. I ran into someone who ran into someone else and someone else. One of us ran into the sculpture and almost knocked it over."

The security guard approached us. "I only wanted to make sure she was okay."

Jayce wrapped her hand around the one I held her face with. She tapped—very intentionally—twice with her thumb.

"Let's go to the main restaurant, sweetheart." I kissed her temple. *What are you doing, Drew?* "There are some chairs set up and you can sit down for a minute."

Chapter 27
Jayce

Drew and I left the banquet room for the main dining room, nodding casually at Scarlett and Malcolm as they made their way in.

"Are you sure you got the tracker on?" It was the third time he'd asked in less than a minute.

"Subject matter expert, remember?" I let go of his hand, not needing to be in that level of contact anymore, and frankly not wanting to be.

He'd been so handsy since Blondie revealed his dirty little secret. *Feeling guilty, Drew?* Was I really nothing more than someone to jump into bed with, so he could move to another woman the next day?

Or was I just conveniently there Thursday?

And then he'd kissed me again. Right on the temple like an intimate moment between two lovers. *What the hell, Drew?*

I snagged a piece of nigiri sushi from a server as she walked by. If I wasn't carrying the little clutch, I would have been double-fisting.

Drew gestured toward the far end of the restaurant, where tall stools were available at the bar. "You need to sit down."

Sitting was the last thing I needed. "This job is driving me batty. All this standing around and watching and waiting. I should be doing something. Accomplishing something."

Drew kept pace with me, an easy feat with his long legs. He leaned close to whisper, "You're keeping an eye out for the thief. That's accomplishing a lot."

"No, that's what Scarlett and Malcolm are doing right now. I'm wandering around pretending to be a clumsy woman who almost knocked over a ten-foot sculpture."

"So we should sit down."

"I need to move."

"Do you want to look over the auction items?"

A long table stretched through this end of the restaurant. Covered in a white tablecloth, a couple dozen smaller pieces of art sat atop it. Next to each, a small sign proclaimed the title, medium, and artist. Underneath, each card had a QR code for the auction. Bids were entered by scanning the code and punching in a value that exceeded the current one. I hadn't installed the app, so couldn't even guess at the going prices.

Probably more than my car, every one of them.

"You know, Drew..." I swiped a glass of champagne from the ridiculous skirt of one of the servers. "Your body language suggests you're listening to me, and yet your words make it obvious you aren't."

"You need to keep a clear head." He took the glass from me. "There are only so many options available to you at an event like this. You can socialize, which includes standing still during a conversation. You can browse the auction items, which requires moving slowly."

"We could do a pass of the lower and upper floors. Make sure the security guys didn't miss anything."

Drew took one long step and stopped in front of me. "Ask Rav if he thinks his guy who did the preliminary survey missed anything."

Over my earpiece, Rav grunted. That meant Drew was right.

"And then ask Brie if she's noticed anyone going into the areas they're not supposed to."

"He's not wrong," said Brie. "We're watching all the comings and goings and no one has left the boundaries we set. I'd have alarms going off here if they did."

Drew had only worked with my team twice. And somehow he knew exactly how long to wait for each of my team members to not only recognize he was talking about them, but to respond.

I folded my arms.

"And we're not debating how well Scarlett and Malcolm are handling the banquet room, or that Emmett and Zaria will be in there next. That was your team's plan. And we're going through with it."

Beyond the auction tables, the long bar with at least twenty seats sat off to the right. To the left, where there had been tables the first time we came in, there was the dance floor and the raised platform where the five-man band played. Dressed in burgundy tuxedos, they'd been playing an eclectic mix of oldies, smooth jazz, with a few R&B standards.

Drew placed the champagne flute he'd stolen from me on an auction table nearby. "The only option if you want to move is—"

I held my hands out to stop him. "Don't even go there."

The corner of his irritatingly sexy mouth quirked up. He held out a hand and bowed slightly. "May I have the honor of this dance?"

"I don't dance." Literally. I'd missed out on every high school dance because I'd been too busy training. Tanner and I had never done something like that, because we were... too busy training. In my dark days after the accident, I hadn't gotten into relationships where we went out to clubs together, let alone any sort of couples dancing.

And since then?

I hadn't had a man in my life.

It was too much of a risk.

He dragged his knuckles down my arm again—lighting my skin on fire—and took my hand. Not the same way we'd done it earlier. This wasn't about communication. It was tender—he was actually *holding* my hand. "Think of it like this. You'll be moving, we'll spin around the dance floor slowly, and we'll be able to watch everything going on in the main dining room. It's nothing but cover."

Scarlett hummed in assent over the line. "It's standard practice when you're working in the front."

I wanted my shadows back. "Okay, but I warn you, it's your toes that are going to pay the price."

"I'll keep it simple." Drew maintained a tight grip on me, so firm I couldn't escape. "Plus, from what I've heard, you have the best reaction time on the entire Reynolds team. I'd be willing to bet that means you'll be a perfect dance partner."

We threaded our way through the crowd of about thirty people on the dance floor. Half were women holding glasses of wine and dancing as a group, while the rest were couples. One couple glided across the floor as though they were professionals, but the rest were regular people—although to be here, they had to be incredibly wealthy, so not quite regular—enjoying the music and the evening.

Drew stopped at the far end, by the windows that overlooked the fountain. The sun was low in the sky, and the light display he'd told me about began outside. He shifted the way he held my hand, put the other at my waist, and we began to move.

Over my earpiece, Will's voice caught my attention. "I'm here."

Brie said, "How's your mom?"

"They're keeping her overnight, so I came home. I knew you'd need the backup."

Brie laughed. She always laughed more when he was working the op with her. "Ashley's here helping. She's amazing."

"Oh." Will sounded pained.

I piped up, attempting to bolster his spirits. "Don't worry, Will. No matter how good Ashley is, she'll never replace you."

"She's right," said Brie. "Two completely different skill sets. And speaking of which…"

They chatted about the photograph I'd taken, catching Will up on everything he'd missed, and talking about his mom. Life would have been easier if he'd brought her back to Halifax, instead of dealing with her health in London, far away from all of us. He had so much on his shoulders.

Drew pivoted us so I couldn't see the fountain lights anymore. "His mom's okay?"

I nodded. "Are you close with your mother?"

Drew's face hardened.

Why did I ask that?

Scarlett, Emmett, and Brie worked for their mother. Will had sacrificed so much to help his mom when she needed it. Rav... Rav may have been chiseled out of rock instead of born from actual humans. Most of our other co-workers had positive relationships with their families, including our safe cracker, who had a strained but close relationship with his.

But me? I hadn't talked to my mother in eight years.

There was no point.

"I don't talk about that." His jaw flexed, and he did exactly what he said he was going to do while we were on the dance floor—he checked the crowd.

That's what I should have been doing. Instead, the warmth of his body and the scent of his cologne were all I could think about. Thursday night had started out so well.

Drew's attention was stuck somewhere on the mezzanine.

I glanced up to where the second floor provided a view of the main dining area. Wyatt and Rav stood side by side, leaning on the railing, each holding a tumbler of amber liquid. "Rav, is everything all right?"

He grunted. That grunt meant he didn't appreciate Wyatt's company. And from the look on Wyatt's face, the feeling was mutual.

Wyatt's gaze locked with mine. There was something in it I hadn't seen before. It wasn't the predatory or even the flirtatious look, it was... sad?

Drew squeezed my hand, bringing my attention back to him and his rich brown eyes. "Tell me: What do you crave in a partner?"

Someone stifled a laugh over my earpiece. It must have been Emmett.

"What?" That had come out of left field.

"A dance partner." He spun me slowly. "Do you prefer someone who spins you? Or maybe dips you?"

My world tipped upside down as he eased me back, my stupid leg kicking up for balance like a dance show contestant.

"Someone who gives you space?" He stepped back, holding me two feet away. "Or someone who..."

He pulled me close, as close as we'd been at his apartment. One hand latched around my waist, pressing me against his hard body.

Don't think about his cock from the other night, don't think about—

Too late.

"Or someone who holds you so tight, they make it clear to everyone in the room that you belong to me?"

"I don't belong to anyone."

He touched his cheek to mine, his mouth an inch from my ear that didn't have the earpiece. "Turn off your comms. I need to talk to you."

"I can't. You know that."

"Then put yourself on mute. Something."

That was Reynolds rule number one. Never turn off the earpiece on a job. "No."

He straightened, lips tighter than his jaw. "Why did you leave Thursday night?"

"We're not having this discussion right now."

"You'll be gone tomorrow." His hand flexed on my back. "I'm not waiting."

Why did he care? What did it matter? Was it a blow to his ego he couldn't handle?

"Brie," said Emmett. "Mute Jayce for five minutes. If something happens sooner, turn her back on."

My stomach upturned. I pressed a hand over my ear, trying to hear something, but the line was dead. I glowered at Drew, taking a step away from him, but he treated it like a dance step, following me. "They shut my earpiece off."

"Then tell me the truth." His brows fell, as though he gave a shit.

"Stop." I pushed my clutch hand against his chest. "Why are you doing this?"

"I thought we had something."

Something temporary. Something not worth more than a few hours' entertainment. "And then you were in bed with your ex the next day."

His whole body tensed, and he stopped in the middle of the dance.

"Yeah, Drew, she told me." A lump formed in my throat, cutting me off. Why? Why did I care? How did this man get under my skin so easily? "Can we just cut the bullshit and go back to being professional?"

"No." He took in a slow breath, staring at the floor beside us. "You want to know the truth?"

"I don't care." I did, but he didn't need to know that.

"She came by my place Thursday morning, telling me she wanted..." His gaze rolled up toward the room-length chandelier and finally to me. "I told her to get lost and now she's angry."

I patted his chest. "Good story."

"Ask Emmett or Rav what I was doing last night."

"Can't." I shrugged. "They shut me off."

"I was at di Sano's, planning on a quiet evening at my favorite restaurant. But they showed up and told me their concerns about you and Wyatt."

Those traitors. I shot a glare at Rav, who raised his glass at me.

It was all a setup.

"If you don't want me the same way I want you, I'll stop asking," he said. "But from how you reacted at my place, I was sure you did—until you left. Tell me the truth. Why did you leave?"

Chapter 28
Jayce

The truth. *It sets you free, Jayce.*

It ensures you know exactly why anyone wants you around.

Or doesn't want you around.

However, my truth wouldn't negate his. Even if Vanessa lied about yesterday, Drew still only wanted me for one thing. I'd sworn off one-night stands and meaningless sex five years ago. I wasn't going back to that, no matter how I felt in his arms.

Or the way he looked at me when he thought I'd been hurt setting the tracker.

Or the way he'd ordered that security guard to let go of me.

"We look silly standing in the middle of the dance floor." Why couldn't I say it? That his words Thursday night—that I was only something to get out of his system—had stung? I *did* always say what was on my mind.

The background hum in my earpiece kicked back in, full of random chatter.

Will's light British accent was the first one that made sense. "I told you it wasn't ready last week."

I bowed my head, focusing. "What's going on?"

"The extraction software won't work," Will said. "This is Gideon Tremaine. He'll have way too much security on his phone for us to access it remotely. Can someone grab it?"

"I can't do it." I glanced up at Drew, who'd gone back to the flexed jaw look, and pointed at my earpiece. *Heaven forbid he think I meant I couldn't answer his question.* Which apparently, I couldn't.

Drew started the dance again.

"I can try, but he's surrounded by people," said Scarlett. "Would Liana's suffice, if she's the only option?"

"Watch out for the big guy against the wall in the suit," I said. "The one with the blond hair and military cut. I think he's private security for the scarab."

"Is something happening?" asked Drew. "Do we need to get back to the chip?"

"No, the team's got it." How ironic. Talking about honesty, then blatantly lying to him. This double-agent mission-within-a-mission crap was for the birds.

Or for Scarlett. She could handle it.

"I'll be down in a minute," said Rav. "I'll provide cover."

"That's what I'm here for," countered Malcolm. "Hold your post."

Malcolm was growing too comfortable at Scarlett's side. It wasn't his place to make those decisions.

Rav had already pushed back from the mezzanine railing, obviously bothered. But without Scarlett overriding Malcolm, he'd stay. He was a good soldier, and his top priority was always Scarlett.

Wyatt also appeared agitated, despite not being involved in the conversation with Scarlett. He mirrored Rav, moving away from the railing.

But then he left.

"Wyatt?" said Rav. "What are you doing?"

I flicked my gaze intentionally to Drew and back to the second floor. "He just left his post. Didn't tell Rav where he was going."

Drew looked up, then tapped his ear. "Wyatt? Where'd you go?"

Brie hummed aloud. "I lost one of the cameras."

"Drew," I said, "ask Craig about the cameras. Brie's lost one."

He did as I asked, waited for a beat, and shook his head. "He's lost one, too, and he's working on getting it back up. The one that monitors the hallway upstairs?"

Brie said, "That's the one."

I nodded to Drew, the prickling energy of an adrenaline spike starting in my shoulders. "Brie, can you see Wyatt anywhere?"

"I'm reviewing footage from the camera that went out," she said. "He was heading for— Oh no."

"Oh no, what, Brie?" I took Drew's hand and walked him off the dance floor. *Don't run, Jayce. You're in public.*

On the mezzanine level, Rav made a beeline after Wyatt.

Drew didn't question my actions—maybe he had the same concerns as I did, or maybe he was trusting my judgment. "Wyatt says he went to the washroom."

"Noah," Brie breathed and a swear word popped out of every team member's mouth.

I picked up the pace. "What's he doing here?

"He's in the blind spot." Brie's speech accelerated. "Wyatt came back on screen once he was out of the downed camera range, so he could be telling the truth. Rav, Wyatt's on the stairs to the main level. Will, coordinate with Craig and get that camera back up."

"Scarlett," said Rav, "I'm going after Noah."

"I'm coming with you." I hauled Drew with me, tucking down a narrow staff hallway that led away from the throng.

"And us," said Emmett. In the background of his comms, Zaria asked what was happening.

Drew halted suddenly, pulling me to a stop. "Details. Quickly. Who's here, what's the problem, and where are we going?"

The chatter continued over my earpiece, but I put it all aside. How much could I tell Drew? What information could I trust him with? "Scarlett's ex works with a band of thieves and kidnappers called the Fenix Group—F-E-N-I-X, not like the bird. He's upstairs in the blind spot. You and I are going to intercept him. So are Rav and Emmett."

"Are you going after him for personal reasons?" Drew lifted a brow. "Or do you suspect he's here for the chip?"

I didn't have a plan. I'd heard he was there and started moving. Scarlett was my planner, but Fenix was a variable she hadn't accounted for. That was too many times they'd gotten past her.

And I wasn't about to let them tank this job on her.

Scarlett's voice broke through the din. "Jayce, he's right. Malcolm and I are headed to the main dining room in case Noah's here for me. Emmett and Zaria are heading upstairs. Rav's already there. We need you and Drew back in the banquet room."

Drew touched his ear and turned slightly from me. "Be careful, Zaria."

"Why?" I asked everyone who was listening. "Why would Fenix be here? You don't think they're behind the threats against the chip, do you?"

From what we'd learned, Fenix hid their data in Tremaine Industries' elusive data storage center. That's why we'd been after access to it. They collected antiquities, so they could have been there for the other items in the VIP display. Maybe they were after the scarab like we were.

But in addition to taking antiquities, they also stole and kidnapped—and possibly worse—to get leverage over people. They could have been there to grab someone.

"No matter what," said Drew. "The chip is our job. If there's a chance he's after it, we need to get in there. Zaria says Emmett and Rav are going after a suspect."

The cameras had too much coverage upstairs for Noah to vanish. He had to be hiding somewhere. And we could catch him. Fenix had to be the ones targeting the chip.

Stop thinking and move, Jayce.

Fortunately, Drew did the thinking for me. He jerked his head toward the shorter route back to the banquet room.

I nodded and we retraced our steps. I tried walking in double time, but the ridiculous shoes slipped on the polished floor.

Drew steadied me and we slowed. "Should have brought those Kevlar socks."

"No kidding."

"Lost another camera." Brie groaned over the line. "This one covering the stairs to the banquet room."

Drew conveyed the same information to me—likely from Craig.

I stripped off the shoes, balancing them and the clutch in one hand, with Drew's fingers in the other. We dodged between couples, groups, auction pieces, and easels. The huge food skirts were little more than pylons.

We weren't going to fail.

Fenix wouldn't win this battle.

Chapter 29
Drew

I stayed close behind Jayce, grabbing her shoes as her arm swung back. "Give me your clutch, too."

She didn't need to carry so much if we were about to dive into action. I had pockets and her little pink dress didn't.

"We're at the top of the—" Zaria's voice in my earpiece cut out.

"Come again?" I said.

Silence on the other end.

"Zaria?"

Nothing.

"Craig? Wyatt? Anyone?"

Jayce glanced over her shoulder at me. "Comms down?"

"Apparently." It wasn't the first time I'd dealt with something like this. My training kicked in and the emotional locker opened up, absorbing as much stress and anxiety as possible. If only it could do the same for the woman in front of me, whose shoulders were growing tighter by the second. With my pockets full, I took out my phone and dialed Craig. And waited. "Craig's not answering his phone, either."

Given the cameras and comms were down, he would have been working to restore things or leaving his post to communicate in person. If the former, it made sense he wouldn't have time to answer.

Still, backup comms should have been a priority.

"Is your team up there yet?" I asked Jayce.

She paused in her stride, allowing me to catch up. I was next to her again as we passed Scarlett and Malcolm on their way out of the banquet room. "They're checking rooms. They'll find Noah, then help Craig if he needs it."

We slowed once we were in the smaller room, Jayce's gaze growing cold. Calculating. I hadn't seen that look since everything went to hell on the Harrington job. I'd told her we had to abort the mission and she'd refused. She got her way in the end and nearly got us arrested in the process.

"He's smart. Plus, he worked with us for years, so if he knows we're here, he knows our moves. He won't come through the main door or the patio doors," she said. "That means we watch the bathroom and staff doors."

"Or the floor or ceiling?"

"Still less likely, but possible." She guided me along the wall to the back of the room, opposite the patio doors. Our monitoring position was between the two doors we were watching, next to the gold and blue painting from earlier. "Rav says he's brought in Marc, who did the pre-event sweeps upstairs and down."

And where was Wyatt? No word he'd rejoined Rav. He wasn't in the banquet room. Although there were so many people, he could have been hidden.

Jayce stood absolutely still, with her back to the wall. Only her eyes moved. She'd complained earlier about not enough movement, but this was a different type of standing still. She was a snake coiled in the grass, waiting to strike.

If we'd been truly undercover, I would have caged her in against the wall and told her she was being far too obvious. Anyone who knew what they were looking for would have picked her out even faster than they could have picked out the security guards at the doors.

I tried my phone again, this time calling Wyatt.

He didn't answer, but he immediately texted me, *Suspicious guy on the fourth floor. Tracking him.*

I tipped the phone toward Jayce, and she conveyed the information to her team. I texted back, *What did the suspicious man look like?*

She said, "The camera covering the stairwell entrance on this floor is down, so Brie's blind. How did the guy get past the guard stationed there?"

"Likely left his post. That seems to be going around." My phone screen remained stuck on my last message to Wyatt. "And Wyatt isn't answering my question."

"I don't like this," muttered Jayce.

"Need a snack?"

She frowned but didn't look at me. From the way the corner of her mouth twitched, though, the tease had alleviated a little of her stress.

"How about your shoes?"

"Standing here barefoot makes me look suspicious, doesn't it?"

"As do the heels poking out of my jacket pockets." I handed them to her. "If we assume the suspicious character is Noah, and he's on the 4th floor, we shouldn't see much action down here anytime soon."

"He was Scarlett's second in command." Jayce slipped on a shoe. "He knows how to plan a heist. If Wyatt saw him go up to the fourth floor, that's because he wanted Wyatt to see him. He's planning something."

I surveyed the crowd in front of me. Half of them were public figures or the significant others of public figures. I knew a quarter by reputation, from past jobs with Bishop and Associates, or from Vanessa's gossip. The other quarter contained faces I only knew from our preparations for the event. "Would Noah be working alone?"

"Not likely."

Which of my three groups would his team be in? "Send me a photo of him and his known associates?"

My phone lit up almost immediately with texts from an unknown number and several photos. Four men in total: Noah, a man labeled *Enzo* with a jagged scar across his cheek, and two unnamed men.

"There's a couple more in an Italian jail."

I forwarded the photos to my team with a warning to keep their eyes open.

My phone buzzed with a call from Wyatt. I answered, holding the phone so Jayce could hear. "Did you find him?"

"I've got him cornered on the fourth floor." Wyatt spoke quickly between labored breaths. "Northwest corner office. I need backup."

Jayce and I looked at each other. Our teams were split between the restaurant's two floors. We were spread too thin.

"This is his plan," said Jayce.

It was a good plan. Draw everyone out of the banquet room and make off with the chip.

"Wyatt," I said, "I'm sending one of the security guards."

"Tell him to fucking hurry!"

I took two steps toward the guard by the staff door.

The lights went out.

Gasps and startled voices filled the room. Dim light filtered through the main and bathroom doors as people streamed out. Even the patio lights shut off.

"Fuck." I halted. "Wyatt, the lights are off down here."

"They're on up—" He grunted, followed by a thud and a sound as though his phone skittered across the floor.

"Wyatt?" I flipped on my phone's flashlight—as did many others. With no response, I hurried to the guard at the door. "I'm with Bishop and Associates. Get someone to the fourth floor. One of the thieves is up there."

He turned on his own light and glowered at me, but used his comms to order one of the security team to help Wyatt. Part of my brain begged me to go up there, to ensure he was okay.

But I stuffed that inside the locker, too.

Jayce said Noah's group were thieves and kidnappers. Would they do more than disable Wyatt?

My stomach churned uneasily, memories of Alex flooding back to me. *Put it in the locker, Drew.* Had he been alone when the Flame of Khvarenah found him? Had he called for backup from someone who didn't come for him?

"Lights off, everyone." A female voice carried through the sound system, along with quiet music. "It's time for what you all came for."

Camera lights winked out throughout the room, plunging us back into near-darkness. A low-pitched hum filled the room, joined by a single violin, drowning out the crowd's whispers.

Liana had promised a show.

Hopefully, that's all this is.

CHAPTER 30

JAYCE

This was my element.

Light so low, most people couldn't see.

Everyone too distracted by Liana's spectacle to notice the world around them.

Music quiet enough I could hear any cues I needed, but loud enough to mask my movements.

"Liana's shut off the lights," I whispered to my team. "I'm going in. Radio silent."

"Be careful," said Brie over my earpiece. "The cameras can't handle low light. I can't see anything."

Rav, Emmett, and Zaria were still searching for Noah upstairs—how many rooms were there? Wyatt was another floor up on someone's tail. Malcolm had Scarlett sequestered in the main dining room—the man was more paranoid about Noah coming after her than Rav was.

That left me.

I stepped out of my shoes and hunched my shoulders, making myself as inconspicuous as possible.

A flash from a sequin here, a jostle of keys there; I could visualize every person I navigated around. Noah was too smart.

He'd have us chasing our tails all night and swoop in at the right time.

But he wasn't getting the best of Reynolds Recoveries again. I'd be standing next to that sculpture if he tried anything.

The lights being out would be a perfect opportunity—did he know it was going to happen?

Two hands landed on my hips, and I froze. Something deep inside told me it was Drew.

"I picked up your shoes." He must have spotted my movement before he turned off his phone light. "I think Wyatt's in trouble."

I straightened—there was no hiding with him there—and craned my neck around to keep my voice low. "Stay behind me."

"I've sent one of the guards upstairs to find him. Can someone from Reynolds go up, too?"

I held up a finger.

Drew was close enough to my earpiece that my team would have caught his request. If anyone was available, they'd do it.

Not me. Not Drew. We had other priorities in front of us.

Liana's voice echoed throughout the room. "A thousand years ago, Western Europe crawled its way out of the Dark Ages. A time of lost information, brought about by the fall of one civilization."

Drew tapped twice on my hip with one of his fingers. *Go forward*, it said.

"Other cultures around the world flourished, while millions suffered. The Renaissance emerged, creating a spark of knowledge and artistry."

I heard a click, a hiss, and then a flame appeared at the center of the room. The music volume raised, strings and horns joining the unseen orchestra. Oblivious to the threats against the sculpture, the crowd oohed and aahed, as the fire reflected off their faces.

Liana stood in the middle of the VIP display, holding a blowtorch. Her voice rose over the sound system. "If we want to ensure humanity never falls into such darkness again, we must preserve our information, our truth, our stories. The EPRC—the Eternal Preservation and Retrieval Chip—is an ultra-durable, ultra-secure storage chip designed with built-in mechanisms to independently store and retrieve data."

There was the sales pitch.

But why the blowtorch?

Drew and I inched closer to the sculpture.

"With this chip, resistant to water, dust, fire, and the ravages of time, we shall never completely fall from light and into darkness again. We will never fall past the twilight!" Liana dialed up the flame, turning in a slow circle, the orange glow lighting up the faces of the crowd.

We were outside the tightest ring of spectators, but the torch was so hot, it warmed my face.

"She's going to melt it, isn't she?" I said.

Was Liana actually the one we had to worry about? Instead of someone stealing it, was she going to destroy it?

"Where's Gideon?" I asked.

Drew pointed over my shoulder to where Gideon stood by the obsidian mirror. Between the light from the torch and its reflection that bounced strangely off the mirror—up and down instead of out—his proud smile was clear. Not a hint of worry. Had he known her plan all along?

This *was* a performance. But more importantly, it was a demonstration.

Over my earpiece, Rav said, "Noah's not here. Emmett and Zaria, help Craig get everything working again. Jayce, you said Wyatt needs help upstairs?"

I tapped twice on my earpiece, and he acknowledged with a grunt. He was all the backup anyone needed in a fight.

A few nervous laughs spread through the crowd as Liana held the torch higher.

"This is history." She finally moved toward her Digital Twilight. "This is the future."

The amber resin along the side of the enormous sculpture reflected the fire, glowing from deep within. But as the flame got closer, it lit up the dragonfly, too.

"Oh shit," breathed Drew behind me.

The dragonfly's head was gone.

CHAPTER 31
DREW

Was the missing dragonfly head part of Liana's performance?

The way she stood there—the blowtorch firm in her unmoving hand, her eyes wide—it was clear this wasn't what she'd expected.

"Lights!" I yelled over the music's crescendo. "Turn the lights on!"

Jayce was already coordinating with her team, watching her phone. "Tracker's live. Cameras up yet?"

I approached Liana in the dim light, speaking slowly. "Turn it off, Liana. We need to find out what happened."

She stared at her sculpture, blinking at the empty spot where Tremaine Industries' revolutionary chip should have been. "All this security..."

"Drew." Jayce nudged my arm.

Gideon joined his wife, clicking off her blowtorch. His hard gaze fell on me. "You were supposed to protect it."

"Drew." Jayce's voice was more insistent. "The cameras are still down, but—"

"What?" A subtle tick at the corner of Gideon's eye and the way he pulled Liana close told me the successful businessman had shifted priorities. He didn't care about the chip. He cared about his wife.

Jayce continued. "The tracker's active, and I've got an overlay of the floor plan."

"Turn the lights on and cut the music." Liana's voice was soft, but the lights came on immediately. She must have had someone on her own comms.

"We'll get it back." I nodded to both of the Tremaines and turned to Jayce. "Where is it?"

"Lower floor." She dodged between astonished partygoers, the level of gossip and musings turning into confused questions the farther we got. No one outside the first few rings of guests seemed to know what was going on.

Although somewhere in the crowd, Vanessa would be mentally recording everything, already preparing the scandal sheet.

The closer we got to the staff door and the emergency stairwell beyond it, the faster Jayce's steps grew. The security guard stationed at the door had his finger to his ear, nodding and speaking quietly. We should have all been on the same channel. He was working with his team independently of both the Reynolds and Bishop teams.

"Put your shoes on." I took Jayce's arm when she didn't slow down and pulled her to a stop. "I know you don't like them, but if our thief has any brains—"

"Still no sign of Wyatt or Noah." Jayce swapped the offered shoes for her phone, slipping into them without a stutter in her step. Despite her complaints, when she wasn't focused on the heels, she moved in them effortlessly. She pointed at the security guard, who looked at me for authorization before opening the door. "Tell your guys the chip's gone. Check bags and pockets of anyone coming in or out."

Staff would have turned left toward the kitchen. To the right, the emergency stairwell was supposed to have another guard stationed at it.

"Guard's left his post at the stairwell," said Jayce.

"He's probably the one who went to check on Wyatt." We reached the door to the stairs at the end of the hallway at a near run. I glanced at the phone and passed it back to her. "The thief's headed westward, slowly. Likely trying to avoid being heard."

Unless Noah had gotten by the team upstairs, he wasn't the one with the dragonfly's head. That meant he had at least one other person working with him. And if there was one, there could've been more. It didn't matter what kind of reaction speeds Rav said Jayce had; I wasn't about to let her charge headlong into the path of whoever snuck off with the chip.

I took the lead, sparing the gentlemanly routine and entering the stairwell first.

How had anyone gotten the head off without us noticing? It should have made a noise if nothing else. And the way the mob constantly murmured about what everyone was doing, wearing, and who they'd arrived with, surely someone would have noticed the sculpture being tampered with.

Unless someone had tampered with it before the event.

"Slow down," whispered Jayce, as we reached the bottom floor. "They've stopped. Scarlett and Malcolm are in the elevator. The rest of the team's still upstairs."

I tucked in closer to her as she pressed her ear to the door. "My comms haven't come back up. Any word on Wyatt?"

She didn't budge, other than to flick her eyes at me. "No. Rav went to the fourth floor and couldn't find him."

"What does that mean?"

Jayce shrugged one shoulder and closed her eyes, leaning in to the door. "Rav's clearing the office space with Marc. They ran into the guard who was stationed on the stairwell—he didn't see Wyatt, either—and they sent him back to his post. Maybe Wyatt didn't need the help as much as you thought."

Or he'd been taken somewhere. Or someone was doing something to him.

Shove it in the locker, Drew. There are men up there taking care of it.

What if they missed something? What if another suspicious character distracted them? What if Noah had so many co-conspirators crawling through this building we were chasing ghosts?

Jayce placed a gentle hand on my chest. "Breathe."

How was the chaos monster the calm one?

"I can barely hear anything over your heart racing." Her words were so quiet, hand so light.

I gripped her hand, pressing it against my chest. Against my heart. It *was* beating too fast.

We had to finish this job so I could say goodbye to her for good. So I could start focusing on my job. On the world around me. On something other than this woman in her pink dress who wasn't just standing still for once, but was helping me relax.

The CIA trained me. I was in control under every circumstance—in every situation I found myself in—except around her.

What was it about her?

"Scarlett and Malcolm are on the ground floor." She tapped two times with her index finger—*Go forward*—despite not needing the hand signal. "The thief's approaching where they're building the bar. Looks like he's heading for the entrance by the fountain."

The lower floor had been an office space, then a coffee shop, a casual restaurant, and was currently being converted into a whiskey bar. The in-progress construction would provide hiding places, but considering the thief carried Jayce's tracker, the hiding places wouldn't be enough.

"Scarlett and Malcolm will come in through double doors by the elevator at the west end," she said. "They'll hold that entrance, and we'll either catch the thief or flush them out. Good?"

"Good. And the rest of your team?"

"Emmett and Zaria are working with Craig to get the cameras and your comms back up."

"And Noah? Do you think he hamstrung both of our teams simultaneously?"

"Yes." Jayce opened her eyes and shifted her hands to the door handle. "I'm going first on three. One."

"No. I'm going first." The last thing I needed was for someone to swing that metal dragonfly's head and smash it into her skull. I wanted her out of my life, but not that way.

"Now is not the time to be second-guessing me. The way you clomp around in those shoes, they'll know exactly where you are." She glowered at me, lifting her phone to show the tracker had stopped moving. "Me, on the other hand? I'll be able to sneak up behind them and—"

"Get your head bashed in by a solid metal sculpture?"

"This is why I didn't want to work with him," she said, obviously bypassing me and speaking to her team. "This is the same shit you pulled on the Harrington job. I know what I'm doing."

I stopped her before she opened the door. "This isn't about capability. It's about keeping you safe."

"Before you say something else that will force my team to put me on mute again, this is about a job. This is about stopping Noah from screwing us over."

It wasn't even about the chip. She didn't care about that.

She cared about her team.

She'd put herself in harm's way for them.

In some circles, that would be called admirable. In our current circle, it made her weak and ensured she made stupid decisions.

In exactly the same way you're making stupid decisions around her, Drew.

"You're the subject matter expert." I took my hand off the door. "I'll be directly behind you."

With a nod, she eased the door open and slipped through it. I followed, remaining almost as quiet as she did. The soles of her shoes were an uncoated leather, silent against the poured concrete floor. Fortunately, the band was still playing upstairs despite everything.

At the far end of the open space, the lights from the fountain around the square shone through white paper blocking the windows. Unlike the restaurant above, the wall facing the river was just that—a wall without an exit.

With only the fountain's pale illumination lighting the cavernous room, the telltale signs of construction loomed around us—tables covered with drop cloths, radial saws, piles of lumber, and chairs stacked against the wall.

As we crept forward, Jayce showed me her phone again.

I squinted around the room. We'd all done a walk-through of the to-be whiskey bar and the office floors above, so I was familiar with the layout. The kitchen was behind us, sitting underneath the Mosaic banquet room. Ahead, midway along the restaurant, a long, unfinished bar dominated the space.

And the thief was hiding behind the bar.

Chapter 32
Drew

I tapped three times on Jayce's back, and she froze. Instead of speaking, I pulled out my phone and typed into a note-taking app, *Why would they have stopped?*

She shook her head and looked heavenward, the light from my phone gently illuminating her face. She took the phone, stacking it on top of her own, and typed, *We can ask when we catch them.*

This was always the problem with her. Move first, think later. If ever.

What if they were armed with more than a chunk of metal? I hadn't brought a gun and we didn't have any security backup. If I tried to get ahead of her, she'd insist on going first. If I tried to stop her, she'd forge on, anyway.

The best way to keep her safe? Go along with her plan until we got close enough and take over at the last minute.

Two figures emerged from the shadows at the other end—Scarlett and Malcolm. We may not have had security with us, but we had backup.

Jayce steered me toward the wall, and we inched our way closer to the bar.

The thief hadn't moved. Didn't make any noise.

What if they stashed the head and were gone? What if all the sneaking was nothing more than killing time? What if they'd already gotten away with the chip?

Five feet away from the end of the bar, I prepared to make my move: to haul Jayce, unsuspecting, out of the way and tackle the thief before he realized what was happening.

In the dark ahead of us, there was a loud thud, like a piece of lumber hitting the ground and bouncing. Sudden, frantic, scraping across the floor followed it.

I grabbed Jayce, propelled her backward, and turned on my phone flashlight as I rushed to the bar.

A hissing blur of black fur shot at me from the counter. I dodged to the side and lost my grip on my phone, sending it clattering to the floor. Something sliced my temple as I rammed into the bar and a piece of flooring—or the lumber—slipped out from underneath me.

I landed hard, my head slamming off something vertical before hitting the ground.

"What the hell, Drew?" Jayce shoved me with her foot.

I sat up, the world spinning, and touched the back of my head. No blood, but a lump was already forming. I hadn't seen the thief, but since Jayce was speaking at a normal volume, someone must have caught him. "Did you get him?"

"Seriously! What was that bonehead move?" Jayce cradled a thin black cat in her arms.

Malcolm helped me up. "You okay?"

"All I saw was the cat!" I straightened my tuxedo jacket, shoving my ego into my mental locker along with everything else. "Where's the thief?"

"Freaking Noah." Jayce pointed at the cat's collar. "No one's here."

Scarlett said, "The tracker?"

A small tag hung from the cat's collar. I flipped it over to read the animal's name. "*Chaos*?"

Jayce rolled her eyes and groaned theatrically. "Look closer."

There was a small black dot at the center of the O. The magnetic decoration came off easily, and I turned it over in my hand. "It's your tracker. We've been chasing this cat?"

Scarlett peeled away, bowing her head and carrying on a muted conversation with her team over their earpieces. Malcolm joined her.

Jayce absently stroked the cat. "They're not having any luck finding Noah."

"Is Brie sure it was him?" I stuffed the tracker into my pocket. Apparently, we hadn't hired the best heist crew. "What if someone else saw you put the tracker on the dragonfly's head?"

"Not likely." She blew a raspberry. "And your face is bleeding."

With the pounding at the back of my skull, I'd barely registered the throbbing across my temple. I tapped a finger at the spot where the cat had clawed me, coming away with blood. It was already sticky. "Fucking cat."

"No less than you deserve for that bullshit move."

"Maybe you didn't attach it securely. Maybe it fell on the floor and—"

"Are you honestly suggesting this cat was wandering around upstairs and no one noticed?" She placed the cat on the counter, its purring growing louder as she stroked its head.

"Why not? You're suggesting a ghost snuck past us, took the tracker off—a tracker, you claim no one saw you put in place—and attached it to the cat's collar?"

"Chaos!" She flung an arm in the air, not disguising her irritation. "It's all part of his plan. Get us running around this building while he makes off with the chip."

"If it was really part of his plan..." Something wasn't adding up. It was all too convenient. There was another level to this job. "This isn't a random cat. He brought the cat, knowing the tracker would be on the dragonfly's head. He planned it so he could put the tracker on the cat."

Jayce's hand froze on the cat's back. "If Noah did all that, he had to be privy to our plans. Who had access? Who knew about the tracker?"

"Your team. My team." Who else was there when Jayce ran through her plans yesterday afternoon? Everyone had been moving around the space. "Liana? Her staff? The carpenters?"

"Liana said no to the tracker." Jayce grew serious, her irritation with me replaced by an intense focus. "Our teams were there—except for Zaria—and Liana. That was it. Even if someone had been listening in, they would have heard Liana decline."

I picked my phone up off the floor. "Whether or not Brie genuinely saw Noah, he's not behind this."

"If Noah's here, he *is* behind it."

I pointed at the cat with my phone, which was greeted by a hiss. Stupid cat. "He's part of an inside job."

"Are you accusing my team of something?." Not only was she in touch with all of her teammates—meaning they couldn't have snuck around and stolen anything without her knowing—but she trusted them implicitly.

Must've been nice.

"I'm not." I huffed out a breath. If it was an inside job, her team wasn't behind it—it was either someone from mine or the security team. Rav and Malcolm had done background checks, but they could have missed something. "Is Brie having any luck with the cameras? Or our comms?"

"Will's working on the comms. He thinks he's almost got it. Rav and Brie are hacking directly into the cameras, rather than piggybacking off Craig's signal."

"Where's Zaria?"

Jayce conveyed the question to her team, and Scarlett looked over from across the room. "With Emmett. They went back to the patio to monitor comings and goings."

"Still no sign of Wyatt?"

Her mouth opened and hung there. Good. It wasn't just me. She was coming to the same conclusion. "He's not in trouble, is he?"

"He knew about the tracker, knew all of our planned movements, knew every one of the staff on the security team."

Jayce began walking backward toward the stairwell. "We need to ask the security team if he left."

I kept up with her, increasing my speed the farther we got. "His little ploy? Calling me just before he was attacked? It was nothing more than that—a ploy. The guard working the stairs went to look for him and that camera's down. He had full access to the emergency stairwell."

Jayce spun toward the door, picking up to a jog. "If he left through the emergency exit, it would've triggered an alarm."

"Unless he disabled it?"

"Or..." She burst through the door into the stairwell.

The exit was half a floor down and let out onto the eastern side of the building. The side with the parking garage.

I dashed down three steps and paused. Something glinted on the floor in front of the exit. I hurried the rest of the way and picked it up. Wyatt's leather bracelet with the silver longhorn. "He went out this way."

Jayce didn't follow me. Instead, she stared upward. "Or it's another misdirection?"

I stowed the bracelet in my pocket, looking up with her as the pieces fell into place. "Rav's friend confirmed the door locks were upgraded."

"But that was only to keep people out."

"And the guards were supposed to stop anyone going up there from inside." I grabbed the railing and started running up two steps at a time. Wyatt hadn't been after anyone on the fourth floor. He just needed the stairwell guard out of his way. "Goddammit."

No. Wyatt wasn't behind this. He couldn't have been.

But deep in my gut, I knew he was.

It wasn't jealousy or memories of him tracing lines over Jayce's palm at the restaurant last night that confirmed he was the thief. Those were firmly inside my emotional locker.

Mostly.

More than anything, it was the memory of him giving me the key to his safe. 'If something ever happened to me,' he'd said. He hadn't been worried about strangers going through his things after his death.

He'd been worried we'd catch him tonight.

CHAPTER 33
JAYCE

Drew sped up the staircase ahead of me, taking the stairs two at a time. What I lacked in height, I tried to make up for in speed, but with each floor, he increased the distance between us.

"Jayce?" said Scarlett over my earpiece. "What are you doing?"

I reached the fourth floor—thank goodness running upstairs was easier than walking in heels. One floor to go, then the door to the roof. "Drew and I are checking a theory. We think Wyatt took the chip and is up on the roof."

"Why the roof?" asked Scarlett.

"There's access to the other parts of the building complex. He can avoid security and find some other way down."

"Wait for backup," she said, in that calm voice she always used when things got out of hand. "Rav?"

"On our way," said Rav. That was good news. *'Our'* meant Marc would be with him. "Someone talk to security and have them cover the other buildings."

"There's not enough of them for that," said Scarlett. "But I'll see if we can get one up to the roof."

"Cameras are up!" Brie practically shouted in my ear. "We're searching for Noah and Wyatt now."

"Do you have the roof?" I asked.

Her feed through Craig's cameras had only included the two floors of the Mosaic restaurant, since it was through the company's security feed. But hacked in, she could have had more. "No, but we've got the exterior cameras on the main floor, plus the office hallways on the fourth and fifth floors."

"Stairwell?" As I rounded the turn midway to the fifth floor, a loud crash came from above. Like a body meeting metal. Was Drew hurt? *Oh shit, we should have waited for backup.* "Drew!"

"He's disabled the panic bar," Drew called out. The crash came again as I came off the landing at the fifth floor. Drew was ramming his shoulder against the metal door. "He's out there. The son of a bitch is out there."

"Rav's on his way." I finally reached Drew, stopping him before he launched at the door again. Two thick nails with red plastic collars stuck out of the bar, preventing us from pushing it to release the door latch. "Save your shoulder."

"Fuck that!" He slammed into the door again. It didn't budge.

"Drew!" I got in front of him before he dove at it again. "It must be barred from the outside."

A door opened somewhere below us. Two deep French voices and heavy, hurried feet told me it was Rav.

Drew paced back and forth, slamming a hand against the door. "Hurry!"

Marc was a few inches shorter than Rav and built like a freight train. He spoke with an accent even thicker than Rav's. "Stand back." He leaned against the door, pushed away, and rammed into it so hard the concrete around us practically shook.

The only movement was above the panic bar.

He and Rav gave it a few more shots before anyone listened to my theory about it being barricaded. Drew stood precariously close, wound tighter than a balance beam spring.

I moved a few steps down. "Brie, any sign?"

"Nothing helpful," she said. "Ash and Will are trying to piece together the timeline. We've only got a one second clip of Noah and can't find him on any other video. We don't know where he came from or where he went."

"And Wyatt?"

"Last we saw him, he was heading down the stairs from the bathroom. And I only have live feeds from the cameras outside the restaurant, so I can't rewind to confirm if he went to the fourth floor."

"And Craig's team?" I'd been too distracted to pay attention to Emmett's discussions with Craig, as they tried fixing the Bishop comms and cameras.

"Looks like their tech was tampered with."

A hand slid across the small of my back and Drew's warm body closed in on mine. "Anything?"

"Wyatt must have done something to your comms." I looked up at him, at his tense jaw and the mix of frustration and anger boiling just below his surface. The pounding against the door continued behind us. We were going to lose this job.

I couldn't lose.

"I have a breach kit in the car," said Rav's buddy. "But it'll take me twenty minutes."

"Go," said Rav. "I'll buy you a beer if you make it in ten."

"Make that a two-four," Mr. Freight Train said as he ran down the stairs, "and you've got a deal."

Wyatt had between ten and twenty minutes before they'd blow the door. How long until one of the security guards got up there through the other buildings—if they could find a way up. How far ahead of us was Wyatt? And how much farther would he get in that time?

I had to stop him. Had to do something.

But what?

"The fifth floor!" I practically shouted.

Scarlett, Rav, and someone else asked what I was talking about.

But there was no time to explain. I went as fast as the stupid little heeled shoes would take me. Down a flight, through the door into the offices.

"What are you doing?" came Drew's voice from behind me.

Along a hall, hang a right after the third cubicle, past an office, and into the kitchen.

Drew lunged ahead of me, barring the glass door to the balcony on the far side of the kitchen. "Don't you dare. It's too dangerous."

I'd made the climb from the ground floor on Wednesday. I knew the facade well enough I could make it up a single flight without thinking. "He might not be up there anymore. Maybe he's already ducked into one of the other buildings."

"It was pouring yesterday." He stood firm between me and the door, bracing his arms against the frame. "The walls will be too slippery. You'll fall."

I flipped the door's lock between his arm and his body, and gripped the handle. The lights from the fountain danced in the background, casting intricate patterns on the buildings across the square. "We're professionals, remember?"

Was I talking about my harebrained idea? Him listening to me as the subject matter expert? Or the look in his eyes that almost seemed to be worry.

"Scarlett," said Drew, even though he wasn't able to hear any response. "She's going to climb the outside of the building. Tell her no."

Instead of Scarlett, Rav answered. "Security slowed Marc down. He's fifteen minutes out."

That meant *'Go.'*

"Drew, the balcony protrudes from the outer wall. I'll stay above it, so if I slip, I'll only fall one floor." Not that I would fall. I never fell.

He shook his head, clenching his sexy jaw. With a slow breath, he let go of the doorframe and held out a hand. "Give me your shoes."

I did as he asked as he pushed open the door. "And my clutch." Before leaving, I tied the skirt of my dress up so it wouldn't get in the way. It was pretty, but it was a pain in the butt. At least it was stretchy, allowing me to move.

The first handhold was eight feet up. A moderate jump off the balcony railing. But with my things in his pockets again, Drew laced his fingers together as a foothold. He lowered his voice, likely in case Wyatt was close to us. "Where do you need me?"

I pointed to a spot by the door and he gave me the boost I needed. Another whiff of his sandalwood and leather cologne. I could get used to that smell.

Fingers into a hole where the brick mortar's crumbled. Foot on the frame of the door. Ease over to the decorative protrusion. Toes into the gap between two rows of brick.

"And I'm waiting right here," said Drew. "I'll catch you if you fall."

Something warm knotted inside my stomach. That was a far cry from yelling at me that he wouldn't call an ambulance. I was *not* happy Drew Donovan was worried about me. He didn't care, not really. He wanted a fling, not to look out for me.

"I don't fall," I muttered.

"Good. That makes my job easier. I'd hate to put out a shoulder catching you."

I tried to hold back my smile, but that warmth in my stomach was growing too fast, influencing muscles it shouldn't have. "Don't worry, I'd aim for your head. I prefer a soft landing."

"Can't stop, can you?" said Emmett over my earpiece. He could have directed the statement at anyone on the open comms, but it was obviously for me. And he was right.

I couldn't stop taunting Drew. I didn't want him to stop taunting me. It made no sense.

Regardless, I was almost at the top and needed to be quiet.

Toes in the crack. Palm the decorative stone boss. Push with the legs. Stay silent. Ignore the stone scraping your knee, Jayce. Reach.

Wrapping my fingers around the roof's ledge, I hung for a moment, relaxing my body and listening. No footsteps. No words. No noise at all coming from the top. The dark evening must've hidden my climb, as the same gasps and screeches which had accompanied my antics Wednesday didn't repeat.

I pulled up slowly. Years of trying to match Rav at pull-ups paid off.

No grunts. No heavy breaths. Shh.

Once my eyes were above the ledge, I glanced around. Fifty feet away, the bulkhead protruded from the roof. A loud thud came from that direction. Rav was still trying his shoulder while he waited for Marc's return.

No sign of Wyatt.

I swung a foot up to the ledge and and crested the top.

Where was he? Had he already run?

With the fountain lights behind me, my shadow danced across the metal roof. *Second foot up, roll over the edge. Stay down, in case he's up here.*

Someone grabbed my hair.

Shit!

CHAPTER 34

JAYCE

You're in trouble. Convey intel.

"He's—" I started.

But he yanked out my earpiece before I could say more.

I tried pivoting under his arm, but I planted my foot in a puddle and slipped.

Something slammed into my left knee.

A scream ripped through me as I crumpled. Pain ricocheted through every cell in my body.

"Jayce!" Drew's yell from below barely registered.

Spots clouded my vision and I curled up, trying to protect my bad leg from the next blow.

"It had to be you, didn't it?" Wyatt's smooth Texas drawl had vanished. He dropped the earpiece and smashed it under his heel. "The big guy, I could have handled. Hell, I wouldn't have even felt too bad if it were Drew chasing me down."

"Jayce!" shouted Drew again.

"Tell him you're all right." Wyatt knelt in front of me, just out of reach. "Tell him you tripped, is all."

I blinked hard against the tears streaming down my face. A million knives slashed through my leg. I shook my head at him, stifling a sob.

He touched my leg and I flinched, but the touch was gentle. "I am so sorry, Jayce. This wasn't how I hoped things would go."

I had to delay him. How? Scarlett and Emmett were the conversationalists, not me. I just talked and rambled.

Wyatt bowed his head and sighed. "I was serious last night."

"Which part?"

"When I told you I wanted to run away and start over fresh. How I needed a strong woman at my side. You remember that?"

"I remember." How long did I have until the crew burst through the door? "You told me about your grandmother."

"She would have liked you." He lifted his gaze to meet mine. "I can take you with me."

"Jayce!" yelled Drew again. This time, it came from behind the bulkhead door and was accompanied by a body slamming into it. "Tell me you're okay!"

Wyatt looked over his shoulder and shook his head. "I need you to tell him you're all right or I'm afraid he'll actually break that door down—despite the barricade bar I added this afternoon."

No wonder Rav and Marc couldn't break through.

I pushed up to sitting, grimacing with every millimeter my leg moved. On the ground next to the bulkhead, where Drew was pounding against the inside of the door, sat the soccer-ball-sized dragonfly head. How did he get it off without making a racket?

What was the smart play? Do what he said? Play dumb?

My head throbbed from the pain coursing through my leg. "Why are you still here? Why haven't you run?"

A body collided with the door again.

"You told me there wasn't anything going on between you and him?"

"There's not."

"Jayce!" Drew called. Was he really the one running into the door over and over?

"Yet he's acting like a worried boyfriend." Wyatt stroked my injured leg, along the shin. His lips tightened. "And with all the things that jackass said about you."

Did I want to know?

"Drew's good at what he does. You can always count on him to follow through on the job." He pulled the chip out of his pocket, turning it over to glint in the moonlight. "He was afraid you'd ruin everything."

A lump lodged in my throat, and I swallowed hard. It was from the pain. Not from the sting of Drew's words.

"Said you can't trust a thief, especially one as reckless as you."

Reckless? Drew was the one who made the stupid, short-sighted decisions.

Wyatt's hand paused on my leg. "I tried telling him how talented you are. That's why he broke us up for tonight. Thought I'd go too easy on you."

I wouldn't have called trying to break my leg *going easy*.

"He said he needed to keep you in line. Keep you on a short leash." He looked over his shoulder as the door rattled again. "That son of a bitch thinks you're the weak link on the Reynolds team. The targeting package he prepared on you was a joke—'not as pretty or clever as Scarlett,' it said."

Not like that was news. I *wasn't* as pretty or clever as her. Not as strong or competent as Rav. Not as smooth as Emmett. Or as smart as Brie and Will.

"Never listens, can't stick to a plan, more concerned with food than—"

"I get it, Wyatt." I may have been the weak link on my team, but so was Wyatt on his. At least *we* had something in common.

"My ride's on the way." He looked into the distance, toward the water. "I could use someone with your talents."

Talents? Right. I squeezed my eyes shut, holding back a fresh wave of tears. Even for the guy who'd stolen the chip out from under us—who'd just given up his entire life—I was only worth what I could do for him.

Focus, Jayce. Breathe through the pain. Get information from him. "Who's coming for you?"

"The people who... hired me for this job." Regret tinged his voice. 'Hired' didn't seem like the right word.

"We can help you. Just give the chip back."

Wyatt stood, locking his arm under mine to help me up. "I'm afraid it's not that easy."

I leaned most of my weight on him. I'd competed with worse injuries than this, but without my leg brace, the pain washed over me in waves. Bile climbed up my throat. "It *can* be that easy."

We inched our way toward the southern wall. What was taking Marc so long? How many delay tactics did I have in me?

"Jayce, I know you've made decisions in your life that you're not proud of. Drew documented all of it for us. Giving up on your gymnastics career, turning to a life of crime, abandoning your family…"

I didn't give up on anything.

Other people gave up on me.

I feigned my leg giving out from underneath me, and Wyatt reacted, easing me to the ground.

"I'm sorry. I didn't realize the leg was that bad. How did you scale the wall with an injury like that?"

Because if I gave into it, no one would need me anymore. "Someone's got something on you, don't they?"

"You don't spend a career in the CIA, even a short one, without making enemies." He crouched next to me. "They've been sending me texts, threatening to expose something I did a few years back. Told me about a linchpin holding the dragonfly's head on. All I had to do was pull it and run for the rendezvous point when the lights went out, and no one would ever find out."

"Tell me who."

"Well now, if I told you that, I'd—"

An explosion buffeted me, knocking me flat. The high-pitched ringing in my ears muffled everything. I clapped my hands on either side of my head, the pain in my leg competing with the disorienting ring. It was too much.

Somehow, I was sitting up again. An arm wrapped around my throat and something cold pressed against my temple.

Wyatt said something. It sounded like a threat. All his kind words were gone.

I was already useless, except as a bargaining chip. "You didn't want me to come with you."

"The bird will be here any second," said Wyatt. "If either of you tries to stop me, she's dead."

I gripped his arm, trying to pull it away from my throat. Failing. "Helicopters don't fly around DC—it's protected airspace. Don't you know anything?"

"We only want Jayce back." Rav put up his hands, showing he wasn't armed. At least not with physical weapons, because I'd seen him take down plenty of men with his bare hands.

Next to him, Marc did the same. "You can keep the chip if you hand her over."

Wait. Where was Drew? Had Rav ordered him to stay back? Had all his shouting my name been part of a ploy?

Of course it was. *You're a reckless thief who can't be trusted, remember?* Drew didn't care.

"As much as I'm sure you're an honest and upstanding pair of men, I think I'll hold on to the little lady a few more minutes." Wyatt hauled me up, inching us closer to the southern ledge. What would he do if that helicopter didn't come?

Would he keep me as a hostage?

Or throw me over as a distraction?

CHAPTER 35
DREW

I skirted the perimeter of the roof, hiding in every shadow I could. We had a plan. It started with the assumption Jayce was unconscious, too badly hurt to respond, or afraid for her life. Either way, she wouldn't have warned him about the breach charges, so Wyatt would have been caught off guard and his ears would be ringing.

After Rav had blown the door, there'd been a few screams from below. But we were four floors above the patio, and the explosion was contained. Maybe people thought Gideon and Liana were setting off fireworks. That was the sort of thing the Tremaines would have done for their party. Rather than running for cover, most of the guests could have been waiting for the visual display.

Our plan was simple. Once we'd seen Jayce was conscious, the two big men held Wyatt's attention and I snuck around to disable him.

What the plan hadn't considered was a gun at Jayce's head.

Push it into the locker, Drew.

After the past week, I had to clear my mental locker out—it was stuffed full to the brim. I needed time away. Somewhere uninhabited.

Why did I let her climb the building? Why did I move out of her way? Why the hell did I give her that boost?

Foolish, stubborn woman. She'd gotten it in her head she was going to do it, and she would have, whether or not I helped her.

But when I'd heard her scream—

That goes in the locker, Drew. Rescue her first. Then you can worry about her.

"That's it, boys," cooed Wyatt. He was fifteen feet from the southern edge of the building, keeping Jayce vertical with an arm around her throat.

She half-hopped, half-dragged herself with each step he took, barely able to move her left leg. That must have been the scream.

Fucking Wyatt James knew about her accident.

I fucking told him.

And then he'd used it to hurt her.

Rage, fiery and intense, surged inside me. There was no way this man was getting away with what he'd done tonight.

"Why don't you lower the gun, Wyatt?" Rav separated from Marc, keeping his hands between himself and Wyatt. They were splitting his focus, causing him to pivot away from me. "Seeing my friend with a gun to her head makes me consider doing something drastic, and no one wants that."

"Like that guy in Budapest?" grunted Jayce, either from pain or from Wyatt's arm. "He pees into a bag."

"In prison," added Rav.

The more they talked, the closer I got. There was no guarantee the roof was rated for a helicopter's weight. If Wyatt genuinely had one cleared for this airspace, they'd have to throw down a rope ladder for him.

"I'm past worrying about prison," said Wyatt.

Jayce's body was shielded from me on Wyatt's left side. Each shoulder check as he backed up was over her head.

He held the gun in his right hand.

And that was the side I was on.

"Tell us who's paying you." Rav stepped toward Wyatt, swiping two fingers across his nose.

That was the sign.

"No fast moves, you fucking grunt," snarled Wyatt.

"Fast moves?" said Marc, who took two steps away from Rav, farther away from me. "Like this?"

Wyatt shifted the gun from Jayce's temple. He'd point it at one of the big men.

I ran at him.

Rav and Marc dropped.

I wrapped an arm around Wyatt's right arm, and he dropped Jayce. The momentum carried us forward and we slammed into the ground.

He fired. The blast shook my eardrums. Enveloped me in the scent of gunpowder.

Screams erupted from ground level.

"You little—" Wyatt's fist connected with my ribs.

I held tight, getting my free hand on the gun and directing it away from everyone. Wrapping my legs around his midsection for leverage, I got my other hand on the gun. I was stronger, but he was desperate.

Rav's primal roar and thundering footfalls bore down on us.

I heaved on Wyatt's gun, fighting to gain control. But he fired blindly, his knee smashing into my stomach. As the air flew out of me, a black-clad body landed on top of us.

The gun clattered to the ground.

Rav pinned Wyatt face down, with one thick arm across my former co-worker's neck. Marc joined him, wrenching Wyatt's hand up to his shoulder blades.

"Now would be the perfect time to tell us who's behind this, Wyatt." Pain licked up my side with each breath. Hopefully, nothing was broken; the bastard had gotten in some good blows. I pulled Jayce's clutch out of my pocket and tossed it to Rav, who caught it without a word. "Jayce's zip ties are in there."

When she didn't complain about me offering her things—even to her teammate—I glanced in her direction. She wasn't sitting up. She was supposed to be telling us she was fine or making a crack about how it was all part of her plan or—

She lay on her side, facing away from me.

Oh shit.

I hurried over to her, heart beating high in my chest, as though it were trying to escape through my throat. *Be all right, Jayce.*

Her eyes were closed. Breathing shallow. Heartbeat slow but steady.

She'd been active the entire time Wyatt held her, so he hadn't choked her out. Had she hit her head when I tackled Wyatt? Had he shot her?

No blood, other than cuts and scrapes. Nothing that looked like a gunshot.

"Jayce," I whispered, running a hand over her cheek. "Wake up."

Nothing.

The other men were talking. Raised voices, harsh demands, blatant threats. It blended with the continued screams and yells from far below.

"C'mon, Jayce." I leaned closer, threading my fingers into her hair, and tried again. "Wake up, sweetheart."

What happened? What did I miss?

She'd been standing, and he hadn't wrenched her neck, so it wouldn't be a spinal injury. What was wrong? I wasn't about to leave her there. I slid my arms under her and stood slowly, letting her head roll against my chest.

"Drew!" yelled Rav, snapping my attention to him. He was pulling Wyatt to his feet. "I asked what's wrong with her?"

Sirens sounded in the distance. Hopefully, there were ambulances with the police.

"I don't know, but I'm getting her—"

Jayce groaned but didn't budge. "What are you doing, Down-avon?"

The tightness in my chest relaxed. "You're hurt. I'm taking you—"

"Put me down." She clenched her jaw and touched her throat, swallowing hard. Her eyes were closed. How'd she know it was me? "Normal men ask for permission first."

"You need medical attention." A streak of pain ran up my side. I'd almost forgotten about it in the panic. Or the adrenaline had been too strong. "I'm taking you downstairs."

"I just need food." Her eyes fluttered open, and my world righted itself. "Put me down."

"But your leg? You were limping."

"An act." She craned her neck to look at Wyatt, who'd grown silent under Rav and Marc's questioning. Her voice remained soft, a sharp contrast to the panic outside the restaurant. "And it worked. So put me down."

"You're not—"

"She said"—Rav handed Wyatt over to Marc—"put her down."

I eased her legs down slowly, not wanting to incur his wrath. Wyatt hadn't given them the fight either of the big men apparently wanted, and I wasn't interested in being their consolation prize.

Jayce stood easily, balling her hands on her hips. But she didn't move from her position and was obviously balancing on her right leg.

As though directed by some unheard communication, Rav came to her side and looped an arm around her waist. "Scarlett's advised the Tremaines we caught Wyatt with the chip. They're trying to calm the partygoers."

"We should get downstairs." Jayce visibly leaned on Rav. Was she too proud to admit she needed help? It made sense, given her ultra-competitive personality.

Or it was still about me. She was too proud to accept *my* help.

"Your shoes are at the top of the stairs," I said to her.

"Where's your earpiece?" asked Rav.

Jayce pointed toward the edge of the rooftop, closer to where she must have climbed over. "Wyatt smashed it."

A popping noise came from that direction, and something shimmered across the ground.

"Brie destroyed it," said Rav.

Red and blue lights bounced off the buildings to the east, the sirens cutting short.

Jayce undid the ties on her dress, and the skirt fell to her ankles. Ripped and smudged with dirt, as well as a few bloodstains from her scrapes, she'd make quite the re-entrance. "Let's go. Hopefully, we didn't"—she glanced at me and her gaze dropped—"ruin everything."

The four of us made our way in. Inside the blown door, I picked up Jayce's shoes, but she refused my help to put them on. Her limp was pronounced, but I knew better than to say anything about it. Too much pride in that woman.

Once we reached the top floor, we detoured into the office area and took the elevator down to Mosaic's main floor. The scene we returned to was a far cry from the one we'd left. One of the auction tables lay on its side, as did several of the chairs. The band had left, replaced by recorded classical music.

Half the guests were gone, the other half likely sticking around to find out what else the Tremaines had in store. Or to watch them fall. Or to figure out what sort of leverage the night's events might grant them.

Rav helped Jayce to a tall stool at the bar. "Marc and I will take Wyatt to the police and return the chip to Gideon. Scarlett and Emmett are with him now, but will be here soon."

I grabbed a bowl of nuts and a platter of treats for her. Placing them on the bar, I slid onto the stool next to her. "I completely missed that Wyatt was behind it."

Jayce scoffed, staring out the tall windows to the west, where the fountain lights were on full display. There wouldn't be as many spectators as earlier, but the automated show didn't care. "Guess I'm not the only screwup."

"You didn't screw up." I leaned on the bar, trying to get in her line of sight. "You climbed a fucking building. It was amazing."

"After you told me not to." She let out a rueful laugh, avoiding my gaze. "Not like I accomplished anything, anyway. He was waiting for a helicopter that never came. If I'd found a way through one of the other buildings in the complex. If I'd waited..."

"If you'd waited, he probably would have opened fire on us the second we walked out." I reached for her, to run my fingers down her arm, but she pulled away.

I'd almost lost her on the roof.

My emotional locker strained at its hinges, my heart leaping up toward my throat. The *whole world* had almost lost her. "You saved at least one of our lives."

"You should check in with Craig."

"I will." That's what I should have been doing. But the thought of leaving her alone? The memories of Wyatt's gun to her head? Of her lying limp on the ground? I needed to be near her. I needed to be sure she was all right.

What the fuck was wrong with me?

"Jayce?" Scarlett rounded a wide pillar that separated the bar from the main dining area.

Jayce straightened. "Yeah, boss?"

"Do you have your knee brace at the hotel?"

"I do."

Scarlett stopped in front of us, Emmett at her side. "You head back and pick it up. Give the knee at least a half hour with ice before you come back."

"I'm fine." Jayce slid off the stool, a faint grimace creasing her face as she landed. "What's the status on Noah?"

"Brie's trying to track him." Scarlett cocked an eyebrow. "And Rav says you're not fine."

Jayce folded her arms. "Rav was hit on the head. He doesn't know what he's talking about."

Emmett scratched his short beard. "Can you take her, Drew?"

"No." Jayce's voice wasn't as firm as the previous times she'd declined being anywhere near me. She wasn't hesitating—she was swallowing back pain.

"Yes." Scarlett waved a hand over her shoulder. "Rav's dealing with the police, Malcolm's interviewing guests to find out if anyone saw Noah, Emmett's going to join him in a few minutes, and I'm busy coordinating. We all have responsibilities here, but the chip is safely in Gideon's hands, so the Bishop team's job is finished. Drew isn't needed here anymore."

Jayce's lips quivered and she blinked several times. She mouthed *Fine*, but no sound came out.

I sighed deep inside. I wanted to hold her and tell her it was all right. Tell her what an amazing job she'd done over and over until she finally listened. "I'll run upstairs and touch base with Craig, then we can go."

"He's in the banquet room," said Scarlett. "Once we advised him Wyatt had been caught, he told security to secure all exits other than via the patio doors, then packed up his things."

"And Zaria?"

"Craig sent her home." Scarlett turned to Emmett. "We should get back to business."

He nodded and the Reynolds siblings left.

"You said you needed food." I held the bowl of nuts out for Jayce. "But you didn't eat anything."

"I'm not hungry." She took an unsteady step away from the bar and paused, staring at the floor. As much as she needed my help, she wouldn't ask.

Where did that leave me? Offer my help and she'd decline. Grab her and she'd complain. Stand around like a lost puppy dog and neither of us would get what we needed.

"Here's what's going to happen, Jayce." I left the food on the counter and stepped next to her. "I'm going to help you to the car."

She frowned but didn't say no this time.

"If someone comments on it, you can say it's under duress." I wrapped an arm around her waist, and she placed hers around my back. "And then I swear we'll never talk about it again."

CHAPTER 36
JAYCE

Damn straight, we'd never talk about him helping me to the car.

Because tonight was the last time we'd ever speak to each other.

I'd failed. Not only had I failed completely, but I did it in front of the man who predicted it would happen. Drew hadn't wanted to let me out of his sight, for fear I'd screw up tonight's op. And that's exactly what I did.

I was *such* a screwup, even the ultra-controlled, knew-every-one-in-town, leggy-blonde-dating former CIA agent couldn't save us from me.

Even Scarlett didn't want me here.

I'd passed out from some combination of Wyatt choking me and the pain in my leg. *You're so weak, Jayce.* What was I going to do now? Tuck my tail between my legs, go back to my hotel room as I'd been told, and order five rounds of room service.

But I sure as hell wouldn't do any of it with Drew Donovan there.

"You're like Wolverine," he said.

"What?"

"Your leg. You're already doing much better."

That was ego, not rapid healing.

"How's your head?"

"Fine."

"We should get you checked out by the paramedics."

"I've lived with this for ten years. It needs ice and a brace."

"I meant your head." His stupid, sexy jaw clenched again. It was baffling how he had any teeth left with how tight his jaw always was.

"Is that a crack about me being thick-skulled?"

He huffed out a breath. "It's a crack about the fact you were unconscious a half hour ago. Head injuries can be serious."

"It wasn't a head injury." I didn't want to say it out loud, but it was the only way he'd drop it. "I passed out."

"So why didn't you eat anything?"

This conversation wasn't going anywhere. I didn't respond and he didn't press. Instead, we continued through the main doors into the banquet room in silence.

A mob gathered around the doors, with Emmett and Malcolm stationed at each one alongside police officers, collecting information before partygoers could leave. Fifty or so people milled about the room, nibbling on food, admiring the artwork, and drifting in and out of the main dining room. How many had run before my team got the situation under control?

Had Noah escaped in the flood of people? Had the blown door and gunshots been part of his egress plan?

Drew veered us toward Digital Twilight—the dragonfly's head conveniently back in place—where Craig was deep in conversation with Liana. "I need to check in."

My gut flip-flopped. I was the subject matter expert, and Wyatt had snatched the dragonfly's head out from under me.

I didn't want to talk to Liana. That was someone else's job. "Leave me in a chair by the wall."

"We'll only be a second." Drew's grip on my waist tightened.

Craig lifted his chin to Drew as we approached, inviting us into the conversation.

Liana's gaze landed on me. *Shit.* Her eyes widened, and she rushed forward. "What happened to you?"

"Nothing. I—"

Drew squeezed my waist. "She caught Wyatt."

"Oh my! Did he..." Liana fanned herself like she was about to pass out or to ward off tears. "Did he hurt you?"

Mr. Clenched Jaw next to me blew out a sharp breath through his flared nostrils. What was all that?

"Nah." I waved a hand to dismiss her question, not wanting Drew to launch into an explanation of my epic failure. "It's an old injury. I need some ice."

Liana looked heavenward, placing her hands over her heart. "Thank you for everything you did."

"No problem." I pointed at Digital Twilight. "Looks like it was an easy repair? Wyatt said something about a linchpin?"

"That was the part I was going to melt, so it..." Liana tilted her head. "How did he know about that?"

I didn't have the answer, but I'd be sure to pass the questions over to Scarlett. Maybe that information would hold some clue about Noah's involvement.

Drew glanced around. "Where's Gideon?"

"There was a small stampede when everything happened up top and a few people on the patio were hurt," said Craig. "Gideon's gone to the hospital to check on them."

"Part of the crisis campaign?"

Craig nodded. "I'm going to stay here and help Scarlett co-ordinate the search for Wyatt's co-conspirators."

"Do you need a hand? I could..." Drew paused, looking down at me. "I'm driving Jayce to the hotel for some supplies."

"Let me think about it," said Craig. "I may send you to the hospital with Gideon to monitor things."

"I'll call when we're done."

"I lost my earpiece upstairs," I said, "so I'm out of touch. Brie couldn't get your comms or cameras up?"

"She's a smart one. Got the British fellow involved, too. But, no luck."

Drew took the earpiece out of his ear. "Byron may be able to figure it out when he gets back."

Craig accepted the offered tech. "Piss poor time for him to be on vacation."

If this was an important job, why hadn't they recalled their tech guy? If Reynolds took on an op they needed me for, it didn't matter what was going on—Evelyn expected me to be there. I'd have to mention that to Scarlett. Although she probably knew already.

"Do you know who I am?" snapped a man behind us. "Take your hands off me."

One of the security staff gestured for a middle-aged man to take his spot in the lineup to leave. "Sir, if you'd—"

The man backed away, yanking his arm so the guard couldn't touch it.

A woman next to him sidestepped to avoid them both and stumbled closer to the stand with the golden bird. She flailed, one high heel buckling underneath her.

I flew out of Drew's grasp, pain streaking up my leg.

She collided with the stand, and it tipped. The bird rocked to the side.

Why the hell wasn't it secure?

My leg wouldn't sustain me, so I dove.

The woman landed on the floor as the security guard caught the bird's stand.

You should have caught the bird, Mr. Useless.

I slammed into the ground and twisted, bracing myself to catch the small statue. It was over fifty pounds. This was going to hurt.

At least I'd succeed at something.

But it landed in my hands with a muted clink instead of a thud. I was once again the center of attention. If I'd had my earpiece in, I would have been talking to my team already. Instead, all I had nearby was Drew. "Drew?"

People surrounded me, no doubt wondering who the crazy woman tumbling through the banquet room was. The rips and blood on my dress were a sight to behold. Other than the woman who'd knocked over the statue, who was nervously checking to ensure I was all right, the crowd seemed more interested in me for the entertainment.

Drew crouched next to me, hands out as he surveyed me from head to toe. "You're—"

"Yeah, yeah," I said. "I'm reckless, and I need a leash."

His head drew back sharply.

Yeah, I know all about your little report on me, Drew. "This isn't the real huma bird statue."

His eyes practically bugged out of his head.

I tossed it at him with one hand.

Drew reacted as I had, bracing for a heavy weight and almost falling over when the light bird landed in his hands. "It's a fake."

"Yup." I let out a slow breath and hung my head. Four VIP items on display. Digital Twilight had a piece yanked off it. The scarab was a stolen item. Now the huma bird was a fake. What was the mirror's story?

Drew hooked a finger in Craig's direction as he stood. He offered me a hand, but I refused.

I could stand on my own, even with only one functional leg.

When Craig joined us, Drew handed over the statue and said, "It's supposed to be over fifty pounds of solid gold."

The security guy in the black suit who'd accosted me for taking photos barged into our group. "If you're not allowed to take photos, you're not allowed"—he swiped the bird from Craig—"to touch the artifacts."

I cocked an eyebrow at the rude thug. No wonder Scarlett did it so often. It felt liberating.

The man looked at Liana as she stepped into our circle.

"We're dealing with more than the chip, Liana." Drew slid his arm around my waist again, holding tight enough I could use him for balance. "This is a fake. Do you have anyone who can verify the genuine gold statue was here at the start of the event?"

"The men who delivered it are here somewhere." She snapped her fingers over her shoulder, and a dark-skinned woman appeared at her side with a cell phone. Liana dialed a number and wandered off, with her assistant and the man holding the statue behind her.

"I don't like this." Craig stared after them.

No kidding.

"The crisis plan will need significant revisions." Craig looked me up and down, then turned to Drew. "Call me when you're ready. It'll be a long night."

"I will."

Craig nodded and left, following Liana.

Drew's thumb rubbed small circles on my side, coaxing the army of ants into their skittering march over my skin. "Do you think it's related to the chip?"

The chip? What about the scarab? Did Scarlett want its murky provenance kept quiet? Did she already tell Gideon or Liana one of their pieces had been stolen from a museum? I needed my earpiece. Needed to be in touch with my team. I didn't know the plan, and I wasn't as clever as Scarlett.

Just like Drew wrote in his report.

"I need to tell Scarlett about this." *Well done, Jayce. Prove to him you don't know what you're doing.* "She'll get Brie searching through footage if she can. Maybe someone..."

"Someone what?"

I blinked up at him. "What if someone replaced the bird while everything was going on? When the lights were out?"

"That would be quite the coincidence."

"Or that was Noah's plan all along." Would Fenix steal it for the gold? And if they did, did that tie in to the scarab? "Or it's another element of chaos."

I took my phone out of my clutch and called Scarlett, updating her on my theories. Not that there was much point. One, Craig had contacted her before I did. Two, he'd told her that Liana confirmed the heavy bird was there at the start of the evening.

And three, the team at HQ was already on it.

They didn't need me.

CHAPTER 37

DREW

The longer Jayce talked to Scarlett, the more her shoulders fell and the more she leaned on me for support. Part of me wanted to solve the mystery of the fake bird, but I shoved that into the emotional locker.

What I couldn't shove in there anymore was her. From the moment she woke up on the roof, she'd been collapsing further and further in on herself. Something happened up there, and it was destroying her.

Once she hung up, I said, "We should get you to the hotel. The sooner we take care of that knee, the better."

"Thought you said I was like Wolverine?" She stuffed the phone into her clutch and placed her hand on my upper back.

I began the slow and steady walk to the patio doors. It would cause an uproar from those wanting to leave, but Emmett and Malcolm would let us through. "Then you tore off and leaped at an ancient Persian statue."

She shrugged.

Dozens of eyes followed us as I excused our way through the crowd. Some smiled at me, some frowned when we passed them, and even more gave Jayce blatant once-overs. Too many people were judging her for the condition of her dress and her messed hair.

"Good thing you caught that thief." I didn't have the details from Craig about his crisis plan. Maybe he wanted to conceal the theft, maybe he wanted to play it up. Either way, I kept my words loud enough that everyone around us heard. "You single-handedly saved Gideon's data chip."

Jayce rolled her eyes, saying nothing.

"Not to mention the golden statue."

Still nothing.

At the door, a police officer waved us through with Emmett's blessing and we walked silently down the patio tiers, through the arch to the waterfront, then turned up the roadway.

The chatterbox remained eerily silent.

"Do you want me to take you to a drive-through on the way?" Maybe a greasy burger would improve her mood.

We stopped at an intersection across the street from the parking garage, and Jayce pulled out her phone.

"Or I can make you something?" I was grasping at straws now—making her a snack or a meal would require picking up groceries on the way to the hotel or taking her to my place. But food was the only thing we had in common.

"Save it, Downie." The light turned for us to cross, but she stayed in place. "I've got a ride coming. You can go help Craig."

"I'm busy helping you."

"I'm a distraction, just like you said." She unwound her arm from my back and took a half-step away from me. "A reckless distraction who can't follow a plan and who ruins everything she touches."

"That recklessness saved—"

She put up a hand, hobbling another step away from me. "That's all I needed to hear. Leave me alone."

I closed the distance between us. "Jayce, let me take you to the hotel."

She pushed me away. "You said you'd never force yourself on a woman."

My stomach twisted. This was about a drive. About helping her walk. I was ensuring she took care of her knee instead of pushing through the pain and injuring it more.

"Leave me alone." A car pulled up. She checked her phone and opened the door. "The chip is safe. I don't need your leash anymore."

Was that all I was to her? Someone holding her back? Had I misread everything?

She got in and slammed the door.

The car sped off, leaving me to my thoughts. Voices, police lights reflecting off the buildings, the breeze on my face—the rest of the world pressed in around me.

The parking garage stood across the street from me. Option one, go home. Crack open a bottle of wine and start my report on what had gone right and wrong tonight.

Option two, drive to the office and use the key Wyatt had given me to discover what he'd hidden in his safe. The answers might be inside. *No, that should wait for the police so they have a secure chain of evidence.*

Option three? I turned in the direction I'd come from. Go back and make myself useful.

The last option won easily, but only because option four—follow Jayce to her hotel, despite her protests—wasn't an option at all.

My dress shoes clacked against the cobbled sidewalk, carrying over the hum of activity down the block. *Focus on this evening, Drew. What happened? Focus on more than just this evening. What was really going on?*

On our way down from the roof, Jayce had told Rav about Wyatt's confession he'd made enemies, intimating those enemies were involved. Wyatt had laughed at that—as had I, deep inside. Of course, we'd made enemies. There were only so many people you could ask to betray everything they believed before someone figured you out.

Was Noah one of those enemies? I'd have to ask Scarlett about his role with the Fenix organization Jayce had told me about. This would have been easier if Jayce were still here.

Or not, since she didn't want to talk to me.

I should have put Thursday behind us instead of pressing the matter.

Focus.

What if Brie was mistaken about Noah? What if it was simply someone who looked like him? What if he'd been there for the bird while Wyatt went after the chip? Was the chip theft only a distraction, so security would have their eye on Digital Twilight, ignoring the other items?

What if neither theft was tied to the threats about the chip? What if they were about Liana's reputation and not Gideon's?

I passed under the giant metal sculpture at the end of Mosaic's patio and under a decorative street lamp adorned with bright pink flowers—like Jayce's dress—and stopped at a short railing at the river's edge. It led down some stairs to a narrow dock, where a few of the night's attendees may have parked their boats.

Moonlight glinted off the slow-moving river. I inhaled, pulling in the subtle earthy scent the river was giving off tonight. Better than the stink of diesel when the boats started up.

One more deception. Being by the water normally calmed me, but up close, it was a far cry from my dreams. I should have moved closer to the ocean instead of staying in DC after I left the CIA.

Or bought a boat and sailed the world.

All alone. No one hiding things or lying to me. Just me against Mother Nature.

"Hey there, handsome," came a low purr.

"Vanessa," I sighed. Of all the people to interrupt my wallowing. "I'm not in the mood."

"Too bad." She leaned back on the railing, running a hand up my arm. "I wanted to check in on you. Vijay said you were too busy to talk?"

Vijay? With all the chaos, I'd completely forgotten about his strange job offer.

"You know, I've always thought you should have been your own boss." She stared off toward the buildings, her gaze unfocused. "Think about it—traveling the world as a crisis manager. Taking on the jobs you want, instead of having to play second fiddle to Craig."

It was a dream we'd talked about more than once. Something I could do from that boat. Anchor in the Caribbean, the

Mediterranean, the South Pacific—and do my thing. There was never any shortage of people getting themselves in trouble and needing help to get out.

How long could that last, though? How many liars and charlatans could I work for before calling it quits? At least working for Craig meant the ethical decisions were his, not mine. I could go home at the end of the day and say I'd just been doing my job.

How many of history's monsters did exactly that?

Was I better than any of them?

"It's not a limited-time offer." She folded one arm, highlighting her cleavage, and ran the other hand over her shoulder. "If you reconsider, make sure you get in touch with him."

"Why?"

She fluttered her eyelashes at me. Not in the way she had in my apartment Thursday morning, but in the way she did when professing her faux-innocence.

"We're not together anymore, Vanessa. Why would you set that up for me?" There had to be an ulterior motive. She always had one.

She shrugged, her gaze roaming over my face. "I've been offered a job in Italy and I'm thinking of taking it."

I straightened. "Italy?"

"A headhunter found me."

"You work online. Why would you move to Europe?"

She smiled, the type of smile I hadn't seen from her in years. A genuine one. "I need a change of scenery. Believe it or not, I'm sorry for what I did."

Sorry because she missed our apartment or my paycheck or my connections, sure. Maybe she was sorry she didn't have me in her bed. But sorry because she'd magically transformed into a good person and regretted what she'd done?

"Amazing cuisine there." She moved closer, so her hip rested against my hand on the railing. "The job's near Naples. I could have a little garden and grow tomatoes and herbs. Maybe grapes. Although I'd need a good cook to make it worthwhile."

"Should be able to find a nice Italian chef to share the kitchen."

"You love Italian food." Her hand crept up my arm again. "Think about the amazing markets you could visit and all the fresh ingredients."

I stared out at the water again, the gentle waves lifting the boats moored next to us.

The job offer, the fake apology, tempting me with Italy—all another poorly executed manipulation.

I'd been in Italy when I found out about my parents' accident. Stuck in Leonardo da Vinci airport for a four-hour layover on my way home from Istanbul, while my world crumbled around me. Vanessa had gotten me home two hours early, but my parents were already gone.

She'd helped me get through the revelation in their wills that they'd adopted me, through my decision to leave the Agency, and through Alex's death.

Two and a half years ago, Vanessa had been my rock.

Now she was an anchor around my neck and Italy was the last place I wanted to see again.

"Where's Jayce?" came a sharp male voice behind me.

I looked over my shoulder.

Emmett stood there with the same threatening expression he had last night at di Sano's. "You can't have gone to the hotel and back already." His words were an accusation, not a question.

Vanessa snaked her arm around mine. "Who's Jayce, honey-bear?"

He scoffed. "This explains so much."

For fuck's sake.

"You remember that mood I said I wasn't in?" I unwound myself from Vanessa's grip. "Craig needs me inside."

"Oh no, you don't." Emmett put a hand out to stop me from leaving, clear we were about to have words.

I flicked my gaze from Vanessa to the restaurant, and she surprisingly took the hint, rather than lingering to hear all the gossip. "Aren't you supposed to be working the door?"

Emmett's eyes narrowed as he crossed his arms. "What sick game are you playing, Donovan?"

"Why don't you clue me in on what game you're referring to, then I'll explain the rules to you."

"Jayce. You were supposed to take her to the hotel."

"She opted for an alternate plan." I gripped the railing's top bar. *Opted* was a gentle word for it.

"And then that harpy?" He jerked his head in the direction Vanessa had left.

"My ex."

"Did you tell her that?"

"Yes, when I threw her out six months ago."

Emmett's eyes fluttered closed as he took a slow breath. "I meant Jayce. Does Jayce know your ex was the one harassing her earlier?"

My fingers tightened around the railing. Vanessa had spoken to Jayce while I was getting my equipment from Craig and claimed we'd slept together this past week. Jayce had gone from cool to cold after that. The same as after she'd been alone with Wyatt on the roof.

"The CIA should demand their money back."

I let go of the rail and dragged my fingers through my hair. I'd started the evening hoping to turn things around with Jayce. They'd progressively devolved all evening, with both our relationship and our job turning into utter flops. Add on my ex and an angry Reynolds sibling who couldn't be bothered to make any sense? This was the worst night I'd had in some time.

"Drew, I've watched you play your little connection games with everyone around you. Look into their eyes, touch an arm, ask questions. You make people feel special, feel like they can trust you. But with her?"

With Jayce? I'd tried everything. Making her dinner, kissing her, telling her I wanted her. Offering to help, carrying her when she was hurt, telling her she was beautiful.

Fuck, the battle of wills in Gideon's office on Monday had been the greatest thrill I'd felt in months. Probably since the last time I'd seen her. She'd risen to the occasion, not acted like a wilting flower.

"With her..." He clenched a fist. "You make her feel small."

"You don't know what you're talking about."

"Tell me the truth: What do you want in a woman?"

I'd asked Jayce almost the same thing. The first time, it *was* about sex. The second time? I'd hidden it behind a question about a dance partner. "You and I are associates, not friends, Emmett. I don't discuss this sort of thing with associates."

"Do you have any friends, Drew? Anyone who could point out what a dumbass you're being right now?"

Didn't need friends for that. I'd been doing a damn fine job all on my own.

"She'll kill me if she finds out I told you this, but since you don't seem capable of figuring anything out on your own, let me paint you a picture." His body loosened, as though he were no longer considering punching me. "She likes you so much it terrifies her."

My heart took a tremendous leap up into my throat. "Then why wouldn't she let me take her back to the hotel?" Why had she run away from me on Thursday?

"Because you're as bad as she is." He leaned on the railing, mirroring my earlier frustration. "After your little escapade at Gideon's and then how much food you made when Scarlett and I came over, I was sure something was going on between you and Jayce. So when she initially refused to go to your place the other night, I had Scarlett insist. I thought you'd treat her well. She told me about the food and wine, but she also told me all you wanted was a roll in the hay."

"I didn't—"

"It broke her heart, so I split the two of you up." He shook his head. "And if that weren't enough to piss my sister off, I saw how you reacted to her and Wyatt at the restaurant, and I knew you were being a stubborn idiot, so I let you change the teams again."

My head spun. With all the angles to the mission, Emmett had been orchestrating a backup play that had nothing to do with the chip? And I'd missed all of it?

"You and Jayce need to get your collective heads out of your asses and do something about this. I'm tired of being the only one with any clue what's going on."

I'd thought I knew what was going on. But maybe I didn't.

"Now, since you haven't stormed off and you're still here listening, I expect your feelings for her are stronger than your ego."

They were. Holy shit, they were.

"But I swear upon everything I hold dear, if you go anywhere near her, thinking you can use any of this info for a quick lay, I'm going to tell Rav how you treated her." Emmett pushed off the railing. "You do not want to see what happens after that."

The threat barely registered. Was there a chance fear was the only thing keeping us apart? "What's she afraid of?"

"I'm sure you did your research on us before we worked together for the first time. Which means you know Jayce grew up without a father, and that her mother was her choreographer and her whole world. You also know after her accident that her mother started working with her sister exclusively."

I nodded. This information was easily available for someone who'd been as well-known as she was.

"You may not know she was seeing the boy she got into the accident with. And no one let her see him after that." Emmett sighed. "I shouldn't be telling you any of this, but she went from non-relationship to non-relationship after that, trying to find somewhere to belong. All she wants is to be of use."

Jayce was an integral part of her team. She caught Wyatt. Why would any of this relate to her not feeling useful?

"What she fears most is what happens when people don't *need* her anymore."

Insisting she was fine after I found her unconscious on the rooftop. Refusing my help. Being sent home with the injured leg.

My heart sank. "She thought I'd only wanted her for one night."

Emmett pointed at me. "And that she'd be useless to you after that."

I looked down the block to the intersection where Jayce had left me. I could go after her. Barge into her hotel room and tell her everything. But what *was* everything? What was it about her that had my body on full alert?

"Don't make me regret telling you all that." Emmett smacked my shoulder and walked back to the Mosaic patio. Back to work with his team.

That's what I should have been doing. I should have gone in to help Craig track down Wyatt's co-conspirators. Figured out what had happened with the golden huma bird statue. Maybe gone to the hospital, like he'd suggested.

Instead, I made my way to the parking garage.

I was going to find Jayce and figure out what *everything* was.

Chapter 38
Jayce

I launched the logic puzzle book against the wall, the pencil clattering as it ricocheted across the corner and bounced onto the table. My brain wasn't into it. The stupid puzzles always helped me come down from the performance high.

Why wasn't it working tonight?

Next up, I curled my toes into the carpet. *Deep breath*. Relax the toes. *Deep breath*. Curl. *Deep fucking—*

My knee buckled under me, and I quickly shifted my weight to the right.

Why would I think anything could make me feel better? Scarlett had thrown me out. What use was a thief who couldn't walk? There was no sneaking with a limp, let alone with the knee brace hampering my flexibility.

No climbing buildings while wearing that damn thing.

It sat on the bed, taunting me.

I'd gotten it out of my bag, but there was no way I was putting it on. I could walk the injury off. A little ice, some ibuprofen, and I'd be good as new.

Eventually.

Wyatt's revelations about Drew spun in my brain. I was only concerned with my stomach. I was reckless. He was afraid I'd ruin everything. Wanted me on a short leash.

Someone knocked on the door.

It wasn't room service—they'd already dropped off both my orders, which I hadn't touched. The late-night waffles had seemed like a good idea, then the even-later-night pizza should have hit the spot. But other than the complimentary bottle of water, my stomach had refused everything.

When Drew and I had sparred in Gideon's office bathroom, I *had* been flirting with him, no matter what I said to Emmett after. It was stupid and foolish. I'd thought he was flirting back, but I was only a job.

A liability to be managed.

The knock came again. They'd leave if I ignored them long enough. It was past the hour anyone should come to my room unless I was expecting them.

"Jayce?" The sound of Drew's voice twisted a knot in my gut. What did he want? Had Scarlett sent him to summon me?

"Go away," I snapped.

I wanted to open the door, punch him in the gut, and prove I wasn't the weak link on the team. But the second I saw his rich brown eyes and the jaw I knew he'd be clenching, I'd lose my nerve. I'd want him to wrap his arms around me so I could pretend I wasn't such an utter failure.

"We need to talk." His deep, gravelly voice lit up pathways in my brain I didn't want to be lit up.

"I'm busy icing my knee."

"And I'm not leaving until you let me in." The light shifted in the small space under the door, followed by a gentle thud. What was he doing?

I checked the peephole. The hallway was empty, except—wait—he was sitting on the floor, leaning against the door. "I told you to leave me alone, Drew."

"Yeah, I tried that."

I kept my face plastered against the door, waiting for him to go. Was he really going to stay there until I let him in?

A couple of women in ultra-short dresses wandered along the hallway, growing silent as they got closer. They slowed and one of them said, "Locked out of your room?"

He waved, acting as though this was a normal Saturday night for him. "Just having a small fight with the girlfriend."

I hollered through the door, "I'm not his girlfriend!"

"Okay, maybe a big fight," he chuckled.

The women stopped and looked at the door. "Have you called the police?"

Drew put both of his hands up. "It's just a disagreement. I said some stupid things to her and am trying to apologize."

The woman in the longer dress smiled at Drew, but the one in the shorter said, "Do you need us to call the cops? Wait until they arrive?"

"No need for that." Drew shot up from his spot on the floor, and the smiling woman stepped back.

The other dug into her purse. Was she going for pepper spray or a gun? *You have to rescue him, Jayce.* I groaned inwardly.

I swung the door open, and Drew stumbled back a half step. "Come in before you get yourself in trouble."

"Thanks, sweetheart."

"Shut up." I forced as much of a smile as I could for my would-be saviors. "Thanks for that, but he's not dangerous."

Except to my heart.

And my brain.

And my ego.

The women nodded and continued down the hallway as I closed the door.

"What do you want, Down-avon?"

He stood in the middle of my hotel room, with his bow tie hanging loose and the top buttons of his shirt undone. His gaze flitted around the room. "You said you were icing your knee."

"Yeah."

"Where's the ice?"

"It melted." I folded my arms. "I need to get more."

"You're not a very good liar, you know that?"

I rolled my eyes. He was right, but no way was I admitting that. "You said we need to talk?"

"Wyatt fooled all of us."

"Seriously? You came all this way to tell me that?"

He shrugged. Shrugged!

I reached for the door handle. "If that's all you've got, you can leave."

Drew lunged forward, his hand landing on top of mine as he pushed the door closed. "You can't take it personally."

"Well, duh." It wasn't as though I was obsessing over how royally I'd screwed up. Or was trying to drown my sorrows in food. Or was foolishly pacing back and forth with an injured leg, while doing logic puzzles, because that usually centered me. "I don't take anything personally."

He took in a breath and held it, gaze raking down my tattered and dirty dress. "Why haven't you gotten changed yet?"

I wrestled my hand out from underneath his—immediately missing the connection—and forced myself to walk normally to the middle of the room. As normally as I could without giving away the truth about my leg. "Because as soon as my leg's ready to go, I'm heading back to Mosaic. My team needs me."

"You can't take it all on your shoulders."

I spun to face him, pain ripping through my knee and up my thigh. I should have put the brace on. "I'm not."

"Your team can make do, just like mine can."

"You heard Scarlett—your job's done. The chip is safe in Liana's hands, and we spoiled Wyatt's theft."

"*You* spoiled it." He finally let go of the door and took a few steps toward me.

"You should be celebrating your big success with Miss Blonds-A-Lot." I sidestepped as he moved closer. "You shouldn't be here."

"You're upset."

"I'm irritated." I bumped into the wall.

He stopped a foot away from me. "Why can't you tell me the truth?"

On a regular day, there were fifty-three different ways I could escape Drew's reach. But tonight? With my leg protesting every time I put too much weight on it? Not a chance. "What do you care? I'm the weak link, right? The reckless thief who can't be trusted and needs to be kept on a short leash?"

His shoulders sagged and his eyelids eased closed.

"Yeah, Wyatt told me what you wrote in your report." I shoved him, which didn't move him an inch. My throat grew tight as a ridiculous prickling started behind my eyes. *No tears, Jayce. You're not weak. Only babies cry.* "You wouldn't let me partner with him because I'd ruin everything."

Drew braced a hand on the wall by my head. "That's not true."

"Not as pretty or clever as Scarlett? Remember that part?" Instead of pushing him again, I hit his chest. That stupid, broad, muscular chest I knew was covered with a light smattering of hair. Two nights ago, my lips had touched his skin there. Tears gathered against my lower lids. I tried blinking them away, but that pushed them over the edge and down my cheeks.

"He's a trained liar, Jayce."

"Just like you." I ran my hand across my eyes, clearing the tears. When things went wrong, I found the reason and corrected it. Ensured it never happened again. That's what I had to do with these feelings for Drew. Figure out why they were screwing with my head and put an end to it. And above all, stop crying.

"Yes, but..." He raised his free hand, slowly, until it was brushing my hair over my ear. "I didn't say those things."

"Say, write, same difference."

"No." His fingers dragged across my cheek, then along my jaw. He cupped my face with both hands, forcing me to look at him. "Yes, I wrote that you're reckless because you are."

My stomach churned and part of my brain wanted to run. But more of it wanted to stay and pretend I mattered to him.

To anyone.

"But the rest of it?" He shook his head, not breaking eye contact. "I also wrote about how independent you are. How you're aggressive, inventive, and you'd go to any lengths to help your team."

Those almost sounded like praise. And the opposite of what Wyatt said.

"You're a quick thinker, brave…" His gaze roamed over my face. "But something holds you back and I couldn't figure out what."

"Nothing holds me back." I wrapped a fist in his shirt.

"Wyatt figured it out." He stroked my cheeks with his thumbs. "You have doubts about your place on the Reynolds team and he used that."

I sniffled. "That's not true."

"You've always had doubts about where you belong, haven't you?"

My throat tightened. We weren't going to hash this out. We weren't going to talk about my mother, my sister, or the men that littered my life after that. Let alone about how most of the Reynolds elite team had grown up together and I was an interloper who needed to work extra hard to fit in.

There was no hugging things out to make the pain magically go away. That was for the movies, not real life.

"You didn't grow up with the support you needed." Drew stepped closer and touched his lips to my forehead. "I know how it feels."

"You know nothing about the real me."

"So tell me." He leaned in so close his hot breath warmed my cheeks. "Who's the real Jayce Monroe?"

The real me? "There's no real me. That's the catch. I'm a tool. People use tools to fix the things that matter most."

"And when you break?"

I took in a shuddering breath. *Kick him out. You don't have to talk about this.* But if I told him, maybe he'd leave me alone. "You don't fix your tool when it breaks. You get a new one."

Drew nodded, running his hands down to my shoulders. "What do you want, Jayce? I keep asking and you keep avoiding the question."

"I want someone to want me." My mother had only wanted my spotlight and when I couldn't give it to her anymore, she took my sister's. All those men I stole for only wanted my skills. Even Scarlett only wanted me on the team so long as I could perform, and when I couldn't, she sent me to my hotel. The tears came for real now. "Not someone who wants what I can get for them. Just me."

Tanner had been my one chance, and I'd thrown it all away because my mother insisted I focus on training.

"*I* want you," whispered Drew.

"No, you don't." My whole body shook in his grasp. "You want an orgasm and I'm conveniently in the same room. It's not the same thing."

I covered my face with my hands, so he couldn't see my pathetic face or the tears that proved what a failure I was.

No one wanted *me*.

CHAPTER 39
DREW

The CIA had drilled the arts of influence and manipulation into me. *Break down a person's public walls, then find a way into the most intimate recesses of their soul.* I could take anything from someone once they'd revealed that part of themselves.

Take her secrets. Take her truths. Like a drug.

But in that moment, I didn't want to take anything.

I wanted to give.

Despite every time Jayce irritated the shit out of me, all I wanted was for her to see herself the way everyone else did. I wanted Emmett's confessions to make a difference.

"If an orgasm were all I wanted, I'd be with Vanessa right now. But I'm not." I eased an arm around her shoulders. Slow movements, everything designed to help her feel better. I dropped the timbre of my voice. "You told me to leave you alone and I tried, but I had to come after you. All the activity and glory, not to mention my job and my ex, are all at Mosaic. Instead, I'm here. Where I want to be."

She stepped into my arms, still covering her face, burying herself against my chest. When I wrapped my other arm around her, she slid hers around my back, under my jacket. She balled her fists in my shirt so tightly she could have ripped the fabric.

How did this feel so right? How did it feel like she belonged there?

The woman was sobbing her heart out, but all I could feel was rightness.

Regardless of what she thought, I was there for her.

"Let it all out. You're safe here." I kissed the top of her head, inhaling the subtle fragrance of vanilla. Not sure why I breathed it in, but I did.

She took in a shuddering breath, holding onto me like I was her lifeline. "Why?"

"You deserve someone to take care of you."

Her mother had all but abandoned her. Her father was nowhere to be found.

My parents had lied, but at least they'd been there for me. They'd loved me. Fuck, they'd *chosen* me and then hid it so I wouldn't question my belonging. Was their lie really so bad? Or were my memories of them just tangled up in all the other shit I'd dealt with? Maybe I had to focus on the good years, instead of carrying so much resentment around.

"I can take care of myself, Drew."

"You've been hurt." I combed my fingers through her hair again, attempting to find something that would soothe her. "I don't know all the details, but I want to make it better."

"Why do you care? You hate me."

It was an arrow straight into my heart, causing some sort of darkness to form deep inside. But then everything finally clicked into place. All the confusion washed away.

She mattered.

Her opinion of me mattered.

No one's opinion was supposed to be important, so long as I got my work done.

I'd held back with Vanessa because I'd never fully trusted her. I knew she'd spill details on her website if I shared too much about a job with her.

But Jayce was the opposite of everything wrong in the world. She was honest, except when she was scared. She was a beacon of positivity, except when I said things that hurt her. Things that weren't true, but were my stupid way of protecting myself.

"Hate you?" I leaned back, pulling away one of her hands so she couldn't keep her tear-streaked face hidden from me.

"In your apartment, you said all you wanted was to get rid of me."

"Get you out of my system, not get rid of you." I sighed and pressed a kiss to her forehead. Something about this woman threw me off balance, and I kept pushing her away, trying to right myself. I couldn't read her like I could read almost everyone else on the planet. "Every time you're near me, it throws my whole world out of whack."

Her fists loosened but didn't release. "What do you mean?"

I didn't know what I meant. Words were my strength, but they were a messed-up jumble in my head. I ran my thumb under her eye to clear her tears and pressed my lips against her opposite temple.

"Why do you keep kissing me?"

I pulled back, taking in her pinched, confused face. "To make you feel better?"

"Or to take advantage of an upset woman?" Her tone sounded serious, but maybe it was the normal, taunting Jayce peeking through.

"I would never force a woman—"

"You want to make me feel better?" As she moistened her lips, she released the death grip on my shirt, her fingers beginning a descent down my back. "Then take advantage."

Thursday night, I'd nearly convinced myself I only wanted to blow off steam with her. But tonight? That wasn't what I wanted at all.

I shook my head.

Sadness clouded her eyes, tears welling against her lids. Rejection was as bad as failure for her.

"I'm not saying no to you, Jayce." There was no space for lies or omissions anymore. I craved her honesty. If I was going to have it, I'd have to pay with my own. "I want to see you naked, sprawled out on that bed. I want to taste every inch of you. Bury myself inside you until you scream."

Her chest heaved, and my cock reacted.

"If you tell me the only thing you want is for me to fuck you so hard you forget what happened tonight, I'll do that for you. I'll do things that make you forget your name." I swallowed, my brain steadily losing the fight to control my body. "And then I'll leave and never look back."

She nodded too quickly. "Get me out of your system. And I'll get you out of mine."

That wasn't the offer I wanted her to take me up on.

Wasn't the one I *needed* her to agree to.

"I want to make love to you, Jayce. Tell you how beautiful you are. Worship at your feet." I pulled her in tighter, my hardening cock pressed against her. "I'd rather spend all night showing you how screwed up I am over you and revel in every second."

That was the truth. I'd cracked open her most intimate side and ended up revealing my own secret.

I wanted her.

And for more than one night.

Her brows fell and she took in a breath like she was struggling to find words. The woman who chattered endlessly didn't know what to say. Her hands trembled at the small of my back.

This wasn't the response I was hoping for. But did it matter? Yes, it mattered. It mattered so much, that I waited, despite how the tightness in my stomach rapidly evolved into a sickly churn.

"You don't..." She blinked, her tears gathering again. "I don't understand."

Neither did I. "You don't need to. Just tell me what you want."

"So much," she whispered, squeezing her eyes shut and rolling her head forward onto my chest. "I swore off sex five years ago when I started working for Reynolds. I don't know if I can break that vow so easily."

"Of course you can."

"I mean..." She looked up at me, her big brown eyes softer than I'd thought possible from her. She was so fucking gorgeous just taking up space with me. Just being vulnerable for a moment. The seconds dragged on as her gaze flitted from my eyes to my lips, to the wall and the ceiling, and back. "Yes."

Yes, to which part? I paused for a beat but wasn't about to debate. I'd give her what I hoped she meant and if she asked for more, I'd give that to her, too.

Her eyes fluttered closed as I leaned in and brushed my lips across hers.

"Yes," she whispered again, threading one arm between us and up around my neck. "Tell me you want me."

"More than air." I ran my mouth up her cheek to her ear.

She pulled out the hem of my shirt, fingers dancing over the buttons. "Tell me I'm pretty."

Frenzied movements didn't belong. I wanted slow and steady, a dance of lips and tongues, hot breaths and soft sighs. I took her hand, slowing her down.

As her eyes searched mine, the intensity built between us. Shared energy charged the air and every nerve in my body felt like a live wire waiting for contact.

"Drew..." The pleading note in her voice shook me to my core.

"You're stunning. More than pretty. More than beautiful." I ran my hands down her sides, under her ass, and picked her up. How many hours had she consumed my thoughts since Monday? How many nights since the Harrington job had I lain awake thinking of her tongue against mine, wanting nothing more than to feel her body beneath me, to hear her moans in my ear?

She whimpered as she wrapped her legs around my hips, her left leg obviously causing her more pain than she'd admit. She dug her hands into my hair, scratching across my scalp, and pulled my face closer to kiss again. Her tongue delved into my mouth, as though she couldn't get enough.

I carried her, and her heels dug into my lower back. She ground against me, my cock begging for me to speed up.

Once she was on the bed, she shimmied out of her dress. Her lips parted as I watched, sending shivers down my spine. She was awe-inspiring, the way the fabric clung to every curve before sliding off to reveal the satin bra and panties beneath.

"Fuck," I breathed, tearing off my jacket and shirt. My gaze drifted along the puckered foot-long scar down the side of her left leg, to the scrapes on her hips, and the bruised skin along her sides. *I should have protected her from Wyatt.* My stomach clenched, but I pushed the guilt into my emotional locker. Guilt wasn't what we needed tonight.

Jayce hooked her thumbs under the sides of her underwear and paused. "Tell me this isn't a mistake."

Did she doubt everything I'd said earlier? Was it because I was the one saying it? Or because anyone had said it?

"This is the first smart decision I've made in a long time." I unbuttoned my pants, but left them on, teasing myself as much as her. "Now take those off because I've been craving you."

She took off her underwear and bra, heat flaring in her eyes.

"Now lie back, sweetheart. Let me take care of you."

"Okay." Her breath hitched as I crawled up her body, pressing kisses along her calves and her injured knee. Her skin tasted like sweat and the hint of sugar I'd imagined.

When my lips reached the top of her thighs, she sighed, and I couldn't hold back my groan. She was already wet—so goddamn ready for me. Her hips jerked forward as I pressed a kiss to her inner thigh. I kept going, dragging my tongue through her slit, up to her clit.

I burrowed my face between her legs and inhaled deeply, taking in the heady scent of her arousal. My tongue traced circles around her entrance and swirled around her clit, eliciting a noise so primal it vibrated through me. Her flavor was heaven, all sweet and salty and so fucking intoxicating.

"Oh god," she moaned, her eyes slipping shut as I plunged two fingers inside her and sucked on her clit.

I licked and teased, determined to make her come as quickly as possible. Once the first one was done, we could take our time. Her body twitched beneath me, hands gripping the sheets tightly as she gasped for breath.

I lapped eagerly at her nub and thrust my fingers in and out, curling them to find the softest spot inside. "Let go, sweetheart."

"Not yet," she groaned. "I want you inside me."

"You need to come first." I had to take away her doubts before she'd truly surrender.

Her fingers dug into my hair and pulled gently, urging me on. She grew louder, her whimpers and quiet cries echoing through the room and straight to my cock, which throbbed in anticipation of claiming her.

I slid one more finger inside her tight core and her walls clenched around them, as she pushed against me, trying to take more of me. I cupped one breast with my free hand, pinching the nipple between my fingers as I worked her clit with my thumb. She arched off the bed as her orgasm approached.

"That's it, sweetheart," I murmured against her. "Let go."

She did, her pussy convulsing around my fingers as she moaned, "Drew. Oh my god, Drew."

I waited for the quivering to subside before removing my fingers, and every one of her muscles went limp. "You're not going to run away now, are you?"

She dropped an arm across her eyes. "I don't think I could if I wanted to."

"Good." I pulled my wallet out of my pocket and fished out a condom. "Because we're not done."

CHAPTER 40
JAYCE

The pulsing in my left knee had all but vanished, replaced by the happy exhaustion of the first non-solo orgasm I'd had in five years. And it was a damn fine one. I peeked out from under the arm I'd rested over my eyes, greeted by the surprising reminder I was naked on a bed with Drew Donovan standing over me.

He was all hard muscle, fire burning in his gaze. "How's the leg?"

"Holding up." Even if it wasn't, I wouldn't have told him. If we only had one night together, I was going to make the most of it.

He flashed me a mischievous grin and tossed his wallet onto the television stand behind himself. "No closing your eyes this time."

"What?"

"I want you to watch my face while I'm inside you." With the condom wrapper between his fingers, he slowly unzipped his tuxedo pants, revealing more of his happy trail and a black waistband. "I want you to see what you do to me."

I'd never done anything like that. Sex was about simple need, not emotion. About soothing my body and calming my thoughts, not... gazing into someone's eyes? Who did that?

He eased his pants and boxer briefs down, his thick cock springing free.

Heat pooled in my core and stupid things flitted through my brain, like saying 'Wow' or launching up to grab him and hurry him up. I'd already climaxed once, so I should have been good. Calm. Relaxed.

There was no playing it cool.

"Wow," I breathed.

Yeah, zero cool.

"That was the other thing I missed in my report." He stepped out of his pants, stroking his cock with a very lucky hand. "You're honest to a fault."

I pushed up on my elbows. "It usually pisses people off."

"You're challenging." His gentle smile and quiet noise of amusement heightened the throbbing between my thighs. "I like it."

Could he have been telling the truth earlier? Could it be possible he was there for me, not *just* for the sex?

Drew knelt on the bed and it dipped under his weight. "I've been looking forward to this."

Looking forward? Since Thursday? Since Gideon's?

"Lie back." His gravelly voice sent a fresh wave of heat through my system. He ran a hand along my left leg, over the bad knee, and lifted it to spread me wide. "You sure you're up for this?"

"Just don't put your weight on the leg and I'll be fine."

"Better be more than fine." He positioned himself between my legs, rolling the condom on before leaning over my body. He propped himself up with one hand while the other ghosted over my abdomen, my breasts, and up my collarbone. When he reached my neck, he cupped the back of my head and guided me to meet his kiss. His forceful tongue, warm and needy, explored my mouth with the same enthusiasm as his fingers had danced inside me.

I wrapped my good leg around his hips, urging him forward, not wanting to break from his kiss to use words.

As his lips finally pulled away from mine, Drew pressed the head of his cock against me, teasing and taunting as he rubbed it across my folds. A low moan escaped my throat at the sensation, and I arched my back, begging him with my body.

He chuckled softly before pushing forward, sinking inside of me.

"Oh yeah," I groaned as he stretched my inner walls, filling me in one smooth motion.

His gaze locked onto mine, never breaking contact, exactly like he'd threatened. He settled his weight between my legs and began to move. Slowly. The steady rhythm made me want to scream with delight. His muscular arms flexed with each thrust, accentuating the power that radiated from him, and I couldn't help but clutch onto his shoulders as I rode out the intense pleasure he was giving me.

Our hips met in a slow grind, both of us adjusting to the new connection between us. My hands roamed down his body, rolling over each muscle, cupping his ass as he moved inside me. "You're so big."

"And you're so wet." He leaned in to press a kiss to my cheek, then raised again to watch me. "Take me deeper."

I shifted, wrapping my leg higher onto his waist, and he moaned in approval. His cock slid deeper with every push, filling me completely. Making me feel fully seen, utterly wanted. I moved my hands to his back, reveling in the smooth ridges of his muscles beneath my fingertips as he buried himself to the hilt and ground against my clit. It sent a shock wave through my core, causing me to clench down on him in response.

"That's it," he murmured, watching me intently as he moved faster. The mattress jostled with each thrust, the room filled with the sounds of skin smacking and grunts of exhilaration. His eyes fluttered closed but snapped open again quickly, locked purposefully on me.

"Holy shit," I gasped as he picked up the pace, stretching me to the limit as he pounded into me. The head of his cock grazed my G-spot with every thrust, sending sparks of euphoria coursing through my body.

Drew's eyes darkened and he leaned down to kiss me, his tongue dancing against mine as his other hand found its way between us, rubbing my clit in time with his thrusts.

I couldn't help but dig my nails into his shoulders.

He broke the kiss again, pulling his face only inches from mine. "So fucking perfect."

We were so close, connected in so many ways. It was more intense than ever before.

As he continued driving into me, I clenched my fingers in his hair, grounding myself. I needed to kiss him, but I needed to watch his eyes even more.

What was happening to me?

I sucked in a deep breath as the heady rush overtook me, and I let it rip apart everything I was. Ecstasy flooded every cell in my body, pulling me under and leaving me writhing beneath him.

He slammed into me with breathtaking ferocity, his powerful body claiming me with each movement. Drew's face contorted as he followed me over the edge, his own release punctuated by a low growl of satisfaction. His muscles tightened with the force of his release, while his eyes struggled to remain open.

Mr. Control, glistening with sweat and utterly losing himself, was the most amazingly primal thing I'd ever seen. Once he was done, he blew out a slow breath and stared at me for a beat.

What was going through his head? Probably as much as was going through mine. A whole lot of *Holy shit, what was that?* mixed with a little *Wow* and a hint of *Let's do that again.*

He collapsed onto the bed next to me, rolled onto his back, and finally closed his eyes. "You're so beautiful when you come."

I shifted onto my side and ran a hand over his chest. "I never took you for a missionary man."

"I'm not." He brought my hand to his lips. Then he pulled harder, so I was tucked in tightly against him. He wrapped his arm around my back and kissed the top of my head. "I'm also not a snuggler."

"So what are we doing, then?"

"Trying to wrap our heads around what happened?"

My head wasn't wrapping around anything.

"We should get dressed and leave. Scarlett's expecting me back at Mosaic, and Craig's likely expecting you. We could pretend this never happened." But I didn't want to. The way we'd connected. The way he hadn't taken his eyes off mine as he came inside me. I'd never had that before. "We got it out of our systems and—"

"That's not what I meant."

"So, what *do* you mean?"

He caught his fingers under my chin and forced my face up. His eyes flicked back and forth between mine, searching. "I mean, what if—"

His phone buzzed from somewhere in the room.

"You should get that."

Drew stared up at the ceiling but didn't let go of me. The phone buzzed again. "They can leave a message."

"It might be important."

He slid his fingers up to my cheek as his eyes reopened. His mouth twitched a few times, as though he was about to say something. But nothing came. He didn't tell me I was important or that this moment was. Just stared.

His phone stopped buzzing, then started again.

"You really need to answer that." I sat up, doing my best—and completely failing—not to gawk at his gorgeous body. A girl could get used to having someone like that around. "And I need to put my knee brace on."

He got up to dispose of the condom and grabbed his phone. "Speak of the devil."

Which devil?

Drew pressed the phone to his ear while he picked up his pants. "What do you need, Craig?"

I limped into the bathroom to grab a robe and paused in front of the mirror. I was still a mess after ripping my dress and skin while climbing the building, plus Wyatt knocking me to the ground. My face was unmarred, but my hair was chaos.

That was Drew's fault. My stomach did a ridiculous flip-flop at the thought.

I grabbed the robe from the back of the door and covered myself up.

What was the *'what if'* he was going to say before the phone cut him off? What if we did this every time I was in Washington? Not that we came to DC regularly, but it was a short enough flight. Or what if I stayed in town for a sex-fueled few extra days? Or what if...

What if I was getting ahead of myself?

What if I was supposed to be focused on my team? On finding Noah? On figuring out why the huma bird had been swapped, the stolen scarab was on display, and why Wyatt had been extorted into stealing the chip?

And how did it all fit together?

And the cat named Chaos wearing the tracker?

There was a thread connecting everything. There was no way there'd been two separate thefts happening at the same time. It was too much of a coincidence.

I dug my fingers into my thigh, into the muscle that continued protesting, despite every doctor telling me it was fine. I'd broken my femur all those years ago, in five places near its midpoint and above. So why was the pain so much lower? How did Wyatt know just where to kick me for maximum effect?

How could I have believed everything he'd said? *Because it sounded so reasonable. So logical.* Of course, he made enemies as a CIA agent. Of course, Drew had said I was reckless.

Climbing a building without gear *was* reckless.

The truth was hidden inside all the lies. Both with Wyatt's words and whatever had gone down at Mosaic. And I had to return to the restaurant and help my team figure it out. I was the thief, and I knew how thieves thought.

When I left the bathroom, Drew had already dressed, including his signature clenched jaw. He dragged his fingers through his hair and nodded absently, staring at the floor.

"I'll be right over." He hung up. When he looked at me, his face softened, and his lips curved into a smile. As much as that tight jaw was smoking hot, his smile was dazzlingly handsome. Heart-stopping, even. With a pinch of comforting thrown in for good measure.

"So you *are* capable of smiling, Downie."

He closed the distance between us and wrapped an arm around my waist, pulling me against him. "Seeing a beautiful woman in a state of near undress does that to a man."

Don't say it, don't say—

"Any ole woman?"

Dammit. Zero chill.

He leaned in to kiss me, his tongue gently exploring before his teeth grazed my bottom lip. "*My* woman."

My?

Wait. What did that mean?

"Craig's at the office, tracking down some information on Wyatt's movements over the last week, and needs a hand." He didn't loosen his grip on me, although the smile faded a little with each word. "Will you be here when I get back?"

Get back?

Jayce, stop repeating everything he's saying.

"I don't know how long we'll be at Mosaic."

"Call me if you uncover anything or need my help." He pressed another kiss to my temple and let go of me. On his way to the door, he took my hand and I ambled the few steps at his side. "Or whenever you're done. No leaving town without a goodbye."

I blew a raspberry. *Classy, Jayce.* "I'm not leaving town without a few more of those orgasms."

"Happy to oblige." He turned the door handle, but gave me a quick peck on the lips before opening it. "And you have to try my Beef Wellington."

"Now you're speaking my language."

"Good." He winked and swung open the door.

Emmett stood there, fist raised to knock. *Shit.* He didn't budge, but as he took in my robe and Drew's open neckline and undone tie, a grin slid up his face. "Good evening?"

"Wonderful evening." Drew kissed my forehead and clapped Emmett on the shoulder as he slipped out.

I turned on my heel and made my way into the room as elegantly as possible. Elegant still wasn't my strong suit, especially with the injured leg.

"How's your knee?" asked Emmett in a sing-song voice. "Work out the kinks?"

"Screw off." I plopped onto the bed and grabbed my brace.

He laughed. "Took you two long enough."

We were not about to discuss my love—or whatever that was—life. "Why are you here?"

Emmett plucked my logic puzzle book off the floor and laid it on the table next to the pencil. "Scarlett got a call from Noah."

"Noah?" I hauled the brace up over my leg, situating the hole over my kneecap.

"He says they didn't need the entire huma bird, so he's offered it up to us."

Pulling one of the brace's Velcro straps taut, I flexed and straightened my knee, searching for the perfect fit. "Sounds suspect."

Emmett shrugged. "Maybe he's still got a bit of the recovery agent in him. Or maybe Fenix really believes they're the altruistic types."

"Despite all the kidnappings and beatings?"

Emmett's nostrils flared. He'd been on the wrong end of both of those things earlier this year. "She took the call in private, so I don't know everything they said. But her gut says this isn't a setup."

And we always trusted Scarlett's gut.

"What's our play?"

"You remember that antique shop you were casing after..." He gestured vaguely over his shoulder toward the door.

After I'd run off from Drew's the first time, he meant. "Yes."

"That's where it is." He sank into the chair by the side table. "Noah said a guy who worked there extracted what they needed, then he left it for us. Since you're familiar with the place, the two of us are going to check it out."

"And recover it if everything looks safe?" I finished with the second strap and stood, testing the leg out.

"That's the plan."

Good. With all the Drew-distractions gone, I'd be as sharp as ever. And with my brace on, there'd be no holding me back. "Give me five minutes to get dressed."

CHAPTER 41
DREW

A few hours next to Jayce Monroe and it was like I'd forgotten all my training. Truth and honesty practically fell out of my mouth. What was I doing telling her all those things—that I'd dreamed of her, that I wanted to make *love* to her?

Had I been trying to make *her* feel better after everything Emmett told me?

Or trying to make *myself* feel better?

Hell.

'What if you stayed in Washington for a few weeks?' I'd almost said. 'Spend some time getting to know each other outside the job?'

What if, Drew?

What the fuck?

Apparently, getting into bed with her didn't get her out of my system. It just lodged her even more firmly inside my brain.

I had nothing to offer her but heartbreak. Parents who'd lied my entire life, a career spent manipulating people, a cheating ex, a best friend whose death was covered up by the government he'd served, and a boss who demanded we twist the truth until it was unrecognizable.

Those were my influences. No better than hers.

Jayce and I were two screwed-up people who tumbled into each other and couldn't tell up from down. It was nothing more than sex. We'd do it again and we'd damn well enjoy it.

Nothing more, Drew. Remember that.

After a short drive, I turned onto the busy street where the Bishop and Associates headquarters were located. Four stories of red brick with arched windows decorating our office level at the top. Shops and restaurants lined the bottom levels of the buildings—many of which had been private homes at some point—all crammed together in the Dupont Circle area.

Before Emmett's lecture, I'd considered opening Wyatt's office safe to see what was inside. Now Craig wanted me to deliver that access. I'd wanted to wait for the police, but as Craig had said on the phone—Wyatt was one of us. Not just a Bishop team member who'd betrayed us, but a former CIA agent who might need protection.

How long had he been plotting behind our backs?

Who had how much on him?

And how did Scarlett's ex factor into this? The dragonfly and the golden bird had to be linked.

I should have asked Jayce for more information while she was in a vulnerable state.

Not like I was thinking with my brain while we were together.

I slowed as I approached the narrow alley where I could access the small parking area between the buildings on our block.

But before I turned in, I spotted a familiar figure.

Vanessa.

Heading into the Bishop building.

She wasn't going into the tiny café on the bottom level, which was still open at this hour. Nor did she pause at the outer door to the office building, which should have been locked.

I picked up speed and continued past her to get a better view.

Through the glass door, she was visible, entering the elevator. Still in her green dress, with a dark shawl around her shoulders. Had she gone back into the party or interrogated more visitors after I told her to leave me alone?

Was she helping Craig dig into Wyatt's past?

Had she learned something important?

I pulled into a parking spot at the side of the road, farther down the block, to watch the office building in my rearview mirror.

Five minutes.

Ten.

She didn't come out. What was she doing in there?

Chapter 42
Jayce

I stared down at the antiques shop from five floors up. From the same building Emmett and I had sat on Thursday night after my disaster with Drew. "You didn't say it was just going to be the two of us."

Very few cars moved along the street, and some late-night revelers sang an unfamiliar song. The city wasn't silent, but it was quieter than the last time I'd sat on this rooftop.

"Does that matter?" Emmett crouched next to me at the roof's edge, binoculars in his hands.

"You could have at least brought me a backup earpiece."

"Rav has all the spares, and he's off chasing Brie's latest lead on Noah."

I pulled a mint out of my pocket—from my body-hugging black spandex outfit, which was way more comfortable than the pretty dress—and unwrapped it. "How is it we're trusting he hasn't double-crossed us here, but we're still hunting him?"

Emmett shrugged.

He acted as Scarlett's second-in-command since Noah left the team—since Noah died, theoretically, but not really-ly—which sometimes meant questioning his sister and sometimes accepting her decisions. It was a fuzzy line, but he danced along its edge well.

"She's still angry, isn't she?" I popped the mint in my mouth. "Wouldn't you be?"

If my fiancé had faked his death, kidnapped my brother, and had my brother beaten, I'd probably be a lot more than angry. I'd never had that serious a relationship and I didn't talk to my sister, but I could imagine. "Any updates on Brie's search for the data storage facility?"

Emmett glanced at me from the corner of his eye.

First, Brie's Trojan had failed. Second, Will shot down the idea of cloning Gideon or Liana's phones, then no one managed to lift one of those phones at the gala. "If Gideon's still at the hospital, I can head there after we retrieve the bird."

"I think Mum's working a different angle. She's looking for something on Gideon."

"Leverage? Dirt?"

"Fenix got away with this bird while you were, what, twenty feet away? After blackmailing Scarlett and nearly burying Dec and Leigh in the Catacombs, let alone what they did to me and Mal..." Emmett let out a slow breath. "Mum wants a back door into the Tremaine servers so she can keep tabs on Fenix."

"Assuming they genuinely store everything there?"

"Brie's pretty sure that part's true."

"If she's sure about something like that, it's enough for me." I let down the binoculars so I could focus with my eyes and peripheral vision. "I'm going to check out the back door. If both access points look good, I'll pop in, grab the bird, and you keep watch."

"Be careful."

I stood and flexed my leg in the brace. It felt a million times better.

Emmett pressed his finger to his ear, turning on his earpiece. "Brie, Jayce and I are in place. Feed the audio from her phone through this channel." He waited a beat, then pointed at me. "Good to go."

I headed for the maintenance ladder, only a little slower than usual. I jogged past a few buildings to an opening to the street, darted across, and reversed my actions to navigate my way between the buildings on the other side.

The quiet was familiar, but disconcerting. When I'd started with Reynolds, we hadn't used earpieces for every job. Six months in, Emmett and I had been stuck inside a museum for five hours because Brie found out about a guard change too late, and we hadn't gotten her texts. After that, the rule about earpieces was instituted: Never take them out, never turn them off.

"You remember the time we had to hole up behind that statue in the little gallery in Antwerp, Emmett?" My phone, secured to my forearm, had a strong enough microphone to pick up everything I said—even whispers.

It was in stealth mode, though, so I didn't receive a response. Brie was probably laughing and Emmett was probably telling me to focus.

Maybe lacking the earpiece was a good thing.

They could send haptic signals through my watch if they needed me, but the phone's screen would remain black until I pressed a specific spot on it. Will's genius design wouldn't risk someone spotting me because the screen lit up.

I skirted the backs of the buildings, past the convenience store where I'd stolen the chocolate bar and past the jewelry store I'd originally considered.

What had changed for Drew between Thursday and tonight? What took him from wanting to get me out of his system to all the sappy stuff he was spouting at the hotel? Maybe it was just another angle—a way to get what he wanted without me taking off—or maybe it was genuine.

Did he really want me? Just me, all my quirks and weirdnesses?

And did it even matter? He lived too far away for it to work out. Although Declan had probably said that about Leigh, who was from Boston. Not to mention Malcolm and Ashley, who'd recently moved to Halifax after falling for Scarlett and Zac.

Still, this was Drew Donovan I was thinking about.

Down-ovan.

The ultra grumpy guy.

Who actually smiled.

Who called me his woman.

Warmth jostled around in my stomach. Drew's smile was one of the most beautiful things I'd ever seen. Let alone that body. And his—

Down, girl. You need to focus.

I climbed another ladder to a roof that overlooked the antiques shop's rear door and long-pressed my phone to wake it from stealth mode. "I'm in position. Any activity on your side?"

"Nothing," came Emmett's reply through the phone. "How much time do you need?"

"We watch for thirty. If there's any activity, I'll need you to approach from the front as a distraction."

"And if there's none, you'll go in?"

"Yup."

When we were done, I'd call Drew. If he was finished with Craig, maybe he'd come back to my hotel. Or I could go to his place and raid his kitchen after he raided my—

A wave of heat shot out from my core, and I had to adjust my position.

Calm down.

Drew was going to be the end of me.

I tapped out a quick text on my phone, letting him know we had a tip about the bird and that I was going to recover it.

That would earn another of his smiles, for sure.

I got comfortable and settled in to observe. Night-vision goggles would have been helpful, but the antiques shop had a couple of windows in the back and a wall of them in the front. If anyone was inside, a light would flick on at some point.

Unless Noah had set a trap for us inside.

Scarlett's gut said he hadn't. Given all the times I'd put my faith in her gut, I wouldn't question it now.

Although she *had* misjudged Wyatt's role in everything.

CHAPTER 43
DREW

I hurried through the back door and skipped the ancient elevator, preferring to rush up the stairs. Why was Vanessa here? It must have been details about Wyatt.

Halfway there, I stopped, staring upward.

Craig knew I was coming into the office. He hadn't mentioned Vanessa. That meant she was heading there of her own volition, and probably as a surprise.

Why would she feel comfortable visiting him at our office in the middle of the night?

They're sleeping together, Drew. It was the only explanation that made sense.

Unless...

I'd never given her a key to our office, but considering she'd lied to me about only having one key to our apartment, what if she'd stolen one of my keys? Or made a copy of it?

What if she was planning to sneak into Wyatt's office and root around for her gossip site?

I redoubled my efforts on the stairs.

How had I let that woman into my bed, let alone into my home? She didn't have an honest bone in her body.

That's exactly why, Drew. Honest people make you want to be a better person and you don't know how to do that.

Honest people like Jayce. Who made me want to stare into her eyes while I poured everything I was into her. Made me want to make stupid declarations I couldn't live up to.

Three times before I'd charged into the building, I'd checked my messages in case she'd sent me anything. Emmett might have shown up to ensure she was all right but more likely, he was there to pick her up. The Reynolds team had learned something or had a lead.

Did she trust me enough to tell me? Not that there was any reason to fill me in. But still, a tiny voice in my head hoped she'd send me an update on what she was doing.

I crested the top of the steps to the fifth floor and stopped dead. *Deep breath. Straighten the tux. And be prepared to walk in on the two of them doing things I shouldn't see my boss and my ex doing.*

The lobby and the main hallway were empty. I canted my head, listening.

Craig's voice was the first I heard, hushed, coming from an office down the hall. "You shouldn't be here."

Vanessa responded, "We need to act fast."

"No, we need to be smart." Craig huffed. "Drew's on his way. He can't find you here."

Whatever they were up to, they were in it together. I walked forward slowly, sneaking so I could hear as much of their conversation as possible.

"What do you want me to do? Hide in the closet?" Sarcasm dripped off her words.

"Maybe if you hadn't been harassing the Reynolds woman he was working with, it wouldn't matter. But after that little show, he won't want to see you."

She sighed. "You sure about this Italy thing?"

I paused. She'd told me a headhunter found her. Was Craig going with her?

"You'll love it," he said.

"I appreciate you bringing me in. I need the fresh start." She chuckled. "And the money."

My phone buzzed in my pocket, and I fumbled to silence it. I only saw Jayce's name at the top of the notification before Craig popped his head out from Wyatt's office.

"Drew," he said, "thanks for hurrying over."

I stuffed the phone into my breast pocket and smiled at my boss. "You're not alone?"

Vanessa appeared from the office and her shawl dropped to her elbows. "I told Craig I had some theories on Wyatt's behavior at the party."

"Oh?" If I wanted information from either of them, treating her the way I usually did wouldn't work. I had to play nice.

"He approached me a month ago." She leaned against the doorframe and folded her arms, causing her neckline to shift dangerously close to revealing something. "Said he was in a bit of trouble. He had a big story—wouldn't give me the details—and wanted my help disseminating the information when he had it."

"And you..." I raised an eyebrow at her.

She shrugged one shoulder. "I told him I'd have to see what it was before I made any promises."

I glanced from her to Craig, as though his face would reveal any lies. "And you think that's related to his attempted theft of the chip?"

Craig nodded. "I doubt it's related to his investigation, but it's possible whoever he had some dirt on put him up to this."

"And you want into his safe in case he was storing the information there?"

"You told me he gave you a key." Craig gestured toward my office. "If the information he had is significant, I don't want the authorities to decide whether it gets buried. We've had enough of that with our own, haven't we?"

I didn't have the type of relationship with Wyatt as I had with Alex, but Craig was right—I couldn't leave Wyatt to the same fate. Not that he'd wind up dead on foreign soil, but that he'd wind up a pawn in someone's game. "You're right. On both counts."

Craig and Vanessa followed me into my office.

Had they been plotting something else before they heard me? Was I too suspicious? Too accustomed to lies, so I saw them everywhere?

I pressed my thumb to the scanner on my safe and it clicked open, revealing Wyatt's key, the research my MI6 contact had done into Alex's death, and all my other documents.

My phone buzzed again. I pulled it out of my pocket to check. It was only a random email notification, but Jayce's text sat beneath it. Since I wasn't hiding anymore, I read Jayce's message as I withdrew the key for Craig. "Good news. The Reynolds team got a tip about the huma bird statue at an antiques shop nearby. Jayce is retrieving it."

"What?" Vanessa's response was too sharp.

A prickle ran up my spine. They *had* been up to something. But what?

Calm head, Drew. Give nothing away.

When I turned around, Vanessa was staring wide-eyed at Craig.

He, on the other hand, was a mirror of me. Professional calm. He extended a hand for the key. "I appreciate your help, Drew."

His gentle smile. The use of my name. The non-threatening posture.

He should have been reacting to Vanessa's panicked stare. Should have responded to her question or waved it off.

Instead, he focused on me.

I wrapped the key in my fist. "Tell me what's going on."

"My employee tried to steal something from one of our clients." Craig left his hand out. "I want to know why."

The best lies were couched in truth. His response was honest, but it wasn't the full truth. And *'our'* client? Nothing more than a manipulation, intended to remind me we were a team.

"And..." Craig's lips tightened. "I'm also going to need the thumb drive with the information about Alex."

Vanessa's eyes widened further. Her unspoken demand that Craig be silent was obvious. How had she been such a convincing liar about her fidelity, but so transparent now?

"Why?" I asked.

Craig checked his watch, then looked at Vanessa. "Be sure we don't lose the statue."

She gave a curt nod and rushed out of the room, heading down the hall. Her stilettos clicked on the floor, growing more rapid the farther away she got.

Lose the statue? What does that mean? Lightbulbs went off in my head. "The comms failure?"

Craig came closer. His movements were slow and deliberate. "All me."

I asked, "The cameras?"

"Also me." Which explained why Reynolds had lost their cameras. Craig ensured they were piggybacking off his feed, so he could take them all down.

"And the lights?"

"Liana told me her plans for the evening." He pursed his lips. "Don't suppose I remembered to share that detail with you, did I?"

With anyone else, I would have prepared for a physical attack. But that wasn't Craig's style. We'd be talking this out. How much truth I'd get was another question—half-truths and evasions were more likely.

"This feels too easy," I said.

"I told Vanessa you'd figure it out. Trying to fool you would only waste time." He checked his watch again. "Time we don't have. I need the information you received about The Flame of Khvarenah."

I left my safe open but didn't retrieve the thumb drive. It remained a bargaining chip, but if I shut him down too fast, there'd be consequences.

Shit. Consequences.

If Jayce had a tip on where to find the golden bird and Vanessa was dispatched to ensure they didn't lose it, the two women could wind up facing off. For Jayce, it was a job. For Vanessa? What was it?

And how could I warn Jayce? Craig and I were facing each other. If I tried typing on my phone or making a call, he'd see it. If he wanted the bird, he wouldn't let me finish the message.

"Where's the bird?" If I knew that, I'd know how much time Vanessa had before she arrived. That would tell me how much time I had to warn Jayce.

"That's of no concern. Someone's coming for the Flame's location and if you're still here when he arrives..." Craig clasped a hand over his watch. Was he trying not to look at it? Where were his tells? There wouldn't be anything obvious—he was too well-trained for that. It would be small things. The watch was one, but a sign like that was easy to fake. "You're a good guy, Drew. A smart one. But he's a loose cannon."

I dangled the key to Wyatt's safe on my finger. "Did you want this, or was it all a ruse?"

"Oh, no, I still need that." Craig rubbed a hand over his face.

The move gave me enough time to tap the microphone on my text app and reposition my thumb over the Send button. It was listening. "And what's Vanessa going to do when she gets to the huma bird's location? Kill Jayce and anyone with her?"

Craig lunged forward and before I could send my message, he had my phone. "Smart. Like I said."

"But not smart enough?"

He dropped the phone and smashed it under his heel.

"Who are you working for?"

"That depends on who's asking." He kicked the remnants of the phone aside. "If I was pressed by someone I trust? I'd say I'm working for my son. His wife's sick and that bird will fetch a lot of money from the right buyer."

The right buyer, whose contact information was on the thumb drive. My stomach churned. "Alex's killers will fund her treatments?"

"That was my plan. But if not…" Craig spread his hands wide, providing a view of the gun at his waist. It wasn't a threat, more a display of openness. "The people I'm working with say its beak is far older than the rest. They claim it's part of a set of ancient artifacts that, when assembled, will raise a phoenix."

"That's not a real thing."

Jayce had told me Noah worked for an organization named the Fenix Group.

And apparently, so did Craig. And Vanessa.

I could have been sick.

"They believe the phoenix—whether the actual bird or something about the pieces when they're brought together—will be capable of curing any disease." He looked down at the remnants of my phone. "The doctors have only given my daughter-in-law six months to live. Chemo's expensive, even with good health insurance."

"So you resort to working with thieves and betraying Gideon's trust?"

"That's not how it is." He clasped the back of his neck and stretched it out. Craig Bishop—CIA legend and my mentor—had fallen for the oldest influence trick in the trade: Approach when someone he loved was sick and needed help. "We could use a skilled operative like you if you'll let me expl—"

The elevator pinged and the doors slid open.

Craig mouthed, *Fuck.*

"Bishop?" came a thickly accented voice.

"Give me the key," Craig whispered, waving a frantic hand. A level of panic flashed behind his eyes I'd never seen before. He then raised his voice. "In here, Enzo."

Enzo. The Reynolds team had told me one of Noah's known associates was named Enzo.

A man with deep olive-tinted skin and black hair stalked into the room. His eyes were narrow, shrewd, and a vicious scar puckered his right cheek. He pulled a gun from a side holster and trained it on me.

Shit. I put my hands out in front of myself to show I wasn't armed. I should have stayed in the hotel room with Jayce.

"Who the fuck is this?" he growled.

CHAPTER 44

JAYCE

I refreshed my phone a few times. Still no response from Drew. Not even a thumbs up. The three little dots had started dancing five minutes ago but stopped.

Now nothing.

I'd really thought he was different. Everything he'd said, everything he'd done... I thought it meant more than a roll in the hay.

Get your head out of your butt, Jayce. He could be busy. Drew was the kind of guy who didn't drop what he was doing for a text. He was serious, intense. If he was talking to you, he'd stay focused on you. *Yeah, he's definitely just busy.*

Or I was out of his system.

"I'm going in. Activating stealth." I long-pressed on the phone's upper corner, darkening the screen and shutting off the volume. They could still hear me, but the phone would look dead until I woke it.

Two haptic bursts from my watch told me all I needed. Two meant *Go forward*.

Three would mean danger.

Four would mean I had to wake my phone, no matter what. Four was never good.

I packed my binoculars in my slim backpack, threaded my arms through the straps, and fastened the clips. During my recon Thursday night, I'd discovered the camera at the back door was for show and I'd picked their deadbolt in thirty seconds.

Getting in wouldn't be a challenge.

I covered my face and hair so the interior cameras wouldn't be able to identify me—if they were working and recorded anything overnight. If the back camera was for show, the interior ones may have been, as well.

The hardest part would be finding the little statue and lugging it out.

I made my way to ground level, across the dimly lit space between the buildings, and to the back door of the antiques store. Picked in twenty seconds this time.

Easy peasy.

I was in without a sound. I locked the door behind myself and stopped.

Listened.

No noise, other than the soft hum of an air exchange unit above me.

I pulled my small red light flashlight from a pocket on my thigh and lit up the room. The back door led into a kitchen, which I moved through quickly. Past that was an office and a workshop. Nothing obvious in either of them.

The shop was long and narrow, its walls and a center aisle covered in shelves and glass display cases. Every horizontal space was crammed with items of various sizes. Vases, boxes, paintings, cutlery. I hadn't even decided what I'd take the last time I was in. It hadn't mattered.

All that mattered on Thursday night was Drew.

He got you out of his system, after all.

As I moved through the space, scanning shelves, I glanced at my phone. No one was in here. I could hit the right spot on my phone to wake it and see if he'd responded to my text yet.

No, the whole team would know you potentially gave yourself away to the interior cameras.

I had to find the bird, recover it, and think about Drew later. Or not think about him. I could board the jet tomorrow morning—or whenever we left—and close this chapter in my life. Officially never come back to Washington again.

The bird wasn't out in the open. Not in the front window. I ducked behind the cash register's counter and my flashlight glinted off gold. Wedged between a metal box and a mug full of pens, the huma bird sat waiting for me.

It didn't have a beak.

It had a beak at the gala, didn't it?

"Found it," I whispered as I rested the flashlight on the counter, illuminating the space behind the register. I placed my pack on the floor, ready to receive the statue, but as I crouched down and got a better look, something else caught my attention.

A white envelope stuck out from underneath the statue.

Did they go together?

I tipped the bird and pulled out the envelope. Someone had scrawled 'Scar' across the front and sealed the back. "There's something here for the boss. I think it's a letter."

Was it from Noah? Was I supposed to open it?

The two buzzes on my watch didn't help. What did *Go for-ward* mean now? Go forward and open it? Or go forward by collecting the bird and leaving? Probably the latter.

Assuming it was from Noah, he'd know Scarlett wouldn't be in the shop. If he'd meant for me to open it, he would have put my name on it. I stuffed the sealed envelope in the bottom of my bag and wrapped my fingers around the little statue.

A door opened and closed at the back.

I grabbed the flashlight. Switched it off and slid it into my thigh pocket. I got low on the floor and peeked around the corner.

The overhead lights didn't come on, but a narrow flashlight beam swept across the room.

It wasn't Emmett. He would have said my name.

But it wasn't someone who was supposed to be there, either.

I tapped three times on my phone screen to alert the team of the danger.

Two bursts on my watch came in response. Emmett would be packing up already, heading for the ladder at the back of the building. He'd be at the front door in five minutes as a distraction.

High heels clicked on the linoleum in the kitchen. Definitely not Emmett, nor Noah. The sound stopped and the flashlight went dark.

Dim light filtered in through the front windows. I eased down to the floor and peered around the end of the counter. Watching. Waiting. An ache spread through my left leg, but I could push through it and run or sneak deeper into my hiding spot.

Where was she?

Who was she?

The flashlight flicked on again and I retreated before the beam hit my face.

"I know you're back there."

I'd only spoken with her briefly, but I recognized the voice. Ms. Legs-a-Lot.

"I only want the bird." The light shifted as she pulled the slide on a gun. She was on the other side of the register. "I'll leave you alone if you hand it over."

"I'm pretty sure it doesn't belong to you." I twisted my head to watch the light over the register, which would tell me when she moved. The counter was free-standing, so I could run left or right around it if I needed to. "And that gun doesn't change anything."

"It changes a lot." She moved closer, surprisingly quiet.

"You're Drew's ex, right?"

Another step closer. "I'm the woman who decides your fate tonight. Either hand over the bird or move to the front of the shop so I can get it."

I'd told the team who it was. I'd told them she had a gun. What else would Emmett need? "It's just you, isn't it?"

C'mon, Emmett. Hurry up.

I felt her next to me as much as I saw the movement. How was she so fast? The flashlight— Shit. The flashlight was on a shelf, not in her hand.

She gestured with the gun. "Stand up and move back."

"Can you help me?" I stretched out my bad leg, running a hand along the brace over my suit. "I hurt my knee at the party."

She frowned, the flashlight casting deep shadows across her face. "It had to be you, didn't it?"

"What are we talking about?"

Blondie crouched down, her ridiculously low-cut dress shifting to highlight her cleavage. She must have used tape. "You smell like sandalwood."

I didn't smell like anything. Every product I used on my body was chosen to ensure I left no trace. "You may be smelling—"

"And sex." She extended the gun in my direction.

Quick scan. Her shoes were off. The dress had a high slit, allowing her free movement. She carried a Glock, so no safety to check, even if there was enough light to tell.

"Get out of the fucking way, shorty." Her voice cracked. She was upset. It wasn't the time to figure out why.

Although that might buy you some time. Or piss her off enough to shoot me.

I put my hands out in front of myself and reached for my pack.

"Leave it. Just move."

"Okay." I nodded slowly, lifting myself to inch backward. "I won't try to stop you."

"Pathetic." She straightened, looking at the statue, then back at me. "I can't believe he opened the Cavallotto Barolo for you."

My hand slipped, and I went down harder than I should have, pain bouncing from my hip down my leg. "The what?"

"Exactly." Vanessa stepped forward as I moved back, keeping ten feet between us. She knelt next to the bird and wrapped a hand around it, as though she didn't realize it was fifty-plus pounds of solid gold. It didn't budge.

Where was Emmett? He should have knocked on the front door by now.

Blondie grunted, using her gun hand to help pull the statue out of its hiding spot. She muttered, "Dancing around each other. Who says shit like that?"

Wait. What? Was she talking about me and Drew? He'd said that to me—that we were dancing around each other—Thursday night. Before he kissed me.

She cradled the bird in her arms, the gun no longer pointed at me. "Heavy little guy, isn't it?"

"What are you going to do with it?"

How did she know it was there? She hadn't wandered the shop searching for it. She'd known I was there. And how had she gotten in the back door?

Noah *had* set us up.

To what end? So I'd find the letter and take it to Scarlett? He'd called her. Why leave a letter?

An arm snapped around Vanessa's torso, and she dropped the bird with a thud. As she sucked in a breath to scream, another hand clamped over her mouth.

I rolled to the side, putting the counter between me and her flailing gun. More grunts sounded, but I kept my head down like I'd been trained.

"You son of a—" wailed Vanessa.

"Let go of the gun." Rav cut her off, in that calm yet irritated voice he always had. No wonder Emmett was slow—he'd gotten backup. "I don't want to hurt you."

"And you won't," she grunted. Was she seriously trying to fight him?

Rav didn't make a noise, but Vanessa squealed.

"You can come out now," said Emmett.

My muscles relaxed and I knelt, massaging above my left knee. "Thanks guys."

Neither of my teammates wore protective gear, so their faces would be on camera if anything was working. That added an extra step for the evening. We'd have to scrub the cameras if they were recording.

"Who sent you?" asked Emmett.

Vanessa squirmed in Rav's grip. "Screw you."

I flexed my leg as I approached them. The brace wasn't enough for tonight. I should have actually iced it, rather than trying to walk off the injury.

Vanessa shook her head, swishing her mane around, and took a deep breath. "You have no justification for holding me."

Rav, looking more ominous than usual in the shadows behind Vanessa, said, "And yet, here we are."

"Do you have your zip ties?" Emmett asked me.

"In my pack." I rounded the counter and dug into the side compartment where I carried small accessories.

"Don't you dare," snarled Vanessa.

"It was Noah, wasn't it?" I said. Who else knew we'd be there?

"That double-crossing prick!" She threw her head back violently.

Rav easily dodged out of the way.

Next, she turned her venom on me. "Drew's a trained manipulator. You know that, right? It's been so deeply ingrained in his psyche he's incapable of doing anything authentic." She grimaced as the zip ties tightened. "Lines like how he can't think when he's around you or making the fucking Beef Wellington. It was all to get you in bed, nothing more."

I knew all this. Deep inside, I'd wanted to be wrong. I'd wanted him to want me. The real me. The—

Wait.

"I told you he didn't make me the Beef Wellington."

It had been a lie when I said it. A distraction. But I was *sure* I'd said it to her. And how did she know what he'd said about not being able to think straight?

She huffed, rolling her eyes.

The Cavallotto. That was the winery he mentioned. A sick rock settled in my gut. There was only one way she knew so much. Drew told her. He'd lied to me about their relationship and—

No, that's not the only way, Jayce. "His apartment's bugged, isn't it?"

Blondie's lips tightened, confirming my guess. After five years of working with professionals like the Reynolds siblings, this woman was too easy to read.

"Why bug his apartment?" I handed the zip ties to Rav.

She didn't know I'd left Drew's place on Thursday night. She thought we'd slept together, otherwise she wouldn't be lashing out. But she knew everything before that. The bug had to be in the kitchen or dining room, where we'd been talking.

The photo of the two of them! Drew had said he'd gotten rid of every trace of her, so she must have planted the photo with a bug. She hadn't heard anything after it was in the drawer.

"Wrongful imprisonment," she growled. "I'll have you all thrown in jail."

My hands shook and volume rose. "I asked why you bugged his apartment!"

"Jayce," said Emmett, in his *calm down* voice.

"It doesn't matter. He's with us now. He'd never say no to—" She clamped her lips shut and raised her chin in a sign of defiance.

Drew had gone to see Craig. He'd said he didn't want to leave. Was that a lie and he was grateful for the excuse? Or was Craig the one he'd never say no to?

Think, Jayce.

She wanted him back. He'd told me as much.

Drew called me *his woman*.

"Craig's behind it all," I whispered, staring at Vanessa in the low light, watching her eyes narrow. I was right.

And that meant Drew had walked into something he didn't understand.

"Shit." I ripped my phone off my forearm and long-pressed, unlocking it. I texted Drew, pacing away from the group while Emmett and Rav questioned Vanessa further.

I called, but the phone rang and rang. No answer. If I was *his* woman and I mattered to him, he wouldn't wait this long to respond to my text. Not after what we did tonight. Not after the way he'd looked at me. Or kissed me.

Or the way he'd held me after.

"Jayce?" Emmett's word snapped me back to the room.

I'd missed something. And I didn't care. "Fenix has Drew."

Rav looked at Emmett, who'd once been held by the thieves, smugglers, and goons.

Emmett's gaze stayed fixed on me. "That's a bit of a leap, don't you think?"

I stepped up to the tall, irritatingly gorgeous woman who thought she could drive a wedge between Drew and me. I pulled off my head covering and pointed at her. "Tell me where he is."

Great. *Now* she refused to talk. That was worse than the taunts and lies.

"Drew was going to meet Craig at their office. Are they still there?"

She grimaced and rose on her tiptoes. Rav must have been exerting pressure on her bound hands. Despite that, she held her tongue.

I didn't have time for this. When had he left the hotel room? An hour ago? Even if he met Craig at the office, how far away could they be by now? I needed a tracker on that man.

"Brie!" I practically shouted into the phone as the thought flew through my brain. He'd put the tracker in his pocket after we found it on the cat. "Drew's got the tracker we put on the dragonfly. Find him!"

"On it," came the reply from my phone.

"Jayce," said Emmett. "Drew's not our—"

"Use my backpack to carry the statue." I snatched the earpiece from his ear and ran for the back door. Voices filtered through my comms and a wave of peace battled with the panic rising inside me. "I'm going after Drew."

"Emmett, do you have the bird?" asked Scarlett.

Tune them out unless they're talking to you. I hit the back door and kept to the shadows in the alley behind the buildings.

A map appeared on my phone with a red dot.

Brie said over the earpiece, "Got a signal, but I can't guarantee it's him."

The dot hovered over Drew's office. Perfect. He was so close, running would be more efficient than calling a car. "It's our best guess."

"Come back here," snapped Emmett. He must have taken Rav's earpiece. "We need a plan."

"That's your job." My job was rescuing my man before he ended up on the wrong end of a Fenix fist. Or gun. "Tell me when you've got one."

CHAPTER 45
DREW

Craig marched across my office, toward the scarred man with the gun. "Put that away, Enzo. Drew's on our team."

"He's not on my team." His accent was thick. Southern Italian?

I should have gotten more details about him from Jayce. The Reynolds crew had been throwing information at me so quickly once Noah appeared, I'd barely kept up.

"And he's not on your team, Bishop." Enzo side-stepped Craig to keep the gun trained on me. "Not your *real* team, sì?"

"Drew had a copy of Wyatt's safe key." Craig turned back to me, widening his eyes as he approached. "We were going to purge the safe of any incriminating evidence."

"And speaking of incrimination..." Enzo shouldered past Craig, raising the gun toward my face. No suppressor, so shooting me would bring unwanted attention, but from the sharpness in his eyes, he likely wasn't the type to care. "Where's the bird?"

"I don't know." I lifted my hands higher, to show the key I had dangling from one finger. Giving them access to Wyatt's private information was wrong, but self-preservation was more important than a few ethics.

Enzo's scarred cheek twitched slightly. He *wanted* to shoot. He'd use any excuse I gave him.

"Vanessa's gone to get the bird." Craig's gaze was steady, his voice calm but firm. "I'm bringing Drew on board. He'll be a valuable asset."

I extended the key to Enzo. The best choice was to go along with Craig's assumption I'd join them. Or his lie, whatever it was. "I convinced Wyatt to give this to me, so I could find out what he knew."

He touched the gun to my forehead.

Stay calm, Drew. You've faced worse. I pointed over my shoulder. "And the information about the Flame of Khvarenah is in my safe. Put the gun away and we can look at it."

Craig exhaled quietly, his relief palpable but unspoken.

Enzo's dark eyes narrowed, but he lowered the gun an inch—a small but significant concession. "If you try anything, you're dead."

"Obviously." I backed up slowly, keeping my eyes on the Italian. With a quick check over my shoulder, I reached into the safe and retrieved the thumb drive. I'd been such a fool for acting at Craig's urging to find out what happened to Alex. What was I thinking I'd do with the information? Who would I tell? What would it matter?

How had I missed that he was manipulating me?

Because he's better at this job than you are, Drew.

I held out my left hand, showing him the drive and the key, breathing slowly to calm my racing heart. "Take them."

"If you're with us, why are you shaking?"

"You're pointing a gun at my head." I lifted my eyebrows, conveying more confidence than I felt.

"The phoenix will rise." The corner of Enzo's mouth quirked up and in a swift motion, he holstered his gun. As he snatched the drive, I noticed a small tattoo on the web between his thumb and index finger—a phoenix. He leaned against my desk. "How long will Vanessa be?"

Craig pulled out his phone. "I'll text her."

Had Jayce gone in alone? She'd told me her team had a tip, but would they all have gone in together? Did they retrieve the bird before Vanessa did? Or did my ex and my new woman have it out again?

Worry about that later.

All attempts to push Jayce into my emotional locker had failed. This was no different. I had to get through this and make sure she was all right. If Vanessa hurt her, I'd—

Focus on survival first.

"Let's open Wyatt's safe," I said to Craig. Hopefully, he had enough pull with Enzo that I'd make it out alive. "How much time do we have?"

"Shouldn't be more than a half hour." Craig pocketed his phone and inclined his head toward the hallway.

With a slight nod from Enzo, Craig and I left for Wyatt's office. His steps were casual, as though a madman wasn't waiting for us to finish.

"What have you gotten us into?" I whispered once we were out of earshot. It was a foolish question. He'd already given me the sob story, and whether or not it was true, he'd stick with it.

Using the word *'us'* was the important part—it reinforced I was on his side. "And what's in Wyatt's safe?"

Light crept into Wyatt's office from the hallway. It was dim, except in the only spot that mattered—the light over the cowboy painting was always on.

Craig guided me around the desk and swung out the painting which hid the safe. He spoke quietly. "Vanessa didn't respond. If she doesn't get the bird, we're in trouble. This is bigger than you can imagine."

"Then let me help you."

He nodded and tapped the safe. "This is how you help. You're doing a great job."

I took a deep breath, inserting the key into the lock. As I turned it, the soft click of the mechanism was like a tiny voice telling me I was selling my soul again. So many lies. Jayce was the only one who was honest with me. I should have confessed more before I left her.

Fuck, I should have realized more and realized it sooner. How much time had I wasted trying to convince myself she was wrong for me?

Craig nudged me to the side and opened the door. He riffled through papers and envelopes, searching for something.

"Tell me more about this organization." I needed intel if I was going to make it through the night. "How is Wyatt involved?"

"Vanessa didn't lie about Wyatt. Mostly." He pulled out a stack of papers, flipped through it, and dropped it onto the desk to pull out more. "The dirt he had was on us, and we had to make sure he didn't reveal anything."

If he put Wyatt through enough to have him steal the chip at the gala, what would he do to me if he thought I'd call the cops the first chance I got? I rested a hand on the paperwork he'd placed on the desk. "Do you need me to go through these?"

"I'm not sure what I'm looking for." Craig paused, hand inside the safe. "I know he gave you the key in case he didn't get away tonight. He must have stashed whatever he found in here and assumed you'd give it to the police."

"He didn't give Vanessa any indication of what it might be?"

"No. He said he'd give her the details when he was sure. That was a month ago."

Maybe Wyatt had discovered Vanessa's role and realized his mistake in going to her.

"How do Alex and The Flame of Khvarenah fit in here?"

Craig peeked inside a manila envelope and added it to the stack on the desk. "Fenix is a dangerous organization. Either you're in, or..."

Or I was dead?

"I couldn't risk"—he lowered his voice further—"certain members finding out about our plan to sell the bird. I heard some whispers about Alex and The Flame, and I knew I could rely on you for the intel I needed."

So he encouraged me to do his dirty work. I stepped back, glancing over my shoulder to check if Enzo was there.

My heart lurched.

Jayce.

Dressed all in black with the brace over her tights. Hair pulled back and sleek. How the hell had she gotten in? She hadn't made a sound. She would have walked right past my office. Past Enzo!

Jayce ducked around the corner, limping slightly. Despite the brace, she moved almost as poorly as she had when we left Mosaic. She was still hurt.

If Vanessa had beaten her to the statue, she would have brought it here by now. Unless Vanessa was double-crossing everyone? That seemed to be a trend.

"Craig, you know I'd follow you to hell and back, right?" I had to keep him on my side, especially now that Jayce was here.

"I knew I could trust you, Drew." He threw more envelopes onto the desk. "I wanted to bring you in from the start."

Get out! I mouthed to Jayce, fighting against every instinct to run to her and grab her.

She balanced on her right leg, her face pinched from the pain. Jabbing a finger in Craig's direction, she mouthed, *Bad guy.*

I know. I waved her away. *Now get out!*

Footsteps sounded from the hall. Panic surged through me. Enzo was coming, and she had nowhere to hide. The black clothes might be enough if she snuck behind the jacket hanging near the door, but if Craig or Enzo looked too closely, they'd see her. Her only other option was behind the couch off to the side, but if anyone walked around it, she'd be done for.

What was I going to do? I had to protect her, but I had to keep myself alive to do that.

"Enzo!" I hurried out of the room, as though I hadn't heard him coming. We nearly collided outside the door. "I can run home for my laptop if you want to read the data on the thumb drive right away?"

At least I could buy Jayce a few more minutes to find the best hiding spot.

He sneered at me and continued walking into Wyatt's office. So much for a *few* extra minutes. "Bishop, hurry up. He'll be here in five minutes."

Craig spun, a sheaf of papers in his hands. "He's early. If Vanessa comes back when he's here—"

Enzo pointed at Craig. "Tell her to stash the bird somewhere. We'll get it later."

Wait. They didn't want the newcomer to know they had the huma bird? Craig wasn't worried about Enzo, it was someone else.

"And you." Enzo faced me, finger still up. "What was your name?"

"Drew."

"Keep your mouth—" His gaze shifted past me, and ice burst up my spine.

Oh no.

Enzo's shoulder rammed into mine as he dashed toward the hangers by the door.

Jayce yelped as he dragged her out of her hiding spot.

"Let go of her!" I shouted. So much for playing it cool.

"Fucking Reynolds Recoveries." He pulled the gun and jammed it against her temple. "I should have killed you in the Catacombs."

Jayce's bad leg buckled, and she stumbled. What if the movement jarred his hand and he shot?

I took a half-step toward them, but Enzo aimed at me.

"Tell me you're working with her," he snarled. "Give me a reason to kill you both."

Jayce steadied herself in a kneel, head wrenched back. "Rav should have left you to die, you asshole."

"How did you know to find us here?" Enzo yanked harder on her ponytail and her veil of bravado collapsed.

"I was looking for intel on Wyatt." She whimpered, adjusting her right leg underneath herself. What was hurting her more? Him practically ripping her hair out, or the forced movement on her bad leg? "I didn't think anyone would be here."

I stood frozen, torn between intervening and maintaining the thin cover I had. She'd given a perfect excuse, and I had to do the same. *Get control.* "I'm not working with her, Enzo. But the more noise she makes, the more likely someone comes to investigate."

"He's right," said Craig. "She's clearly hurt. What's she going to do?"

Craig knew Jayce was planning to recover the huma bird statue. But he wasn't asking her where it was or about Vanessa. Why? Did he already know something? Even if he didn't, he didn't want unnecessary bloodshed, and that was important.

"She snuck in. How hurt can she be?" Enzo jabbed the gun to her head again and pulled upward, hauling her to her feet. "Maybe we should have a little fun with her."

The ice on my spine shifted to fire. *Calm down, Drew.* I released the fist I'd instinctively curled and unclenched my jaw. If he touched her any more than he already was...

But he had a gun.

At her head.

He'd be too fast. There had to be some way to distract him or get the gun away from him. But if I did, would Craig back me up? Or side with Enzo?

The elevator dinged and everyone looked to the door of Wyatt's office.

Two sets of footsteps came down the hallway this time.

A male voice called out, "Craig? Enzo? Are you here?"

"In here, Noah." Enzo didn't release his grip on Jayce or holster the gun. "And we have a snoop."

A handsome blond man in his early thirties walked in, the same Noah the Reynolds team had sent me a photo of. Was this about to make things better or worse? They didn't want him to know they were after the bird. Had he been the one who gave the Reynolds team the tip about its location?

But it was the woman behind him that nearly made me gasp out loud.

Liana Tremaine.

What the hell was going on?

Chapter 46

Jayce

"Fifteen minutes, Jayce," said Emmett over my earpiece. "Just hold out for fifteen minutes."

Pain screamed up my leg and through every follicle on my head. I'd had guns pointed at me before but never by someone as unhinged as Enzo. He'd kidnapped for Fenix, beaten people with wild abandon, and pushed old women into rivers. Was he a killer, though?

Probably.

"You idiot," growled Noah. He marched over to Enzo and swiped the gun away. "Have you never listened to anything I've told you?"

"Che cazzo fai?"

"Let go of her." Noah shoved the gun flat against Enzo's chest, the scarred Italian releasing me and taking hold of his weapon. My former teammate, the liar of all liars, reached for my ear and snatched my earpiece. Next, he pulled my phone from my forearm and ripped off my watch. He whispered into the phone, his tone menacing, "Brie, all her tech is about to be dropped out of a window. You may want to trigger their destruction. And just a warning—if you send anyone in here, Jayce is dead."

My team knew where I was and that I was in trouble. That was the important part.

Actually, the important part was that I didn't have to listen to the Reynolds siblings cussing me out for running into the Bishop office like a lovesick fool.

Scarlett had shut up after I pointed out the time she ran off after Noah in Venice. But only for a half-second.

Noah, shaking his head, crossed to the windows of Wyatt's office, opened one, and threw all of my connections to the outside world away.

Will was going to be pissed. He'd have to replace a lot of stuff for me.

"I told you not to let them keep their tech. Her whole team was listening in." Noah returned to the center of the room and helped me up. Why was he suddenly pretending to be a good guy? He'd sent Vanessa to take me out at the antiques shop. "Jayce, have a seat on the couch. If you move, Enzo has permission to shoot you." He glowered at Enzo. "In the leg only."

"She claims she was here about Wyatt." Enzo's lip curled and his fingers flexed on the gun. Not good. "We should question her more vigorously. I think she's lying."

Definitely lying. Scarlett had fed me the line, which was better than the complete blank I had in my brain when Enzo lifted me by my hair.

"Hypocritical, don't you think?" Drew stood next to the other men, far too comfortable with them. He *was* on my side, right? "Craig told me we're building something that will heal, and yet you use violence to reach that end."

Enzo took a half-step toward Drew, but Noah put up his hand.

Noah said, "You're Drew, right? The one who was working with Jayce tonight?"

"I am."

"Craig speaks highly of you." Noah had always been intense and still was, but he had a peace about him I didn't remember. As though he'd truly found some higher calling. Or believed he had. "He's told you what we're about?"

"A little." Drew tucked one hand in his pocket. Was he genuinely working with them? The panic in his eyes when he spotted me said no, but everything about him now said yes. "And I want in."

Noah looked at Craig, who nodded, then back at Drew. "Have you lost someone?"

"My parents died in a car accident just over two years ago." Drew's lips tightened and he swallowed hard. Was that true? He seemed like he was fighting to control his emotions—but he was *always* in control. Unless he was playing them? "Could the phoenix have saved them, too?"

Liana approached Drew, rubbing a hand down the length of his arm. "It can save everyone."

Noah turned to me. "It could have saved your Olympic dream, Jayce. Saved Tanner's leg."

I felt my body lean forward, as though something deep inside of me wanted what they were talking about, despite my brain knowing it was insane. "What?"

"Everything we're doing"—Noah came closer and knelt in front of me—"is to create a world without suffering. Where disease no longer limits humanity's potential. Where the sick and injured are healed in moments, not over years."

"That's not possible." If my leg had healed properly, I could have followed the path I was supposed to be on. My mother wouldn't have abandoned me for my sister. I wouldn't have done all those awful things. If there was no disease, Coach McInnis would be alive.

Noah placed a hand on my left knee. "It is."

But it wouldn't have changed who my mother really was. I wouldn't have met the Reynolds team. I looked at Drew. I wouldn't have met him. Tanner was a great guy, but I hadn't felt the same way about him as I did about Drew.

Oh my god, was I in love with Drew Donovan?

And why was I only realizing that when I was surrounded by Fenix goons?

Liana touched Noah's shoulder. "The plane's going to be ready in an hour. We should go to the airport."

"Where are we heading?" asked Drew.

Enzo scoffed. "That's not how this works. Bishop can't bring you in that easily."

Noah stood, inserting himself between Enzo and Drew, who looked like they were about to fight. The testosterone was thick in the air, but where would it end?

And how many minutes had passed? Where were Emmett and my team? Or were they holding back because of Noah's threat?

Craig joined the men, not showing the same commanding presence I'd seen from him over the past week. "Wyatt had photos of us. Me, Liana, Vanessa, and Enzo."

"This proves nothing," said Enzo.

"There's a thumb drive in with the photos." Craig held up a manila envelope. "He probably printed the photos so someone would be curious about the drive they were stored with."

"And where is the pretty Vanessa?" Enzo raised his chin at Craig, a threat clear in his tone. "Why isn't she here yet?"

Liana sat next to me, dropping her small handbag onto the couch. "How's your leg?"

"Are you seriously working with them?" I kept my voice down while the men talked.

She took a slow breath and looked at the ceiling. "Have you ever lost someone you loved?"

Everyone I'd loved.

"Someone..." Her gaze fell to my knee. "Someone important to me is very sick, and this is our last shot."

"You have enough money to afford the best healthcare in the world."

She sucked on her bottom lip. "If it was someone I could tell Giddy about."

That made no sense. Who would she keep a secret from her—

"You're having an affair?"

She put her hand on mine. "Can you forgive me?"

"For what?" I barely knew her. Her infidelity didn't matter to me.

"For using your team to cover my shame." She squeezed my hand, tears building against her lower lids. "I helped Craig and Noah set Wyatt up. Kept my plans under wraps to ensure the most chaos possible. Manipulated my friends into donating items for the auction and the art display. Craig helped me, and I... I didn't want anyone to get hurt."

She masterminded all of this? Hurt and betrayed so many people? And what did I do? I wrapped an arm around her shoulder.

"We organized everything to have the huma bird delivered so we could retrieve the phoenix's beak. Coordinated the lights and the music so we could cover up—" She shuddered as tears fell down her cheeks. "If it doesn't save him, I don't know what I'll do."

"Vanessa said you're selling the whole thing." Why would they do that when they had Liana's money behind them? There must have been a prenuptial agreement at play.

"No." Liana shook her head quickly, wiping her eyes with her free hand. "It's going back to its owner. They can do some minor restoration, and no one will ever know."

Enzo's voice dropped as the men shifted into an argument, stealing my attention from Liana. "Small people can't stand in our way."

"The FBI and Interpol are not *small people*, Enzo." Noah cupped the back of his neck. "If we keep the huma bird, they'll be on our tails. If we sell it to those zealots, they're as likely to sacrifice us for touching it as they are to pay us. Use your brain."

The Fenix Group wasn't as tight-knit as we'd thought they were. Noah and Enzo were the ones in command but obviously didn't see eye-to-eye on everything.

Was there a way to use that?

Maybe. Maybe not.

But there was something nearby I could definitely use.

If I made it out alive—they were confessing an awful lot in front of me.

"He'll be all right." I slid my other arm around Liana, under her arm, and bounced my shoulders like I was crying, too. "I understand. I lost everything in a car accident twelve years ago, and I'd give anything to fix it."

Liana held on tight.

I eased my lower arm down her side. Checked the reflection in the windows across the room—the men were arguing, not paying any attention to the crying women. *Perfect.*

Her handbag was open at the top. I dipped a hand in and found my target, retracting it quickly. My sleeves were too tight to slip anything into them, but I lifted my shirt and tucked it into my waistband.

In the reflection, Drew glanced at me. He shifted his weight, moving mere inches, but concealing my actions from Enzo. He *was* on my side.

I sniffled, playing up the sorrow for Liana and the other men. For Drew, I flicked my pinky finger twice. *Please remember that's our signal for needing physical cover and it means I'm ready to run.*

A siren wailed in the distance, and everyone looked at Noah. If we'd needed proof he was in charge, that was it. And from the way he'd protected me from Enzo, despite the threats which were hopefully hollow, that was important.

"We should go." Noah offered a hand to Liana, who stood with him. "We have a car downstairs."

"In case those sirens are for us"—Enzo grabbed me by the hair, hauling me forward—"we should take her."

"Ow, shit, stop!" I stumbled, crashing to my knees, and the tears started for real. The gun was almost better. I grabbed his wrist so he couldn't rip anything out. No one intervened this time. Not even Drew.

Good, Drew. Keep them thinking you're on their side.

Enzo forced me to stand and I played up my limp. Every step was like knives stabbing my leg, but I pretended it was worse. Noah and Liana took the lead, while Drew and Craig trailed behind us.

"Where are you going?" whispered Drew. "I can meet you."

"If you're serious, I'll contact you once we're settled." Craig raised his voice, no longer speaking privately. "What about Vanessa?"

"She knows where the rendezvous is," Noah said over his shoulder. "If she misses the flight, that's on her. I have the beak and we can't sacrifice it falling into anyone else's hands."

Blue lights flashed through the windows of Drew's office as we passed. The elevator doors opened and everyone filed in.

"I'm going to miss this place," said Craig.

As the door slid closed, Drew slammed a hand against one of them, halting their progress. He spun, punching Enzo square in the nose. The scarred Italian released me as he reeled back, holding his face with both hands. Liana cried out.

Noah and Craig?

No idea.

Because Drew yanked me out of the elevator, charged around a corner, and shoved me through the heavy door into the stairwell.

"Get them!" bellowed Enzo. "They know too much!"

"Can you make it?" hissed Drew, tucked in behind me while I took the stairs two and three at a time.

Easy peasy. No words came, every step rattling through my entire body. My head was about to explode. *Use the railing for leverage. Land light on the left, propel with the right. I can do it, Drew.*

A body collided with the door one floor above us and gunfire shattered the night. The bullet pinged off metal and footsteps thundered on the stairs.

"She's already injured, Enzo!" yelled Noah. "Put that thing away."

As we hit the landing between the first and second floors, I miscalculated. I landed hard on my bad leg, and it crumpled underneath me.

Drew stopped and grabbed my arm. "I'm not leaving you."

But it was too late. Enzo paused a half-flight above us, leveling his gun. "Cazzo Madre di Dio!"

Drew's head spun toward Enzo and he dropped on top of me, pain searing through my leg, my head, and every cell of my body. All I saw was a blur of red swinging down from the stairs above Enzo at the same time the muzzle flared. My ears rang. Vision swam with tears.

Through a gap between Drew's arms covering my head, I saw Noah.

With a fire extinguisher?

"Go! Now!" Noah ground out.

"Drew," I said. "Get up. We need to run."

He groaned but was on his feet in seconds.

Noah lifted Enzo in a fireman's carry. "Make sure Scarlett gets the letter."

What the hell?

Before I could ask questions, Drew lifted me, hurrying down the last flight of stairs, as though I weighed nothing. Above us, I heard the door to the second floor open and close. Noah and Enzo were gone.

The sirens grew louder as we reached the ground floor. There was an emergency exit at the back and a door into the front lobby of the building.

Drew checked the small window to the front and pulled away, flattening us against the wall. "Craig and Liana are out there."

"Should we go out the back?"

"Will Noah and Enzo be there?"

"Noah knocked him out and took him onto the second floor. He'll be out for a while."

Drew finally looked at me. "He what?"

"Fire extinguisher to the head." A shiver ran through me. I needed more adrenaline. "Just when you covered me."

Drew grunted—the same way Rav always ignored praise—and pushed open the rear door into the alley space behind the buildings. He snuck along the wall and ducked down a narrow alley that served as the parking lot entrance.

The night grew brighter. Streetlights, lit-up buildings around his office, police lights. We did it. We made it out.

"You can put me down now," I said. "I can walk."

"So stubborn." He hefted me, resettling my weight in his arms. "You walked all the way here—"

"Ran." It was silly, but I wanted him to know how hard I'd worked, despite it all going to shit.

Drew shook his head and rolled his eyes theatrically. "I've never had anyone look out for me like that. The least I can do is pretend I'm saving you now."

Pretend? He'd done a pretty damn good job of genuinely saving me from Enzo.

He continued walking toward the street, and when we saw the police cars, he blew out a long breath. "What did you take from Liana's purse?"

To tell him or not? It wasn't likely he'd blab to anyone at this point. I slipped Liana's phone from my tights. "The scarab at the event was stolen from a museum in Cairo. We were considering a contract to recover it, and Liana might have the information we need."

"That's a crime. You can't just poke around in her phone."

"And you never did that in your former job?"

His jaw clenched. "That was about preserving the Nation, not about—"

"It's all about the greater good, right?" Plus, we were still looking for intel on the data storage center. Liana's phone might not have contained anything useful, but it was worth a shot. We'd have to act fast, though. Once Gideon found out the truth about Liana, he'd likely have her data shielded or fried or whatever the hell those tech security people did.

Drew frowned. "I expect that's what Craig thought he was doing."

"You okay?"

He pressed his lips to the side of my head and said nothing.

Emmett and Rav rushed across the street, from where they'd been talking to a police officer.

Rav reached for me. "I've got her."

"That's okay." I waved the big man off. "My boyfriend's got me."

Drew's head jerked back. "Boyfriend?" he said in unison with Emmett.

"Isn't that why you spouted off all the lovey-dovey stuff in the hotel?"

His brows drew down.

"Plus, you threw yourself in front of Enzo for me."

A tiny smile appeared on Drew's gorgeous face. "I guess that's all true, isn't it?"

"The sentiment is sweet," Rav said as he took me from Drew, "but your boyfriend is bleeding. He needs medical attention."

"Geez Louise, Drew!" I pulled at his jacket, turning him so I could see the wetness decorating his tux sleeve. "Why didn't you tell me?"

Drew rolled his left shoulder and grimaced. "It's just a graze. I'll be fine."

"Scarlett's waiting by the ambulance." Emmett pointed beyond the police cars. "Let's get you looked at."

"What happened with Vanessa?" I asked.

Emmett glanced at Drew. "Does he know?"

No. I'd been too busy trying to save him, then trying to stay alive, to mention our encounter with his ex. "Noah's the one who sent us the tip about the huma bird. For some reason, he also sent Vanessa after me—with a gun."

"No." Drew walked next to us and took my hand. "That was me, not Noah. Before I figured out Craig was behind everything, I told them about your text message."

"If you got the message, why didn't you respond to me? Warn me she was on her way?"

"Craig destroyed my phone before I could." Drew was trying so hard to maintain a calm, stoic exterior, but his jaw wasn't clenching the right way. He wasn't frowning the way he normally did. He was breathing differently. Maybe it was partially the gunshot wound, but maybe he was reflecting on how much he'd lost tonight.

We'd fallen right into Fenix's hands. They had the beak, even though we recovered the bird and the chip. And Drew lost his ex-girlfriend, his boss, and one of his co-workers.

"Vanessa said she was going to sell the bird."

Drew nodded absently.

Holding his hand while Rav was carrying me was awkward, but I couldn't let him go. I had him. We were safe. We were with my team. "And I think she bugged your apartment. She knew things we talked about Thursday night."

I wanted to say more and put everything out on the table so we could deal with it, but the way Drew's gaze unfocused, it might have been too much. He just squeezed my hand again and brought it to his lips.

The door to the building's lobby opened, and Craig walked out, his hands held up. A line of police officers watched him, guns drawn. Liana came out next, sobbing her guilty little heart out.

"We left Vanessa tied up in the antiques shop," said Emmett. "Then we called the police and reported a break and enter. We left the statue with her, so it'll be returned."

Everything had worked out the way it was meant to. We did our job and protected the chip, somehow took down three members of Fenix, and I had a boyfriend. For the first time in over a decade, I had a man who thought I was beautiful and wanted to make me happy.

Even if it was only until we left for home.

If he could get over everything that happened tonight.

CHAPTER 47
DREW

The water beat down on us from the side, but I kept my grip firm under Jayce's thighs. I had her pinned against the gleaming tiles of my shower, just like I'd fantasized.

Her lips froze on mine, tiny gasps coming with each thrust.

"That's it," I moaned. "Take it all."

"So good." She clutched the back of my neck, taking some of the weight off my injured arm as I drove into her. "Now slow down."

I did as she asked, slowing my rhythm. I leaned away to watch her eyes struggle to stay open.

"Deeper," she whispered, angling one leg higher up my back.

I rocked into her, setting a pace that was both maddeningly slow and incredibly intense. "Like that?"

"Harder." Her voice was barely there between heaving breaths. The steam billowed around us. Like my dream.

My grip tightened on her thighs as I moved with more purpose.

She pulled me closer, fingers clawing at my back. "More," the word slipped out as a shudder ran through her.

I complied without hesitation, surging into her with a fervor I thought I'd lost years ago. I couldn't get enough of her.

"Close," she whimpered, her body shaking. Each push brought a moan from her lips that echoed off the shower walls.

"Let go," I told her, my own control wavering with each second.

When she did, I shattered with her—a shared moment of ecstasy that left us breathless, clinging to each other under the stream of water.

Then we were there, just breathing. Just being together, connected, with nothing but raw honesty between us.

Her legs slipped from around me and I pulled out before setting her gently on her feet. She remained silent, but her fingers traced idle patterns on my chest, grounding me.

"Good?" It was a stupid question, but it was the only one my brain could come up with.

"The best." Her lids fell closed for a moment, and I leaned in to kiss her temple. Her hand traveled lower, brushing against my abdomen, and to the base of my shaft. "But I need to get back to those waffles you made."

I kissed her softly, pulling her closer until our bodies molded together under the hot spray. She tasted like lust and want and something that felt suspiciously like love. Plus a hint of sugar from breakfast. With her held close, I let the water cascade over us, washing away any lingering tension.

She wrapped her arms around my neck, and we swayed in a rhythm all our own.

"Stay," I breathed into her ear. Did I really say that? And how long did I mean?

"But there's whipped cream and strawberries in the kitchen."

"I meant Washington." I pulled back to look at her. This honesty thing was going to be a problem if I kept making ridiculous requests like this. "Don't leave today."

Her brows fell and she blinked rapidly. "I have to go back for work."

Work? She had a thriving career, and what did I have? An ex, a boss, a co-worker, and a former client pending bail hearings. Byron—who'd cut his vacation short and was returning today to help deal with the chaos—and Zaria were the only ones in my life who were clear of charges. Lots of acquaintances and associates, but no real friends. No family. Nothing.

What I had was Jayce, but she was leaving this afternoon.

That was what I wanted, though, wasn't it? I could sell everything and buy that boat I'd thought about. Take Vijay up on his offer and work my way around the world. Or just leave without telling anyone and not worry about more lies or betrayals.

The Reynolds team had done a thorough sweep of my apartment and only found a single bug—in the photo of Vanessa and me. That must have been why she was at my place last week, sneaking it in. Before I'd tossed it into a drawer, she'd set it up at the perfect angle to watch all of my planning for the event that hadn't happened at the office. When Byron arrived, he'd sweep the office, and likely find more.

"Of course, you have to go." I turned off the water and grabbed two towels hanging nearby. "Breakfast will be cold, though, so I'll make some more."

"Cold waffles and hot sex." She ruffled the towel through her hair, a tight smile on her face. "Sounds like a perfect morning to me."

It *was* perfect until I ruined it by questioning what happened next.

I pulled on a pair of blue cotton lounge pants and she wore the matching shirt. It fell practically to her knees. It was so fucking adorable. And the little black panties I knew were under it? Even better.

Jayce Monroe was sexy, but unassuming. Not like Vanessa, who knew how gorgeous she was and treated every moment like an opportunity for me to tell her. That lost its appeal quickly.

We made our way to the kitchen and the waffle maker.

"Has anyone ever told you this floor's way too cold?" She put her hands on the counter and hopped up, settling in to watch me work. Her knee was almost at full strength.

"You did." I winked at her. "Thursday night."

She blew a raspberry in return. "Didn't think you were listening."

We'd spent most of the last two days together. An EMT had bandaged my arm where the bullet grazed me, and I'd forced her to ice that damn knee. There had been meetings with her team, statements for the police, and some furious words I heard more than saw from Evelyn Reynolds. I'd asked about the letter Noah mentioned, but no one was talking.

Craig, Liana, Vanessa, and Wyatt were all in custody, but somehow, Noah and Enzo had evaded the police. The huma bird statue was shipped back to its owner without the beak.

"Were you tempted at all?" I pulled a bowl and flour from a lower cabinet, then eggs and milk from the fridge.

Jayce snorted a laugh. "You were with me when I totally gave in."

"I didn't mean the shower." I continued pulling ingredients and tools, centering myself in the process of cooking for my woman. "The whole thing about the phoenix. Your leg, Tanner's leg…"

"Meh." She shrugged one shoulder. "They're lunatics."

"Can you grab the cinnamon?" I raised my chin toward the cabinet behind her. "What if there's some truth to the story? Some ancient medicine lost to time?"

Her gaze unfocused for a moment, then she shifted out of the way of the upper door. "For how much you love cooking, this is an awfully small kitchen."

Message received. She didn't want to discuss it. Which meant she *had* been tempted. It was a seductive concept—the end of suffering. If Fenix was as altruistic as Noah and Liana sounded, they wouldn't have been operating in the shadows. Enzo wouldn't have been so quick to pull the gun or to fire at us.

Think about that after Jayce is gone. You don't have much time before she has to leave.

"The kitchen's big enough for now." I cracked fresh eggs into the bowl. The plan had been to save money for a house and a family. So long as it was just me, I didn't need more space. "I thought maybe we could go to the spy museum after we eat. It's interesting, if you've never been."

"That might be fun." She opened the cabinet and retrieved the cinnamon. "As long as you drop me off at the airport by three."

I whisked the eggs, incorporating cinnamon and nutmeg. "What if I didn't?"

"You said that already." She offered the tall bottle of vanilla, full of Madagascar beans and unflavored vodka. "And I told you I have to go home today."

I rested the whisk against the side of the bowl and moved closer to her, settling between her legs. "I've been thinking a lot about the Harrington job and how everything went down."

She placed the bottle on the counter, gaze darting side to side—searching for an escape from the conversation.

"It finally dawned on me around three this morning that what I wanted that night was to protect you, maybe even from yourself." I used my knuckles to turn her face to me. "But I see now you're completely capable of taking care of yourself all on your own."

Not just capable of taking care of herself, but taking care of me. Of running blocks through a town in the middle of the night, to warn me I was in danger. Throwing herself into the fray to protect me.

When had I ever had that? Sure, my parents had loved me, but they hid such a big truth my entire life. Vanessa cared about herself, not me.

Fuck, if Alex had someone who looked out for him the way Jayce looked out for me Saturday night, maybe he'd still be alive.

"I'm actually not. I'm reckless, like you said." Her gaze fell, and I nudged her chin. "That's what my team's for. To protect me from myself."

I pressed my lips to hers. "I want to be part of that team, Jayce."

She nodded slowly. "I can talk to Evelyn, but—"

"Not the Reynolds team." I chuckled and kissed her temple. She didn't understand. "I want to be on the Jayce team. The team that spends every day with you, learning all your idiosyncrasies—"

"There's a lot of those." She squirreled up her face, still trying to avoid my honesty.

"I know. And I want to learn everything. I want to cook for you, bake for you, and make love to you every day. I want to make sure your feet are warm, your leg doesn't hurt, and your heart never aches."

No matter how uncomfortable it was, this was my only chance to tell her everything. My mental locker was straining at the hinges. Some part of me dreamed of being free of it. The part that could have died Saturday night if a reckless thief hadn't come to my rescue.

And Noah. Enzo would have killed Jayce and me in the stairwell if Noah hadn't rescued us. A man I didn't even know.

"Jayce, I don't want to keep living this fake life. I left the CIA because I wanted to get away from the lies. But all I did was exchange lies for spin, and nothing got any better. Until you."

Her mouth slowly eased open, but no words came.

"You're the most open and honest—"

"I hold a lot in."

I tapped her nose. "Would you let me finish?"

"Will it be long?" She inclined her head toward the bowl. "I'm hungry."

"No, you're not. You're deflecting." I placed a hand on either side of her face, forcing her to meet my gaze. "I know that, because you ran on an injured leg to save me. You showed me how you feel about me. There's no need for words."

"I've never had a boyfriend before."

I kissed the tip of her nose. "And I hope I'm the last one you ever have."

She took in a sharp breath. "That sounds kind of serious."

"I'm kind of a serious guy."

Was it too much? Too soon?

Screw it.

"If you can't stay here, what if I come back to Halifax with you for a while? Maybe a couple of weeks?"

"We have nothing in common, Drew." She pulled my hands from her face. "How would that ever work?"

"So we find common ground. We both grew up in the light. You fell into the shadows, and I skulked into them intentionally. We can start there and spend every day keeping each other out of the dark."

She placed my hands on her hips and wrapped her arms around my neck. "In the twilight?"

"I don't care." I slid my hands to her ass. "As long as you're there with me."

CHAPTER 48
EMMETT

I walked a few steps toward the jet and paused, taking in the expansive hangar, the simplicity of our Gulfstream, and the sun shining through the giant open door at the front. Another job mostly well done.

A wild ride, but successful in the end.

Jayce and Drew climbed the stairs into the jet, his hand grazing her back, and I smiled. They'd wasted too much time living in their dark pasts, thinking they didn't deserve the happiness they obviously felt together.

Good job, Emmett.

Life was too short for that bullshit.

Something metal clanged in a corner and a jolt ran up my spine. A fist flew at my face and a bag went over my head. Next would be the boot in the ribs.

No, it won't, Em. You're safe. You're with your team. I wasn't in the room where Fenix had held me. Not on the plane they flew me to Venice in, or the villa where I waited for Scarlett to come for me.

I slid my hand into my pants pocket. Casual move. Standard Emmett Reynolds.

But my fingers grazed the textured face of the poker chip hidden inside. It was blue with white pips. A flame decorated its center. Five thousand printed on one side. A small hole poked through its middle.

I scanned the open space again.

And breathed.

Malcolm passed me at a clip, head down, towing his wheeled bag. Strange. He was never far from my sister when we were off the clock.

The click of Scarlett's stilettos behind me came to an abrupt halt. "I need to talk to you."

I turned to face her, hooking a thumb over my shoulder. "Trouble in paradise?"

She stepped closer, keeping her voice down. "He's not happy about Noah."

"Oh?" I feigned surprise. "Your current live-in boyfriend wasn't happy you followed along with your formerly dead ex-fiancé's plan?"

She cocked her eyebrow. The infernal Mum Eyebrow. It meant *Stop being sarcastic* and *Butt out of my love life* and maybe a hint of *Yes, it was hard on him, but I'm trying to pretend I'm as strong as our mother.*

"Oh, fine." I placed my messenger bag on top of my suitcase. "You needed to talk?"

Rav stopped next to us. "Is everything all right?"

"We're good. We'll be right behind you." Scarlett touched his arm and smiled.

Rav dipped his head in the subtle way he questioned her.

"Really. We'll be right there," she said.

He nodded and continued to the plane. He'd been one of her closest friends as a kid and always had a protective streak. Something happened between them before he joined our team. Not romantic—they'd never had that kind of relationship—but something deeply personal they never spoke of that created an unshakable bond. Since my ordeal with Fenix, everything between the two of them became more intense.

Malcolm had told me in confidence it bothered him, but after a few trips out to the pubs that wound up as pseudo-counseling sessions, I'd convinced him there was nothing to worry about. She and Rav could make out as cover on a mission, but after the job was done, they never looked at each other like they wanted more.

Having two men so devoted and protective of my sister made our work easier for me.

Once Rav was climbing the steps to the jet, Scarlett continued. "Noah's letter said he was behind the tip about the scarab. He expected us to find out it would be at the gala, and that would bring us there. His plan was for us to be part of his deception all along."

And we fell into that, didn't we? "He just didn't expect us to be on someone's payroll?"

She nodded. "He's provided the name and location of the man who has the scarab."

"I thought we got that from Liana's phone?"

"We got enough off her phone before it was wiped to confirm what Noah said." Scarlett glanced over my shoulder at the plane.

"Oh, shit, sis." I rubbed my fingers over the chip again. "You still want to go after it?"

"It *was* stolen from a museum in Cairo. Our team already confirmed that part."

"So why lend it out for public display?"

"Either they don't know or they don't care." She shrugged. "One of our first steps will be to find out which."

"You told Noah in Venice that you wouldn't work for him. And now? Now we're taking jobs from him?" This conversation was getting worse by the second.

"There's a reward. And as Mum likes to say"—she gestured at the jet—"the jet doesn't run on fairy dust. We have enough intel to plan a recovery."

"No wonder Malcolm's upset."

She frowned. A reaction she rarely gave around anyone but her best friends and family. "Malcolm doesn't know the details."

"Details? Who gives a shit about the details? You're hiding letters from your ex-fiancé."

"Reynolds Recoveries is a family business. That means family comes first."

"That man wants to be your family." I gripped the poker chip harder with my hidden hand. Why did she have to be so thick about things? "Don't you get that?"

Malcolm was *so* serious about their relationship, he'd already talked to me about whether he should ask my permission or Mum's. I'd said yes. Mum would say yes if it were advantageous in some way. I'd told him to focus on getting Scarlett completely over what Noah did to her. But here she was, letting the snake back into the garden.

She was amazing at reading a mark, but the people around her? She'd missed everything between Jayce and Drew, and now she was risking her relationship with Malcolm without even realizing it.

Either that or she was sabotaging things.

"The target is a wealthy businessman with homes in at least six countries. One of them—where he normally keeps the scarab—is in Monte Carlo."

"No one's hired us to get that back, and you're already calling the man a target?"

"Returning the huma bird was prepayment."

"That's a relief." My eyebrow involuntarily rose to punctuate my point. "We're not just doing his dirty work, because he's our client now?"

"He's not. I said he was *behind* the tip, not that he was the one who contacted us."

"Wonderful." Now we were playing semantics, so she could defend him. It hardly mattered whether he'd called us or told someone else to. "He's our broker now?"

"The letter said there's a fracture in The Fenix Group and Drew confirmed it. The kidnappers and extortionists are on one side. They wanted to sell the bird to a group in Iran, while Noah's faction wanted to return it to its owner. Noah believes in the goodness of their cause."

I ripped my hand out of my pocket and raked my fingers through my hair. "Goodness of their cause? Are you fucking kidding me? They broke two—"

"Keep your volume down!" she snapped, her hands flying up as though they could calm me down.

I hissed back, "They broke two of my ribs, fractured my orbital bone, and threatened to kill me five times a day! I still have headaches from the fucking concussion!"

Her shoulders dipped—I didn't have to look at her feet to know those toes were scrunching, just like how Mum taught her to conceal her emotions. *That's it, Scar, bottle it all up.* "That wasn't him."

Noah hadn't touched me. It was mostly Enzo and a few shots from the other two working with them. That was hardly an excuse. He was the reason they grabbed me in the first place.

"It doesn't matter if it was his fist or boot or someone else's." I shoved my hand into my pocket and gripped the chip one more time. "Noah's one of their leaders, you said. He's as guilty as the rest."

"That's the thing," she said. "Jayce said he and Enzo were the only ones with the phoenix tattoos. Same thing in Venice and Rome—no one else had tattoos. She and Drew also said the two of them were obviously in charge. So if he and Enzo are at the top of the organization and they're battling things out, I think Noah's trying to make a play."

"Let me get this straight…" I sucked in a slow breath, attempting to calm my heart. "He's not just our client now, but that snake has you wrapped so firmly around his little finger that we're going to help him take over the organization behind my kidnapping, who tried to kill more than one of us in Rome, and who tried to shoot Jayce two days ago?"

She cocked the damn eyebrow again. "He saved Jayce's life. And Drew's."

"I'm done." I turned and grabbed my messenger bag, tossing it over my shoulder. "We can talk about this at home."

"Em." She gripped my arm, and I paused. "There's no way Malcolm or Rav will agree to me going to Monte Carlo to lead a mission based on Noah's information. That means it'll be your job."

"Tell Mum."

"I did." Her voice held a note of apology. As it should have. She should have talked to me about this.

I faced my sister. "Mum's already approved it, hasn't she?"

"Scarlett? Emmett?"

We both looked toward the plane, where our flight attendant, Patricia, was beckoning us to board.

Scarlett waved and nodded, then held out a hand to encourage me forward. "I think Mum's looking for a reason to go on the offensive after... after everything you mentioned. But now that we know there's blood in the water? She's ready to attack."

"Great." I had a lot of pull in the company, but if Scar and Mum had decided, my role was to support them. Question them, suggest different approaches, ensure the job went off as smoothly as possible—but in the end, support them.

She moved closer. "And he warned me they're looking into her background."

"Which background? Dad?"

"Mum's." She leaned toward my ear, her voice barely a breath. "Her time with MI6."

My step stuttered. I hadn't heard that right. "Her what?"

"We swore we'd never dig into their past, Em," she said, "but Fenix is."

Our father had been in jail for espionage since I was twelve. He'd worked for CSIS and she worked as an accountant with the British High Commission in Ottawa. After Dad's arrest, she'd left that job. After the sentencing, she'd moved us to Halifax. Yearly visits, no tears, and what did she do for a living after that? None of us knew.

Until she opened Reynolds Recoveries.

Scar, Brie, and I had promised each other we wouldn't use our resources to find out. Someday, Mum would tell us the truth, and we'd wait. No scouring the dark web, no pressuring sources, no research.

Our family trip to London when I was fourteen included planning how to steal the Crown Jewels. We'd thought it was a funny game. In Paris the next year, we watched tourists milling about the Eiffel Tower and identified which ones weren't protecting their bags well enough. A Louvre tour with discussions about how to detect forgeries, scavenger hunts around Dublin, and visiting banks in Switzerland.

Every year, the trips were moments for us to bond, but they became more serious as we grew up. Brie started getting nervous when Mum paid too much attention to someone. Scarlett started stretching her wings and taking the lead on interrogations. And Mum taught us how to read people. How to hide our emotions.

I didn't want to know the truth. I wanted my mother to be an eccentric woman who loved the three of us unconditionally underneath her harsh exterior.

Scarlett went up the metal steps ahead of me, through the galley, and into the passenger cabin. Everyone was seated comfortably—Jayce and Drew on the divan in the mid-cabin, while Rav and Malcolm sat in the aft.

Fenix had taken me, but my family followed and got me out. Not just my blood family, but the family inside this jet. Reynolds Recoveries had done what they needed to do to save me.

I took a long step and caught up with Scarlett. I whispered to her, "I'm in."

She nodded without looking at me and passed the men at the back. Pausing at the door to the private cabin, she laid a hand on Malcolm's shoulder. He gave her a tight smile and stood. They slipped into the cabin and locked the door behind themselves.

I slid into a big seat opposite Rav. "Did Scarlett tell you about Monte Carlo?"

"The scarab?" Of course, he knew.

"Yeah. We've got a job to plan."

Epilogue
Jayce

The car rolled to a stop and I considered keeping my eyes shut. It was oh dark thirty and after a four-day whirlwind mission in Grand Cayman, I was exhausted. I'd texted Drew when we left the island, but hadn't heard from him.

I wasn't even sure what country he was in.

"Wake up, slacker." Emmett nudged me from the driver's seat. "I still need to drive home, so I'm not sitting in your driveway all night."

"That's your fault." I stretched my arms and yawned. "I was going to grab a rideshare."

Emmett chuckled, "Open your eyes already."

They fluttered open, and the world came into focus. It was too dark outside. I lived in a condo in town, but that's not where we were. Thick pines blocked out the view on two sides, opening up to a two-story house with gables and enormous windows. Beyond it... nothing.

This wasn't right.

"Where are we?" I sat up straighter, swiveling in my seat to take in the long driveway behind us. "Is this where you bury the bodies?"

Emmett laughed and pointed to the house.

A porch light came on.

The front door opened and a figure appeared.

Drew.

My heart beat higher in my chest, and excited energy began pinging around inside me. The same energy that flooded me every time I saw my boyfriend.

"What the—" hell was going on?

He'd stayed with me for a month after our return from Washington. Two weeks ago, he'd left on a business trip of undetermined length to an undisclosed location. My team went radio silent when we landed in Grand Cayman, so as much as I'd hoped to see him at my place when I got back, I hadn't expected it.

Definitely hadn't expected to see him at someone else's place in the middle of nowhere.

"I make no bones about playing matchmaker in Washington, but this one's all him." Emmett popped the trunk release. "Get your stuff. I'll see you at the office in a couple of days."

I pulled a piece of gum out of my pocket and unwrapped it.

Bad idea. There was a man to kiss out there.

I dropped the gum into the little trash behind the center console and opened the door.

Drew hadn't come out to grab my bags. Strange. He said he enjoyed doing things like that for me.

It was early August, hot and muggy outside, but the scent of salt air told me we were close to the water—not that it was a stretch in Halifax. I towed my bag across the end of the driveway and onto the interlocking brick walkway. "Too busy looking mysterious in the big house to help a girl out?"

"Welcome home, sweetheart." He smiled, and the closer I got, the more the butterflies flitted over my skin.

When had the ants switched to butterflies? Or had they ever really been anxious ants? Not that it mattered, because the sight of him had become the most wonderful thing in my world. "How much did you pay Emmett to drive me out here?"

He stepped out of my way as I rolled the bag in. No kiss. No hug. Only courtesy.

What was going on?

"Where's my hug?" I looked around, confusion spreading through my brain. Scents overwhelmed me. I closed my eyes and inhaled deeply. Baking bread. Cookies. Cinnamon rolls. "Am I dead?"

The house seemed bigger on the inside. A vaulted ceiling stretched the length of the left side, from an office to a great room with couches and a huge television. On the right, a formal dining room with a table and ten chairs. Separated from the dining room by white pillars was a sprawling kitchen. At the far end, a granite fireplace sat dormant. A wall of windows spread out from either side of the fireplace, providing a sweeping view. There was just enough moonlight to tell the house overlooked the water.

"Not dead, no."

"How was your... um..." I yawned again. "How was your little cloak and dagger trip?"

"Good." His jaw clenched, but not in the serious or frustrated way. In the way it did when he was holding back a smile. "I started in Ottawa, visiting some folks with CSIS. Professional courtesy, plus quelling some fears about a former spy going to work for an incarcerated spy's wife."

My heart skipped several beats. "Did Evelyn..."

"She sent me an offer less than an hour after I told Scarlett I was coming back with you." He took a step toward me and ran his fingers down my arm. "But I wanted to get a feel for things before making any commitments."

"Things?"

"Us."

"You know you haven't hugged me yet?"

"You drive me crazy." He smiled, but came no closer. "And it didn't get any easier when I was staying with you."

My first instinct was to promise I'd clean more. Listen more. Do more of something so he wouldn't end what we had so soon. Instead, I shrugged. "I am who I am."

"Shoes off," he whispered.

What?

He flicked his gaze to my feet and my standard black sneakers. "Take them off."

There was no point in arguing, so I did as I was told. I placed the heel of one foot against the toe of the other and slipped the shoe off. When my sock touched the floor, I understood. "In-floor heating?"

He took my hand as I removed the other shoe and curled my toes against the hardwood. "You like your feet warm."

"I do." Before I could pull him to me, he started from the foyer, past the dining room.

"And you like my cooking."

"Almost as much as your baking."

He stopped as we rounded one of the pillars and reached the kitchen's huge marble-topped island. He'd set out trays with cheeses, meats, and crackers, along with two glasses of red wine. Cooling racks held fresh cookies and sugar-dusted pastries.

Two wall ovens were on, as was an element on the gas stove, heating something in a small stainless pot. A pot filler extended from the tiled backsplash and a range hood decorated in paneling to match the cabinets hung from above. Along the back wall of the house, the big sink sat in a long row of lower cabinets with a dishwasher and wine fridge, but above it was all windows. Plus an ultra-fancy coffee maker. *I wonder if it makes nitrogen bubbles.*

This kitchen was a chef's dream.

With the view of the water, it must have been Drew's dream. Although the food he was making was from one of my dreams. "If I'm not dead, am I still asleep?"

He let go of me and crossed to the stovetop. "Emmett texted before you touched down. I wasn't sure what you'd like, so I made a little of everything."

"What I'd like?" It was two in the morning. What I'd wanted when we arrived was sleep. I dropped my shoulder bag on the island. "I'd like my hug hello."

"We need to finish this conversation first."

That was never a good sign. "Can you give me the TL;DR?"

"I went to DC after Ottawa, to hand the final pieces of Gideon's crisis plan over to Zaria." Drew took the lid off the pot, steam curling up from some bubbling liquid. "With Craig facing such a long list of charges—extortion, theft, conspiracy, industrial espionage—Bishop and Associates is done for. But

Zaria and Byron think they can make a go of things with a few new hires."

"You're not going back?"

"I also met with Gideon about my investigation into Liana's role in everything. One of the many tidbits I discovered was her little house she used for painting retreats." He waved his hand, gesturing around the room. "Apparently she'd have five or six friends stay here regularly and they'd set up a wall of easels on the big stone patio out back."

"This is Liana's house?" I tried suppressing a yawn. I was too tired for this to make sense. The great room behind me had two huge leather couches. I could sleep on one of those.

"It *was*. I also discovered one of those friends was her lover." He put the pot lid back on and turned to me, leaning on the island.

"And we're waiting for him to show up?"

He shook his head slowly. "In public, Gideon's doing a fantastic job of playing the shocked husband, while the tabloids rake her over the coals. Behind the scenes? He's already changed his will to cut Liana out, made an anonymous donation to Craig's daughter-in-law's medical bills, and is pushing his EPRC into full production. He's also so pissed with Liana—and happy with my work—that he offered me the house at a price I could afford."

That, plus a job offer from Evelyn? He was moving to Halifax? So why was he keeping his distance?

"Drew, I am too tired for this. Can you lay it out for me?"

"I thought about visiting Vanessa while I was there. It sounds like her angle was only monetary—she didn't buy into the phoenix crap. I don't know everything the prosecutors have on them, but she and Liana are up on the same charges as Craig. Wyatt might be the only one who's out of prison inside five years, and I expect he'll leverage the intel he gathered on the others to ensure that happens."

"No word on Enzo or Noah?"

"None."

I pulled out one of the bar chairs tucked neatly under the island's breakfast bar and sat before I crashed on the floor. "What now?"

"Sweetheart, I want to do work that matters. I want to unravel lies, not make more of them." He balled his hands into fists. "I need a fresh start, so I packed up my wine collection and told Gideon I needed a few days to decide about the house."

I yawned, unable to keep the fatigue at bay.

"And I went to see my parents before I left."

I leaned forward on the island.

After he'd been in Halifax for a few weeks, he'd finally told me the truth about them. The good times, the bad times, and the shock after their deaths. He hadn't visited their graves since he discovered they'd adopted him.

"I want to move on. I don't want to carry that anger anymore. So I forgave them." He blinked several times and looked out toward the water. "But the truth is..."

"Letting go is hard?" Guilt over what happened to Tanner had gnawed at me for twelve years. But in the past month and a half, it had finally started to fade. Emmett suggested my relationship with Drew had something to do with it; I'd told him he was psychoanalyzing me again.

"It is." He fluttered his eyelids and dragged a hand across his eyes. "Everything's fallen into place too easily. Too suddenly. I'm waiting for the shoe to drop. To find out your company isn't really the good guys. Or for Gideon to take back this offer. For you to tell me I'm jumping into our relationship too fast."

"Never fear the leap. That's what my coach used to say."

Drew nodded, looking down at the counter. He wasn't being standoffish. He was being scared.

I slid off the stool and walked around the island to run a hand over his back.

He pulled me into his arms—his strong, muscular arms that made me feel safe and so wanted—and buried his face against my hair.

"The only thing to fear—" My throat tightened and the backs of my eyes prickled. I held onto my man with all the strength I had. "The only thing to fear is standing still."

He nodded. "I used to think you threw my world off balance."

"I'm good at that."

"No." He kissed the side of my head. "The last two weeks—being away from you? I realized my life's been out of balance for a long time. You were the one trying to straighten it for me."

No one had ever accused me of anything like that. Annoying them, entertaining them, distracting them, sure. But definitely not making them better.

He whispered, "I want you to move in here with me."

Butterflies took flight inside my stomach. Was he serious?

He squeezed me tighter. "You don't need to answer right now."

"Commute must be a bitch."

Drew pulled back, chuckling. "It's only twenty minutes to your office."

"My old commute was five."

"You're so spoiled in this city." He ran a hand through my hair and kissed my temple.

"Nah. The office is in a convenient spot." I snaked a hand out of our embrace and ran my nails over his short beard. "So why haven't you kissed me yet?"

"I didn't want to manipulate you. I wanted your honest opinion."

"You didn't think the food would sway me?"

He looked around and shrugged. "Maybe a little."

I'd been taking tiny leaps for years, trying to ensure I didn't fall into my dark days again. Why would I even think I would? I had a job and friends I loved. I got to travel the world and meet interesting people. The Reynolds team cared enough about me that they brought my boyfriend home and offered him a job. Sure, part of that was how awesome he was, but part of it was for me.

They didn't want me only for what I could do. They wanted me for me.

Just like Drew did.

Moving in with him would be a big leap. Too big? Or just the right size?

"Did you make croissants?"

He laughed quietly, that gorgeous smile of his lighting up his face. "With chocolate hazelnut inside, yes."

"All right." I gave him a curt nod, failing miserably at looking serious. "I'll move in with you."

The oven beeped, but Drew leaned in, pressing his lips to mine.

"Is that seriously an oven timer again?"

His tongue traced my upper lip. "Let it burn."

"If those are my croissants…"

He grabbed an oven mitt, pulled the baked goods from the upper wall oven without checking for doneness, and dropped them unceremoniously on the counter. All while keeping his gaze fixed on me. "You didn't take off this time."

I wrapped my arms around his neck and sighed. "Turn off the stove, too. We've got two weeks to make up for, roomie."

He flicked it off and moved the pot. "No more standing still?"

"It's never been my strong suit."

He grabbed me by the waist and lifted me to the counter.

I was caged in between a cheese plate, a cooling rack covered in chocolate chip cookies, and my boyfriend. Life was pretty good.

Drew picked up a cookie and held it out for me. Still warm, it was soft and chewy. Sweet, with a surprise of something nutty inside. The chocolate dripped out as he pulled it away from me. "You like?"

"I love." I took it from him and put it back on the rack, then draped my arms around his neck. Food wasn't what I wanted.

He stepped between my legs and stared into my eyes, the corner of his sexy lips drawing up slowly. "Was there another word to come after that?"

The last time I'd said it was probably to my mom or my sister when I said goodbye. Before that would have been Tanner. *I love you* didn't hold good memories for me.

"Jayce Monroe..." Drew's hands skimmed up my thighs to my waist. "You told me you wanted someone who wanted you. Just you, and not things you can give them."

I nodded. Where was he going with this?

"Well, I want two things from you." His thumbs brushed lazy circles over my shirt, his intense gaze not faltering. "Your honesty and your love. Do you think you can give me those?"

Could Drew and I make new memories? Here in this huge house, just the two of us? Or traveling the world, working for Reynolds Recoveries? Part of my brain wanted to make a crack about lacking a filter between my brain and my mouth, so the honesty part was always easy.

Instead, I savored the butterflies swirling around my stomach and leaned in. No more leaping away. I inhaled deeply, the scent of leather and sandalwood mixing with the aroma of baked goods. "Okay, maybe 'you' goes at the end."

"I think we need to add vulnerability to that list of what I want." He pulled me closer to the edge of the counter, so we were nearly flush. "And in case there's any doubt, I love you, too."

Then he finally kissed me.

His tongue slid into my mouth and caressed mine, a low moan deep in his throat warming me from the inside out. He tasted like chocolate chips and fine red wine. Like expensive coffee with a dash of vanilla and a hint of forever.

Maybe it was a dream. Maybe it wasn't.

I'd take it either way.

Because I had my man. And he was the best damn dream I'd ever had.

THE END OF BOOK 3

BOOK 4: Emmett and the team head to Monte Carlo in pursuit of the scarab. But there's a surprise waiting for them there... and it's not Fenix (at least, it's not *just* Fenix).

Sign up to be notified when Emmett's story is available at
https://janetoppedisano.com/newsletter_preorder/

BONUS SCENE: Oh, that dastardly Harrington job. Who do you think remembers it right? Did Jayce's cockiness almost get them caught? Or was it really Drew's fault?

Join Janet's author newsletter and get
The Harrington Job short story plus behind-the-scenes details at
https://bf.janetoppedisano.com/hli4zufbbo

AUTHOR'S NOTE

Jayce and Drew. What can I say?

Writing a book is a lot like riding a roller coaster. It starts with all the excitement and anticipation of what the book will be. Before long, it turns into abject terror—and a certainty this book is the worst thing I've ever written. But when it's over, all I want is to read it again. I'm in love.

When I did my final read-through on this novel, I closed the book (digitally), and said to myself, "I think Jayce and Drew are my favorite couple."

Of course, Sam and Antonio expressed their displeasure with that statement... then Dani and Ellis... etc etc. I will not pick favorites, but trust me when I say I loved this couple.

Maybe it had something to do with everything going on in my life while I was writing it. There was a lot of self-reflection, a lot of doubts, and also a lot of learning who I am as an author. Or more importantly, who I *want* to be.

Hopefully, if you're still reading at this point, I landed in the right spot. I created a good book that held your interest. If I did, I'd appreciate it if you dropped me a line. Because that's who I want to be—an author who takes her readers on a wild ride that makes them want to get in touch and tell me how much they loved the ride.

Before I call this book done, I'd also like to say a few thanks to the people who helped me get through this one! Mr. Oppy and Oppy Jr. for their constant support; my amazing first readers, Paula and Patricia; my fantastic book coach, editor, and all-around amazing woman, Miranda; and all of my followers and subscribers on Ream.

And finally, I'd like to thank you, dear reader. Without you, I'd just be listening to the voices in my head and calling it a day. It means so much to me that you've enjoyed my story, and I hope it brought some light to your day.

About Janet

Janet Oppedisano hails from Canada's East Coast and has lived in five provinces, from the Maritimes to the Prairies. Growing up with a Mountie for a father and marrying a Navy diver, it's no surprise she writes romance with a hint of danger and mystery in it. Not to mention strong heroes and equally strong heroines.

When not writing, you can find her... thinking about writing. And indulging in her favorite pastimes, like baking, traveling, hiking, playing with her dog, and watching her hockey goalie son on the ice.

Oh, and it's pronounced oh-ped-ih-SAH-no. Exactly the way it's spelled. Honest!

You can find Janet and all her social media profiles at: https://janetoppedisano.com

www.ingramcontent.com/pod-product-compliance
Lightning Source LLC
Chambersburg PA
CBHW031830310726
48972CB00005B/1230